COLLATERAL
DAMAGE

Fire and Ice
Judgment Call
The Old Blue Line (A Novella)
Remains of Innocence
No Honor Among Thieves (A Novella)
Random Acts (A Novella)
Downfall
Field of Bones
Missing and Endangered

J.P. BEAUMONT MYSTERIES

Until Proven Guilty
Injustice for All
Trial by Fury
Taking the Fifth
Improbable Cause
A More Perfect Union
Dismissed with Prejudice
Minor in Possession
Payment in Kind
Without Due Process
Failure to Appear
Lying in Wait
Name Withheld
Breach of Duty
Birds of Prey
Partner in Crime
Long Time Gone
Justice Denied
Betrayal of Trust
Ring in the Dead (A Novella)
Second Watch
Stand Down (A Novella)
Dance of the Bones
Still Dead (A Novella)
Proof of Life
Sins of the Fathers
Nothing to Lose

J. A. JANCE

COLLATERAL DAMAGE

POCKET BOOKS

NEW YORK   LONDON   TORONTO   SYDNEY   NEW DELHI

Pocket Books
An Imprint of Simon & Schuster, Inc.
1230 Avenue of the Americas
New York, NY 10020

This book is a work of fiction. Any references to historical events, real people, or real places are used fictitiously. Other names, characters, places, and events are products of the author's imagination, and any resemblance to actual events or places or persons, living or dead, is entirely coincidental.

First Pocket Books paperback edition October 2023

POCKET and colophon are registered trademarks of Simon & Schuster, Inc.

For information about special discounts for bulk purchases, please contact Simon & Schuster Special Sales at 1-866-506-1949 or business@simonandschuster.com.

The Simon & Schuster Speakers Bureau can bring authors to your live event. For more information or to book an event, contact the Simon & Schuster Speakers Bureau at 1-866-248-3049 or visit our website at www.simonspeakers.com.

Interior design by Erika R. Genova

Manufactured in the United States of America

10 9 8 7 6 5 4 3 2 1

ISBN 978-1-9821-8916-7
ISBN 978-1-9821-8917-4 (ebook)

For Robert Hamilton,
my favorite Bone Doc

COLLATERAL DAMAGE

PROLOGUE

ST. PAUL, MINNESOTA

Tuesday, October 31, 2017, 7:30 p.m. (CST)

At seven thirty on Halloween evening, 2017, Danielle Lomax-Reardon was still at work. She felt guilty about not being home to see her two boys, Dan and Andy, head out for trick-or-treating in their carefully constructed *Star Wars* costumes, but she knew Luke would take an armload of pictures, ones the whole family would share while nibbling away at whatever goodies the boys collected in their jack-o'-lantern-shaped buckets.

This was the job-versus-family tug-of-war every working mother had to fight on a daily basis, and on this occasion, Danielle's work obligations had won out.

Hearing a murmur of voices coming from down the hall, she cleared her desk, left her private office, and made her way down the hall to the main conference room. It was a bare-bones kind of place, furnished with nothing but a collection of mismatched chairs and a refreshment table, but Danielle knew it was a place of hope and new beginnings for many of the people who had ventured inside, and these Tuesday night support-group meetings were an integral part of the process.

This shabby gathering place had once been the posh front parlor for one of St. Paul's grand old mansions. Now it was the centerpiece of the Dahlke House, a shelter—both residential and drop-in—for victims of domestic abuse, established in honor of Sophie Dahlke's long-suffering mother. Outsiders might have been surprised to learn that the shelter's executive director herself often facilitated this Tuesday night support-group meeting, but Danielle felt it was important to be there in person. When it came to domestic abuse, she, too, was a survivor.

The desperate women who finally ventured inside the shelter often felt trapped and hopeless, believing there was no way out. Many turned up in clothing meant to hide the bruises on their arms and legs and wearing layers of makeup designed to conceal the fading but still visible marks on their faces. Unfortunately, the room's cheap fluorescent lighting usually undid their attempts at physical camouflage. For Danielle, who had once walked in their shoes, it was easy to see through their equally futile efforts at concealing the damage to their souls.

Several of Danielle's clients had confided that, upon meeting her for the first time, they had almost turned and fled. To them it had seemed unlikely that the poised, stylishly dressed, confident woman reaching out in welcome would understand where they were coming from. How could she possibly have anything in common with their own horrific realities? Facilitating Tuesday night support-group meetings gave Danielle an opportunity to address those erroneous assumptions.

Not only had she once been a victim of domestic violence, so had her best friend. Alysha Morgan had suffered through months of unrelenting domestic abuse from her boyfriend, Zeke Woodward, in a relationship that had eventually ended in homicide. At the time, both Danielle and Alysha had been working as exotic dancers in a strip joint in Pasadena, California. Late one night an enraged Zeke had turned up in the parking lot and fired six close-range shots into Alysha's body. Danielle had been the sole eyewitness to that horrific event, and her presence that awful night had inevitably led her to the life she lived now and to her work at Dahlke House.

Sometimes, during group sharing, Danielle told her own story and sometimes she didn't. At the beginning of any given meeting she was never sure which way things would go, and that was the case that Tuesday evening as well.

As she entered the conference room, Danielle was greeted by a small burst of laughter from a group of women gathered around the refreshment table. Danielle regarded laughter as a good sign—it showed the beginnings of recovery, of people beginning to find ways to embark on paths to new lives. Three of the women at the refreshment table were Dahlke House graduates, ones who had spent six months or more in the shelter's residential treatment program. Their continued participation in support-group meetings benefited their own recoveries but also offered encouragement to newcomers.

What was now Dahlke House had once been the fashionable residence of Henry Gottfried Peterson, a railroad baron considered to be one of the city's business titans. Outside the walls of their stately home, Henry and his wife, Madeline, had been greatly admired members of the city's high society. At home, Henry had been a monster, bullying and abusing both his wife and daughter, with his son, Alfred, eventually mimicking his father's abusive behavior.

Sophie, the daughter, had grown up in that toxic family dynamic where what went on in public was the opposite of what went on at home. Determined to escape, she had married her high school sweetheart, Steven Philip Dahlke, weeks after they both graduated high school. Months later, Steven was shipped off to World War II, never to return. He perished in the Battle of the Bulge, as did Sophie's brother.

By age twenty-three Sophie was a childless widow, living at home with her parents and doing what she could to protect her mother from her father's increasingly angry outbursts and drunken rages. The abuse only ceased when he suffered a fatal stroke. By then Madeline was a shadow of her former self, living out the remainder of her life as a reclusive invalid. Sophie, living in a private suite of rooms inside the mansion, functioned as her mother's primary caregiver. After her mother's death in 1958, the stately home that had once belonged to her parents became Sophie's alone.

In the early sixties, with the onset of the women's movement, Sophie learned to her surprise that many of her contemporaries, also members of the city's high society, had grown up in similarly challenging circumstances where the specter of physical violence lay hidden behind a thin veneer of wealth and respectability.

As the reality of their mutual histories gradually emerged, the women were shocked to realize that if their privileged mothers had been unable to exit abusive marriages, what chance did those less fortunate have? With that in mind, several of them banded together to do something about that very issue, offering support for abused women trapped in similar situations.

As a founding member of this fledgling organization, Sophie happily opened both her pocketbook and her home. While she continued to occupy her upstairs apartment, the ornate ground floor morphed into office space and public meeting rooms for women in need. When Sophie passed away in 1978, she left the mansion itself as well as the remainder of her fortune to the organization that now officially bore her name. Over time, the mansion had been remodeled to include several residential units, and Dahlke House remained at the forefront in the battle against domestic abuse not only in St. Paul itself, but throughout the Twin Cities area.

As the organization's executive director, community outreach became Danielle Lomax-Reardon's primary focus, and that was at the forefront of her mind when she entered the conference room that night, greeting attendees she recognized and introducing herself to first-timers.

One of those was a quiet-spoken Muslim woman dressed in traditional garb who seemed poised to flee at a moment's notice. Seeing the woman's sorrowful, downcast eyes, Danielle suspected there were black-and-blue marks hidden beneath her hijab and long-sleeved burka. Danielle went out of her way to greet the reticent newcomer and put her at ease.

"I'm so glad you could join us tonight," Danielle said with a welcoming smile, taking the woman's slender but clammy hand in her own. "My name is Danielle. And yours is?"

"Baan," the young woman whispered. "My name is Baan."

"I hope you'll come again, Baan," Danielle said, and it was at that moment she decided that this was one of those times when she would share her own story. Some of the women in attendance might have heard the tale before just as she had heard theirs, but that was all right. Danielle had learned that there was often something new to be learned from each retelling.

The version she told that night was a short one. She related how she had dropped out of high school and fled an abusive household, choosing to live on her own at a very young age. She went on to tell about going to work as an "exotic dancer" and of taking up with a married man, a cop named Frank, who had beaten her senseless on more than one occasion.

Eventually Danielle told about witnessing her best friend's horrific death and about her interactions with the caring homicide detective who had interviewed her that awful night. The tears she'd shed in the aftermath of Alysha's death had washed away Danielle's makeup. At the end of the official interview, the detective had inquired about the telltale bruising on her cheek, and in a moment of utter despair, she came clean about the crooked cop boyfriend who was her own tormenter. It was that conversation that had changed the arc of her life forever, leading her out of that abusive relationship and into a brighter future and eventually to her work at Dahlke House.

"It just doesn't get any better than that," she finished, "but sometimes you have to let go of the bad in order to find the good."

After Danielle told her story, several others shared theirs as well. Throughout the proceedings, Danielle noticed that Baan said nothing but listened intently. Being able to share her own story might come later, but for now Danielle was grateful that by coming tonight Baan had taken a tiny baby step forward on her own behalf. Everyone had to start that difficult journey somewhere.

"Do come again," Danielle said, catching up with Baan as the younger woman darted toward the exit. "You're always welcome."

Baan replied with a nod of her head, but that was all.

It was ten thirty before Danielle finished putting away chairs, emptying the coffee urn, and shutting off lights. Wearing a light coat and with her purse slung over her shoulder, she stepped outside into the crisp fall nighttime air, pausing long enough to lock the door behind her.

As she turned to go, she noticed the shadow of a male figure silhouetted against a nearby streetlight and barring her path to the sidewalk. Without warning, a barrage of bullets slammed into her body, propelling her backward. As her body slid to the floor of the porch, it left behind a bright red stain on the shelter's oaken door.

Danielle lived long enough to see her attacker turn and disappear into the distance. She tried to call out but couldn't. Lights in other nearby houses and buildings came on as alarmed neighbors tried to figure out what had just happened, but Danielle Lomax-Reardon knew it was too late. She would be dead long before help arrived.

In those few moments as her lifeblood drained

away, although Danielle had no idea who had pulled the trigger, she understood who was responsible—her former boyfriend. Frank Muñoz had sent someone to kill her, and why wouldn't he? After all, he was in prison in California, and she was the one who had put him there.

CHAPTER 1

LAS VEGAS, NEVADA

Wednesday, January 1, 2020, 8:00 a.m. (PST)

Frank Muñoz's first New Year's Day out of the slammer was a quiet one. He got up, made coffee, and had a bowl of cold cereal—Frosted Flakes—for breakfast. His mother, Lupé, had never bought Frosted Flakes back when he was a kid. She claimed they were too expensive. "Have a tortilla," she'd always said. "They're better for you than all that sugar." Of course Frank realized now that a steady diet of tortillas wasn't very good for you, either.

After breakfast he switched on his flat-screen TV and settled in to watch the Rose Parade. His moderately priced, fully furnished apartment on Shadow Lane was only a stone's throw away from Las Vegas Metropolitan Police headquarters. Having lived in lockup for the past sixteen years, being in this clean and comfortably furnished apartment was like living in the lap of luxury. His choosing to live within walking distance of the local cop shop made it appear as though he had nothing to hide—which was exactly what he wanted people to believe.

Frank watched the parade from beginning to end, not so much to see the floats but to catch glimpses of the city of Pasadena itself. Living in self-imposed exile here in Vegas, Frank still missed the place where he'd gone to work fresh out of college. And being occupied with the parade meant he wasn't keeping an eye on his watch and wondering what was going on. After today, he'd be one step closer to achieving his goal—three down and one to go. By the end of the week, once all four of his tormentors were out of the way, his job would be over, and his score would be settled.

Melinda, his younger sister, called just as the parade was winding down. "Are you coming over to watch the game?" she asked. "Menudo, tamales, and tacos—all homemade and all you can eat."

He understood why she was calling. Melinda was the baby of the family. Although much younger than Frank, she was incredibly bossy and felt morally obliged to look after him. The problem was Frank didn't really like her, and he could barely tolerate her husband, either—his brother-in-law, Ricky. But when Frank had been coming up for parole, Melinda and Ricky had suggested he consider moving to Vegas, and that's why he'd asked to be set up with a parole officer there—to be close to family. Melinda had provided a plausible excuse, but the real reason for Frank's wanting to settle in Vegas was far more complicated.

Years earlier, and two days before his trial had been due to start, Frank had sat in a jailhouse interview room with his attorney and a US prosecuting attorney who was there to pitch a plea deal.

"We've examined your financials," the prosecutor said. "We know for a fact that you've been receiving substantial amounts of hush money from the people behind BJ's, and we have witnesses who are prepared to testify to your having subverted an upcoming vice raid, which allowed ample opportunity for the illegal gambling operation to disappear long before officers arrived."

That was all true. Frank had been a longtime regular at a local strip joint called BJ's, but he was also a cop. He had noticed that many people who came through the place exhibited zero interest in the dancers. They all went directly upstairs to a room marked PRIVATE. AUTHORIZED ENTRY ONLY. Frank recognized a good number of those folks. They were well-known locals, respected politicians and businessmen, whose reputations would suffer irreparable harm if they were caught up in a raid on an illegal gambling den.

One afternoon in the locker room while preparing for his shift Frank had happened to overhear two of the vice guys discussing an upcoming operation—a planned raid on BJ's. The owner, Betty Jean Parmenter, was a tough old bat who, back in the day, had been a well-known stripper herself. While still in her prime, she had managed to marry into the mob. Her long-deceased mafioso husband and his pals had provided the start-up funds that launched BJ's originally, and for years it had operated as both a gambling den and a mob-friendly money-laundering establishment.

The very day Frank overheard the vice guys' discussion, he had shown up in Betty Jean's office unannounced and sounded the alarm. Once he did so, she had examined him with a disturbingly intense look.

"We know you're a regular," she said finally. "We also know you're a cop. How come you're telling me this?"

Frank had shrugged. "Just thought you should know is all," he replied.

He hadn't known if she'd pay attention to his warning, but when the promised raid occurred, that private upstairs room had been wiped clean as a whistle. The next time Frank stopped by the club and it was time for him to pay his tab, he didn't have one. Instead the barkeep handed him an envelope with his name on it. Inside was a cool $10,000 in cash.

That Christmas Frank had used his unexpected windfall to play Santa in a big way. The kids at home had all gotten everything on their wish lists, and he'd found a pair of one-carat diamond earrings for Danielle, his sweet little side dish. He'd given her the earrings while they were dining at a fancy restaurant on a night when he'd had a bit too much to drink.

"These are lovely," she said, "but how can you afford to be so generous?"

With the booze loosening his tongue, he'd told her the whole story. Sitting in the interview room that day, Frank knew Danielle Lomax had to be the one who had fingered him.

"What we've got you on so far," the prosecutor continued, "is enough to put you away for the next twenty years, give or take. We're willing to cut that down to ten if you'll agree to name names."

William Banks, Frank's supposedly pro bono attorney, had been in the room at the time, ostensibly taking handwritten notes on a legal pad. When the prosecutor's spiel ended, Banks spoke for the first time.

"I'll discuss your plea offer with my client," he said. "We'll let you know."

Once the prosecutor had left the room, Banks slid

the legal pad over to Frank so he could see what he'd written there:

> *We are prepared to pay $500,000 in cash due upon your eventual release if you don't name names.*

Obviously Banks didn't believe the audio/video feed in the interview room had been turned off once the prosecutor left the room, and neither did Frank. What's more, he didn't have to think twice about the offer.

Thanks to that little bitch Danielle, he was for sure going to prison. As a former police officer, once inside Frank would automatically be on an endangered species list. As for the people making this very quiet counteroffer? They had every reason for wanting him to stay silent and he suspected they were good for the money they were offering. If they somehow reneged on the deal after the fact, he could always come after them. The statute of limitations might have run out on some of their current illegal activities, but by the time he got out of the joint, there were bound to be more where those came from.

At that point, Frank had placed his hand on the legal pad and pushed it back toward his attorney. "I'm not taking the prosecutor's deal," he said aloud, "and I'm not naming names. I'll take my chances and go to trial."

"That's totally up to you," Banks had said, closing the legal pad and slipping it into his briefcase. "It's probably just as well to have this over and done with. See you in court."

Even before the counteroffer was on the table, Frank had already made up his mind to plead guilty, but for strategic reasons, he waited until the day of the trial before actually doing so. He wanted to know exactly who the feds had lined up to testify against him. That morning, as he and Banks waited in a conference room before entering the courtroom, Frank had asked if he could see the prosecutor's list of proposed witnesses. Obligingly Banks had handed it over. On it were several names Frank recognized—Danielle's, of course, but also those of two homicide cops from Pasadena PD— Jack Littleton and Hal Holden.

The night of Alysha's parking lot shooting, Frank had been at the club, but he had managed to disappear into the woodwork before homicide cops ever appeared on the scene, so someone—Danielle, most likely—had brought his presence to their attention. Frank had no doubt the homicide cops were the ones who had alerted the feds to what went on behind the scenes at BJ's.

When Frank returned the witness list, Banks had handed him a business card on the back of which was a handwritten note containing the name "Nicholas" and a phone number. Because the area code was the same as Melinda's, Frank understood this was a Las Vegas number. His sister's presence may have been an excuse for wanting to move to Vegas, but the phone number on the card was the real reason he'd done so.

"Hang on to this," Banks had advised. "When you get out, call the number. Ask to speak with Nicholas and tell him I sent you. He's someone who'll give you a helping hand."

Frank studied both the name and the string of numbers for a long time, burning them into his memory before returning the card.

Banks appeared puzzled as he took it back. "I thought you'd want to keep it," he said with a frown.

"I am keeping it," Frank told him, tapping the side of his head, "in here where it'll be safe."

That's all that had been said aloud, but Frank had understood what was really going on. Nicholas, whoever he might be, was the guy in charge of overseeing Frank's payout.

Years later, out on parole and after arriving in Vegas, he'd finally gotten around to calling that memorized number. The phone was answered by a woman who said, "Hi-Roller Fitness. May I help you?"

"I'd like to speak to Nicholas."

"Nico's not in right now," she said. "May I take a message?"

"My name's Frank Muñoz," he told her. "William Banks is a friend of mine. He suggested that I give Nicholas a call."

She took Frank's number, saying she'd pass it along. An hour and a half later he got a call from an unknown number.

"Good afternoon, Mr. Muñoz," a pleasant male voice said. "Nicholas Fratelli here. Glad to make your acquaintance. I understand you may be in need of some assistance. Do you happen to be in Vegas at the moment?"

"Nearby," Frank replied. "I'm currently staying in Henderson with my sister."

"Do you have transportation?"

After their mother's death, Melinda had held on to Lupé's twelve-year-old Honda, and had used it as her kids' vehicle of choice when they were learning to drive. By the time Frank showed up, the kids had moved on to newer vehicles, and Melinda had signed the Honda over to him. Having an old beater suited him. It wouldn't do for someone fresh out of the slammer to be driving around in something flashy.

"Yes, I do," he answered.

"Why don't you drop by the Hi-Roller Fitness location on Alta tomorrow afternoon around two and let's see what we can do?"

The next day Frank had shown up at the appointed hour. Nico Fratelli knew everything there was to know about the payout. It didn't take long for Frank to realize that the fitness part of the gym was little more than a front, providing appropriate camouflage for a well-organized money-laundering operation. Unlike a bank, Hi-Roller didn't come with the convenience of ATMs, and although there were twenty-some locations in the Las Vegas metropolitan area, the one on Alta was the only one where funds were actually disbursed.

After that initial contact, whenever Frank needed money, he would drop by the gym and make a discreet visit to the attendant in charge of the back room. To most of the people who frequented the gym, Frank was buff enough that he looked like he belonged. That was one thing being in prison had done for him. With nothing else to keep himself occupied, he had worked out for hours almost every day, and he had been released in far better physical condition than when he'd been arrested.

"Just so you know," Nico said, "a number of our local constabulary have back-room privileges, but if you don't bother them, they won't bother you."

Knowing that made Frank uneasy, but he shrugged it off. "Fair enough," he said.

"One more thing," Nico added. "That number you used to call me?"

"What about it?" Frank asked.

"Lose it. If you need to speak to me again, just mention it to the guy in charge of the back room. Got it?"

"Got it," Frank had replied.

Obviously his silence on the phone to his sister had gone on for far too long. "Well," Melinda pressed impatiently, "are you coming over or not? The kids would love to see you."

That was Melinda being bossy again, and the last bit about the kids was an outright lie. Frank's niece and nephew were both in college now, and they weren't at all interested in their uncle Frank or in anyone else, for that matter. Most of the time they kept their noses buried in their cell phones or iPads and were totally oblivious to everything around them.

"No, thanks," Frank replied. "I'll just hang around here."

"Are you sure? I hate to think of you being alone on New Year's Day."

"No, really," Frank insisted. "I'll be fine. I appreciate the invitation, but I just don't feel all that much like socializing today. Maybe next time."

"Next time I may not have homemade tamales," Melinda warned.

Frank laughed at that. "Okay," he said. "I'll take my chances."

"All right, spoilsport," Melinda retorted. "Go ahead and be a hermit. See if I care."

"But I'm still going to watch the game," he told her. "Who are you rooting for, the Ducks or the Badgers?"

"Oregon, of course," Melinda told him. "I'm from the West Coast. Why would I cheer for Wisconsin?"

Frank was relieved when the call ended. It was coming up on noon now. Rose Bowl Game or not, whatever had happened in Arizona was most likely already over and done with. Once he knew the final outcome of that, he'd be ready to move on to the final chapter. He was a bit concerned about the two events happening in such close proximity, but he didn't believe the cops would make a connection between them. Why would they?

So today it was Hal Holden's turn. Later this week would be Sylvia's. To Frank's way of thinking, it was high time his ex-wife finally got hers, too.

CHAPTER 2

SEDONA, ARIZONA

Wednesday, January 1, 2020, 9:00 a.m. (MST)

Once Hal Holden punched the code into the keypad, the gate slowly swung open wide enough to admit his turquoise '76 Lincoln Mark V. He eased the old-fashioned vehicle, one he affectionately referred to as his "Luxo-barge," through the narrow opening and up the steep incline to his client's home. Only a few days earlier, when he'd dropped off the same customer, snow had made the driveway impassable, and he'd been forced to use his other vehicle, a four-wheel-drive Escalade. Because of that model's popularity with funeral directors, he referred to the Caddy as "the hearse," but only in private.

When a severe winter storm had blown through Arizona just before Christmas, Hal had been forced to use that one exclusively for several days while shuttling holiday travelers back and forth between the Verde Valley and Sky Harbor Airport in Phoenix. On this clear New Year's Day, however, that storm was history. No doubt plenty of white stuff still lingered up on the Mogollon

Rim as well as in and around Flagstaff, but Sedona was at a lower elevation. Down here ice on roadways and private drives had melted away.

Hal steered the Lincoln into the residence's spacious turnaround and shifted into park. Then, with the engine still idling, he waited for his client, B. Simpson, to put in an appearance. Hal checked his watch—B. had a midafternoon flight on British Airways. He was someone who always wanted to arrive at the airport several hours early, and that suited Hal just fine. When passengers booked trips too close to their scheduled departures, the ninety-mile drive to Phoenix could devolve into a nail-biting nightmare. Today's trip would be much less stressful.

Both men were well over six feet tall. With the Lincoln's bucket seats pushed all the way back, they'd be able to enjoy a comfortable ride in what Hal considered to be a glorious piece of American engineering. For Hal, driving this piece of highly polished US of A sheet metal was as much of a patriotic experience as saluting the flag.

A widower now for seven years, Hal had taken up an airport-shuttle-driving gig five years earlier, and not because he needed the money. With his beloved Rosie gone, he was lonely and bored. While putting in his twenty-five years as a cop for the Pasadena Police Department, Hal had never imagined being able to retire someplace in the Arizona desert or having the luxury of a Cadillac Escalade as his day-to-day vehicle with his antique Mark V reserved for special occasions. That wonderfully refurbished Lincoln, complete with a brand-new vinyl top and old-fashioned white-wall tires, had been a gift from Rose in honor of Hal's sixtieth birthday, the last birthday the two of them had celebrated together.

Of course, retiring to Arizona had also been a gift from his wife. Despite the fact that Hal and Rose had been lifelong residents of the same city, they might never have met had it not been for one of those proverbial "little old ladies from Pasadena."

The little old lady in question happened to be one Edith Givens, age seventy-eight, who had suffered a massive stroke in the parking lot of her neighborhood Walgreens. When her deadweight foot landed full force on the gas pedal of her Lexus, it had shot into the storefront building through the glass-doored entrance and mowed down both sides of the cosmetics aisle before finally coming to a stop against the back wall next to the pharmacy.

When the incident happened, Hal, a longtime homicide detective with Pasadena PD, had been next door having a pre-shift cup of joe at Starbucks. Consequently, he was the first officer to arrive on the scene. As the on-duty pharmacist at Walgreens, Rose Turnbull was there, too. Together they had provided first aid until EMS arrived to take over and transport Edith to the nearest hospital.

Once the excitement had died down, Hal invited Rose to join him for coffee at the undamaged coffee shop next door, and the rest was history. Rose, a widow, and twice-divorced Hal had married a bare two months later. Due to having received treatment in the immediate aftermath of her stroke, Edith Givens had made a remarkable recovery, and she had been the guest of honor at their wedding.

Rose and her first husband, Alex, had met and

married while they were attending pharmacy school. The childless couple had made a successful life together with both of them working as pharmacists. Due to Alex's careful management of their finances, the two of them amassed a good deal of money during their working years. When Alex passed away, Rose could easily have stopped working, but she didn't. She enjoyed what she was doing, and she wasn't ready to give it up, but she had told Hal up-front that once she did retire, she was moving to Arizona, like it or not. As it turned out, the idea of moving to Arizona suited Hal just fine.

Rose's small bungalow in Pasadena happened to be on a large lot in a desirable neighborhood. After two days on the market followed by a bidding war, it had sold with no contingencies for an eye-popping amount that enabled them to pay all cash for a small, older home that backed up to the golf course in the Village of Oak Creek.

For the next few years Hal and Rose went on several cruises, but all that came to an abrupt halt when she was diagnosed with stage four liver cancer shortly before Hal's sixtieth birthday. That was when she had gifted him with the Mark V. Two months later, Rose was gone, leaving Hal financially secure but broken-hearted because their happily ever after had ended so soon.

During Hal's days in law enforcement, he had golfed occasionally and badly, but once he and Rose moved to the village, he'd gone ahead and taken up golf since the course was literally just outside their back door. Both before and after Rose's passing, he played with a group of fellow retirees, old geezers from the neighborhood, who enjoyed lunching together afterward more than they enjoyed playing the game.

Over burgers and beer they would reminisce about what they'd done prior to retirement. Unlike his golfing chums, Hal wasn't interested in talking about his old days. He had seen enough bad things during his time on the job, and he didn't want to relive them. Once Hal pulled the plug, he was done. He wasn't interested in chatting about those things with a bunch of guys who had never worn a badge and didn't know the first thing about what he'd witnessed along the way. Nor was Hal interested in striking up conversations with other retired LEOs. He was out of it and wanted to stay that way.

The closest he'd come to rejoining some of his old colleagues had been last fall when someone had sent him an envelope containing a copy of a *Los Angeles Times* article concerning the death of his longtime partner, Jack Littleton. Hal and Jack had worked together for years. Jack, five years older than Hal, had been regarded as the "old man" of the duo while Hal had been called the "young 'un." They had gotten along fine when they worked together, but neither had bothered staying in touch after retirement.

According to the article, on October 3, 2019, Jack, a widower living alone and reportedly suffering from ill health, had been found dead in his home, the apparent victim of a gunshot wound to the head. According to the ME, he had died several days before the body was found. Officers on the scene presumed his death to be a suicide, although the coroner's office later listed his manner of death as undetermined.

Hal had been saddened by the news, but he was no more surprised by the outcome than the responding officers had been. These days, suicides among former law enforcement officers were all too common.

The very end of the article provided details about Jack's funeral services. For a brief moment Hal had considered attending but eventually decided against it. Far too many retired officers, haunted by things they could never unsee or unfeel, often resorted to suicide as their only escape hatch. At officer memorials suicide was always the elephant in the room, and Hal didn't want to be part of that conversation when it came to Jack Littleton. He wanted to remember his old partner as the man he had once been—back when both of them had been tough, honest cops, working together and devoted to the job. When faced with Jack's funeral, Hal had used the needs of his shuttle passengers as his excuse for not attending.

The truth was, these days he regarded the people who rode in his vehicles as *his* customers. Initially he had worked for an established company and had driven their vehicles. Over time he learned that Verde Valley's weekend travelers came in two distinct categories. Vacationers tended to be rowdy, rude, and occasionally downright obnoxious. Hal much preferred the more serious commuters—people who lived in and around the Sedona area but had jobs and business interests that took them to other cities or other continents during the week. Although those two groups weren't at all compatible, they tended to come and go from the airport at about the same time.

Commuters heading back to the airport for work purposes on Sunday afternoons were often already in work mode while the vacationers were likely to still be living it up. Shuttle companies were interested in filling their vans to capacity, even when doing so meant having passengers with two very different mindsets in the same vehicle. To Hal's way of thinking, that was bad for business.

Eventually he had decided to leave the vans and his previous employer behind and branch out on his own. Along the way, Hal siphoned off a number of those serious commuter types, taking those along with him—B. Simpson included.

B. and his wife, Ali Reynolds, ran High Noon Enterprises, a tech company of some kind, and B. traveled internationally on almost a weekly basis. Hal had no idea why B. went by his initial only rather than a first name, but that was none of the limo driver's business, and he didn't ask. Occasionally B.'s wife traveled with him. In those instances, Hal used the Escalade because he thought it rude to expect paying passengers to climb into the back seat of a two-door car, but when B. traveled solo, it was always in the Mark V.

Early on, while engaging in idle chitchat, Hal had learned that B. was something of a car buff, speaking fondly of a high school friend whose ride had been a seventies vintage Lincoln. The next time Hal drove B. to Phoenix, he had picked him up in the Mark V as a treat. Now it was a regular occurrence.

A light tap at the passenger window roused Hal from his reverie. He exited the car and hurried around back to open the trunk. B. handed over his customary luggage, a larger rolling bag and a much smaller carry-on, but he held on to his briefcase.

"Happy New Year," Hal said. "How's it going?"

"Pretty well," B. answered. "Can't complain. How about you?"

Hal grinned. "Still on the right side of the grass," he remarked. "Where to today—British Airways?"

Camille Lee, the young woman who handled B.'s travel arrangements, had sent Hal a complete itinerary, but it was always best to verify, just in case.

"Right," B. told him. "British it is. I'm due in London for a reception tomorrow evening."

"Okey-dokey," Hal said. "I'll have you at the terminal in two shakes of a lamb's tail."

After loading the luggage, Hal slammed the trunk closed and then returned to the driver's side of the vehicle. Once he'd fastened his seat belt, he glanced in B.'s direction to make sure he was properly belted as well. When B. opened his briefcase and pulled out his iPad, Hal got the message. On this trip, B. would be working rather than visiting, so Hal put the Lincoln in gear and nosed it back down the driveway.

They had turned onto the main drag and were just coming up to speed when B.'s phone rang. "Hey, Stu," he answered. "Happy New Year to you, too. How are things down on the ranch?"

A ranch? Hal wondered. That was news to him. Hal knew about High Noon Enterprises, which operated out of an office park in nearby Cottonwood. He had dropped B. off and picked him up from there on several occasions, but he'd had no idea the couple was also involved in owning a ranch.

"Yes," B. was saying, "just having High Noon invited to the ransomware roundtable is a huge honor, but you've got that right. We'll be a very small fish in a pool full of sharks."

Hal was not a tech kind of guy. He didn't know what ransomware was exactly, but it sounded bad. The word took Hal back to a dark time. He'd still been working patrol when he'd been the first responding officer at the scene of a reported kidnapping. The boy's parents had coughed up $10,000 in ransom but ended up losing their nine-year-old son anyway. The kid had been found dead—bound, gagged, stabbed to death, and left in a dumpster—two days later. And even though the two perpetrators had eventually been brought to justice, the fact that they were both doing life in prison without parole didn't even the score as far as Hal was concerned.

Pulling himself away from that unwelcome memory, Hal focused on driving, making his way through the roundabouts that were some highway engineer's optimistic daydream for fixing Sedona's growing traffic issues. As far as locals were concerned, they were a constant annoyance since many of the area's out-of-town visitors were completely in the dark when it came to negotiating roundabouts.

B. ended his phone call and glanced in Hal's direction. "Hope you don't mind if I work."

"Not at all," Hal told him. "I'm good."

As B. once again immersed himself in his iPad, Hal continued driving. With New Year's Day falling on a Wednesday, the afternoon's mass exodus might not be that bad. In any case, they were traveling early enough to miss most of it.

Beyond the Village of Oak Creek and just past the entrance to the Hilton, a grubby, mud-spattered, crew-cab Silverado with New Mexico plates pulled in behind him and parked on the Luxo-barge's back bumper. Hal had an issue with tailgaters. For one thing, they were usually in a hell of a hurry, but if this guy—and the driver was definitely a guy—thought sticking to the Mark V like glue was going to make Hal drive any faster, he had another think coming.

Good luck with that, Hal thought to himself. *There aren't many passing zones between here and I-17.*

Of course, having other vehicles following too closely behind the Lincoln wasn't an unusual occurrence. Younger drivers in particular often wanted to gawk at his shiny motoring antique. Later, when they finally got around to passing him, they'd often do so with a friendly wave or a nod or even a thumbs-up. Eventually, maybe that's what this guy would do, too.

But just because someone was following him didn't mean Hal was going to change his driving habits. He always stuck to the posted speed limit no matter what, and that's what he did this time, keeping his speed at a steady fifty-five. Even so, when they reached the first of the passing zones, the pickup made no effort to go around.

Okay, then, Hal thought. *Enjoy your unobstructed view of my Continental kit.*

By the time Hal was ready to merge onto southbound I-17, several more cars were lined up behind the crew cab. There had been several passing zones along the way but none were long enough to allow more than one vehicle to pass at a time. Since the pickup hadn't gone around the Lincoln, no one else had been able to do so, either.

Once southbound on the freeway, Hal accelerated at a leisurely pace, giving the drivers lined up behind him ample opportunity to pass. Three of the vehicles stuck behind the Silverado immediately sped up, merged into the left lane, and surged around both of them, but the pickup remained right where it was—still following way too close, especially now that both vehicles were traveling at the posted limit of seventy-five.

What's with this guy? Hal wondered.

Just then the Silverado eased into the left-hand lane. For a moment it was invisible in Hal's blind spot, but when the truck came into view again, it had pulled up alongside the Lincoln and was straddling the lane marker. At that point, some long-buried law enforcement survival instinct came into play, warning Hal that something wasn't right. Just then the Silverado veered sharply into the right lane as though intending to smash directly into him.

A PIT? Hal thought in disbelief. *He's trying to pull off a damned PIT maneuver?*

As a trained police officer, Hal Holden knew all about the Pursuit Intervention Technique. That's where a pursuing cop car slams into a fleeing felon's rear bumper with enough force to swing the other vehicle into a spin. During his time on the job, Hal had successfully performed PITs on numerous occasions, but never as the targeted vehicle and never at seventy-five miles an hour.

Hal's reaction was instantaneous. Taking the only evasive option available, he hit the brakes, hoping that by slowing the Lincoln's momentum, he'd be able to mitigate a catastrophic crash. Instead, as the Lincoln suddenly slowed, the speeding pickup missed the back bumper and slammed into the front fender instead.

Gripping the steering wheel for all he was worth, Hal tried shouting a warning to his unsuspecting passenger, but his words disappeared in shrieks of shredding metal. The Silverado's glancing but powerful blow sent the speeding Lincoln across the rumble strip and through a guardrail. For a moment it became airborne as it plunged off the edge of a steep embankment. It landed nose down in a ditch and turned end over end once before flipping to its side. The vehicle rolled three more times before finally coming to a halt that sent a pillar of dust flying skyward.

Hal Holden wasn't aware of any of that. He was out cold and down for the count.

CHAPTER 3

COTTONWOOD, ARIZONA

Wednesday, January 1, 2020, 9:00 a.m. (MST)

New Year's Day might have been a holiday for lots of people, but not for Camille Lee. Cami had grown up in a dysfunctional family as the object of a parental tug-of-war between a pair of unhappily married parents who, for reasons she never understood, refused to go their separate ways. Their daughter seemed to be the only thing they had in common, and both had been gravely disappointed when she had refused to follow the life plan either of her parents had individually laid out for her.

Cami's parents were of Chinese descent. Her mother's forebears had immigrated to the US in the early part of the twentieth century. While attending college, Cami's mother, originally named Xiu Ling, had changed her given name to a more American-sounding Susan or Sue. As of now, Professor Susan Lee was a tenured professor of French at Stanford University, and she was appalled that her daughter exhibited no interest whatsoever in following in her mother's academic footsteps.

Cami's father, Cheng, a professor of computer science at Stanford, had come to the US from Taiwan as an exchange student. He and Sue had met in college. When his student visa ran out and he was about to be shipped home, the couple had exchanged vows in what was generally acknowledged to be a green card marriage. Unlike most of those unions, however, theirs hadn't ended once Cheng became a US citizen. They had persisted in sticking together through thick and thin for, as far as Cami was concerned, no apparent reason.

Growing up in that troubled family atmosphere, Cami had escaped into her studies, isolating herself in her room while her parents quarreled endlessly in other parts of the house. Cheng and Sue didn't do Christmas, and they didn't do New Year's, either—at least not on January 1, but Lunar New Year was another story. When that came around, the couple somehow buried the hatchet long enough to make the trek into downtown San Francisco to watch the parade and have dinner at Cami's grandfather's restaurant. In the course of the afternoon, while her mother was out shopping and her father was doing whatever he did, her grandfather, Liu Wei (known to his many customers as Louie), would regale Cami with stories of his decades in the restaurant business, often sharing his usually top-secret recipes with his granddaughter and teaching her how to cook.

Now living far from home, when Lunar New Year came around, Cami made sure to celebrate on her own. This year she had already asked for two days off. January 24th would be devoted to cooking. On the 25th, she would show up at High Noon Enterprises' corporate office laden with a New Year's feast large enough to feed one and all and cooked to Liu Wei's exacting specifications.

That meant that on this day—one of no particular importance to Cami—she had the High Noon complex all to herself. Stu Ramey, the company's second-in-command, had originally been scheduled to work that day. Although the company was an internationally known cybersecurity powerhouse, its physical presence was a low-key operation in a Cottonwood office park where High Noon ran long on computers and short on personnel. Banks of CPUs whirred endlessly, searching out possible cyberattacks on customer networks scattered around the world. It was only when the watchful algorithms discovered a possible incursion did audible alarms summon immediate human intervention.

A few days before Christmas, Cami had overheard Stu's part of a conversation with his aunt Julia. Julia Miller, a crackerjack horsewoman somewhere in her seventies, ran Racehorse Rest, a nonprofit racehorse rescue operation located near Payson on the far side of the Verde Valley. Caring for retired and often injured racehorses was an expensive proposition, and Stu was one of the benefactors who kept the outfit afloat.

"I'm sorry, Aunt Julia," Cami had heard him say. "I'm scheduled to work New Year's Day. Attending an event like that the night before would be too much."

At High Noon, computers took up the vast majority of the floorspace. Workstations for the crew of people who supervised said computers were located in such close proximity to each other that carrying on private telephone conversations wasn't an option.

"What kind of event?" Cami asked once the call ended.

Stu sighed. "Aunt Julia is holding a big New Year's Eve gala at the ranch, and she'd really like me to attend, but I already told her I have to be here early the next morning. It just wouldn't work."

Stuart Ramey was brilliant when it came to computers, but he had limited social skills. When Cami was first hired, her main responsibility at High Noon had been helping Stu interact with people, especially face-to-face. In the years since, he had made enormous progress, some of which Cami credited to his working with the damaged animals at his aunt Julia's ranch. When Cami first met him, it would have been unthinkable for him to be invited to a gala, much less for him to consider attending one.

"You should go," Cami advised him. "I can take your shift."

"But it's a holiday," Stu objected. "You're scheduled to have the day off."

"It's no big deal," Cami had told him. "Call Aunt Julia back and tell her you're coming."

Much to Cami's amazement, Stu had done just that. Of course, Cami's apparent generosity on that score had an ulterior motive. It gave her a perfect excuse to call her own mother and tell Sue that her daughter wouldn't be coming home to attend her grandmother's birthday party, which happened to be scheduled for New Year's Day.

But just because the first of January was a holiday for most of the world didn't mean that Cami needed to be any less vigilant. Cybercrooks didn't seem to celebrate holidays. In fact, they often scheduled attacks to coincide with times when offices would be shuttered or lightly staffed. That way, whatever damaging cyber-bug they installed on targeted networks would have time to settle in and do their damaging work before victims were any the wiser.

Needing a pit stop and a fresh cup of coffee, Cami did one last survey of the master control panel before leaving her workstation and padding in her flip-flops out of the computer lab, first to the restroom and then on to the break room.

As Cami walked along, she was grateful for the skilled orthopedic surgeon who had repaired her damaged leg months earlier when she had escaped a kidnapper by throwing herself out of the back of a moving pickup. Due to the seriousness of her injury, she'd originally been told that she might never walk again. Much to her surprise, the leg had healed nicely, and she had since resumed her Krav Maga workouts, gradually increasing their intensity. Now she was pretty much back to her pre-surgery skill levels.

In the break room, Cami raided the fridge for a container of yogurt and one of Mateo Vega's mother's homemade tamales. The two made for an unlikely but good combination, and she snacked on that while she brewed a new batch of coffee to replace the one that had turned to brackish dregs in the pot. Then, with replenished coffee in hand, she returned to the lab.

When she had first come to work at High Noon, the never-ending racket of Stu Ramey's police scanner had bothered her. For reasons Cami never understood, he kept the device playing in the background twenty-four/seven. That had been the case when he'd had the lab all to himself, and it continued even though more employees had been added to the mix.

At first the constant verbal back-and-forthing had driven Cami nuts. For a time she had even considered wearing earplugs, but eventually she'd adjusted to it. Now the radio chatter was just so much white noise in the background, and most of the time, she didn't even notice it. Occasionally, however, when something bad happened and the distant voices took on a life-or-death urgency, whatever was playing out on the scanner caught Cami's attention. That was exactly what occurred as she reentered the lab.

The first voice she heard was that of a female 911 dispatcher. "The Air Evac helicopter is twenty minutes out," she said. "Traffic on I-17 is stopped in both directions. The helicopter should be able to land directly on the roadway."

A major traffic pileup of some kind must have happened, Cami realized, but why? As far as she knew, there were no weather-related problems. Still, if the major highway between Phoenix and Flagstaff had been shut down on the last day of an important holiday, whatever it was had to be serious.

Back at her desk, she checked her monitor visually while still listening in on the scanner in the background and trying to pluck more details from the law enforcement jargon flying back and forth. Eventually she was able to sort out that a single-vehicle rollover accident resulting in serious injuries had occurred just south of the interchange between State Route 179 and I-17. A mile farther south, yet another vehicle, which might or might not have been involved in the original mishap, had been found completely engulfed in flames. The burning vehicle had ignited a fast-moving brush fire, which was now the cause of the freeway shutdown.

At that point Cami became concerned. One of her responsibilities at High Noon was making employee travel arrangements. She knew that B. was scheduled to depart Sky Harbor on the afternoon British Airways flight from Phoenix to Heathrow. Because she'd made both his flight reservations and airport limo arrangements, she knew the exact timing of Hal Holden's pickup at B.'s home in Sedona. If they were now stuck in that traffic backup, there was a good chance B. would miss his flight.

Cami checked her phone. There were no missed calls, and her ringer was turned on, so no one had tried to call her. She was tempted to try calling B.'s number but held off on that. Maybe she was wrong to be worried. Maybe they'd been far enough ahead of the accident to miss it altogether. If not, and if B. needed her to rebook his flight arrangements, Cami was sure he'd be in touch.

Nonetheless, she went over to Stu's workstation and turned up the volume on the scanner, making it easier for her to hear the transmissions. She listened in as cops on the scene reported the Air Evac helicopter's arrival as well as its departure a few minutes later with two seriously injured passengers on board and headed for the trauma unit at St. Gregory's Hospital in Phoenix.

Cami was tempted to turn the scanner volume down after that, but she left it alone. She was still listening in when a call went out requesting a tow truck to be dispatched to the scene in order to retrieve a 1976 Lincoln Continental.

A '76 Lincoln? Cami was dumbfounded. That had to be Hal Holden's car! How many '76 Lincolns were still out on the road? That's when Cami reached for her phone. With trembling fingers, she dialed B.'s number.

"Hello." The voice on the other end of the line was unfamiliar.

Cami's heart fell. "This is B. Simpson's phone," she said urgently. "I'm one of his employees. Who are you?"

"This is Officer Darrel Collins with the Arizona Department of Public Safety," the stranger answered.

"My name is Camille Lee. As I said, Mr. Simpson is my employer. What's happened to him?"

"Please hang on, Ms. Lee," Officer Collins said. "Let me put you in touch with my supervisor."

CHAPTER 4

LAS VEGAS, NEVADA

Wednesday, January 1, 2020, 1:00 p.m. (PST)

Once the Rose Bowl ended, Frank put on his sweats, left the apartment, and walked to Hi-Roller. There was a workout room in the apartment complex, but the equipment and atmosphere there didn't compare to that of a fully operational gym.

During the short walk, like it or not, he found himself wondering about Sylvia and the kids—the two who were his and the one who wasn't. What were they up to today? They didn't exactly stay in touch. Once Sylvia refused to post bail for him and had filed for divorce, he hadn't heard from any of them the whole time he was in prison. The last Frank knew, Sylvia was supposedly living somewhere near Portland, Oregon, with her second husband. The kids were all in their twenties now, probably grown up and out of the house. If he had put his mind to it—and his Internet search engine—he could probably have gone looking for them, but he didn't. For the time being he needed to stay hands-off. The less interest he showed in them, the better.

At the gym, he did some stretching and then spent some time lifting weights. His strategy there was to increase the number of reps as opposed to increasing the weights. When he finished that, he put himself on a treadmill and walked for an hour straight. Walking worked for him now the same way it had while he'd been in the joint. Early on he had decided that in addition to being hard on his knees, running or jogging didn't use up enough time. Both in prison and out, Frank Muñoz had way too much time on his hands.

Thanks first to his mother's and later to his wife's tortillas, Frank had been a bit on the pudgy side when he was first arrested and even more so by the time he was transported to Lompoc. At first, as a newly imprisoned ex-cop, Frank had barely dared to leave his cell. Each time he showered, he expected to be met with a shiv. Ditto for eating in the mess hall. Living in that kind of fear was bad for the digestive system, and the food was abysmal. Naturally, Frank lost weight.

Eventually, though, his fear level decreased. No one seemed interested in coming after him, and finally he figured out why—Frank wasn't a snitch. He had pled guilty without taking a deal or naming names. In prison circles, that gave him a certain amount of status. On the inside, being a snitch was far worse than being ex–law enforcement.

The big problem for Frank had been how to pass the time. There was a library, but books had never held much interest for him. There was a TV in the rec room during certain hours, but he remained wary of being in such close quarters with that many fellow inmates. There was a basketball court in the yard, but basketball had never been his thing, so he had spent his yard time walking. Finally one of his fellow walkers said, "Why don't you come to the gym?"

He'd accepted the invitation, and working out worked for him. It helped pass the time in ways yard-walking never had. Over time, and with constant working out, his body began to transform. By the time Frank was released on parole, he was in excellent shape, and his Hi-Roller workouts were helping him maintain his prison-based level of physical fitness.

For Frank, treadmill time was thinking time. He held it sacrosanct and always wore a pair of earplugs to discourage others from engaging him in unwanted conversation. Naturally, given what he'd been thinking about on his short walk from his apartment to the gym, once Frank was on the treadmill, his thoughts returned to Sylvia Garcia Muñoz Rogers. No matter which way you cut it, Frank's troubles always came back to her.

Growing up in Riverside, the Muñoz family and the Garcias had been next-door neighbors. Ramon Garcia, Sylvia's older brother, and Frank had been best buds. They had regarded Sylvia as an obnoxious pest and the bane of their existence. Ramon was five years older than Sylvia and Frank was four. Mrs. Garcia expected Ramon to function as Sylvia's protector. That translated into his being a glorified baby-sitter most of the time, and the boys had to drag her along with them wherever they went.

Once while Frank and Ramon were riding bikes, Sylvia wondered why she couldn't ride one, too. When Ramon told her it was because she was too little, she'd gone crying to their mother, complaining that Ramon had been mean to her. Ramon got in trouble and Sylvia ended up with a new bike, one that came complete with training wheels. In junior high, on Halloween, the two boys couldn't go trick-or-treating with their pals because they'd been put in charge of Sylvia, dressed in a Cinderella-style ballgown. While in high school, even though Ramon had played trumpet in the band, Mrs. Garcia had insisted he take Sylvia along to the football games. Since Frank often rode with Ramon, he was stuck riding with Sylvia, too.

Frank had been a good student and a fair-to-middling football player. He'd won an academic scholarship to UCLA where, intent on going to law school, he'd majored in criminal justice. Frank's father was a long-haul trucker. His mother was a stay-at-home mom. The scholarship wasn't a full ride, by any means, but it had enabled Frank to go on to college.

His junior year at UCLA, when Frank came back to Riverside for homecoming weekend, something amazing had happened. Sylvia was no longer a pest. Instead, she had grown up and morphed into a dark-haired beauty—a head-turning, hot little number with generous curves in all the right places that attracted boys wherever she went.

Once she laid eyes on Frank at a post–homecoming dance gathering, however, every other guy at the party vanished from view—including the poor sap who had brought her there in the first place. She ditched him in favor of riding home with Frank and stopping off to do some hot-and-heavy necking along the way. From that moment on, the two of them were a couple. Frank gave her a promise ring the following summer. As far as everyone in the neighborhood was concerned, they were bound to get married, sooner or later. Unfortunately sooner came earlier than expected.

The next April Frank made a special trip home to take Sylvia to her senior prom. She had been gorgeous that night in a bright red floor-length gown, and Frank had presented his tuxedoed self, complete with a red bow tie and a matching red pocket square. That evening Sylvia didn't want to dance nearly as much as she wanted to drink. They bugged out early and drove to a teenage hangout just outside town where they sat in the back of Frank's aging Cutlass and imbibed shots of tequila.

They had come prepared for that part of the evening festivities. Frank, old enough to buy booze by then, had provided the tequila while Sylvia had brought along both a saltshaker and a fresh lime concealed inside her tiny beaded handbag. Frank hacked off slices of lime with his pocket knife, and they had sipped their tequila—lots of it—straight out of the bottle.

That night when the necking threatened to go beyond hot and heavy, Frank had tried to back off. "Don't worry," Sylvia had whispered in his ear. "I'm on the pill." Which, depending on your point of view, turned out to be either a little white lie or else a very big one. Two months later Frank came home eager to share the news that he'd just been accepted to one of the coveted spots at the UCLA School of Law. That was when Sylvia dropped the bomb, telling him that the pill must not have worked because she was pregnant.

There was never a question about Frank's doing the right thing. Doing otherwise wasn't an option because his dad would have killed him. The couple tied the knot in front of a justice of the peace in Palm Springs two weeks after Sylvia's surprise announcement. Frank knew before he ever said "I do" that fatherhood and going to law school wouldn't work. Married and with a baby on the way, he needed a job in a hell of a hurry. With his criminal justice degree in hand, he applied for work at any number of police agencies and ended up being hired by Pasadena PD.

At first he and Sylvia were happy enough. They found a tiny apartment and set up housekeeping. On a beginning police officer's pay, money was tight. Sylvia wasn't interested in earning a degree. She offered to go to work to bring in some needed funds, but the only job she'd ever held had been a short stint at a local fast-food joint while she'd been in high school. She probably could have gotten a gig doing that, but the idea of her having to work was unacceptable to Frank's macho pride. His mother had never worked outside the home, so why should his wife? Besides, once the baby was born, he reasoned, the amount of money Sylvia would bring home from a minimum-wage job would barely cover the cost of childcare. So the die was cast—Sylvia stayed home while Frank worked.

When their baby boy arrived, Sylvia insisted that they name him Ramon, after her brother. At the time, Frank was as proud as any other brand-new papa. Recently graduated from the police academy, he passed around blue-wrapped cigars to everyone in the squad room. The first of Ramon's two younger sisters, Cristina, came along two years later and Lucinda in another two after that. But it wasn't until after the births of the two girls that Frank began to wonder if he'd been sold a bill of goods.

Even as newborns, Cristina and Lucinda looked like tiny versions of Frank's mother, their grandma Lupé. Ramon, on the other hand, didn't resemble anyone in the family—not on his father's side, and not on his mother's, either. Before long Frank began to wonder if the boy was even his. He had always believed that he and Sylvia were in an exclusive relationship, but what if that wasn't true? What if Sylvia had already suspected she was pregnant by someone else by the time prom rolled around, and what if the consensual sex they'd engaged in that night had been her way of getting Frank on the hook?

Once those doubts crept in, things between Frank and Sylvia started going downhill. They quarreled all the time. She claimed he picked on Ramon and spoiled the two girls, and that was probably true. Every time Frank looked at the kid, he wondered. Being a cop, Frank had learned about DNA early on. Finally those years of working around crime scenes and collecting evidence pushed him toward having a paternity test, but for a long time he didn't go through with it because he was torn, wanting to know the real answer almost as much as he didn't.

In high school Sylvia Garcia had been beauty queen material, but having three kids in little more than four years had resulted in a certain amount of wear and tear in that department. She was only five-three to begin with, and the weight she gained in pregnancy never went away. When you added thirty pounds or so onto an already voluptuous figure, the end result wasn't great, at least not in Frank's opinion, and that was about the time he began visiting local strip joints, especially BJ's.

One day Frank came home from work and presented all three kids with brand-new battery-powered tooth-brushes. After collecting the old ones, he took them to a pal of his in the crime lab who performed an off-the-books DNA test. When the results came back, it was clear that whoever Ramon Muñoz's father was, he sure as hell wasn't Frank Muñoz.

Not long after that Frank told Sylvia he was spending the weekend fishing with some of the guys from work. Instead, he visited a nearby office of Planned Parenthood and had a vasectomy. On the sign-in form, he listed himself as divorced so Sylvia wouldn't be able to weigh in on the subject. She wasn't the least bit upset when he came home two days later without any fish, but if she'd known about the snip job, she might have been. As it was, Frank was suddenly shooting blanks, and she was none the wiser. Neither was Danielle, for that matter, because by then he was already seeing her on the side.

From then on, marital relations in the household went from bad to worse, but getting a divorce was out of the question. There was no way Frank's cop salary would support two households. So he and Sylvia had stuck together—unhappily so—right up until she deserted him once he was in jail, and that hit him hard. After all, she had turned to Frank when she was in trouble, forcing him to abandon his long-held dream of becoming a lawyer, but what happened once he needed her help? Sylvia had walked away from him without a second glance.

That was one betrayal he would never forget or forgive, and it was one for which she would pay the price.

CHAPTER 5

SEDONA, ARIZONA

Wednesday, January 1, 2020, 9:00 a.m. (MST)

For the first time ever, when Ali kissed B. good-bye and watched him ride away in Hal Holden's aging Lincoln, she was relieved to see him go. B. had been home longer than usual, for three whole weeks—the two prior to Christmas and the week after Christmas as well. All that togetherness should have been great, but a lot of it hadn't been.

Ali had been thrilled to have him on hand to host High Noon's annual Christmas party for employees, family, and friends. This was the first holiday season after the death of Ali's father, and the party had been Edie Larson's initial major solo event without her beloved Bobby at her side. Although Edie had done her best to put on a good game face, Ali had known how much her mother was hurting. Having B. there playing host had allowed Ali to run interference for her mom.

Once the party was over, however, B. had spent most of his waking hours, both at home and in the office, working on a presentation for an upcoming international ransomware conference. As he worked, he became more and more irritable and restless. Since B. was generally completely unflappable, Ali had finally asked what was going on.

"I'm fine," he told her. "Everything's just fine."

Obviously everything wasn't fine, but she let it go. Now that he was finally on his way to deliver the damned presentation, she hoped he'd be in a better frame of mind the next time she saw him.

As the aging Lincoln disappeared from view, Ali closed the door and came inside, amazed to realize that, except for Bella, their miniature dachshund, she had the house to herself. Not only was B. gone, so was their majordomo, Alonzo Rivera. After spending several days over the holidays with relatives in Phoenix, Alonzo was due back home later that evening.

Reveling in her unaccustomed solitude, Ali headed for the master bath and the jetted soaking tub she had installed at great expense years earlier. This seemed like a golden opportunity to put the seldom-used tub to use. Bella happily followed Ali down the hall and into the bathroom, but once she realized a bath might be in the offing, the dog took herself out of harm's way.

After filling the tub and adding a sprinkling of lavender-scented bath salts, Ali climbed in and turned on the jets, allowing the steamy water to pound her legs and back. It was only as she closed her eyes and relaxed that Ali finally allowed herself to acknowledge how glad she was that the holiday season was over.

Christmas without her father had affected more people than just Ali and her mother. Much of the time, Ali had slapped a smile on her face and simply gone through the motions. Christmas dinner itself, without

Bob Larson in his customary spot, had been more somber than celebratory. So it was with some relief that Ali focused on getting back to the usual grind. Tax season was coming. As High Noon's CFO, that was always a big chore.

Soaking in the tub, she eventually lost track of time. When a ringing cell phone jarred her out of her reverie, Ali was dismayed to see the phone laying on the bathroom counter well out of reach. Rather than breaking her neck to scramble out of the tub and answer, Ali decided to let the call go to voice mail. She suspected one of the twins might be calling to wish their grandmother a happy New Year. Deciding their good wishes could wait and refusing to be rushed, Ali added more hot water to the mix and resumed her pleasant bath.

Ali's plan for the remainder of the day was to take down and box up the Christmas decorations. Alonzo would have been happy to tackle that job, but it was something Ali herself needed to do this time around. She already understood that, in the process of putting away many of those long-treasured decorations, she would also be boxing up countless memories of her father and of her parents together. If she needed to shed a tear or two in the process, she wanted to do so in private.

With the water cooling again, Ali was about to climb out of the tub when the doorbell rang—and not just once, either. It sounded as though someone was pressing the button over and over. She climbed out of the tub and was reaching for a towel when Bella began to bark. A moment later, she heard Stu Ramey's voice over the racket.

"Ali, are you here?"

Stu? Ali was astonished to realize he had entered the house without waiting for the door to be opened. *What the hell is going on?*

"I'm just getting out of the tub," she called back. "Hang on."

Giving up on using a towel, Ali wrapped her dripping body in a terrycloth robe. When she hurried out of the bathroom, she found Stu standing in the bedroom doorway with Bella doing her best to hold the looming intruder at bay.

"Sorry to barge in like this," he apologized. "I used the keypad on the garage."

One look at the man's anguished face told Ali something was terribly wrong. "Stu," she demanded, "what's going on?"

"It's B.," he replied. "There's been an accident on I-17. Cami spoke to the incident supervisor on the scene. B. and Hal Holden are both alive, but they're in bad shape and currently being airlifted to St. Gregory's in Phoenix. Get dressed. We need to go now."

Ali could hardly believe her ears. For a moment she could neither move nor speak. "Oh, no!" she whispered finally, clutching at the doorjamb to keep from falling. "Are you sure?"

"I'm sure," Stu said grimly. "Come on."

In all the years Ali had known Stu Ramey, she had never heard that kind of urgency in his voice. "Okay," she managed finally. "Give me a second to get dressed."

Stu set off down the hallway with Bella still at his heels. In the bedroom Ali's hands shook so badly that it took far longer than a second for her to get dressed. In the bedroom she pulled on a pair of jeans, a Sedona High sweatshirt, and a pair of tennis shoes. Before climbing into the tub, she'd used a scrunchy to pull her hair into a bun on the top of her head. Now she switched that over to a ponytail. As for makeup? She didn't bother.

Returning to the bathroom to grab her phone, she noticed she had missed a call from Cami some fifteen minutes earlier. Doubtless, when Ali hadn't answered, Cami had dispatched Stu to come find her.

As Ali's initial panic subsided, she realized there was no way of knowing how long she'd be gone. With that in mind, she took a few moments to collect an overnight bag from the closet and fill it with a few essentials—a change of clothing and underwear, her makeup bag, and the clear plastic containers of liquids and hairspray she used to get through airport security. Exiting the bedroom, she detoured through the library long enough to add her computer, her iPad, and a tangle of chargers to the jumbled mix of hurried packing.

Even then Bella was still barking. Halfway down the hall, carrying both the overnight bag and her purse, Ali realized she'd need to figure out what to do about the dog. Obviously she couldn't take Bella along to the hospital, and without Alonzo, she couldn't leave her home alone, either. There was no doggy door in the house. The neighborhood's many predators made it too risky to allow the tiny dog outdoors on her own.

As Ali puzzled about that, the dog fell silent. Arriving in the kitchen doorway, Ali saw why. Stu had taken a piece of string cheese from the fridge and was using small pieces of that to silence the dog. Bella was now happily eating out of his hand.

Stu glanced up as Ali entered the room. "We need to hurry," he urged. "I-17 is shut down in both directions.

Traffic is being diverted through Cottonwood. If we go the back way through Sedona, we'll miss some of the logjam, but we'll be in the thick of it once we get closer to Cottonwood."

"We're going the back way, then?" Ali confirmed.

Stu nodded. Realizing that route would take them directly past her mother's place, Ali made up her mind and called her mother.

"Happy New Year," Edie said as she came on the line.

"Thank you," Ali said, "and the same to you, but I need your help. There's been an accident on I-17. B. has been injured and is being airlifted to St. Gregory's in Phoenix. Stu and I are on our way there, and Alonzo is out of town. Would it be okay if I dropped Bella off with you?"

"Oh my goodness!" Edie exclaimed. "Of course, come right over."

After that, Ali handed her luggage to Stu while she collected a grocery bag containing dog essentials—two metal dishes, some kibble, and a leash. Then, lugging both Bella and the dog-care bag, Ali followed Stu out of the house.

"Your mom's place, then?" Stu asked, once Ali clambered into the passenger seat of Stu's enormous Dodge Ram.

She nodded. "Alonzo can pick Bella up from there when he gets home from Phoenix."

As Stu drove, Ali held Bella close to her chest, letting the dog's presence calm her enough to ask questions. "Okay," she said finally, "what happened?"

"Cami heard about the accident over my scanner," Stu explained. "She tried calling you first. When you didn't answer, she called me. I had just gotten home from Payson. I must have exited the freeway just minutes ahead of the accident."

"Where was it?"

"Just south of the Sedona interchange on I-17."

"What caused it?" Ali asked. "The weather's fine. The snow and ice all melted. Did they have a blowout?"

"I don't know," Stu replied. "According to Cami, the accident is being reported as a single-vehicle rollover."

"But why would a single-vehicle accident in the southbound lanes have the freeway shut down in both directions?"

"A mile or so south of the original incident, a second vehicle caught fire and started a fast-moving brush fire. That's what caused the closure."

Ali was barely listening just then. She was caught up in remembering the last words she had whispered to B. as she kissed him goodbye: "Travel safe."

"Any details about the injuries?" she asked after a pause.

"Cami says the word 'serious' came through over the scanner."

"Serious rather than life-threatening?"

"Let's hope," Stu said. "I've turned Frigg loose on the case. As soon as she has anything definite on that, she'll report in. I also asked her to locate B.'s electronic devices, back them up, and brick them. We can't afford for any of High Noon's proprietary information to be sitting in the back of some unsecured cop car or locked up in an evidence room for the duration of an accident investigation."

Frigg was the pet name used to refer to Stu's private artificial intelligence. The fact that his AI could remotely access and control B.'s electronic devices was a scary proposition as far as Ali was concerned, but in this case, her ability to do so counted as a blessing.

"Good thinking," Ali said.

Moments later they pulled up to the entrance of Sedona Shadows, her mother's assisted-living facility. Edie was standing just inside the sliding front door. Before Stu's truck came to a full stop, she dashed out to meet them.

"How bad is it?" Edie asked anxiously as Ali climbed down from the truck. "Is B. going to be all right?"

Ali shook her head. "I don't know. Details are pretty scarce right now, but I'll let you know how he is once I find out. But thank you for doing this," she added, handing over both the dog and her accompanying bag of goods. "Alonzo is due home this evening, and he'll come collect her, but here's some food for her to eat in the meantime."

With the exchange made, Ali hugged her mom and then climbed back into the truck. Moments later she and Stu were on their way.

CHAPTER 6

LAS VEGAS, NEVADA

Wednesday, January 1, 2020, 2:00 p.m. (PST)

Frank didn't exactly advertise that he was fresh out of prison, not at the gym and not at his apartment complex, either. He doubted that any of his fellow tenants guessed their neighbor was a recent parolee because he did his best to fit in. He was pleasant when meeting people on the stairs or in the breezeways. And that's what he did on his first New Year's Day on the outside, too—he did his best to fit in. He greeted the people he met with a cheerful "Happy New Year." Since everybody seemed to be ordering up pizza and/or wings to be delivered for the game, so did Frank.

By kickoff time, he had all the necessary trappings on hand, including a freshly opened bottle of Coors. Once the game started, anyone walking past his living room window would have spotted a seemingly devoted football fan seated in front of his flat-screen TV, totally engrossed in the game. Except he wasn't—not at all. Frank's mind was a good seven hours away from Vegas, back in Lompoc—back in the pen.

There had been all kinds of rules in prison, most of which, Frank soon discovered, were meant to be broken. Inmates were not supposed to have access to electronic devices or the Internet, but some of them did, and with the exchange of a sufficient amount of bartered goods, the haves were often willing to share with the have-nots.

Once Frank managed to move beyond the terror of being a dishonored cop on the inside, something unexpected happened. Suddenly the degree in criminal justice he had earned all those years earlier became a valuable commodity. Inmates had legal questions. The prison library was stocked with a collection of law books, but when it came to finding answers, most of Frank's fellow prisoners had no idea where to start.

Lompoc was a federal correctional facility. Many of the people imprisoned there were guilty of financial transgressions—fraud, corruption, tax evasion, money laundering, drug dealing, and the like. There were a number of disgraced lawyers in the prison population, including an impeached superior court judge and a prosecutor or two. Any of those folks would have had more legal expertise than Frank did. At first he was surprised that prisoners brought their legal questions to him, but finally he figured it out.

Every one of those incarcerated legal beagles were there on reduced sentences after negotiating plea deals. To a man, all of them had named names. Given a choice between doing business with a crooked cop who wasn't a snitch or a crooked lawyer who was, Frank Muñoz was the hands-down winner.

Over time he realized that he had moved up the ranks and was now a member of Lompoc's elite ruling class. That gave him access to any number of goods and services. It was also how Frank learned about Gregg Atkins.

Atkins went to Lompoc as the founder of a now-defunct Ponzi scheme. When it went bust, no one was more dismayed than Gregg himself, but not because the money from his fraudulent investment scheme was missing from his clients' accounts—that had been the intention from the beginning. What infuriated him was that the funds from those ill-gotten gains that he had expected to keep for himself were gone, too—and not just gone—they had ended up in someone else's pocket. Gregg had been under the impression that his wife, June, his loving partner in crime, had been transferring those funds into accounts the two of them held in common. That assumption had turned out to be wrong.

Instead, those monies had ended up in accounts owned jointly by June and her boyfriend, a handsome, much younger man named Stefan, who had been the couple's off-shore banker. When the feds closed in to shut down the Ponzi scheme, June and Stefan had fled to his home country, the off-shore banking haven of Montenegro, leaving Gregg alone to take the rap. While he ended up being sentenced to a seventeen-year stretch in prison, June and Stefan appeared to be living happily ever after, safely out of reach of US extradition proceedings. As soon as he ended up in Lompoc, he told anyone willing to listen that the moment he got out, he would make it his life's work to get even with June and her boy toy.

But then along came Gregg's cancer diagnosis—pancreatic, stage four. Everyone who heard about it—inmates and prison staff alike—expected Gregg to petition for compassionate release, but he didn't. Instead he stayed right where he was—inside the walls of Lompoc—and went on the warpath from there.

Gregg was no fool. Before the Ponzi scheme's collapse, he had squirreled a bit of money away in something June had regarded as entirely bogus—cryptocurrency. At the time it had been a relatively small amount, and he'd made only that single deposit. Shortly after that, however, cryptocurrency had exploded. Dismissed and forgotten by June, the value of that one deposit had mushroomed. It was accessible to anyone with the proper codes and an Internet connection.

As his health deteriorated, Gregg let it be known that he was in the market for a hit man, and he had money to pay for the same. Not only that, time was of the essence.

As it happened, if you knew the right people and had the means, hit men were among the goods and services available on the open market inside the Lompoc Federal Correctional Complex.

Less than two weeks later, the bodies of June Atkins and Stefan Lazovich were found in their luxury hotel room inside the fortified fishing village of Sveti Stefan off the coast of Montenegro. They had both been stabbed to death. Three days later, when Gregg Atkins breathed his last, there was a smile on his face, and the Lompoc inmates who were in the know all understood why.

Although Gregg was a prime suspect in the double homicide, he was dead and gone long before the authorities came calling. As far as Frank knew, the case remained unsolved, and even though a number of prison inmates knew all about what had happened, no one breathed a word.

Frank was not directly involved in any of this, but he was well aware of it. It pleased him to know that not only had Gregg succeeded in getting even with the people who had wronged him, he had also gotten away with it, and that gave Frank Muñoz something else to think about. Up to that point, he'd been totally focused on getting fit and getting out. Now he was focused on getting even.

When a ringing phone jarred Frank back to the present, he was astonished to discover it was already halftime. He'd watched the first half of the football game with his eyes wide open and his mind elsewhere. Naturally, his caller was Melinda.

"Where are you?" she asked.

"Where I said I'd be," he told her, "at home."

"I thought maybe you were headed for a sports bar and didn't want to hurt my feelings."

"No sports bar," Frank said. "I'm eating pizza and wings instead of tamales."

"Okay," she said, "just checking."

When the call ended, Frank sat there for a while thinking about Melinda and wishing she'd mind her own business and leave him the hell alone.

CHAPTER 7

PHOENIX, ARIZONA

Wednesday, January 1, 2020, 11:00 a.m. (MST)

Under normal circumstances, the drive between Sedona and Phoenix takes a little under two hours. That day it took close to four. As Ali and Stu headed out of Sedona on 89A, there was already more traffic than usual. By the time they hit Cottonwood and turned onto SR 260, it was bumper to bumper with more than one fender-bender along the way making things worse.

Once on the road, Ali tried calling the hospital. Whoever answered the phone, citing HIPAA regulations, had been unable to provide any information on B.'s condition. When that didn't work, she was forced to wait for Frigg's hacking abilities to access St. Gregory's admission records.

The idea that the AI could do so made Ali almost as uncomfortable as Frigg's being able to remotely access and deprovision B.'s electronic devices, but desperate as she was to know what was happening, Ali was willing to turn a blind eye. With Stu driving and talking to Frigg,

Ali dialed the Yavapai County sheriff, Dave Holman, to ask if he could give her the inside scoop.

Years earlier, while Dave was still a homicide cop, he and Ali had been involved in a brief romantic entanglement, one that had ended amicably. In the years since, they had both married other people while managing to remain friends. Now he had been elected sheriff.

"I heard about what happened," Dave told her, "but I'm short on details. I didn't want to try calling you until I knew more. Priscilla and I are on our way home from Palm Springs. With I-17 still closed, we're heading back to the department in Prescott by way of Wickenburg. No telling how long that will take."

"Who was the first deputy on the scene?" Ali asked.

"Deputy Hawkins," Dave answered.

Ali had hoped the officer in question would be someone she knew, but this wasn't a name she recognized. "Maybe I could call and see if he could provide any additional information."

"Not him," Dave corrected. "Deputy Merrilee Hawkins is definitely a her. I'll have Priscilla text you her number as soon as we get off the phone. That's the best I can do from here. Fingers crossed that B.'s okay."

"Thank you," Ali breathed. When call-waiting buzzed with Cami's name showing in caller ID, Ali dropped Dave's call and took the second one.

"Have you heard anything?" Cami asked.

"Not yet," Ali answered. "I tried calling the hospital and didn't get to first base. Stu has Frigg working on the problem."

"Keep me posted. How's traffic?"

"Worse than expected. Feels like we've been on the road forever, and we're barely through Cottonwood."

Moments later Priscilla's text arrived. At that point Ali switched over from Cami's call and dialed Deputy Hawkins. When no one answered, Ali left her name and number. Then she settled back in her seat and attempted to corral her thoughts.

What if she lost B. without warning the same way her mother had lost her dad? Ali knew Edie was struggling to put one foot in front of the other, but her folks had been retired for a number of years. Ali would be left with a complex business to run. Would she be able to manage it on her own?

High Noon had been B.'s baby from the beginning. He had built it from the ground up into the multimillion-dollar enterprise it was today. In addition, he had sought out the loyal bunch of talented techie misfits who worked for them and kept the wheels turning on the bus. Ali herself was a journalism major without a hint of tech credentials on her CV. If she were left in charge, would anyone—customers and competitors alike—take her seriously? And if she failed at taking the helm and High Noon was forced to shut its doors, what would become of their employees?

Cami would be all right, Ali supposed, but what about Lance Tucker and Mateo Vega? Would prospective employers take their talents and skill sets into consideration, or would they focus on their unfortunate histories—Lance's juvenile incarceration or the sixteen years Mateo had spent behind bars on a wrongful conviction for second-degree murder?

And then there was Stu. She glanced over at the man himself. His hands were glued to the steering wheel and his eyes focused on the traffic-clogged road ahead of them. His formal education had ended with his earning a GED, but he was nonetheless a self-taught computer whiz who had been B.'s right-hand man for the better part of two decades. Would anyone take his natural talent into account, or would they focus on his lack of formal credentials and his somewhat odd personality traits and simply write him off?

The buzz of her cell phone interrupted Ali's train of thought. "Hello?"

"Deputy Merrilee Hawkins," a wary voice said. "Who are you, and how did you get this number?"

"I'm Ali Reynolds, and Sheriff Holman gave me your number," Ali answered. "My husband, B. Simpson, was a passenger involved in that rollover accident on I-17."

"I thought you said your name was Reynolds."

"It is. B. and I don't share the same last name. I've not been able to get any information from the hospital, and since you were the first deputy on the scene, I was hoping you might be able to fill me in."

"It was a terrible wreck," Deputy Hawkins said, "and you're probably worried sick, but I can't be of much help. By the time I got there, DPS was already on the scene and had taken control of the situation. They shifted me over to traffic detail. I was still doing that when the Air Evac helicopter took off, but I managed to pick up a few details. Someone said that although the driver was still unresponsive, the passenger seemed to be coming around. He was confused and injured, yes, but at least he was communicating."

Ali allowed herself a relieved breath. Communicating was good, and this was more than she'd known before.

"Thank you so much, Deputy Hawkins," she murmured.

"Sorry I can't be more helpful," Deputy Hawkins said. "I was returning from responding to a domestic dispute outside Camp Verde. Coming north I remember seeing two vehicles parked on the far shoulder of the freeway. It looked like someone might be stranded with car trouble. At the time there was no sign of a fire. I was about to pull over to check when I heard about the rollover. I went there instead."

"Again," Ali said, "thank you for the good news, Deputy Hawkins. It means the world."

"What good news?" Stu asked once the call ended.

Ali repeated what Merrilee Hawkins had told her. "You're right," Stu agreed. "If B. was awake and talking at the scene, that's an excellent sign."

In Cottonwood proper, they'd had to wait through four complete stoplight cycles before being able to turn left onto what was now a totally gridlocked State Route 260.

"Anything from Frigg?" Ali asked.

"Not yet," Stu said. "Once she has something on his condition, I'll put her on speaker, but in the meantime, she has managed to locate and deactivate all of B.'s devices."

"Good," Ali murmured, feeling better. Not only was High Noon's proprietary information secure, thanks to Merrilee Hawkins, Ali now knew that although B. had been injured, at least he wasn't dead. Things for Hal Holden sounded far more bleak.

Ali's phone rang again, this time with her son's name in caller ID. "I just talked to Grandma," Christopher said. "How's B.?"

Ali felt a pang of guilt that she hadn't contacted her son earlier, but until that last phone call she'd had nothing to report—at least, nothing good. She passed along what she'd just been told.

"Athena and I are on Christmas break until next Monday," he said. "If you need me to come down to Phoenix to help out, let us know."

"I will," Ali said. "Thank you."

As that call ended, she heard Stu saying, "Thank you, Frigg. I'm putting you on speaker."

Moments later, Frigg's computerized voice came through the Dodge Ram's sound system. "Good morning, Ali," she said. "I'm so sorry to hear about your current difficulties."

You and me both, Ali started to say, but then she remembered she was speaking to a machine—a polite machine, but a machine nonetheless. "Thank you," she said.

"Mr. Holden was severely injured and is in critical condition. At the scene he was unconscious and having difficulty breathing, requiring intubation prior to transport. Mr. Simpson's injuries are not reported as life-threatening."

"At least they're both alive," Ali said. "Thank you, Frigg."

"Will there be anything else at this time?"

"No," Ali replied.

"Very well," Frigg said, "but if there are any additional updates, I shall certainly pass them along."

As Frigg signed off, Stu gave Ali a sidelong glance. "How are you doing?"

Ali allowed herself a moment of reflection before answering. "Medium," she said. "Thanks to Frigg, I can stop holding my breath, but can't these people drive any faster? How long is this going to take?"

"According to the GPS, with current traffic conditions, we'll arrive at the hospital in two hours and twenty minutes."

Great, Ali thought. *It could just as well be forever.*

By then word about B.'s accident had spread, and Ali's phone began blowing up with calls of concern. She answered a couple of them, but everyone wanted to know the same thing—how was B. doing? Since Ali wasn't supposed to have the information Frigg had just supplied, there was no way for her to answer those questions honestly. After telling her third caller that she would have to get back in touch once she reached the hospital, Ali switched the phone over to vibrate and let the calls go to voice mail. She preferred not answering to telling lies.

CHAPTER 8

PHOENIX, ARIZONA

Wednesday, January 1, 2020, 2:30 p.m. (MST)

When Stu and Ali finally arrived at St. Gregory's, the Dodge Ram's rooftop was too tall for the parking garage. Stu dropped Ali at the hospital's front entrance and then went in search of on-street parking. At the reception desk, Ali managed to negotiate the HIPAA restrictions. After being informed that Mr. Simpson was out of surgery and in recovery, she was directed to a waiting room.

Stepping off the elevator a minute or so later, Ali was greeted by the familiar face of Sister Anselm Becker. The nun rose from her chair on the far side of the room and hurried over to envelop Ali in a comforting hug.

Ali and the now eighty-something nun had met years earlier at the bedside of a badly burned woman. Despite their many differences—age, religion, and occupation—the two women had surprised everyone, including themselves, by becoming the best of friends.

Sister Anselm lived in St. Bernadette's Convent in Jerome, just up the road from High Noon's headquarters. At the behest of now-retired Archbishop Francis Gillespie, Sister Anselm's life was devoted to traveling from hospital to hospital, where she served as a patient advocate for people in need. After Archbishop Gillespie's retirement, his successor had continued Sister Anselm's mission. These days she made her rounds accompanied by a much younger associate, Sister Cecelia Groppa, who handled the driving.

That day, however, Sister Anselm was the last person Ali had expected to encounter in the ICU waiting room.

"What are you doing here?" Ali asked.

"What do you think?" Sister Anselm replied with a laugh. "Waiting for you."

"How did you get here?" Ali wanted to know. "How did you know something was wrong?"

"Cami," Sister Anselm replied.

Despite the seriousness of the situation, Ali almost laughed aloud. The previous April Cami had ended up with a badly broken leg that had required surgery, followed by a stint in a wheelchair. Once released from the hospital, when it became clear that she'd be unable to manage on her own, Sister Anselm had shown up at her house uninvited and taken charge. Both women were stubborn, and sparks had flown in all directions. Now, though, if Cami had run up the flag to Sister Anselm about what happened with B., the two of them must have buried the hatchet.

"Cami called me right after she called you," Sister Anselm continued. "Sister Cecelia and I were at home at St. Bernadette's, so we packed up and headed here, coming by way of Prescott. Most of the time going that way would have taken much longer, but not today."

Ali glanced around the room. "Where's Sister Cecelia now?" she asked.

"She's with Mr. Holden," Sister Anselm told her. "She's been in touch with his daughter, Sheila, who is on her way here from DC and due to land at Sky Harbor shortly before nine tonight. Until she arrives, Sister Cecelia will be looking after her father."

St. Gregory's was a Catholic hospital, and both nuns were known entities to the staff. If Sister Anselm said they were supposed to be there, it was unlikely anyone would have objected. Ali had no idea how the two nuns happened to know the name, location, and travel plans for Hal Holden's daughter. The Sisters of Providence probably didn't have access to an AI, but one way or the other, they had sussed out Hal's supposedly confidential information.

"I'm glad you're here," Ali said, sinking gratefully into a nearby chair. "Any word about B.?"

"His surgeon told me that he came through the splenectomy fine, but he'll probably be in the recovery room for at least another hour," Sister Anselm reported. "He has several broken ribs, but the damage to those isn't nearly as serious as Mr. Holden's and apparently will require nothing more than taping. His fractured shoulder is another matter entirely. The orthopedic surgeon examined the X-rays and will operate on that once B.'s condition stabilizes."

"What kind of surgery?" Ali asked.

"To determine if the bone can be set or if the shoulder will require replacement," Sister Anselm explained. "Either way, that will have to happen later on down the road."

Ali felt a flood of relief. This was far better news than

she had expected during that long, tortuous drive to the hospital.

"How are you?" Sister Anselm asked.

"I'm not sure," Ali said. "It's been an emotional roller coaster."

"Have you had anything to eat?"

"I've had coffee," Ali admitted, "but that's it."

"We should go to the cafeteria, then," Sister Anselm declared. "I'll get a buzzer from the nurse so we can be notified if B. is moved from recovery to his room while we're gone."

Ali nodded in agreement. It wasn't like her to allow herself to be pushed around, but she was too spent to voice even the smallest objection. Just then, however, her phone vibrated again. She'd kept the ringer off, letting the calls go to voice mail and occasionally scrolling incoming calls and texts to see if any of them needed to be returned immediately. This time, when she saw Alonzo was on the line, she answered immediately.

"Hey, Ali," Alonzo said. "You've probably heard about the traffic mess on I-17. I'm still planning on being home tonight, but it'll be later than expected. They're saying the fire is out, but it's going to take hours for traffic to clear."

"About that traffic problem," Ali said. "There are a few things you need to know."

After filling Alonzo in and making sure he had her mother's contact information, Ali and Sister Anselm went down to the cafeteria. The holiday pickings were slim. Ali settled for a tuna sandwich and a cup of coffee. The sandwich was dry and tasted like cardboard. She choked down half of it and tossed the rest. Ali was returning from the trash bin when Sister Anselm's buzzer sounded.

"They'll be moving him to room 703 in a matter of minutes," the nun told Ali. "Why don't you go on up while I check on Sister Cecelia? B. will probably be awake, but don't be surprised if he's a bit on the groggy side."

On the seventh floor, Ali saw that room 703 was still empty. Heading to the nurses' station to ask if plans had changed, she spotted a seemingly disconsolate Stu Ramey sitting alone in the waiting room and staring bleakly at the floor.

Ali's heart was flooded with guilt. During the grueling drive from Sedona to Phoenix, she had been totally focused on her own issues. Only now did she realize that she hadn't been the only one looking at a potentially catastrophic loss. Out of concern for Ali, Stu may have done a good job of hiding his feelings before, but now his desolation was painfully obvious.

Of course he was worried sick about possibly losing B. Stu's parents had died while he was still a baby, leaving him to be raised by loving grandparents but ones who'd had very little guidance in coping with a child who happened to be incredibly smart but also autistic. Stu had grown up with virtually no social skills, and once his grandparents passed away, he'd been lost. He had been living in a homeless shelter as an abandoned teenager and working for minimum wage when B. had become aware of the boy's self-taught computer skills. After plucking him out of the shelter, B. had given Stu both a job and a place to live. Over time B. had also gifted Stu Ramey with a sense of purpose and a chance at a semi-normal life.

B. Simpson was Ali's husband, but he was enormously important to Stu—boss, friend, benefactor, and in a very real way the only father figure the younger man had ever known. If B. didn't make it, Ali would lose her spouse. Stu Ramey would lose his anchor.

"Hey, Stu," Ali said solicitously. "Are you all right?"

He started as though awakened from a sound sleep. "I'm okay, I guess," he muttered. "Just worried. Where were you?"

"Sister Anselm was already here at the hospital when you dropped me off," Ali said, taking the seat next to his. "We were down in the cafeteria. They're supposed to be bringing him up from recovery any minute. Have you called Cami?"

"Just did," Stu answered. "I thought people up there would want to know what we heard from Deputy Hawkins."

Ali gave herself another black mark for focusing on herself and not paying enough attention to others. "Thank you," she said. "I should have handled that myself."

"It's okay," Stu replied. "At least I was able to do something."

The elevator door opened and a bed was wheeled into the corridor. Spotting B.'s profile, Ali rose and followed, then stood in the doorway waiting for the attendants to get things settled before actually entering the room.

"If you're not a sight for sore eyes," B. said with a smile when he saw her.

"How are you feeling?" Ali asked.

"Not that bad," he replied. "The pain meds they use around here really are something."

Sister Anselm had warned Ali that B. might be somewhat groggy. She had expected him to be higher than a kite, but that didn't appear to be the case.

"Mr. Simpson?" a male voice inquired. Ali turned and found a man dressed in a suit and tie standing in the doorway. She recognized him as a cop long before he opened his mouth.

"I'm Chief Detective Warren Biba, an investigator with the Arizona Highway Patrol, from the District 12 office in Prescott," he said by way of an introduction. "Mind if I ask you a few questions about what happened earlier today?"

B. was fresh out of recovery. Ali's first instinct was to tell the guy to get lost, but B. was willing to talk.

"It's fine," he said, "but I'm not sure how much help I'll be. Things are still a bit fuzzy."

When Detective Biba shot a meaningful look in Ali's direction with an unspoken suggestion that she take her leave, Ali chose to ignore it.

"B.'s my husband," she said, folding her arms in front of her. "I'm staying."

"Suit yourself," Biba agreed grudgingly.

There was only a single visitor chair in the room, and Biba helped himself to that. He crossed his long legs before producing both a small leather-bound spiral notebook and a ballpoint pen from his coat pocket.

"So why don't you walk me through whatever you remember about today's events?" he asked.

"Let's see," B. said. "Hal and I were on our way to . . . to . . ." He frowned as if searching for the words.

"To the airport," Ali supplied.

Biba shot a warning glare in her direction. "And where were you going?" he asked.

B. paused uncertainly again. "I'm not sure."

"London," Ali said. "You were on your way to London."

"Please allow your husband to answer the questions, Mrs. Simpson," Biba cautioned.

Ali was fast losing patience. "My name is Ali Reynolds," she told him brusquely. "I didn't change my name when we married, and he didn't change his."

Biba turned back to B. "So you were on your way to London. Business or pleasure?"

Once again B. seemed to struggle to come up with a suitable reply, and he looked beseechingly in Ali's direction.

"Business," Ali answered. "We run a cybersecurity company located in Cottonwood called High Noon Enterprises. B. was on his way to participate in an international ransomware conference that's being held in the UK."

Biba frowned. "You're calling him B., using his initial rather than his given name. Is that correct?"

Ali was in no mood to relate the unfortunate history that had forced B. to resort to using his initial in place of a first name. That was a private matter and none of the detective's business.

"If you had bothered to check his driver's license, you'd see B. is his legal name. He changed it years ago."

Ali's tone of voice wasn't lost on Detective Biba, and he didn't press further.

"Can you tell me if there's anyone in your circle of acquaintants who might wish you harm?" Biba asked.

Ali was startled. "Harm?" she demanded. "Wait a minute. Does that mean what happened today wasn't an accident—that someone deliberately ran them off the road?"

"It's a possibility," the investigator conceded, "and that's what we're trying to determine." When B. didn't reply immediately, Biba gave him a gentle prod. "Well, Mr. Simpson?"

Looking lost, B. shook his head. "I can't think of anyone," he said.

"What about a business associate?" Biba asked.

"No one who works for High Noon Enterprises has any kind of issue with B.," Ali interjected. "We're a small, close-knit organization."

"What about competitors, then?"

"Cybersecurity may be a cutthroat business," Ali said firmly, "but I can't imagine one of our competitors putting out a hit on someone."

Biba's disapproval of Ali's involvement in the interview was apparent, but he backed off and changed course. "What about Mr. Holden, then?" he asked, once again addressing B. "How well do you know him?"

"Not all that well," B. said without any prompting. "I use him as a driver from time to time."

"Do you know of anyone who might wish to harm him?"

"So then you really do suspect this wasn't an accident?" Ali insisted.

Biba sighed. "We've recovered evidence that suggests that Mr. Holden's vehicle was deliberately forced off the highway," he allowed.

B. shook his head. "I don't know of anyone who would have issues with Hal. He's a super-nice guy."

"No financial difficulties as far as you know?"

"None," B. answered.

"What about romantic entanglements?"

"As far as I know he's a widower, and I have no idea if he's involved with anyone."

"What about you?"

"Believe me, I'm a happily married man," B. replied, "but I'm really tired now. Could we finish this some other time?"

With that, B. effectively dismissed the detective by simply closing his eyes and apparently drifting off. If B. was done, Ali was, too.

"That's enough!" she announced. "As you can see, he's tired and needs to rest."

"I'm a cop, and I'm trying to do my job here," Biba objected.

"And I'm a wife doing mine," Ali countered. "Yours will have to wait until later. You need to leave—*now*. If my husband couldn't remember where he was going when he left home this morning, he's clearly in no condition to answer any further questions."

Making no effort to conceal his annoyance, Warren Biba closed his notebook and returned both that and the pen to his jacket pocket. Then he unfolded his legs and stood up. "Are you always this protective of your husband, Ms. Reynolds?" he asked.

Since Ali was still standing, they were now glaring at each other across the white expanse of B.'s hospital bed. "I am when I need to be," she said unflinchingly. "Now get the hell out."

"I'll be back," Biba replied.

Over the decades that sound bite from *The Terminator* had become the punch line to thousands of jokes, but coming from Chief Detective Biba that afternoon, it sounded like a threat.

In the course of her lifetime, Ali Reynolds had

become a keen observer of people. As a matter of course, she usually liked law enforcement officers. After all, she'd been one of those herself for a brief period of time. But for some reason, Chief Detective Biba didn't give her a warm fuzzy feeling, and to all appearances, he felt the same about her.

"Believe me," she said. "I'll be here waiting. You can count on it."

She watched the man stride out of the room and down the corridor toward the elevator. When she turned back to B., she was surprised to find that his eyes were wide open. Clearly he wasn't nearly as out of it as he had seemed while the detective was present.

"Finally," B. said, sounding surprisingly alert. "I thought he'd never leave."

"Wait," she said. "Was that whole 'I can't remember' thing a put-up deal?"

"Pretty much," B. admitted. "I wanted to get rid of him."

"He seems to think what happened on I-17 wasn't an accident," Ali said.

"I don't think it was, either," B. said.

Ali was startled. "Really?" she asked in dismay. "You believe Hal's vehicle was deliberately targeted?"

"I do, and that's why I want you to get on a plane and go to London, the sooner, the better."

That was the last thing Ali expected him to say. "Wait," she objected. "It was bad enough when you were talking to Biba and couldn't remember up from down, but now you're downright delusional."

"I'm not."

"Why on earth would I want to go to London?"

"Because you need to ride herd on the ransomware conference."

"Me?" she asked. "Now you really are nuts. This is an international cybersecurity conference, and I'm an electronically challenged liberal arts major who occasionally has trouble with the controls on the microwave."

"But I still need you to go," B. insisted. "High Noon is an important part of this conference, and people will be expecting a principal to be there. If I can't go, you have to. Besides, don't sell yourself short. Once those arrogant jackasses take a look at you, you'll have them eating out of your hand before they know what hit them."

"I don't want anyone eating out of my hand," Ali hissed, "and I'm not going anywhere. You're my husband. You've been injured and are in a hospital. I'm staying right here."

"Please, Ali," B. begged. "I really need you to go."

"Why?" she insisted.

"Ask Stu," B. replied. "He knows all about it."

Just like that, B. Simpson threw his longtime friend and protégé under the bus. Even worse, a moment later, the meds really did take over. Without a hint of feigning, B. Simpson fell fast asleep.

CHAPTER 9

Out in the waiting room at St. Gregory's, Ali found Sister Anselm and Stu Ramey huddled in deep conversation. "I need to speak to Stu in private," Ali announced.

Recognizing Ali's no-nonsense tone of voice, they both looked at her in alarm. "What's going on?" Stu asked. "Is B. all right?"

"He probably will be," Ali replied, giving Stu a cold stare, "but I'm not so sure about you."

Sister Anselm took the hint and beat a hasty retreat. "I believe I'll go see if Sister Cecelia could use a hand," she said and scuttled off.

Ali turned on Stu, her eyes alight with fury. "The guy who followed me into B.'s room turned out to be an investigator for the Arizona Highway Patrol, Chief Detective Warren Biba. According to him, what happened to Hal and B. on the freeway this morning most likely was no accident. Biba believes another vehicle deliberately forced Hal's Lincoln off the road."

"You're kidding!" Stu exclaimed.

"No, I'm not," Ali responded. "He's also under the impression that the attack was intended for B. He wanted to know if B. had any enemies—if there was anyone who wished him harm. B. said no, but that may not be true. After Biba left, B. began insisting that I go to London in his place, as though we're really at risk here. So what's going on, Stu? B. says you're the one who happens to know all about it. Would you care to enlighten me?"

Rather than responding aloud, Stu ducked his head and seemed to be doing an in-depth study of his shoelaces.

"So tell me," Ali continued, "why should the least tech-savvy person on the payroll be the one racing off to represent High Noon's interests at the ransomware conference? B. claims that with him in the hospital, someone else must be there. He made it sound like a matter of life and death. Considering what happened on I-17 today, maybe it is."

Once again Ali paused, waiting for a response, but Stu remained stubbornly silent.

"So here's the deal," Ali concluded. "B. says you're the guy in the know, and since I'm completely in the dark, you'd better start talking."

At last Stu raised his head. When his eyes met Ali's furious gaze, they were full of regret. "I'm sorry about all this, Ali," he apologized. "We didn't mean to leave you out of the loop, but B. needed to discuss the situation with someone. With you completely caught up in looking out for your mom, he settled on me."

Ali wasn't at all mollified. "Needed to discuss what?" she demanded.

"The situation."

"What situation?"

Stu sighed. "B. believes one or more of our competitors may be trying to put us out of business. In terms of name recognition, being asked to speak at the ransomware conference was a big step forward. It moved us out of the minor leagues and into the majors, but if we fail to do well at the conference, or worse, if we end up being a no-show, it'll play directly into the hands of what our critics, including some of our biggest competitors, are saying about us."

"Which is?"

Stu took a steadying breath. "Ever since we were able to resolve that internal ransomware issue at A & D Pharmaceuticals without bringing in law enforcement and causing a media meltdown, Albert Gunther has been singing our praises far and wide."

"That seems like a good thing," Ali offered.

Stu nodded. "On the surface it is," he agreed, "and it's been good for our bottom line."

As High Noon's CFO, Ali was well aware of a recent overall uptick in business. By any measure, things were booming. "From where I'm standing, that looks like a good thing," she said.

"Yes, but some of our newly acquired customers came to us as a direct result of the A & D situation. They moved to High Noon after either canceling or not renewing long-held contracts with other firms, including some of the leaders in the cybersecurity field."

"So we've rocked a few boats," Ali said. "Isn't that what competition is all about?"

"Unfortunately, some of the boats we're rocking are big ones, and they're not happy about it. Lately one individual in particular has been taking swipes at us in industry journals as well as the general media."

"What individual?"

"A hotshot tech blogger named Adrian Willoughby. He's been pushing the premise that the A & D situation was bogus—that we didn't fix anything because there wasn't a problem in the first place. He's also offended by the fact that a tiny outfit located somewhere in the wilds of Arizona and operating with a handful of employees is stealing customers from firms with hundreds of employees."

"What's his beef?" Ali asked. "We're gaining customers and the other companies are losing them because we're more cost-effective. Without carrying the same amount of employee-based overhead, we can charge less for our services. So tell me about this Willoughby guy," Ali urged.

"He bills himself as a kind of tech guru," Stu replied. "He claims to be unbiased, but B. suspects that someone—probably a pissed-off competitor—is paying Willoughby under the table to give us bad press. In one of his recent blogs he hinted that an upstart US-based company headed by a former gamer—a flimflam man—is operating a bait-and-switch scheme by luring customers to sign up with the promise of low prices but without the ability to actually deliver the requisite services."

Ali's immediate reaction was to be outraged that anyone would refer to B. as a flimflam man. "Can we sue him for libel?"

"Probably not—he didn't mention us by name, but since High Noon is the only cybersecurity company run by a former gamer, it's pretty clear who he meant."

"And this is what had B. so worried all during Christmas?"

Stu nodded.

"But it's hardly a reason to commit murder," Ali replied.

"That may be," Stu agreed, "but there's a lot of money at stake here. Willoughby has managed to create the expectation that High Noon will fall flat on its face at the conference, and our not showing up would turn that prediction into a self-fulfilling prophecy."

"That's why B. is so adamant about my going to London?" Ali asked.

Stu nodded. "He's been working on his presentation for weeks. It's probably on either his laptop or his iPad. Once Frigg retrieves it, all you'll have to do is stand and deliver."

"Why don't you do it?" Ali asked. "You know a hell of a lot more about all this than I do."

"I'm not a public speaker, and you are," Stu declared. "Not only that, you're a full partner in the company, and that would carry some weight in terms of optics. At events like this, that's a big deal."

"I understand the importance of how things look," Ali replied, "and maybe I could deliver B.'s paper in a sensible fashion. After all, I read news scripts for years back in the day, but what happens when the presentation is over? How's it going to look if someone in the audience asks me a question I'm unable to answer? In terms of optics, that would be a disaster."

"I hadn't thought about the Q and A," Stu said with a frown, "and you're right, that could be dicey." He fell silent for a moment, then his face brightened.

"What if we had Cami do the presentation?" he

asked. "Your being there will count from a public relations standpoint, but Cami will be able to handle whatever questions anybody throws at her."

Ali could see that sending Cami to pinch-hit was an inspired solution. With Cami delivering the presentation and with Ali there to provide gravitas, maybe together they'd be able to cover all the bases B. usually handled on his own.

"All right," Ali said at last. "I can see that having both of us go is probably the best solution, but if the conference starts tomorrow, how do we make it happen?"

Once Ali was on board, Stu was ready to move forward. "You'll need to use a private jet," he said decisively. "Given that it's New Year's Day, that might be problematic, but if anyone can line one up in a hurry, I'd lay money on Frigg."

"Okay," Ali agreed, "put her on the case. But here's something else to think about. Let's suppose Detective Biba is right and B. was the target of what happened on the freeway today. How would anyone outside High Noon itself know when and how he was traveling?"

"I've already had Cami and Lance do a system-wide check on all High Noon–affiliated devices. No sign of a hack there," Stu said. "We'll be examining Hal Holden's devices next."

"If B. really was the target, what are the chances that whoever's behind it might send someone else after Cami or me while we're on the ground in the UK?"

"I hadn't thought of that," Stu said. "Maybe we should look into hiring bodyguards."

Ali was all in now, too. "Okay," she said with a nod. "I'll try contacting Sonja Bjornson with WWS."

"Who's that?"

"She's with Wonder Woman Security. They're the ones who looked out for me when I was in LA during that Gilchrist mess. Sonja has high-profile female clients all over the world."

"Okay," Stu said. "Sounds good."

"And since there will be two of us," Ali said, "some-one needs to let the hotel know we'll need two rooms instead of one."

The elevator door slid open, revealing Sister Anselm. As she started in their direction, Stu excused himself and then walked across the room with his cell phone pressed to his ear. Ali had no doubt he was summoning Frigg.

"How's Hal?" Ali asked.

"His condition is still critical. He has a closed head injury as well as what's known as a 'flail chest.' The steering wheel broke so many ribs that his chest wall has gone floppy, severely impacting his ability to breathe. That's why he's on a ventilator. So what's happening here? How's B.?"

The term "critical" sent a shiver through Ali's body. If B. had been the actual target of the attack, did that mean Hal's injuries were due to the fact that he had been driving B. to the airport? Ali quickly brushed the disturbing thought aside in favor of answering Sister Anselm's question.

"The last I saw he was out like a light, but you need to know things are a bit unsettled at the moment."

"Why?" Sister Anselm asked. "What's going on?"

"Depending on aircraft availability, Cami and I may or may not be flying to London tonight."

Sister Anselm was clearly dismayed. "You're heading

off to London with B. in the hospital here? Why would you do that?"

"Because he wants me to," Ali explained. "In fact, he almost made it mandatory."

"All right," Sister Anselm said finally. "Go you must, but you can count on my hanging around here until he's out of the woods. Understood?"

Ali felt a rush of gratitude. "Thank you," she murmured. "It'll make it easier for me to go if I know you're here, but it's not exactly a done deal. It's such short notice that we may not be able to locate an aircraft."

"Don't give that idea a second thought," Sister Anselm said with a reassuring smile. "When it comes to the Ali Reynolds I know, where there's a will, there's always a way."

CHAPTER 10

While Ali and Sister Anselm had been speaking, a nurse entered B.'s room, no doubt intent on taking his vitals. She was still there, checking the monitors, when Ali and Sister Anselm arrived on the scene and found B. not only awake but seemingly in a jovial mood.

"Hey, you two," he said with a grin. "Where've you been?"

"Out in the waiting room," Ali answered. "The last I saw, you were sound asleep."

"Yes," B. agreed, "but I'm awake now. I had a dream about hiking the Grand Canyon. It was beautiful. You should have seen all the colors."

Sister Anselm turned to Ali. "Those are the pain meds talking," she advised. "Having vivid dreams is pretty standard."

B. turned to the nurse. "When's dinner?" he asked.

"I'll check," she said, "but you won't be having solid food tonight. It's probably noodle soup with Jell-O for dessert."

"Beggars can't be choosers," he said. "How's Hal doing?"

B.'s mood darkened as Sister Anselm filled him in on the driver's condition. "It sounds like he's in a lot worse shape than I am."

"He is," Sister Anselm agreed, "and he's in for a long, difficult recovery."

"And we'll do whatever we can to help," B. said. Then, turning to Ali, he added, "What about London?"

"I'm going and so is Cami," Ali answered. "At least, we're going to try."

"When do you leave?"

"Frigg is trying to book a charter, but since it's New Year's there's no telling if she can make it work. In the meantime, Sister Anselm says she'll hang around and look after you while I'm gone. It occurred to me that if someone was after you, they might come looking for Cami and me, too, so I'm going to contact Sonja Bjornson about providing a security detail while we're there. I'll be in attendance for the PR value while Cami will deliver the presentation and answer all incoming questions."

B. looked relieved. "Sounds like you have everything under control."

There was a tap on the door. "Dinner," a male attendant announced.

He brought in the tray and arranged it on the table attached to B.'s bed. B. uncovered the bowl of soup and then glanced at the two women. "I probably shouldn't eat in front of you."

"Not to worry," Sister Anselm assured him with a smile. "We grabbed something in the cafeteria earlier."

Just then Stu appeared in the doorway and beckoned to Ali.

"What is it?"

"Frigg's got a lead on a Gulfstream," he said. "It was scheduled to fly a skiing party from San Diego to Aspen tonight, but there was a death in the host's family. The plane is fueled up, on the ground in San Diego, and available on a moment's notice."

"Book it," Ali said without hesitation. "Will we be flying out from here in Phoenix or from Flagstaff?"

"I checked the weather. Either one will work. Which do you prefer?"

"Let's make it Flag," Ali said. "That'll give Cami and me a little more time to pack."

"Okay," Stu agreed, "but we'd better head out soon."

Ali turned back to B. "I guess we're leaving, then," she said. Bending over the bed, she gave him a quick peck on the cheek.

"Thank you," he said.

"You're welcome," she said, "but you'd better do everything Sister Anselm says while I'm gone. If you don't, there'll be hell to pay when I get back."

Stu was just ending a phone call when Ali stepped out into the hall. "We're good, then?" she asked.

Stu nodded. "The flight's confirmed."

"Have you talked to Cami?"

Stu nodded again. "Briefly," he said.

"Has the charter company sent a flight plan?"

"Not yet."

"Have Frigg send me a copy when it comes," Ali said. "I'll need that when I contact Sonja."

As they stepped into the elevator, Ali said, "This is one of those high-travel days. I can't believe Frigg was able to book a flight on such short notice."

"She's something else, isn't she?" Stu said proudly.

Ali couldn't help but remember a time when, worried about Frigg's unorthodox capabilities, Stu had been determined to pull the plug on the AI on a permanent basis. Now they were both glad he hadn't.

"She certainly is," Ali agreed, "and the next time you talk to her, be sure to tell her I said thanks."

CHAPTER 11

LAS VEGAS, NEVADA

Wednesday, January 1, 2020, 6:00 p.m. (PST)

The game ended with the Oregon Ducks beating the Wisconsin Badgers by a single point, 28 to 27. Once it was over, Frank turned off the TV and logged on to his computer where he checked the newsfeeds from both Flagstaff and Phoenix, looking for any sign that his intended hit had actually taken place. Unfortunately, the only newsworthy topic of the day seemed to be a huge brush fire that had temporarily shut down freeway traffic in both directions between Phoenix and Flagstaff. Frank doubted the fire had anything to do with Hal Holden. Disappointed and wanting to clear his head, Frank left the apartment and went for another walk, this time just around the apartment complex.

The divorce Sylvia had initiated came through only months after Frank's transfer from a holding cell in LA to Lompoc. Surprisingly, seeing the decree in black and white had gone a long way toward helping him settle into prison life. At the time she filed, Frank had not yet been found guilty in a court of law nor had he entered his guilty plea, but Sylvia had decided well in advance that his going to prison was a foregone conclusion. She hadn't bothered asking for child support or alimony. She already knew that with him doing time, no financial support would be forthcoming.

Somehow that had helped Frank put his own situation in perspective. If he had not been incarcerated and had been ordered to pay alimony and child support, he would have had to work overtime shifts or take on private security jobs just to make ends meet. In Lompoc he had assigned tasks to do—working in the mess hall or the laundry mostly—but those were nothing jobs. It wasn't much, but here he had a roof over his head. On the outside, he would have had to do his own cooking. Here he had three squares a day, and although the food was admittedly bad, it was probably better than anything he could have concocted on his own.

Frank wasn't earning a steady paycheck, but he had a big payday coming. How many of the guys he'd met at the academy could walk away from a new job after only fifteen or twenty years with a cool tax-free $500,000 just sitting there waiting for them? Not very many, he guessed. So, although being in prison wasn't all hunkydory, it could have been a hell of a lot worse.

After learning about Gregg Atkins's successful outcome, Frank realized that although he didn't have a Bitcoin fortune available to fund a revenge campaign, he did have that $500,000. The problem was, he didn't know if he'd be able to access any of his payout prior to being released. To that end, he sent a letter to William Banks, his now semiretired defense attorney, asking for a meeting to discuss a possible appeal. That was bogus, of course, since he had pled guilty.

Nonetheless their attorney-client discussion was conducted in an interview room rather than a visitation one. Despite the fact that no recording equipment was supposed to be present, they nonetheless conducted their business by writing notes back and forth on one of Banks's many yellow legal pads:

FM: Can I receive periodic advance payments?

WB: I believe so. How much?

FM: That depends.

WB: When?

FM: As needed.

WB: How much?

FM: Don't know yet.

WB: How will I know the person asking is for real?

FM: I'll have them tell you that St. Nick suggested they stop by.

Frank figured the name St. Nick was close enough to Nicholas for Banks to get the message, and he did. "Got it," he said, returning the yellow legal pad to his briefcase. "Glad to be of service."

"What about the bill for your coming today?"

"Not to worry," Banks replied with a grin. "That's still covered."

Frank had felt the slightest twinge of worry when he heard that. Obviously William Banks was every bit as crooked an attorney as the former legal beagles now locked up inside the Lompoc Correctional Complex—he just hadn't been caught yet. The question was, if he ever did wind up on the wrong side of an FBI investigation, was he or was he not someone who would name names?

During the meeting, Banks had given Frank enough of a thumbs-up for him to go ahead and create his mental kill list—starting with Danielle Lomax. He had no idea what had become of her after his arrest, and that was a problem. How does a hit man find a target if you can't tell them where said target happens to be?

A certain amount of sleuthing on Frank's part revealed that someone named Salvatore Moroni, a lifer in Lompoc, was the guy who'd been Gregg Atkins's fixer. Sal's name may have been common knowledge inside the joint, but no one squealed on him. That was probably more due to the laws of self-preservation rather than any kind of loyalty. If Moroni could wave a wand and knock off two people in a luxury hotel in faraway Montenegro, he could probably arrange for a similar event to occur somewhere in the US of A.

First, though, Frank needed to make Sal's acquaintance. He was subtle about it by finding a way to be seated at Sal's customary table in the mess hall. After a casual introduction, Frank spent several months establishing a sense of rapport between the two of them. On that score, Frank's reputation for not being a snitch helped immeasurably. One day, when both he and Sal were in the gym, walking on side-by-side treadmills, Frank was finally able to get down to brass tacks. Sal's response was completely straightforward and to the point.

"Can you pay the freight?" he asked.

"How much?"

"Ten per," Sal told him, "payable in advance, all cash and in untraceable bills. Can you do that?"

"I think so," Frank said.

"Where's the pickup?"

Frank gave Sal William Banks's name and location, as well as the St. Nick code word, and warned him that whoever was doing the pickup would need to stop by a day or so in advance to give Banks a heads-up.

Frank liked the fact that Sal listened and nodded in response to all his questions but made no paper- or tech-based notations. Like Frank, Sal trusted his head to remember things more than he did any kind of outside reminder. That was reassuring since nothing hidden inside the man's head would be at risk of falling into the wrong hands.

"How will this work?" Sal wanted to know.

"Have your messenger stop by Banks's office in the next couple of days to introduce himself and work out the exact time and date for the pickup."

"Fair enough," Sal said. "Once that happens, we can move forward."

Since Sal's business was killing people rather than finding them, his first hurdle was all about locating the target. Danielle Lomax had seemingly dropped out of sight the moment Frank was arrested, so finding her wasn't easy. For another five grand, Sal hired the services of a hacker who, according to him, could find anyone anywhere. Within days the hacker had located Danielle—happily married now and living a new life in St. Paul, Minnesota. That was where she was found, and, to Frank's immense satisfaction, that was where she died.

Sal let him know the job was done but provided few details. After being let out on parole, Frank had searched through newspaper archives in the Minneapolis–St. Paul area to suss out the details. According to them, Mrs. Lomax-Reardon, the executive director of a local women's shelter and mother of two, had been gunned down by an unidentified assailant late in the evening of October 31st in 2017 as she left the shelter after facilitating an evening support-group meeting for survivors of domestic violence. The homicide was considered to be an act of random violence. No perpetrator had ever been identified, and the homicide remained unsolved.

Frank read those words with a euphoric sense of satisfaction. After setting Frank up to spend years of his life rotting in prison for more than a decade, Danielle had blithely moved forward with her own life. For Frank, spending fifteen thousand bucks to take that life away from her had been worth every penny.

At first Danielle's death was enough to satisfy Frank's thirst for revenge, but eventually that urge returned. After all, Danielle wasn't the only one responsible for sending Frank to the slammer. Jack Littleton and Hal Holden, fellow cops at Pasadena PD, were also involved. With Jack especially there had been a long-standing feud.

Shortly after graduating from the academy, Frank had been one of the officers called to a reported homicide that had started out as a barroom brawl. As cops converged on the scene, one of the onlookers had gotten physical. Frank, who'd always had a bit of a temper, had lit into the guy and was cleaning his clock when Jack intervened, dressing Frank down right there in front of God and everybody, while the bleeding guy, still present and smirking, had been giving Frank the finger behind Jack's back.

"I'll be reporting your actions to your FTO, Officer Muñoz," Jack had growled at him. "If you pull another stunt like this, you'll be booted off the force in the blink of an eye. Got it?"

"Yes, sir," Frank had replied.

The two men seldom crossed paths after that, but Frank remained convinced that Jack Littleton had it in for him. Frank had been at BJ's on the night of the Alysha Morgan homicide. His name and contact information had been taken down by one of the uniforms at the scene, but Frank had managed to leave the area without being interviewed. When he learned that Littleton was the lead investigator on the case, he had fully expected to be put under a microscope, but that hadn't happened.

For a time he had wondered about that. Danielle had actually witnessed the shooting, so he knew she had been interviewed, but when he had asked her about that, she'd gone all squirrelly on him. Within a matter of weeks, she'd quit her job, moved out of her apartment without leaving a forwarding address, and disconnected her phone without so much as a *vaya con Dios*.

Sometime later, when the feds came calling, Frank put it all together. Danielle must have blabbed to Littleton and Holden about Frank's involvement in the goings-on at BJ's. It didn't take much for Frank to realize that the homicide cops had most likely brought the FBI into the picture, and now they were the next names on Frank's kill list. With his parole in the offing, he went back to see Sal.

"Where you gonna be once you get out?" Sal asked.

"Vegas," Frank had answered.

"No shit?"

"No shit."

"My daughter lives in Vegas," Sal said, "and she works with me on this. What say we cut out your middle man and have Rochelle collect the cash from you directly?"

"Works for me," Frank said, "but if I'm on the outside and you're on the inside, how do we make contact?"

Sal had given Frank detailed directions that included Frank's buying a computer. After that they communicated through draft files in a mutually accessed email account to plan and successfully carry out the hit on Jack Littleton. Still living where he'd always lived, Jack had been easy to find and easier to take down. Hal Holden was another story. He was now living in a small town in Central Arizona where he kept completely irregular hours. For Hal, Frank had been forced to fork over an extra five thousand bucks just to get a detailed look at the man's schedule.

But Frank's new computer came with a terrific side benefit that had nothing to do with communicating with Sal. One of his first Internet searches had brought him to a small but important article on the second page of the *Pasadena Times*:

FORMER COP'S DEATH RULED AS UNDETERMINED

The LA County Medical Examiner's Office has ruled last week's death of former Pasadena Police Department officer and retired homicide detective Jack Andrew Littleton as undetermined. Mr. Littleton died of a single gunshot wound to the head.

The body was found when neighbors, noticing unread newspapers accumulating on his front porch, requested a routine welfare check. At the time officers entered the victim's residence, he had been deceased for at least three days.

Mr. Littleton, age 71, retired from Pasadena PD in 2009 after twenty-five years of service, initially in patrol and later in investigations. During his years as a homicide detective, he is credited with closing fifty-three cases, including the brutal 1995 slaying of Hollywood starlet Loralei Day.

According to sources inside Pasadena PD, when officers entered the residence, Mr. Littleton was found dead in a recliner in the living room with a gunshot wound to the head and with his service weapon on the floor nearby.

The house was locked at the time responding officers arrived. There was no sign of forced entry nor did there seem to be a disturbance of any kind having occurred inside the home.

No suicide note was found at the scene, but Mr. Littleton was known to have been in de-

clining health for a number of years preceding
his death.

Funeral services are pending.

In Frank's opinion a ruling of suicide would have
been better, but "undetermined" was a good second
best. Sal's hired hand had been enough of a pro to make
sure the crime scene was properly staged. As the weeks
went by the lack of any additional coverage indicated
that the case had gone cold.

With Littleton dead and Holden hopefully on his
way out, Frank was three-quarters of the way there.
Sylvia Garcia Muñoz Rogers was the last target standing, and Sal's latest draft file communication indicated
that her death would occur later this week.

For Frank Muñoz it couldn't come soon enough. He
was tired of waiting.

CHAPTER 12

PHOENIX, ARIZONA

Wednesday, January 1, 2020, 5:00 p.m. (MST)

Ali and Stu had merged onto I-17 and were headed north when a message from Frigg containing the flight plan details arrived on Ali's phone. After dialing Sonja Bjornson's number, an answering service told her Sonja would call her back shortly.

"Any more news?" Ali asked when that call ended.

Stu nodded. "Frigg has obtained a list of conference attendees and is creating dossiers on all the company execs expected to be there. Those should be ready for you by the time you board the plane."

"Will Adrian Willoughby's information be included?"

"Yes," Stu said. "In addition, Frigg has retrieved a copy of B.'s presentation from his computer, so Cami will be able to study that while you're on board."

"In other words, we'll both have some homework to do," Ali observed.

Turning back to the flight plan, Ali saw they were scheduled to depart Pulliam Airport, FLG, at 9:00 p.m.

on January 1, arriving at London City Airport, LCY, at 4:30 p.m., London time, on January 2, with a scheduled fuel stop at Teterboro Airport in New Jersey along the way. Seeing their scheduled arrival time, Ali switched over to the conference details, noting that a private opening reception was scheduled for 7 p.m. on January 2 in Il Bar at the Bulgari Hotel.

With the timing of that in mind, Ali called Cami. "Are you packing?"

"I am," Cami replied.

"About that, according to the flight plan, we should be on the ground in time for us to attend the opening reception, so pack accordingly."

"Which means?"

"Suitable business attire for the meetings themselves and something dressy for the reception," Ali told her.

"By suitable, I'm assuming you mean something other than jeans and flannel shirts?" Cami asked with a laugh.

To counter the considerable heat generated by the computer lab, High Noon's thermostats were kept at a cool 68 degrees year-round, so business attire there was long on warmth and short on fashion.

"Yes," Ali agreed. "Something slightly dressier than that, but what about the hotel? Were you able to reserve another room?"

"Nope," Cami replied. "Right now the hotel is fully booked, but the conference already had B. in one of their suites. It comes with one and a half baths and a separate sitting room that includes a pull-out sofa. I'll take the sofa and you can have the bedroom, unless you'd like me to look for another nearby hotel."

"No," Ali said, "the suite will be fine."

Ali went on to update Cami on B.'s and Hal's current medical situations. "By the way," she added, "thanks for bringing Sister Anselm into the picture. She was already at the hospital when Stu and I got there."

"Not a surprise," Cami responded. "Sister A. is one amazing woman."

Ali was taken aback to hear Cami refer to Sister Anselm by a pet name—something Ali herself had never done. Obviously the disconnect between the two women was a thing of the past.

Just then Ali's phone let her know that Sonja was calling.

"I have to take this," Ali told Cami. "It's Sonja Bjornson."

"Wait," Cami said. "You're hiring a bodyguard?"

"Trying to," Ali said. "Under the circumstances, it seems like a good idea." With that, she switched over to the other line.

"What's up?" Sonja asked. "From what my answering service told me, it sounds like you need a security detail sooner rather than later."

For the next ten minutes or so, Ali provided all the pertinent details, and she and Sonja began getting the situation sorted. Ali was in the process of hanging up when the screen of her iPad flashed red, indicating Frigg was sending out an urgent message. Out of deference for Stu's fondness for J. K. Rowling's Harry Potter, those flashing red messages from Frigg were always referred to as howlers. Ali read this one aloud for Stu's benefit.

An anonymous source at the Arizona Department of Public Safety is now reporting that a burned-out and abandoned 2012

Chevrolet Silverado pickup was the cause of the midmorning brush fire that shut down I-17 in both directions between Phoenix and Flagstaff. The vehicle had been reported as stolen from a construction company parking lot in Kingman, Arizona, earlier today.

The fire-damaged wreckage of the truck was found approximately a mile south of what previously had been considered to be a one-car rollover accident that seriously injured two people.

The two individuals in that vehicle, airport limo driver Hal Holden of the Village of Oak Creek and tech entrepreneur B. Simpson of Sedona, were both airlifted to St. Gregory's Hospital in Phoenix with serious injuries.

At this time, investigators are not releasing any details about the possible connection between the two incidents, but they are currently operating under the assumption that the two are related.

So far there is no indication as to what caused the fire, and there has been no sign of any individuals who might be connected to the stolen truck.

The investigation is ongoing.

"So the wreck really wasn't an accident," Ali murmured aloud, "and unless I miss my guess, Chief Detective Biba is going to be pissed as hell that details of his investigation are now being made public."

CHAPTER 13

QUARTZSITE, ARIZONA

Wednesday, January 1, 2020, 11:00 a.m. (MST)

As a pillar of smoke rolled skyward from the torched Silverado, Dante Cox and Tyrone Jackson high-fived each other in the front seat of the speeding Subaru. With Dante at the wheel and Tyrone slouched in the passenger seat, they felt like a million bucks. They'd done the job exactly the way they'd been told, and once they got back to LA, they'd each have two thousand dollars to show for this little all-expenses-paid vacay through Nevada and Arizona.

Just outside Anthem, Dante turned off at a truck stop for some breakfast. They'd been up all night and were starving. The drive from Kingman to Flagstaff had been scary. They were both from LA. Neither of them had ever seen snow in person before. The highway had been dry and clear but the piled snow on either side of the freeway had freaked them out. What would happen if they got stuck in it? Wasn't Arizona supposed to be desert? How could there be this much snow?

After breakfast while Dante gassed up, Tyrone bought a celebratory six-pack for them to sip on along the way. In Phoenix they turned onto I-10 and headed west. Eventually, as the beer asserted itself, the adrenaline in their bodies began to wear off. The third time the Subaru's tires meandered over the rumble strip and startled Dante awake at the wheel, Tyrone had had enough.

"That's it," he said. "Next motel we see, we're stopping. No sense in getting ourselves killed or picking up a DUI along the way."

Minutes later a gas, food, and lodging sign indicated they were approaching a place called Quartzsite. Neither had ever heard of it before, and when they drove into town, it looked like a dusty set for some low-budget, end-of-the-world movie.

"Not here," Dante objected. "This place is crap. Let's keep going."

"Nope," Tyrone told him. "Come on, man. We're beat. I say we sleep for a couple of hours."

Grudgingly Dante turned off. They ended up at a hardscrabble motel called Trail's End where the lady at the reception desk took Tyrone's cash and barely glanced at his ID. Tyrone had seen that old black-and-white movie called *Psycho* once, and their dingy room—shower stall included—reminded him of that, but there were two double beds covered with floral bedspreads. Within minutes both of them were fast asleep.

Three hours later they were awakened by the chirp of Tyrone's burner phone. "Where the hell are you?" Big Eddie demanded. Big Eddie Gascone was the guy who had gotten them not only the gig but also the phones.

"At the Trail's End motel in a town called Quartzsite," Tyrone replied. "We stopped to grab some sleep. We were both running on empty."

"Stay where you are," Eddie ordered. "I'll come get you. It'll take me a couple of hours, but we need to ditch that stolen car."

"Why?" Tyrone asked. "What's going on?"

"It's all over the news. That burning truck started a huge brush fire that shut down a major freeway. It caused quite the uproar. If the car you're driving was spotted at the scene, cops are probably on your tail right this minute. If you try to cross into California, they'll nail you at the highway checkpoint at Blythe."

"What should we do?"

"Like I said, stay right there. When I'm close, I'll tell you where to meet me. I don't want to end up being caught by your hotel's surveillance cameras."

Tyrone didn't bother telling Eddie that Trail's End probably didn't have surveillance cams.

"We'll be there," he said. Then, putting down the phone, he rolled over on his side and promptly fell back asleep.

CHAPTER 14

BEAVERTON, OREGON

Wednesday, January 1, 2020, 6:00 p.m. (PST)

In Beaverton, Oregon, Ramon Muñoz was beyond relieved by the time the football game ended and his sisters finally packed up and headed north to their respective homes in Olympia and Seattle. They had arrived together on Monday afternoon, and now they were gone. By the time they backed out of the driveway, Ramon had become a firm believer in that old saying about company and fish wearing out their welcome after three days.

With his stepdad's knee-replacement surgery scheduled for Friday morning, Ramon knew that his mother would have preferred having her daughters visit over Christmas rather than New Year's, but both had had other plans. Tina had spent Christmas with her fiancé's family in Shoreline, Washington, and Lucy's presence had been required for some kind of shindig at the governor's mansion in Olympia.

Watching the Rose Bowl Game together should have been fun, but it hadn't been. Their stepfather, Larry Rogers, was a University of Oregon alum, so he was a Ducks fan all the way. Ramon had attended Lane Community College in Eugene, so he was a Duck through proximity rather than matriculation. "The girls," as Ramon generally called his sisters, had both attended college in Washington State—Lucy at Evergreen State College in Olympia and Tina at the University of Washington.

During the game, more out of spite than anything else, they had rooted unashamedly for the Badgers. When Oregon won with that single-point lead, they had taken it personally and had huffed out shortly after the game ended. Their mother may have been saddened by their abrupt departure, but Ramon wasn't, and he doubted Larry was, either.

As far as Ramon was concerned, he had always considered his sisters to be a pair of spoiled brats. That might have been cute when they were little, but it wasn't cute now. To his way of thinking, they were overeducated snobs and lazy to boot. The whole time they'd been home, they'd sat on their butts, letting their mother wait on them hand and foot. Mom had done all the cooking and cleaning, with neither daughter lifting a finger.

Ramon had helped out, of course, but since he still lived at home, having "failed to launch" as the girls jokingly called it, they assumed those chores rightfully fell on his shoulders. And neither of them had offered to hang around and help with Larry's upcoming surgery, either. Apparently, that was also Ramon's responsibility. During their visit, he'd tried to not let his sisters' constant jibes bother him, but they did. Their double-teaming him was nothing new. They had been doing it for as long as Ramon could remember.

Lucinda had a four-year degree in political science

from Evergreen, and Cristina was working on a master's in psychology at U-Dub. Both of them sneered at Ramon's lowly AA degree from Lane Community College, but his two years of higher education had given him exactly what he wanted—the ability to do a job he loved with police agencies large and small all across the Pacific Northwest.

And no matter what Tina or Lucy thought or said, Ramon was no freeloader. Yes, at age twenty-seven he lived behind his parents' main house in an ADU cottage Larry had created for his ailing mother by remodeling what had once been a woodworking studio into a livable, handicap-friendly studio apartment. Grandma Rogers had passed away two years earlier. When Ramon had mentioned that he was shopping for a new apartment, Larry had told him he was welcome to move into the cottage and stay for as long as he wanted.

Ramon earned enough from his consulting jobs that he could easily have moved out, but he happened to know—as his sisters evidently did not—that things were a bit tight for his parents right now. Larry was only in his early sixties, but ongoing health issues had necessitated his taking early retirement, meaning that his retirement income was lower than he and Sylvia had anticipated. Despite their somewhat straitened circumstances, Larry had insisted on paying the freight for "the girls" to go to school—at out-of-state schools, no less—because he didn't want them starting out in life with a mountain of student-loan debt. Ramon thought it ironic that his sisters could make fun of *his* so-called failure to launch without noticing their own, but he kept that opinion to himself.

Although Ramon's folks weren't nearly as well off as they had once been, they still lived in a neighborhood where people were expected to keep their houses and yards in good repair. Ramon helped with expenses by paying rent, but he did a lot of physical labor as well, filling his nonworking hours with chores that were now beyond Larry's physical capability.

His folks had been forced to let their longtime yard guy go, so Ramon did that, keeping the lawn trimmed and mowed as well as raking leaves and pruning trees as needed. In the fall he turned off the irrigation system and blew out the pipes so they wouldn't freeze over the winter. And he made sure the gutters on both the main house and the cottage were in good working order.

His industry didn't go unnoticed. On more than one occasion, strangers driving past had stopped to ask if he was interested in working in their yards as well. They were noticeably surprised and more than slightly embarrassed to learn that Ramon actually lived there as opposed to being some hourly paid Hispanic guy doing random yardwork.

Ramon was loading the last of the football party dishes and glassware into the dishwasher when his mother poked her head into the kitchen. "Thanks for doing that," she said. "Dad's knee was really bothering him. He went to the bedroom to lie down for a while. Having the girls around wears him out. Truth be told, they grind me down, too."

Make that me three, Ramon thought.

"It's still early, though," Sylvia continued, "so if you wouldn't mind bringing some of the boxes in from the garage, I'd like to get a start on taking down decorations. With Dad's surgery on Friday . . ."

"Say no more," Ramon said cheerfully. "Will do."

He was more than willing. That's exactly what he

needed—some time alone with his mother while they took down decorations. There was something he needed to discuss with her, an issue that couldn't be mentioned in front of anyone else, Larry Rogers included.

Ramon had understood from an early age that, as far as his family was concerned, he was the odd man out. Presumably, at the time he was born and maybe for a short time afterward, Frank Muñoz had been proud of his baby boy, but by the time Ramon was old enough to remember, Cristina and Lucy had arrived. The two girls were inarguably the apples of their father's eye with Ramon a distant third. Frank doted on them, and they could do no wrong, and it didn't take long for Tina and Lucy to understand the lay of the land. From then on, Ramon's relationship with his sisters became one of constant open warfare—him versus them.

In the meantime, relations between his parents weren't all sweetness and light, either. Frank and Sylvia Muñoz had a volatile relationship punctuated by lots of heated arguments and raised voices that, on more than one occasion, had devolved into physical violence.

Ramon's father was a cop. To Ramon's way of thinking, that meant Frank should have been one of the good guys, but he wasn't. When he slapped Sylvia's face or came after Ramon with his belt for some offense or other, Frank Muñoz seemed more bad than good. As a result, the boy grew up being afraid of his father and stayed out of his way as much as possible.

Ramon was in fourth grade when things at home had gone from bad to worse, and that was when his grade school—one within easy walking distance of their home in Pasadena—became Ramon's refuge. His teacher, a wonderful woman named Mrs. Lawson, must have noticed things weren't good for him, and she had taken him under her wing.

Before getting her teaching degree, Mrs. Lawson had been an art major, and she recognized and encouraged Ramon's natural talent for drawing. She gifted him with his first pocket-sized sketch pad and allowed him to spend time in her classroom after school, giving him space to sit quietly and draw to his heart's content.

Even as a child Ramon had been intrigued by faces—by old faces with lines and wrinkles on them and by smooth, young faces as well. He paid attention to how eyes and ears were placed. He studied the shapes and sizes of noses and how people's expressions changed when they laughed or frowned. Soon he was sketching at home as well as at school, capturing images of his family members while they were living their everyday lives.

That's when he had first noticed something odd. When he studied his sisters' faces, they could have been twins. Some of their facial features, especially their cheekbones, bore a clear resemblance to Grandma Lupé's. As for their eyes? The set of those came straight from their mother, while their skin tone matched their father's.

But when Ramon looked at himself in the mirror, only a few of his facial features lined up with anyone else's. He had his mother's eyes and nose but that was it. His face was squarer than his father's. His nose wasn't nearly as sharp, and his skin was darker, too. Ramon bore no resemblance to any of his near relatives, including his mother's brother, the uncle for whom he'd been named. His looks seemed to set him apart from his family rather than allowing him to blend in.

Ramon was in fifth grade when the family's life in

Pasadena fell apart completely. Suddenly their father was in jail awaiting trial on some kind of criminal charge Ramon didn't understand. At school he became a pariah. Boys who had once been Ramon's pals no longer wanted anything to do with him. Tina and Lucy still had each other. Their brother was on his own.

When their mother announced that she was getting a divorce, selling the house, and moving the family to Oregon, the girls had been devastated. Ramon had been thrilled. He was more than ready to leave Pasadena and everything in it behind, including Frank Muñoz and his belt.

Once the family arrived in Portland, Sylvia had gotten a job working for an escrow company, and that was where she met Larry Rogers—at work. The couple dated for some time before Sylvia finally allowed her new beau to meet the kids. Tina and Lucy had been wary of Larry to begin with and still maintained some distance, but Ramon had welcomed this new man in his mother's life from the start. Larry was older, sandy-haired, and a bit on the chunky side, but he was an incredibly kind man without a mean bone in his body, and he loved Sylvia Garcia Muñoz with all his heart.

Financially speaking, Larry was clearly better off than Frank had ever been. Compared to the cramped two-bedroom house the family had inhabited in Pasadena, Larry's spacious mid-century modern on Beaverton's NW Telshire Drive seemed downright palatial. Not only that, Larry loved spoiling his new family, giving them lavish gifts they could never have afforded otherwise.

Unlike Frank, Larry took a genuine interest in Ramon. He was in junior high when his stepfather stumbled onto the fact that Ramon loved art and had zero interest in team sports. At that point, Larry had sprung for private art lessons—a small but loving gesture that permanently altered the trajectory of Ramon's life.

Mrs. Clarke, his new art teacher, soon noticed Ramon's keen interest in faces and his skill at drawing them. "You know," she told him one day, "you could probably earn a living doing this."

"Like being an artist in a studio or something?" Ramon had asked.

"More like in a police station," she said.

That's when she had explained what police sketch artists do. When Ramon expressed an interest in following through on that, Mrs. Clarke had mapped out a path for him to get there, including enrolling at Lane Community College where he had earned an AA degree, with a double major in art and human anatomy.

During his second year in Eugene, a series of rapes occurred on campus. When campus cops had asked the art department for assistance in creating a composite sketch, one of Ramon's instructors had recommended him for the job. He had spent hours working with the two victims, slowly using a charcoal sketch pad and a book of suggested facial features to create a black-and-white rendition of their attacker's face.

Once released to the public, Ramon's sketch was instrumental in helping to identify and ultimately arrest the suspect. When the rapist's mug shot was shown on a television newscast side by side with Ramon's sketch, he along with everyone else had been astonished by how close he had come to re-creating the bad guy's features. That was the moment Ramon knew for sure that Mrs. Clarke had been right all along when she had directed him onto this path.

By the time Ramon was twenty-one, he was already self-employed, building a consulting business that allowed him to function as an on-call sketch artist for any number of small law-enforcement agencies that, due to budgetary constraints, were unable to keep one on staff.

And it was while doing that job—working with cops and dealing with forensics and DNA evidence—that Ramon once again began examining his own face and wondering about it. Finally, in late November, he had taken the plunge and sent a DNA sample off to Ancestry.com. The results had come back the previous Friday, but with his sisters due to visit, he'd kept quiet about it until now.

Although Ramon had more or less expected the news, he'd still been shocked once he saw his DNA profile in print. He was 100 percent Hispanic, all right. Half of his ancestors, the ones on his mother's side, had immigrated to the US from either Sonora or Chihuahua in Mexico. Immigrants on his father's side hailed from Central America, from El Salvador, to be exact.

El Salvador? Ramon wondered, staring in disbelief at the paper in his hand. *What about Jalisco?*

Grandma Lupé, his paternal grandmother, had told Ramon countless stories about how she and Grandpa Pepe had made the long trek north from Jalisco to the US, crossing the border at Yuma. For several years they had worked in the lettuce fields around Yuma before finally making their way to better work and better lives elsewhere. And that was what Ramon wanted to discuss with his mother that night. Either Grandma Lupé had lied about Jalisco, or else Ramon's mother had lied about everything.

Taking down and putting away decorations took less time than getting them out and putting them up, but Ramon kept his own counsel about the DNA issue until after the job was done and Larry had retired for the night. Only then, when he and his mother were alone in the kitchen and sharing glasses of eggnog, did Ramon finally spill the beans.

"I got my DNA results back from Ancestry dot com last week," he mentioned casually.

His mother responded to those quietly uttered words with a sharp intake of breath. Her face paled. Her hand shook as she carefully set her empty glass down on the table. For a long time she simply sat there saying nothing.

"I never meant for you to find out," she managed at last. "I always hoped you wouldn't."

"But I did," Ramon replied, more brusquely than intended. "So why don't you tell me the rest of it, Mom? If Frank Muñoz isn't my father, who is?"

Sylvia didn't answer immediately. "He was my boss at work," she said finally, her voice barely audible. "He was my manager in the fast-food restaurant—the taco shop—where I worked when I was a senior in high school. One night after work, he raped me."

Ramon suddenly felt as though his heart had been ripped from his body. He had thought he'd be hearing about his mother having an affair of some kind and that his birth father had been her lover, but this was far worse. He had never imagined his mother as a possible rape victim. Now Ramon was the one stunned to silence.

"It happened in the back room of the restaurant one night after everybody else left," Sylvia continued. "I thought it was my fault—that I had somehow caused it to happen. I quit my job the next day, but I was so ashamed that I didn't tell anyone. Then, when I realized I was pregnant, I was scared. I couldn't stand to give up the baby or have an abortion, so . . ."

"So you married Frank Muñoz and told him I was his?"

Sylvia nodded brokenly.

In that moment Ramon understood for the first time what a terrible price his mother had paid in order to keep him—a price, it turned out, they had both paid.

"Does he know?"

"Maybe," Sylvia said with a shrug. "We never discussed it."

Ramon took a moment to gather himself. He remembered those poor, damaged girls from Eugene, the ones he'd had to interview while creating that composite. Their raw pain had been palpable, and here he was learning that his mother had suffered through a similar nightmare. Even so, he plunged on.

"Who is he?" Ramon asked at last. "What's my father's name? I want to find the son of a bitch and punch his lights out."

"Sergio," Sylvia answered. "His name was Sergio Gomez, but you won't be able to find him."

"Why not?"

"Because he's dead," she said. "He died in prison of hepatitis. He'd been sentenced to life without parole for raping and murdering two other girls. I'm lucky he didn't murder me."

With those few spoken sentences everything Ramon had ever wondered about his family life suddenly clicked into place and made sense. Standing up, he walked around the table, where he knelt in front of his mother's chair and took her tear-stained face in his hands.

"I'm so very sorry about this," he said softly. "You were a terrified eighteen-year-old girl. Faced with impossible choices, you did the best you could, and I'm grateful for that. Thank you for keeping me. Thank you for not letting me go."

"I couldn't," she said hopelessly. "You were an innocent baby. What happened wasn't my fault, and it wasn't yours, either."

With that, Sylvia fell sobbing inconsolably against her son's shoulder. While she let go of more than two decades of heartbreak and grief, Ramon felt a sudden sense of relief—his birth father may have been a worthless piece of crap, but at least he wasn't Frank Muñoz.

At last Ramon pushed his mother away. "Don't worry, Mom," he said. "I won't mention any of this to a soul unless you tell me it's okay."

"Thank you," she whispered.

In that moment Ramon had a whole new appreciation for Larry Rogers. Ramon had been almost thirteen years old when he first met the man who would become his stepfather. From the beginning, Larry had always been far more of a father to him than Frank Muñoz ever was. A desperate Sylvia Garcia may have married the wrong man the first time around, but she had gotten it right the second time, and for that her son was incredibly grateful.

CHAPTER 15

FLAGSTAFF, ARIZONA

Wednesday, January 1, 2020, 8:30 p.m. (MST)

At eight thirty that evening, Stu Ramey dropped Ali and Cami off at the Fixed Base Operator. After carrying their luggage inside, he didn't wait around for the pilots to show up or to watch their plane take off. Instead, he climbed into his truck and headed out. On the way to Flag, he had checked in with both Lance and Mateo to see how things were going at work. Assured that everything was under control, Stu stopped off at his house in the Village of Oak Creek rather than continuing on to Cottonwood.

The news that the incident on I-17 had been a deliberate act as opposed to an unfortunate accident had cast a whole new light on the situation, leaving Stu sick with worry. If B. Simpson had been the intended target, as Detective Biba seemed to believe, how had a potential killer or killers known not only that B. would be traveling in Hal Holden's vehicle, but also the exact date and time when they'd be driving on that particular stretch of roadway?

Stu had already ordered a complete scan of all company-owned electronic devices to see if any of their systems had been compromised. No incursions were found, unless, of course, someone was using software similar to Lance Tucker's GHOST, which would have made tracking impossible. Barring that, however, it seemed reasonable to assume that High Noon's network remained secure.

Where was the leak, then—on one of Hal Holden's devices, maybe? It had been easy for Stu to order security checks on High Noon's company-owned devices, but that wasn't the case with Hal's electronics. He was a vendor as opposed to an employee, and any search of his devices had to be conducted under a cloak of secrecy. That was why Stu had assigned the task to Frigg earlier in the evening, but it wasn't until he was driving back from Flagstaff that she responded.

"Good evening, Stu," she said. "I hope you're having a pleasant evening."

The evening wasn't pleasant at all, but Stu went with the flow. "I am, thank you," he replied aloud. "What have you got for me?"

"It took time to access Mr. Holden's equipment," Frigg said, "but I have located a keylogger."

Keyloggers register every keystroke made on an individual keyboard, thus giving whoever is behind it complete access to any information typed on an individual computer, which is then passed along to any connected devices.

"Can you tell where it's from?" Stu asked.

"I don't have a final answer on that," Frigg replied. "I'm still following up on it. So far I've managed to trace it to an IP address in Albania."

Albania? Stu thought. *Why would someone in Albania want to track the movements of an airport limo driver from the Village of Oak Creek, Arizona?*

"That means," Frigg continued, "if Mr. Simpson was the actual target, all of his travel arrangements would have been available to anyone having access to Mr. Holden's hacked computer."

Stu gripped the steering wheel as the news settled in. "Good work," he muttered.

"Will there be anything else?" Frigg inquired.

Stu thought about that for a time before he answered. That Albanian IP address suggested a sophisticated, international connection that was more likely to lead back to B. than to Hal Holden, so maybe Biba's single-minded focus on B. as the target wasn't that far off the mark after all. Still, the keylogger had been found on Hal's devices and not on B.'s, so while the official investigation remained firmly fixed on B., maybe someone else should take a hard look at Hal Holden.

"There were two people in that wrecked Lincoln," Stu said. "That means one was the intended victim and the other collateral damage. The official investigation is operating on the assumption that B. was the target and Ali is the only viable suspect."

"According to the latest data," Frigg intoned, "twenty-eight percent of all homicide victims die at the hands of someone they know, often a spouse or a love interest, so focusing the investigation on Ms. Reynolds would be a logical course of action."

"Logical maybe," Stu countered, "but what if it's not right? We know about the keylogger. Warren Biba doesn't. Whoever installed that on Hal's computer is most likely behind all of this. We need to find out who that is, and in order to do that, I want to know everything there is to know about Hal Holden."

"Of course," Frigg replied. "I'll get right on it. Would you like me to send my results as they come in?"

After Aunt Julia's late-night party in Payson the night before and this extremely stressful day, Stu knew he needed sleep in the worst way. "Just queue them up for me," he said. "Once I get home, I'm going straight to bed. I'll look at your findings in the morning."

"Very good, then," Frigg told him. "Drive safely and sleep well."

CHAPTER 16

PRESCOTT, ARIZONA

Wednesday, January 1, 2020, 9:00 p.m. (MST)

At nine o'clock that night, when Chief Detective Biba assembled his team in the conference room at the Arizona Highway Patrol's District 12 headquarters in Prescott, he was not a happy camper. This was supposedly a holiday, but he had been on duty since midmorning. He wasn't thrilled about that, and his wife, Dena, was off the charts.

He was also now the lead detective in charge of investigating not one but two major incidents that had occurred almost simultaneously earlier in the day on I-17. One of them, a single-vehicle rollover, had resulted in two seriously injured people being airlifted to the nearest ER trauma unit. The other, a vehicular fire, had occurred about a mile south of the original incident. The brush fire resulting from that had snarled north- and southbound traffic in Central Arizona for hours on end.

With the two incidents attracting massive media attention, his team was stretched thin. It consisted of four uniforms—the troopers who had originally responded to the scene, two detectives; the CSIs who had investigated each of the two damaged vehicles; and the weird little tech guy who had spent the day assembling and analyzing any dashboard camera video and all available security footage of the vehicles involved. Unfortunately, someone in that very small group of people was supplying inside information to outsiders.

"All right, people," Biba announced as they settled into their chairs, "listen up. I want to know the identity of the so-called anonymous source who's leaking information to the media!"

The room went completely silent in the face of Biba's accusatory gaze. No one moved so much as a muscle, and no one responded.

At last Biba continued. "The lab has now confirmed that paint fragments discovered on the left front fender of the wrecked Lincoln Mark V from the single-vehicle rollover is consistent with paint used on 2012 Chevrolet Silverado crew cabs. A stolen, burned-out, and abandoned crew cab of that make and model was found a mile south of the wrecked Lincoln only a few minutes after the original incident. We know that, the crime lab in Phoenix knows that, and now anyone in the country who happens to have an Associated Press newsfeed on their cell phone does, too."

The room remained locked in silence. Eventually Biba spoke again.

"So here's the deal. I'm a detective, and I'm very good at what I do. Once I identify that anonymous source, he or she will be gone. Understood?"

This time several heads nodded in silent agreement. Leaks to the media during important investigations were always a bad idea.

After another long, uncomfortable pause, Biba went on. "We've got two patients in St. Gregory's in Phoenix. One is in serious condition; the other is critical and on a ventilator. That means we're looking at two counts of vehicular assault. If the guy on the ventilator croaks, it becomes vehicular homicide. So what have we got? Let's start with you, Peach Fuzz."

He pointed to the department's twentysomething tech whiz, a guy whose name was Darren Curtis, and someone Biba never addressed by name. Looking nervous and miserable, Darren rose to speak, having to clear his throat several times before any words emerged. "I've examined the surveillance footage from Kingman Redi-Mix, the company that owned that stolen Silverado. At 10:26 p.m., December 31st, their security cameras recorded a pair of headlights approaching the property but the vehicle remained out of camera range. Two individuals, both wearing hoodies, emerged from the unidentified vehicle and used a bolt cutter to unlock a gate and gain entry to their grounds.

"They entered a 2012 Silverado crew cab, gray in color, and drove it away. Stealing the vehicle was evidently their sole purpose. Since no effort was made to enter the building itself, no alarms sounded. Two minutes after cutting through the perimeter fence, the suspects were gone. The first vehicle left the scene shortly thereafter. At the time the pickup was stolen, it was equipped with Arizona plates.

"The owner of Kingman Redi-Mix, Mr. Kenneth Spelling, has the company's security surveillance feed sent to his home computer overnight and checks it first thing every morning. At eight thirty today, he noticed that the crew cab was missing and reported it as stolen.

"At 2:37 a.m., the dash cam license plate reader on a Highway Patrol vehicle recorded the Silverado with the correct plate number driving eastbound on Interstate 40 fifteen miles west of Flagstaff. It was traveling at the posted speed limit at the time and appeared to have only one occupant.

"At eight fifteen this morning, the manager of the Super 8 motel in Flagstaff called nine-one-one to report that two hotel guests, visitors from New Mexico, had awakened this morning to discover that license plates had been stolen from two separate vehicles, parked side by side in the motel's parking lot. Unfortunately, the motel's surveillance system is currently inoperable. However, two badly damaged New Mexico plates, matching the ones reported stolen this morning, were located at the scene of the vehicular fire on I-17."

"If two vehicles were involved, where's the other one?" someone asked.

While a relieved Darren sank back into his seat, Biba took over.

"No idea," he said, "and that's the crux of the matter. What Peach Fuzz told us suggests a good deal of premeditation on the suspects' part. Stealing those plates at the last minute was designed to avoid an LPR encounter that might have registered the discrepancy between the vehicles in question and their accompanying plates. In other words, this was not a random event."

Biba paused long enough to survey the room. "What else?" he asked.

One of the CSIs raised her hand. "The fire was started by someone stuffing a lit, accelerant-soaked rag into the gas tank opening. Within a matter of seconds the whole thing went kaboom. The fire burned hot enough to destroy any possible evidence, and it also served as a major distraction, allowing the suspects to flee the scene without being apprehended."

"No evidence of any kind was found in the truck?" Biba asked.

"None," the CSI replied with a shake of her head. "And any tire tracks left at the scene were obliterated by the arrival of first responders."

"What do we know about our hospitalized victims?" Biba asked.

This time Detective Steven Flack spoke up. "The driver and owner of the Mark V is one Hal Holden, a sixty-seven-year-old widower and retired cop from Pasadena, California, who resides in the Village of Oak Creek. He runs a small, privately owned limo outfit called Oak Creek Car Service. He was driving his passenger, Mr. B. Simpson, to Sky Harbor where he was expected to board a London-bound British Airways flight. Holden's wife, Rose, passed away from cancer several years ago. He has a daughter from a previous marriage, Sheila Rafferty, who resides in Washington, DC. I was unable to speak to her directly, but when I called to notify her about the incident, I was advised that she was already on her way."

"Before you made contact?" Biba asked.

Steven nodded. "Correct," he said.

"I'd like to know who reached out to her," Biba said. "Given both the timing and the distances involved, it's unusual for someone to beat law enforcement to the punch when it comes to delivering that kind of news."

"I'll look into it," Steven said.

"Does this Holden guy have a girlfriend?"

Flack shook his head. "No, sir, not so far as anyone knows. According to neighbors, he's an ordinary guy who spends his time either golfing or driving to and from Sky Harbor."

"What's the deal with Simpson?"

This time Detective Julie Morris took the floor. "He's considered to be high profile in the Sedona/Cottonwood area," she offered. "He and his wife, Ali Reynolds, are fairly well-to-do, living in Sedona but owning and operating a small tech company called High Noon Enterprises with headquarters in Cottonwood."

"What kind of tech?" Biba asked.

"Cybersecurity," Detective Morris answered. "As far as I can ascertain, most of their business is international in nature, and Mr. Simpson travels extensively, going in and out of the country on an almost-weekly basis while his wife handles operations here."

"You said they're well-to-do," Biba said. "How well off are they?"

"Most of their customer base appears to be located outside North America, and fares for transatlantic and transpacific flights don't come cheap," she said.

"Any financial difficulties?"

"Since today's a holiday, I couldn't access any of those records," Julie said. "I'll look into their finances and real estate holdings tomorrow."

"Any marital difficulties?"

"None that I've heard about so far."

"What about their electronic devices?"

The other CSI, Megan Holly, raised her hand. Theoretically Warren Biba was a happily married man. Megan was a sexy little number who sometimes made him wish he wasn't.

"Yes, Megan," he said, nodding in her direction. So far she was the only person in the room he had addressed by name. That fact may have escaped Warren Biba's notice but not anyone else's.

"Two cell phones were found at the scene," Megan reported. "The one belonging to Mr. Holden appears to be functional, but we won't be able to access it until he's able to give us permission or until we can obtain a warrant, whichever comes first."

"What about the other one?" Biba asked.

"Mr. Simpson's phone was apparently operational initially because one of the uniformed officers at the scene reported receiving a call on it. However, by the time it was taken into evidence, the phone was no longer working."

"Why not?" Biba asked.

"It would appear that the device had been disabled. That, along with Mr. Simpson's laptop and iPad, had all been returned to their factory settings."

"In other words, they'd been wiped?"

"Correct."

For the better part of thirty seconds, Warren Biba sat there quietly tapping the tabletop with the end of a ballpoint pen while he mulled that information. *Only someone with something to hide would wipe their devices at the scene of a car crash.*

"Anything else?" he asked eventually. This time no one responded.

"All right, then," he said, "we'll hit this again first thing in the morning, but in view of the fact that Simpson's devices were clearly tampered with and Holden's weren't suggests that Simpson was our intended victim, but make no mistake. While I'm looking for a suspect, I'll also be looking for our leaker. Once I find him or her, there will be consequences. Understand?"

Again people nodded but said nothing. Almost everyone in the room, other than Warren Biba, was well aware that Megan's former college roommate was now a newspaper reporter in Phoenix, and they were all waiting to see what would happen if and when Biba found out.

"All right," he finished. "That's all. Go home and get some rest, and in case I didn't mention this earlier, happy New Year."

As people began to gather their goods and file out of the room, Biba was still deep in thought. Homicide investigations always work from the inside out, starting with members of the victim's inner circle before moving on to more distant friends and relations. And who was the nearest and dearest member of B. Simpson's inner circle? That would be his wife, of course.

Biba's mind flashed back to his earlier visit at the hospital and to the way Ali Reynolds had quickly jumped in to answer questions that seemed to have stumped her husband. He hadn't liked her attitude or the scathing way she had looked at him as she summarily ended the interview. Biba's thoughts returned to the present just as Julie Morris and Steven Flack were about to leave.

"Hey," Biba called after them. "Hold up a minute."

Steven and Julie reversed course. "Yes?" Julie asked.

"I'd like you to take a deep dive into B. Simpson's wife," Biba said. "I had an unpleasant encounter with her down in Phoenix earlier this afternoon. I'd like you to bring her in for a voluntary interview tomorrow. I want it done here at the station and on the record so we have her locked into her story."

Julie Morris nodded. "Because it's always the wife, you mean?"

"Or the husband," Biba agreed, "but in this case, I think there's a very good chance it's the wife."

CHAPTER 17

FLAGSTAFF, ARIZONA

Wednesday, January 1, 2020, 9:00 p.m. (MST)

The chartered Gulfstream departed Flagstaff's Pulliam Airport at nine p.m. on the dot. While a big-eyed Cami, riding in a private jet for the first time, examined her surroundings, Ali switched on her iPad and stole a look at the email from Sonja Bjornson that had arrived while they were still in the FBO.

> One of our approved car service providers will meet your aircraft at London City Airport and will transport you to the hotel. They have your tail number and can track your flight, so don't worry if there are changes in your ETA.
>
> Angela Patterson, your assigned operative, will meet you at the hotel. We've arranged for her to register at the conference as your personal

assistant. She'll be in attendance with you at all public events.

Sonja

The plane took off, rising quickly from the lit atmosphere surrounding the airport into darkness broken only by the glowing red light on the wingtip visible outside her window. Gradually, as Ali's eyes adjusted, countless stars began to glimmer in the sky overhead.

Once the chime indicating cruising level sounded, the Gulfstream's flight attendant was up and at 'em. When beverages were offered, Cami—focused on her upcoming presentation—ordered coffee, while Ali opted for a glass of Merlot. They chatted over finger sandwiches and fresh fruit before settling in to work.

As Ali went through the travel briefing Frigg had provided, she focused for the first time on the Bulgari's address in Knightsbridge, as well as the accompanying neighborhood map. When she caught sight of a street called Brompton Road, she realized she'd been in that same area years before during a homecoming trip for her former majordomo, Leland Brooks. The two of them had gone to dinner at the posh penthouse flat in nearby Brompton Square that belonged to Leland's great-nephew, Jeffrey Brooks, a solicitor, and his partner, Charles Chan, a restaurateur.

Leland had come into Ali's life as part of a package deal when she had purchased her home on Manzanita Hills Drive. For years he had served as Ali's butler and right-hand man, but after retiring, Leland had returned to the UK to care for the love of his life, a man named

Thomas Blackfield, whom he had been forced to abandon decades earlier.

A week or so prior to Christmas, Ali had received a
card from Leland telling her that Thomas had passed
away several months earlier and that he had accepted
Jeffrey and Charlie's invitation for him to come stay
with them in London for a while. In the early fifties,
when Thomas and Leland's relationship had been pried
apart, homosexuality was still a criminal offense. Things
for Jeffrey and Charlie were far different. Reading the
note, Ali had been relieved to know that, after years
of caring for others, Leland now had someone looking after him, and although she had meant to send a
sympathy card earlier, she had not yet gotten around
to doing so.

Studying the map, Ali realized that the distance
between the hotel and Leland's current place was probably something less than a ten-minute walk. Once she
understood the logistics, Ali decided that sometime
during the conference, she'd play hooky long enough to
visit her friend and deliver her condolences in person.
That would mean more to both of them than sending
a card.

At that juncture, Ali reclined her seat and allowed
the long day's worth of emotional turmoil and two
glasses of Merlot to get the best of her. The next thing
she knew, the flight attendant was shaking her awake.

"Excuse me, Ms. Reynolds. We'll be landing in Teterboro soon. Please raise your seat back to its full upright
position and make sure your electronics are turned off
and properly stowed."

Ali looked down and was surprised to find that while
she'd slept, the attendant had covered her with a blan-

ket. Across the aisle, Cami's seat was already in its full upright position. Although she was still sleeping, she, too, had been covered with a blanket.

Both Ali and Cami disembarked during the fuel stop. Once back on board, they reversed roles. Done working, Cami left her seat and stretched out full length on the plane's long bench seat. Ali fired up her computer and began going through the dossiers Frigg had prepared for her perusal. It was slow going and boring beyond words.

For the most part, name-brand cybersecurity elite were highly educated executive types with seemingly beautiful wives and picture-perfect children—at least as far as Frigg's research had discovered. To a man—and they were all men—they seemed totally ordinary, and not one of them looked like a potential murderer.

Only Adrian Willoughby appeared to have anything dodgy in his background. He had been let go early on by what was then a tiny tech start-up that had eventually morphed into a massive conglomerate. No reason was given for his abrupt departure from the firm, but a nondisclosure agreement was involved, which probably indicated that a sum of money had changed hands. Willoughby's career as a tech blogger had launched shortly thereafter, probably underwritten by that unspecified monetary settlement from his previous employer.

From the photos Frigg had gathered, Willoughby appeared to be in his early to mid-forties, and his bland face gave no hint of any murderous proclivities. He had a very attractive, somewhat younger wife and three highly photogenic kids. However, Frigg had discovered there was probably trouble in paradise since the wife had recently filed for divorce.

By the time Ali fought her way through the last of the dossiers, the blended aroma of brewing coffee and reheating quiches was wafting from the galley.

If you have to go racing off somewhere far away in the middle of the night, Ali told herself, *this is the way to do it.*

CHAPTER 18

LONDON, ENGLAND

Thursday, January 2, 2020, 3:45 p.m. (GMT)

Ali and Cami's original ETA at London City Airport had been 4:30 p.m. Due to driving tailwinds, the aircraft actually touched down at 3:47. It was raining pitchforks and hammer handles when they disembarked. Their hired car had pulled up next to the plane, but the driver nonetheless escorted them across the tarmac to the waiting vehicle under an immense golf umbrella. Then he drove them to the FBO, where an immigration officer quickly granted them entry into the UK.

Despite their early arrival at the hotel, Angela Patterson, their bodyguard, was already on hand to greet them. She was a tall, lithe, fashionably dressed Black woman who looked like a model who'd just stepped off a catwalk. Striding along in a pair of incredibly high heels and with an enormous leather purse slung over one shoulder, she glided across the lobby's polished granite floor with the sure-footedness of a leopard on the prowl. Cami seemed surprised by the woman's appearance, but Ali was not. When it came to hiring operatives, Sonja Bjornson usually went for stunning good looks that masked a formidable opponent.

After making polite introductions and inquiring about their flight, Angela took charge of the check-in process and led them to the elevator. Up in their suite, the three women waited for the bellman to depart.

"You're not carrying any weapons, are you?" Angela asked.

"No, ma'am," Ali said. She already knew better than to bring handheld weapons into the UK, and she had passed that information along to Cami.

At that point, Angela reached into her purse and extracted two tiny, tissue-topped gift bags, each of them sporting a Christian Dior label.

"Sonja sends her regards," Angela said as she handed each of them one of the diminutive packages.

Cami was the first to unwrap her gift and pull out a tiny glass spray bottle. When she made as if to open it, Angela held up a cautioning hand. "Please don't," she said. "What you see isn't what you get."

"What is it?" Cami asked.

"Wasp spray," Angela answered. "Carrying firearms is frowned upon in the UK, but there are no laws against carrying wasp spray."

Cami studied the vial. "Wouldn't a vial of bear spray be that much better?"

Angela laughed aloud at that. "Here in the UK we don't have bears, but we have plenty of wasps, which makes wasp spray much easier to come by. Please keep your 'perfume' bottles close at hand, and don't leave the room without them."

"Including tonight at the private reception?" Ali asked.

"Most definitely," Angela replied. "And if either of you happens to be without a suitable evening bag, I'll be glad to pop out and get you one."

"We both came properly equipped," Ali assured her.

Angela left then, after saying she'd be back to collect them at seven sharp. Once she was gone, Cami made straight for the chintz-covered sofa. "I'm beat," she said, digging an eye mask out of her purse. "If you don't mind, I'm going to grab a nap. Wake me at six, would you?"

"Will do," Ali said.

Leaving the sitting room to Cami, Ali retreated to the bedroom, closing the connecting door between them. A glance at her phone told her that with the eight-hour time difference, it was just past eight a.m. in Phoenix. St. Gregory's Hospital would be up and running by now. No doubt B. was awake, but since he was minus his cell phone, she dialed Sister Anselm's number.

"Good morning, Ali," the nun said cheerfully. "I trust you traveled safely?"

"We did. How's B.?"

"He had a bit of a rough night," Sister Anselm replied, "but he's sleeping now. I probably shouldn't wake him."

"Please tell him I called," Ali said. "I'll have Stu make arrangements to deliver a cell phone and iPad to the hospital, but I don't know how long that will take. What about Hal?"

"His condition remains stable but critical."

"Okay, keep me posted."

When the call ended, Ali sat gazing out the window

at a rain-shrouded Knightsbridge. With the rain pelt-
ing down, a ten-minute walk seemed much less inviting than it had on the plane. Besides, since Leland was
currently staying with someone else, making a surprise
drop-by visit seemed wrong.

She didn't have Jeffrey's direct phone number handy,
but she knew that his partner was a well-known London restaurateur. Using her iPad, she located a phone
number for the Charlie Chan's restaurant location in
Knightsbridge and called.

The woman who answered the phone was more
interested in making dinner reservations than she was
in fielding a phone call for Mr. Chan himself. After
putting Ali through the third degree to ascertain that
she was really a friend rather than a salesman trying to
jump the line, the hostess finally agreed to take Ali's
name and number. Her attitude changed remarkably
for the better when Ali gave a room number and mentioned that she was staying at the Bulgari.

Less than ten minutes later, the phone rang. "Ali,"
Charles said, "how good to hear from you! You're here
in London?"

"I am," she said, "in your neighborhood, too. I'm
hoping to see Leland while I'm here, but I wanted to
check with you to make sure my turning up wouldn't
be an inconvenience."

"Not at all!" Charlie exclaimed. "Leland will be
thrilled to see you, and you're welcome to drop by
whenever you wish."

"How's he doing?" Ali asked. "I heard from him just
before Christmas, letting us know about Thomas's passing."

She heard a momentary hesitation before Charlie responded. "Thomas's death hit him pretty hard," Charlie conceded. "Once he came back to the UK, he threw himself wholeheartedly into being a full-time caregiver. I'm afraid that cost him dearly."

Ali knew from things Leland had mentioned in earlier letters that life with an ailing Thomas had been anything but easy.

"When Jeffrey and I went to Bournemouth for the funeral," Charlie continued, "the poor man was a mess. That's when we decided he should come stay with us. At the time, we told him it was just a temporary measure, but it's not, Ali. He needs us, and if he ends up requiring more care than we can provide, we'll find it for him. For now, though, he seems content, and at last our little Jonah has something in common with the other kids at school—a grandfather."

For Ali this was all welcome news.

"When would you like to come by?" Charlie asked after a pause.

"Tomorrow afternoon, maybe?" Ali asked tentatively. She had studied the conference schedule. Cami was due to deliver B.'s presentation in the early afternoon. Once that was over, Ali suspected she'd be able to slip away unnoticed.

"Sure," Charlie replied. "I'll give myself the day off and cook something at home. With Jonah around, Jeffrey and I find eating there much more pleasant than dining at the restaurant."

"Sounds wonderful," Ali said, recalling the amazing Peking duck Charles had served the last time she had dined with them.

"Plan on dropping by around four or thereabouts," Charlie continued. "You and Leland can enjoy afternoon tea. Then, since you'll most likely still be dealing with jet lag, we'll eat early—around seven."

"Done," Ali said. "See you then."

Off the phone, Ali busied herself by checking in with Stu and letting him know about getting a replacement phone and iPad delivered to the hospital. She checked in with both her mother and with Chris and Athena. After that she took the time to reply to dozens of emails and texts. Word of B.'s accident had gotten out and people wanted to know how he was doing and whether there was anything they could do to help. There wasn't, of course, but she thanked them one and all for offering.

By then it was time to awaken Cami so they could get gussied up for the reception. Ali's little black dress wasn't exactly a coat of armor, but it felt like one. After applying a final layer of lipstick and picking up her chic wasp-spray-equipped evening bag, Ali was ready to go. Out in the sitting room, Cami was dressed in a floor-length emerald-green gown, the same one she'd worn to High Noon's Christmas party. She looked spectacular, but Ali knew that the dress's main appeal for Cami had to do with the fact that it completely covered the long, narrow scar where her broken leg had been surgically repaired.

When Cami, Angela, and Ali made their fashionably late entrance into the silver-curtained enclave of Il Bar, more than a few heads turned in their direction. Angela was exceptionally tall, Ali was moderately so, and Cami was exceptionally short, and all were suitably dressed for the occasion. Entering a room where suit-clad males vastly outnumbered their female counterparts, the trio's arrival made an impact.

Cami didn't stay long. She accepted a single glass of champagne before making a beeline for the appetizer spread where she dished out a plate of food. She picked through it daintily enough, but minutes later she went back upstairs to continue working on her presentation.

Her departure left Ali momentarily uneasy. What if someone asked her a question she couldn't answer? Still, in her years as a news anchor in LA, Ali had spent enough time dealing with Hollywood A-listers to know how to work a room. With Angela sticking close at hand, Ali made her way through the crowd, smiling, shaking hands, and chatting while Angela did the same. Along the way, she learned that, over the years, she had picked up enough cybersecurity jargon to blend seamlessly into the crowd.

Each guest was given a name tag lanyard upon entering the room. That allowed Ali the ability to recognize the people who had been described in Frigg's pre-conference dossiers. The men were welcoming and polite. Several guests questioned her presence as opposed to B.'s. She explained in neutral words that he was dealing with a health issue that made traveling currently impossible. None of them seemed to be aware of the traffic incident on I-17. That changed when Adrian Willoughby himself sidled up to her. She recognized him from the material Frigg had provided.

"I understand B. was involved in an unfortunate accident," he said. "I do hope he'll be okay."

Since no one else had made mention of the incident, Ali went on full alert, but she kept her face neutral. "I'm sure he will be," she assured him smoothly, smiling over the rim of her champagne flute. "He really wanted to be here, but his doctors wouldn't hear of it."

"What about his presentation?" Willoughby asked.

"Not to worry," she said. "High Noon is a collaborative effort. The presentation will be handled."

The man paused long enough to sip his own beverage. She guessed the amber liquid in his rocks glass was something stronger than champagne.

"And she is?" he added, nodding admiringly in Angela's direction.

"My personal assistant," Ali offered. "She makes traveling ever so much easier."

"I'm sure she does," Willoughby said. "Care for another glass of champagne?"

"No thanks," Ali said. "With jet lag and all, I'm sure one glass will be more than enough."

It was, too. Forty-five minutes later, having done her wifely and corporate duty of seeing and being seen, Ali caught Angela's eye and nodded toward the exit. She had fulfilled her assignment. Fifteen minutes after returning to the suite, Ali Reynolds was stretched out on the bed and fast asleep.

CHAPTER 19

COTTONWOOD, ARIZONA

Thursday, January 2, 2020, 6:30 a.m. (MST)

On Thursday morning, as Stu headed for the kitchen to brew his first cup of coffee, Frigg's computerized voice greeted him through his recently inserted earbuds.

"Good morning, Stu. You're up early. I hope you're having a pleasant day."

He wasn't, actually. In fact he was a bit on the grumpy side due to an incoming text from Lance that had awakened him earlier:

> You probably need to go back to the hospital today, but Mateo and I could use some help. It would be great if you could spell us for a few hours.

"So-so," Stu muttered under his breath in response to Frigg's teeth-grindingly cheery greeting.

"Would that be in regard to creating some type of garment?" she inquired.

Stu sighed. There were bits of idiomatic English that remained baffling to the AI.

"Nothing to do with sewing," he replied. "I'm fine. Thank you for asking."

"I have one hundred seventy-three documents lined up in the queue waiting for you. Would you like me to begin sending now?"

"That many? What's in them?" Stu asked.

"The collection includes police reports and media coverage of homicide cases handled individually and jointly by Hal Holden and his onetime partner, Jack Littleton."

One of the things Stu appreciated about Frigg was that, as far as information gathering went, she was always thorough—in this case, perhaps overly so.

"Wait," he objected. "I asked you to do a deep dive into Hal Holden. I suppose those jointly handled cases are fine, but why his partner's cases?"

"In view of the fact that someone may have taken Mr. Littleton's life last October, you should probably look into his cases as well."

"Are you saying he's dead?"

"Yes, Mr. Littleton was found deceased in his home in Pasadena, California on October 3, 2019. He died of a single gunshot wound to the head. His manner of death has been filed as undetermined and the case remains unresolved at this time."

"Whoa!" Stu exclaimed.

There was a pause. "Would you like me to terminate this conversation?" Frigg asked.

Now Stu was the one who was puzzled. "Terminate? Why?"

"*Whoa* is a command issued to an animal, often a horse, telling it to stop."

Stu sighed. "It can also be used to express surprise or dismay, and dismay is what I meant. You're telling me no one can figure out if Jack Littleton's death was a suicide or homicide?"

"That is correct," Frigg replied, "and that is the first item in the police report queue. If you'd like me to send it . . ."

"No," Stu said, "not right now. I need to go into the office for a while. I'll let you know when I'm ready for you to start sending. Where did Littleton die again?"

"Pasadena, California."

"Thank you, Frigg. I'll let you know when I'm ready."

"Very well," Frigg said. "Drive safely."

Sometimes Stu couldn't help but regard Frigg as an overly attentive mother figure, keeping watch over his every move, because that's exactly what she did, including tracking his devices as he drove back and forth to work. Shaking his head, he grabbed his loaded coffee cup and headed for the door.

Driving toward Cottonwood, he considered what she had said. If there were 173 files in the queue, that meant Hal and Jack had been homicide detectives for considerable lengths of time and working as partners for at least part of it. If the traffic incident on I-17 had been a disguised but so far unsuccessful attempt on Hal Holden's life, what were the chances that the undetermined death of his onetime partner had been a successful one?

Using the truck's sound system, Stu connected to his cell phone and asked Siri to locate and dial a non-emergency number for Pasadena PD. Once the call was answered, he asked to be put through to the lead investigator into Jack Littleton's death. Fortunately

Detective Hollingsworth was on duty and eventually he came on the line.

"Ray Hollingsworth here," he said. "May I help you?"

"I'm calling about the Jack Littleton case," Stu replied. "Is there anything you can tell me about that?"

"Are you a friend or relative?" Hollingsworth asked.

"Neither," Stu said. "My name is Stuart Ramey. I work for a tech company in Arizona. Are you aware that yesterday Jack Littleton's onetime partner, a guy named Hal Holden, was involved in a serious vehicular incident that may very well have been an attempt on his life?"

"I hadn't heard a thing about it," Hollingsworth said.

"Is it possible there might be a connection between the two incidents?"

There was a pause on the line as Hollingsworth considered the best way to deal with this unexpected development. "As you may or may not know," he said eventually, "Mr. Littleton's manner of death was ruled as undetermined. We're still investigating the matter. Since it's an open investigation, I'm unable to discuss any further details, but what's this about Hal? Is he all right?"

Had Stuart Ramey been more socially aware, he might have caught the very real concern in that last question and understood that Hollingsworth and Hal had a personal connection. Unfortunately, that tiny detail went right over Stu's head. Offended by the idea that information flowed in only one direction, he hit back.

"I'm unable to provide any additional details at this time," he replied curtly and ended the call. After all, turnabout was fair play.

Stu found the office in Cottonwood in crisis mode. Mateo was grabbing a much-needed nap while Lance had his hands full dealing with a late-breaking attempted cyberattack on a customer's network in Taiwan. Working together, Stu and Lance, later joined by Mateo, spent the next fifteen hours thwarting that and numerous similar cyberattacks on other customer networks from around the world. Engrossed in their work, the day passed without Stu ever checking back with Frigg. There wasn't enough time.

CHAPTER 20

LAS VEGAS, NEVADA

Thursday, January 2, 2020, 7:30 a.m. (PST)

The second of January dawned clear and cold in Vegas. Frank had been out of prison since the first of November, but he still appreciated being able to climb out of bed and have his feet land on soft carpet instead of bare concrete. Standing in the shower, he anticipated this would be a good day. First he'd walk over to the gym and work out. On his way home, he'd have breakfast at the diner.

Out in the kitchen, he started a pot of coffee. While it brewed, he logged on to his computer and checked the newsfeeds from Phoenix, the same ones he'd used the night before. Unfortunately, what he read there put a blight on what had started out as a wonderful morning. Both of the injured victims from the previous day's I-17 wreck were still alive, one in serious condition and one critical but stable. There was no way to tell which was which. After reading that, Frank slammed his laptop shut with more force than necessary. For the first time, Sal had let Frank down, and he was worried.

What if Hal recovered enough to be able to talk? What if someone asked Hal if there was someone who wanted him dead? He would probably say there was. Most homicide cops accumulated a list of enemies over time, but with Jack Littleton's recent death still under investigation, what were the chances someone might ask if they'd had any enemies in common? Hal's mentioning Frank's name might be that tiny particle of falling ice that sets off a massive avalanche, and if Danielle's name ever came up, he'd be toast.

Having reached that worrisome conclusion, Frank returned to his computer and typed a three-letter message into Sal's draft file.

WTF?

While he waited for a response, Frank considered his options. He had already decided that, once his scores were settled, he wouldn't stay on in Vegas. The remainder of his payout would go a lot further somewhere with a lower cost of living. He had imagined that when Sylvia's situation was handled, he'd make a leisurely exit. Maybe now he should speed up that process.

Eventually Sal replied:

I know. Those two screwups are off the board.
You can expect a full refund.

Frank wasn't sure what the sentence about screwups meant, but a full refund was more than he'd expected. He was glad to know that Sal was an honorable man when it came to keeping his word, but that promised refund wouldn't be of much use to him if he was back in the slammer. Not only that, he had already paid for the contract on Sylvia, and she was up next.

What about S?

Not to worry. In process.

Moments later the draft file emptied, meaning the conversation was over. It was easy for Sal to say Frank shouldn't worry, but at this point Sal had nothing to lose. Frank did, and the more he thought about the first part of Sal's message—about the "screwups" being off the board, the more concern he felt. That terminology meant they were dead, which might create more complications.

Finally, after considering his situation for the better part of an hour, Frank headed for Hi-Roller, where he went straight to the back room and told the attendant he needed to speak to Nicholas—urgently. A few minutes later, while Frank was back out front on his favorite treadmill, another attendant handed him a cordless phone.

"Hey, Frank," Nicholas said once Frank came on the line. "I hear you wanted to speak to me. What's up?"

"I need to leave town on a permanent basis."

"Leave town or leave the country?" Nicholas inquired. He was nobody's dummy. No doubt the first problem was easier to solve than the second.

"The latter, I guess," Frank answered, "preferably somewhere beyond the reach of the US Marshals."

"So you're looking for the full-meal deal," Nicholas said. "New identity, fake passport, and transportation?"

Yes, Nicholas had done this before. "All of the above," Frank said.

"When do you want to leave?"

"The sooner, the better."

"Fast and good will be expensive."

"No problem," Frank said. "You know I'm good for it."

"Where do you want to go?"

"I'm not too fussy about a final destination. Any suggestions?"

"Indonesia would be a good bet," Nicholas answered.

Indonesia didn't sound especially inviting. Vegas was hot and dry. Indonesia sounded hot and humid.

"Why there?" he asked.

"That's where the balance of your payout is," Nicholas replied. "We're not dumb enough to keep that much money lying around here in the States."

"In that case, Indonesia is sounding better all the time."

"What about your parole officer?" Nicholas asked. "Any upcoming meetings with him?"

"With her," Frank corrected. "Miriam Baxter. I'm scheduled to meet with her the first week of every month. I see her on Monday."

"Okay," Nicholas said, "I'll set your departure for some time after that."

Frank knew more about his current state of jeopardy than Nicholas did. "I'd like to leave right after that if possible," he said. "That way I'll have a month-long head start before anyone starts looking for me."

"All right," Nicholas agreed. "I'll do my best, but it's gonna cost you."

"It's only money," Frank said.

"Okey-doke," Nicholas said. "I'll get on it and let you know when arrangements are in place."

Frank returned the phone to the front desk. Along the way he worked on revising his initial opinion about that final destination. *Between living in Indonesia and going back to prison, there is no contest!*

CHAPTER 21

PRESCOTT, ARIZONA

Thursday, January 2, 2020, 9:00 a.m. (MST)

Chief Detective Biba had barely set foot in the office on Thursday morning when he was summoned to appear in Captain Bill Dunn's office. Dunn ruled District 12 with an iron fist, and Biba knew he was about to be dressed down.

"What the hell is going on with your people?" Dunn demanded as soon as Biba took a seat. "What part of not discussing an ongoing investigation with the media don't they understand?"

"I know all about that leak," Biba replied, "except for the identity of the worthless SOB who did it! When I figure that out, he'll be out of here."

"He'd better be," Dunn agreed. "Aside from what's already on the news, has any progress been made in solving this case?"

"Not so far," Biba admitted. "I checked with the hospital on my way in. So far both victims are still alive, although one is still critical and on a ventilator. As soon as I touch base with my folks here, I'll head down to

Phoenix to have a talk with the guy who's not currently in the ICU. I tried interviewing him yesterday, but he was fresh out of surgery and wasn't much help."

Because his wife kept butting in and answering questions for him, Biba thought, but Dunn didn't need to hear about that.

"Keep me in the loop," the captain ordered. "So far today I've fielded over a dozen calls from media types asking about a press briefing, but I'm not scheduling one of those until I have something meaningful to say."

"Yes, sir," Biba said, rising to his feet. "I hear you loud and clear."

On the way back to his office, he stopped by the bullpen. Detective Julie Morris looked up from her keyboard as he approached.

"Making any progress?" Biba asked.

Julie shook her head. "Not much."

"What about that interview with Ali Reynolds? As far as I'm concerned, that's step number one."

"Tried but didn't get anywhere," Julie replied. "When I called High Noon's office, I was told she's out of the country."

"Out of the country?" Biba echoed. "When did that happen?"

"Sometime last night," Julie answered. "Around nine she flew out of Flagstaff on a private jet, bound for London."

"She fled the country?" Biba demanded.

"Not exactly fled," Julie corrected. "The woman I spoke to was . . ." She paused long enough to consult her notes before continuing. ". . . Shirley Malone, High Noon's receptionist. She explained that Ms. Reynolds was on her way to pinch-hit for her husband at a tech conference of some kind in London."

"Why didn't either she or her husband mention that when I spoke with them yesterday afternoon?" Biba inquired. "Is she really going to a conference, or is this her high-priced way of avoiding doing an interview? When's she due back?"

"Shirley didn't know for sure," Julie answered. "If you can afford to use private jets, I guess you don't have to worry about making reservations in advance—you just come and go whenever you please."

Biba nodded. What was true in the world of travel held true in the justice system as well. Regular people, the ones who flew economy, if at all, usually turned up for police interviews or court appearances accompanied by public defenders. First-class fliers came to court shielded by high-priced lawyers. Elites, however, the real jet-setters, were usually able to avoid interviews and court appearances altogether. He suspected that was exactly what Ali Reynolds was doing.

"What are you working on there?" Biba wanted to know, changing the subject and motioning toward Julie's monitor.

"Since we still don't know the real target here, I'm looking into the backgrounds of both men. Simpson grew up here in the Verde Valley before moving to the Pacific Northwest and starting a video gaming company. A dozen years or so ago, he sold that, came back home, and started High Noon Enterprises, which he and his wife now own jointly. From what I can see of their finances, they're seemingly in good shape."

"So no obvious money problems," Biba said. "What about Holden?"

"Born and raised in Pasadena, California. He's a retired cop who spent twenty-five years serving with Pasadena PD. He and his third wife, Rose, retired to the Village of Oak Creek in 2005. She's deceased now, and he's been driving an airport limo for the last several years."

"Nothing stands out about him?"

"Nothing at all, at least not as far as his years on the job are concerned. He started out in patrol and was working in homicide when he retired."

"He sounds like a big nothing burger."

"That's how it looks to me, too."

"What can you tell me about Ali Reynolds, Simpson's wife?"

"I've started on her but haven't gotten very far. Why?"

"Because I got a weird vibe from her," Biba answered. "From what you've said, Simpson makes a far more likely target than an over-the-hill cop."

"Okay," Julie agreed. "I'm on it."

Just then Detective Flack let out a triumphant whoop from his own cubicle. "Hot damn!"

"What's going on?" Biba asked.

"I've been going back through all the witness statements from yesterday."

"And?"

"After our two patrol officers, Yavapai County Deputy Merrilee Hawkins was the next officer to show up at the scene. She had been traveling northbound on I-17 and spotted the Silverado and a red SUV parked on the shoulder of the southbound lanes. She was about to go back to see if they needed help when the call came in about the rollover, so she headed there instead.

"After reading her statement this morning and going

on a hunch, I put out a BOLO for stolen red SUVs and just now got a hit. Half an hour ago a red 2018 Subaru was reported stolen from the long-term parking lot at McCarran International Airport in Vegas. It left the lot at 18:30 on New Year's Eve. The owner told officers that the car was equipped with STARLINK, Subaru's vehicle-location system. A few minutes ago, officers from the La Paz County Sheriff's Office reported finding that vehicle abandoned on a dirt road west of the transfer station in Quartzsite."

"Quartzsite?" Biba repeated. "That's in the middle of nowhere. Why would it be there?"

"Who knows?"

"Great catch, Steve," Biba said. "Now get on the line and tell responding officers to keep their hands off that vehicle. You should also advise them that the surrounding area should be considered a crime scene. In the meantime, I'll call District 4 in Yuma and ask them to dispatch people to impound the vehicle. If it was involved in our incident, chances are the perpetrators wiped it down before abandoning it, but if they were in a hurry, I'll bet they didn't wipe everything."

"Anything else?" Flack asked.

"If they stole the Subaru in Nevada and the Silverado in Kingman, Arizona, they covered a lot of territory and must have stopped off somewhere. Let's go on the hunt for surveillance footage. I want to get a look at these guys."

With that, Warren Biba headed into his office. He had planned on driving down to Phoenix to take another crack at interviewing B. Simpson, but for now that could wait. If this investigation was finally going somewhere, he wanted to be here at his desk directing traffic.

CHAPTER 22

PHOENIX, ARIZONA

Friday, January 3, 2020, 7:00 a.m. (MST)

B. Simpson had had a rough night. His whole body was battered and bruised. His damaged shoulder was taped to his body in order to keep it stable and prevent further injury. Between that and his surgical incision, it had been impossible for him to find a comfortable sleeping position. It wasn't until Sister Anselm had finally insisted that the night nurse administer additional pain meds that he'd gotten some rest. Then, once he'd fallen asleep, an attendant had shown up with his breakfast tray at seven sharp followed shortly thereafter by the surgeon who had removed his spleen who reported he was doing "just fine."

You could have fooled me, B. thought grumpily. *And whatever happened to the concept of people resting comfortably in their hospital beds?*

He wanted to call Ali and see how things were going in the UK. Most likely Cami had already made her presentation, and he wanted to know how she'd done, but he couldn't call because the replacement phone Sister

Anselm said was coming had not yet arrived. He was back dozing again when yet another scrub-clad visitor arrived at his bedside, a doctor B. didn't remember having seen before.

"Hello," the newcomer said. "I'm Dr. Robert Hamilton, the orthopedic surgeon assigned to your case. I'll be performing the surgery on your damaged shoulder and upper arm, unless you have a personal bone doc who you'd rather do the honors."

"I don't have a 'personal bone doc,'" B. replied grudgingly. "I've never needed one."

An unfazed Dr. Hamilton smiled at B.'s brusque manner. "You need one now," he said cheerfully, "and I'm your man. I've spoken to the surgeon who performed your splenectomy. His assessment is that we can go to work on repairing your arm and doing your shoulder replacement as early as tomorrow morning."

"Shoulder replacement?" B. echoed. "I thought it was just broken."

"The goal in fracture treatment is to put things together well enough to start motion early so as to prevent the joint from turning into a lump of scar tissue. Your arm bone or humerus was broken into a dozen pieces which might be fixable. The socket or glenoid was smashed like a stomped-on Christmas cookie. It is unfixable. In order to get the joint moving it's best to replace the damaged parts. You're not a tennis player, are you?"

"No," B. replied, "but I'm also left-handed. For the first time in my life, I guess that's a good thing."

"Left-handed or right-handed," the doctor replied, "with a new shoulder and the proper rehab you'll have a functional shoulder after rehab. Exercises will start the day after surgery."

"How long?"

"Three to six months, give or take, but that's only if you are absolutely, one hundred percent committed to doing physical therapy."

From where B. was lying, three months sounded like forever.

"So I'll see you tomorrow, then, seven sharp?" Dr. Hamilton finished.

"Sounds good," B. muttered under his breath.

Sister Anselm returned. "How are we doing?" she asked brightly.

"*We* are not doing well," B. groused. "The orthopedic guy just told me he'll be doing a shoulder replacement tomorrow morning. Did you know about that?"

Sister Anselm shrugged. "I more or less figured it out," she said.

"Why didn't you tell me?" B. asked.

"Because," Sister Anselm replied with a smile, "I was pretty sure you'd shoot the messenger."

"Probably," B. sighed. "So how about lending me your phone so I can see how Cami did?"

"Right-o," Sister Anselm said, handing it over. "Here it is."

CHAPTER 23

Ali's and Cami's English breakfasts were delivered to their suite. Cami, uncharacteristically quiet, barely touched her food. Ali attributed her lack of appetite to a case of nerves about the upcoming presentation.

Ali had expected the conference room to be in a portion of a much-larger ballroom, but once they entered, she saw that was not the case. The narrow room had soaring windows on both sides, allowing a full view of London's winter-gray skies. Conference participants were seated around a long banquet table with printed plaques indicating seat assignments. Ali and Cami were seated together, with Angela at a chair under the windows directly behind them.

Due to jet lag, Ali had a tough time staying awake during the morning sessions, and she caught Cami on the verge of nodding off from time to time as well. Luncheon, served in an adjoining private dining room, consisted of salmon baked in lemon caper butter and accompanied by roasted potatoes and steamed broccolini. For conference fare, the food was probably amazing, but due to nerves, both Ali's and Cami's plates remained mostly untouched.

By the time one thirty rolled around and Cami was introduced, she appeared to have conquered her jitters, while Ali was still a wreck. Once Cami launched into her talk, however, she spoke as easily as if addressing a roomful of high-powered executives was an everyday occurrence. The hours of study on the plane had paid off, and although she had carried a stack of note cards to the lectern with her, she seldom consulted them.

Sitting there listening, Ali's own nervousness settled and she felt a growing sense of pride. She knew something about Cami's challenging home life growing up. Since coming to work for High Noon, she had matured into a poised and confident young woman, and her performance that day was flawless. During the Q and A, she fielded the incoming barrage of inquiries with complete aplomb.

During the afternoon break that followed, Ali was approached by George Smythe, the CEO of International Cyber Security and someone Ali had met on several previous occasions.

"How's B. doing after that car wreck of his?" he asked.

Naturally that question raised Ali's hackles. "You heard about that?" she asked.

"I believe Adrian mentioned something to me about B.'s involvement in an automobile mishap. I would have expected you to stay at his side."

You hoped, Ali thought. "That's what I expected, too," she replied aloud, "but he insisted I come. He felt the conference was too important to miss."

"Well," Smythe went on, "that young woman who stood in for him today was quite impressive. I trust you're not keeping her locked up in a computer lab. With communication skills like that, she'd make a crackerjack saleswoman."

"You might be right," Ali agreed.

Just then her silenced phone vibrated in her pocket. A quick check revealed Sister Anselm's number on the caller ID, so she hurried into the corridor to answer.

"Hey," B. said. "How'd Cami do?"

"She was terrific," Ali replied. "In fact, George Smythe just suggested we take her out of the lab and put her in sales, but enough about us. How are you?"

"The doctors have finished their rounds. The surgeon says I'm doing well, but the orthopedic guy says I need a shoulder replacement immediately if not sooner. That's scheduled for tomorrow morning."

Ali's heart fell. "If you're having more surgery, I should be there."

"You don't need to . . ." B. began, but Ali cut him off.

"Look," she said, "you know as well as I do that I'm only here as window dressing. Everyone who just heard Cami's bravura performance knows she's the real deal. I should be able to catch a flight home tomorrow."

Ali more than half expected B. to object, but he didn't. "Thank you," he said. "Sister Anselm is great, but the truth is, I'd rather have you here."

I'd rather be there, too, Ali thought. "Anything new on the investigation?"

"Not as far as I know," B. answered. "So far Detective Biba hasn't put in another appearance, but it's still early. He'll probably stop by later. What about your bodyguard situation? Did Sonja deliver?"

"She did. Her gal's name is Angela. Upon arrival she presented us with tiny vials of wasp spray disguised as bottles of designer perfume for when she's not around."

"Wasp spray?" B. repeated.

"Yes," Ali replied. "In places where you're not allowed to carry handguns, wasp spray is supposedly the next best thing."

"But a bodyguard is better," B. said, "so if you do end up leaving early, be sure that Angela person hangs around to keep an eye on Cami."

"I will," Ali agreed.

"So do the two of you have plans for this evening?" B. asked.

"I don't know about Cami, but I've given myself permission to play hooky. Leland Brooks is in town, staying at his great-nephew's place just a few blocks from here in Knightsbridge. I've been invited to afternoon tea followed by dinner."

"Are you going alone?" B. asked.

"That's the plan," Ali said. "I can't very well show up with an extra mouth to feed."

"How are you getting there?"

"It's only a short walk . . ." she began, but B. stopped her.

"Do not walk," he insisted. "If Angela isn't going with you, take a cab."

"Okay," Ali conceded, "a cab it is." Just then people began heading back into the conference room. "Have to go," she told him. "Our break is over."

She stayed for a while after that, but just before three Ali slipped out of the conference room and went upstairs, where she changed into something a little more casual. While in the room, she left a note telling

Cami about B.'s next round of surgery and asking her to book Ali on the next available flight home.

A few minutes later, when Ali's cab arrived at Brompton Square, she saw that Jeffrey and Charlie's building was still aglow with holiday decorations. She was standing outside the entrance, searching for the right bell to ring, when the door opened, revealing a pale imitation of the Leland Brooks she once knew.

The years between that moment and when she'd seen him last had taken their toll. The old man who stepped outside to greet her may have been smiling a hearty welcome, but he looked frail and spent. Painfully thin and leaning heavily on a cane for support, Leland Brooks now bore little resemblance to the aging hero who had once appeared out of the darkness to rescue Ali from grave danger. No, that earlier version of Leland Brooks was no more.

"Come in, come in," he said in greeting. "I'm delighted to see you."

"You were waiting in the lobby?" Ali asked, after a brief embrace.

"Of course," he said. "You didn't expect to come upstairs unescorted, did you?"

Leland's looks may have changed, but his gentlemanly manner had not. He led her over to the elevator, waved her inside, and then pressed the button labeled *PH*—the penthouse level.

"I can still manage the interior stairs," he explained as the lift rose, "but sometimes I cheat and use this. Normally I'd invite you into my downstairs sitting room, but Jonah fell asleep on the sofa. The two of us spend a good deal of time together, and I'm afraid the place is a bit of a mess."

Jonah, Ali knew, was Charles's and Jeffrey's son. As Ali's majordomo, Leland had always kept her home in perfect order. It was difficult for her to imagine his apartment in any kind of disarray.

"The boy's not alone, is he?" Ali asked.

"Certainly not," Leland replied. "Anna, his nanny, is there. She'll bring him upstairs once he's awake."

The elevator door opened directly into a penthouse unit alive with the welcoming aromas of food preparation. That had been true the last time she had visited, but the apartment itself was vastly different. Before it had been the picture of pristine elegance, something out of *Better Homes and Gardens*. Now it was lived-in, comfy, and cluttered with a scatter of kid-friendly debris, including a Big Wheel parked with its nose tucked in under a beautifully decorated Christmas tree. Seated on a sofa, Jeffrey was engrossed in trying to corral a pile of loose crayons and clear them from a glass-topped coffee table.

Caught in the act, he looked up sheepishly as they entered. "I meant to have all of this cleaned up before you arrived," he apologized, "but I came home later than expected. Please make yourself at home, Ali. Once I finish tidying up, do you prefer tea or cocktails?"

"Given my jet lag, I'll stick to tea," Ali told him, and Leland followed suit. The two of them settled in a pair of easy chairs while Jeffrey continued straightening the room. Based on the abundance of toys, Ali suspected that Jonah Brooks-Chan was destined to be something of a spoiled brat.

Parking his three-pronged cane next to his chair, Leland leaned forward and asked, "What brings you to London?"

Ali gave him an abbreviated and somewhat watered-down version of what had happened to B., treating the incident as an unfortunate accident rather than an attempted homicide. There was no need to burden Leland with all that.

"And how are things going for you?" Ali asked, turning the focus of the conversation back to him.

Leland's lined face darkened. "I miss Thomas dreadfully, of course," he said, "but I'm so grateful to have been able to care for him for as long as I did. I have you and Mr. Simpson to thank for that, of course. Had you not gifted me with that trip home, he and I never would have reconnected. Can you guess which TV show was our absolute favorite?"

"I give up."

"*As Time Goes By,*" Leland said with a sad smile.

That made perfect sense. She and B. had enjoyed watching that one, too—the story of a loving couple who had lost track of each other during the Korean War only to be reunited decades later. In that respect, their story and Leland and Thomas's were remarkably similar.

"Not surprising in the least," Ali said.

"Toward the end, though," Leland continued, "even watching television became too much for him. It was all very difficult, and I'm afraid it took more out of me than I realized. If Jeffrey and Charles hadn't gathered me up and brought me here after the funeral, Thomas's death might well have been the death of me, too, but of course they'd already been through much the same thing."

Jeffrey and Charles had met in Thailand, where both had lost previous partners to a catastrophic tsunami. No wonder they'd taken pity on Leland.

Just then, a towheaded boy appeared at the top of the stairwell, popping into view and then racing across the room toward them. "Uncle Lee," he said, skidding to a stop in front of Leland's chair. "Are you going to read me a story?"

"Not now, Jonah," Leland said. "We have company. I'd like to introduce you to a friend of mine, Ms. Reynolds."

Turning to look at Ali, the boy came to attention. "Good afternoon, Ms. Reynolds," he said seriously, offering a tiny hand. "I'm Jonah, and I'm very happy to meet you."

Spoiled or not, the kid had excellent manners. Ali took his proffered hand and shook it. "I'm glad to meet you, too, Jonah," she said.

"Do you know my dads?" he asked.

"Yes, I do," she replied. "I visited here years ago, before you were born."

"You talk funny," Jonah said. "Are you from America?"

"Yes, I am," Ali told him with a smile. "That's where I met . . ." She had to think for a moment about what to say next. ". . . your uncle Lee."

With introductions out of the way, the boy propelled himself up and onto Leland's lap, where he snuggled comfortably under the old man's chin.

"Are we having tea now?" he wanted to know.

"I believe that's the plan," Leland replied.

"Good," Jonah said. "I'm starving."

Tea consisted of delicate cucumber finger sandwiches and freshly baked scones still hot from the oven, and it was delivered by a demure young woman Ali suspected had been borrowed from the waitstaff at the nearest Charlie Chan restaurant to act as their server for the evening.

Jonah stuck around long enough to devour several scones before heading pell-mell back down the stairs.

"He's very bright," Ali observed as the boy disappeared from view.

"He is that," Leland agreed. "I'd never spent much time with little ones before this, and it can be a bit tiring on occasion. Fortunately, he and Anna will be taking their dinners downstairs this evening, so we'll have a chance to visit."

And visit they did. Ali caught Leland up on all the goings-on in Sedona, filling him in on the circumstances surrounding the loss of her father and the relatively recent arrival of Ali's second grandson. Leland wanted to know how Alonzo was holding up as far as keeping the household running smoothly, and he was thrilled to hear that Bella was still alive and well.

A little past six, Charles emerged from the kitchen and took a seat as Jeffrey served aperitifs. "We have a perfect division of labor," Jeffrey explained. "I handle beverage service, and he does the cooking. Fortunately for me, he still loves to cook. What are we having?"

Charles favored Ali with a conspiratorial grin. "I didn't want our visitor to think I'm a one-trick pony, so we're going all-English tonight—wine-glazed beef Wellington, potato puree, and crispy Brussels sprouts with a lemon cream sauce. How does that sound?"

"Wonderful," Ali told him, "and it makes me thankful that I only had one of those scones."

After sharing a delightful meal and giving Leland what she feared would be a final hug, Ali returned to the hotel. By 8:30 she was back in the suite, where she found Cami on the phone with her laptop open in front of her. Ali started to ask a question, but Cami held up a silencing finger.

"Okay," she was saying into the phone. "We're good to go, then."

"What's happening?" Ali asked once the call ended.

"You're booked business class on a 7:30 a.m. Delta flight tomorrow from Heathrow to LAX," Cami told her. "I've got a charter flight lined up there to fly you from LA to Phoenix. Someone from the charter company will meet you at baggage claim and take you to the civil aviation part of the airport for your Phoenix-bound flight. Easy-peasy. I've also booked a 4:30 a.m. wake-up call here at the hotel and a 5:00 a.m. car service pickup, so you'd best get packing. Depending on how things go, you should be on the ground in Phoenix somewhere around noon. With any kind of luck, you might be there before B.'s even out of recovery."

"Thank you," Ali said. "You really do work magic."

"Should I tell Angela that she's off-duty once you leave?"

"Nope, she's to stay on the case."

"But I don't really need a bodyguard," Cami objected.

"You may not think so, and I may not think so, but B.'s the boss, and he thinks you do."

"All right, then," Cami agreed with a toss of her head. "Whatever B. says goes."

CHAPTER 24

PHOENIX, ARIZONA

Thursday, January 2, 2020, 3:00 p.m. (MST)

It took time to get the Highway Patrol's team of CSIs from Yuma to Quartzsite so they could process the scene, and it took even longer to have the Subaru towed back to the District 4 impound lot. In the meantime, Julie had managed to track down some very interesting details on B. Simpson's life insurance situation.

Midafternoon, Detective Steven Flack popped his head into Biba's office to announce that he had managed to locate a truck stop in Anthem where the stolen red Subaru had pulled off I-17. Once Biba had a chance to review the surveillance video, he gave himself permission to leave his desk and head for Phoenix.

It was late in the afternoon before he finally arrived at St. Gregory's. Thanks to Detective Morris's research, Warren Biba felt he was loaded for bear. With Ali Reynolds out of the country, he expected to have a straight shot at interviewing B. Simpson. Unfortunately, Sister Anselm was there in Ali's place, and she seemed disinclined to leave the room.

"How are you feeling today, Mr. Simpson?" Biba asked.

"Okay so far," was the answer, "but I'm scheduled for another round of surgery tomorrow morning."

With the nun occupying the only visitor chair, this time Biba was the one forced to remain standing—not an optimal situation for conducting a successful interview.

"I understand your wife's been called out of the country," he began.

Simpson nodded.

"I'm surprised there was no mention of that when I was here yesterday."

Attempting to shrug his injured shoulder, B. winced. "She's in London," he said, "filling in for me at a conference. Having her go in my stead was a last-minute decision, one we made after you left."

"When will she be back?"

"Tomorrow maybe," B. replied, "but I'm not sure."

"Must be nice to be able to grab a private jet and hop over to London at the drop of a hat."

"It's business," B. returned. "This is a high-profile conference, and it was important that High Noon have a presence. Ali and I are full partners in the business," he added. "I handle most of the outside sales while she manages the home team."

"Is that why you do so much traveling?"

"It is."

"I understand there's quite an age gap between you and your wife," Biba said.

The abrupt change of direction caught Simpson momentarily off guard. "Fifteen years," he said finally, "but since the age difference doesn't concern Ali or me, why should it interest you?"

"You know," Biba said dismissively, "the whole age-gap thing."

"What are you saying?"

"With an older woman waiting back home, it seems possible that on one of your many trips, you might have strayed off the straight and narrow with someone a bit younger."

"You're suggesting I'm screwing around behind Ali's back?"

"I'm investigating an attempted homicide," Biba replied. "When it comes to motive, money is right at the top of the list, with jealousy a close second."

"I'm not having an affair," Simpson declared, "and we're not having money problems, either."

"Speaking of money," Biba said, "how about if we talk about that?"

"What about it?"

"I understand you carry a substantial amount of life insurance."

"Of course I do," B. answered. "Who doesn't? There are two large individual policies and probably a small amount of group insurance as well."

"Tell me about the individual ones," Biba suggested.

"I believe one has a face amount of about $500,000 while the other is for $2,000,000. Ali is the named beneficiary on both. The smaller one is for her personal use while the key-man policy primarily benefits the company."

"If that's the case, shouldn't High Noon be the named beneficiary?" Biba asked.

"As High Noon's CFO, Ali is in charge of finances. If her position were to change, so would the beneficiary designation."

"But why so much?"

"You may think that's an exorbitant amount, but it's not. Each year I'm personally responsible for bringing in about a million bucks' worth of new business. In the event of my death, that policy is designed to give her two years to find a replacement. And if you think Ali's after the insurance proceeds, forget it. One of the reasons she's CFO is that she's good at math. Given a choice between grabbing the insurance money for herself or maintaining the business, there's not a doubt in my mind which one she'd choose."

"But . . ."

"No buts," B. said. "You've been here for less than ten minutes, Detective Biba. In that time, you've accused me of being unfaithful to my wife and suggested that my wife is trying to have me murdered in order to collect the insurance proceeds. As far as I'm concerned this interview is over. Either show yourself out, or I'll have Sister Anselm here escort you out."

Biba didn't argue the point. "Very well, Mr. Simpson, I'll go," he said, "but please advise your wife that, upon her return, we'll want to speak with her at her earliest convenience."

"Oh, I'll tell her, all right," B. answered sarcastically, "but here's a word of warning, Detective Biba. You should probably be careful what you wish for, because you might just get it."

CHAPTER 25

BEAVERTON, OREGON

Thursday, January 2, 2020, 8:00 a.m. (PST)

As far as his work was concerned, Ramon Muñoz had learned that things were generally fairly quiet in the early part of January, so he spent most of the next morning in his cottage, using his computer to investigate the life and times of Sergio Gomez. What he found wasn't pretty.

Ramon's close connections with various law enforcement agencies gave him access to computer databases not accessible to the general public. Poring through those along with police reports and court documents, Ramon was able to piece together a fairly comprehensive biography of his biological father.

At the time Sergio was born, his own father was already in the US illegally. His wife came north, expecting to reunite with her husband. Unfortunately, her husband, a field hand, had died in an automobile accident two months before Sergio was born. As a consequence, the life husband and wife had planned to live together never materialized. Around the time Sergio turned five, his mother disappeared with no explanation, leaving her son to grow up in a series of foster homes, the last one in Pasadena.

Life there had been stable enough that Sergio had graduated from high school and spent a semester enrolled in junior college. After dropping out of that, several jobs in the fast-food industry had given him enough experience for him to be offered the night manager job for a locally based fast-food joint known as Tacos to Go. That was where he had hired Sylvia Garcia, and that's where he had raped her. She may have been his first victim, since Ramon could find no record of anyone else ever lodging a complaint against him prior to that incident or after it, either, for that matter, because, from that point on, apparently none of Sergio's other victims lived to tell the tale.

After a short-lived career in the fast-food business, Sergio had drifted into the world of gangs and drugs. In 2006 a gangland brawl landed him in jail on felony assault with intent to kill, an arrest that triggered the mandatory collection of his DNA. A check with CODIS linked him to the rape kits collected from two separate homicide victims. Lulu Sanders, age fourteen, had been raped and murdered in July 1995. Isabel Griffith's death occurred three years later, in September 1998. She was sixteen years old at the time of her death.

Sergio had been charged and convicted of both crimes. He died of hepatitis in the California Correctional Institution in Tehachapi, California, on April 1, 2007, less than five years into his sentence of life without parole.

Good riddance, Ramon thought, closing the lid on his laptop. *Not nearly what you deserved, you son of a bitch, but I'll take it.*

After that, Ramon went for a run. As his feet pounded away on the cold, wet pavement, he attempted to take everything he had learned about his parents' histories and apply it to his own life. He had a girlfriend—Molly Braeburn—an officer for Gresham PD. She'd been on leave for the past two weeks, caring for her mother in San Diego who had just undergone surgery for colon cancer. Molly was due home on Saturday evening in time for her shift on Sunday.

The couple had met some six months earlier when Ramon had been hired to do composite sketches of a pair of home invaders who had broken into houses to terrorize and rob elderly residents. Molly and Ramon had met in a break room and instantly hit it off. They'd been a couple ever since. She was Ramon's first serious relationship. He'd thought about asking her to marry him over the holidays, but with her mother seriously ill in California, he had decided to delay popping the question.

Now he was glad he had waited for more than one reason. Molly was on the pill. At least she said she was, but what did he know? What if she wasn't or if it just didn't work? What if she turned up pregnant the same way his mother had? What would happen then?

The two of them had never discussed any of those what-ifs, but Ramon realized now they should have. If she did conceive out of wedlock, would they still go ahead and get married? And if they didn't marry, would Molly want to keep the baby, put it up for adoption, or would she choose to have an abortion? Ramon wasn't sure about any of that, and he might not have any say in the matter, anyway.

And if they decided to go ahead and get married,

what would happen then? Were they ready? What kind of marriage would it be—as good as his mother's with Larry Rogers, as bad as his mother's with Frank Muñoz, or something in between? And most of all, what kind of parents would they be?

Then there was the matter of his mother's history. What was he supposed to do about that? Ramon was willing to keep her secret as far as Larry and his sisters were concerned, but what about Molly? If they were serious about getting married and having a future together, didn't he have an obligation to tell her? And wasn't it better for her to learn about it directly from him rather than have it show up later on from some outside source?

Back from his run, Ramon put on work clothes and went out into the yard to do some long-neglected pruning. Working on that helped settle his nerves. As the day progressed, he was surprised to find himself feeling almost lighthearted. The emotional encounter with his mother had somehow lifted a terrible load off his own shoulders, but he kept wondering if she had mentioned any of it to Larry. Since she had kept the awful truth from her son, what were the chances she had done the same thing to her husband?

Once it started getting dark, Ramon went to his own place to shower, then he headed for the main house. With Larry's upcoming surgery in mind, Ramon had gifted his mother with a spa day for Christmas, and today was the day she was redeeming it. After a long weekend of nonstop cooking, she had announced prior to leaving the house that she'd be bringing home takeout for dinner.

Ramon found Larry sitting in his recliner and

watching the local news. "Hey," he said, "you were just on TV."

"I was?" Ramon asked. "How come?"

"Not you—one of your cases, one from last summer, the one in Cannon Beach," Larry said. "They finally caught the guy. Hold on, I'll run it back."

Just before the start of the school year, a seven-year-old kid named Chip Andrews had been playing on the beach near Haystack Rock on the Oregon coast. At some point, Chip had returned to the family's rented condo to retrieve a kite. On the way through the parking lot, he was accosted by a stranger who had attempted to lure him into a vehicle. The kid had been smart enough to take off running. Later, when he told his folks about what had happened, his mother had insisted on filing a police report. No onlookers had witnessed the event, and Chip was unable to identify the make or model of the car.

At that point, Ramon Muñoz had been called in. He had spent the better part of four hours working with Chip to create a composite drawing of the man in question—a white male with blue eyes and stringy long blond hair. Ramon had been impressed by the details the kid had been able to recall—including a gap between the assailant's two front teeth and a scar that ran from the bottom of his left ear to his chin.

Finishing the drawing had marked the end of Ramon's personal involvement in the case, which, as a general rule, was how things worked. If the suspect was captured eventually, most of the time no one from the various cop shops involved bothered to let Ramon in on any of the details. He learned about case outcomes the same way everyone else did—either on TV or in the local newspaper, the *Oregonian*.

That was the case today. As the news broadcast resumed, the anchor was saying that four months after the fact, the suspect in a Cannon Beach attempted kidnapping had been apprehended and charged. The suspect turned out to be a recently paroled convicted child molester from Longview, Washington. In the course of the news clip, they showed the suspect's current mug shot side by side with Ramon's composite drawing. Between Chip's detailed recollection of the man's appearance and Ramon's ability to translate the boy's words into lines on paper, the resemblance between the two was uncanny.

"Great job," Larry said, when the story ended and the newscast went to a commercial break. "How on earth do you do that?"

"It's all thanks to you and Mrs. Clarke, Dad," Ramon told him. "If you hadn't sent me to her for art classes, none of this would have happened. Care for a beer?"

"I wouldn't say no," Larry said.

Ramon returned with two beers. After handing one to Larry, Ramon settled on the sofa with his, realizing as he did so that Larry was uncharacteristically somber.

"Are you worried about tomorrow?" Ramon asked.

Larry studied the beer bottle for a long moment before finally nodding. "I guess I am," he admitted, "but don't tell Mom. I'm not exactly what you'd call slim, you know, and no matter your age, there's always a certain amount of risk with being put under anesthesia. So yes, I'm dreading the surgery, but I can't live like this. My knees are so bad I can barely get around. I'm not getting any younger, and at your mother's age, it's not fair for her to be saddled with a crippled old man, so tomorrow's a first step."

Ramon had always known there was an age difference between his mother and Larry, but it had never seemed to pose a problem between them. Now, however, for Larry at least, apparently it did.

"Sounds to me like you're doing the right thing," Ramon said after a pause, "and I'm sure you'll be in good hands."

"True," Larry agreed, "but I'm over sixty, overweight, borderline diabetic, and hypertensive, so if I don't make it, promise me you'll look after your mom. The girls are too caught up in their own lives to bother helping out. Don't get me wrong. Sylvia's not helpless by any means, but she could use a little backup from time to time. She's still relatively young and good-looking. Once I'm gone, I don't expect her to spend the rest of her life mourning over me, but please keep an eye out for her. I don't want her hooking up with some worthless asshole."

"Because she did that once already?" Ramon suggested.

Larry nodded. "And that guy was a doozy!"

"So how about this?" Ramon asked. "How about dropping all this gloom-and-doom stuff and focusing on living instead of dying? How about if we plan on having you around and running the show for the next thirty years or so?"

"I'll drink to that," Larry said, raising his bottle in a mock toast. "And you're sure you don't mind driving us back and forth to the hospital in the morning?"

"Not at all," Ramon replied. "That way Mom can concentrate on worrying about you instead of worrying about parking."

"What's for dinner?" Larry asked after a pause.

"Beats me," Ramon said. "As she was leaving, Mom said that after spending the whole weekend cooking, she was bringing home takeout."

An even longer pause ensued. "Still," Larry said at last, "I'm surprised neither of the girls offered to hang around for a day or so longer to help out."

That reality about his sisters hadn't surprised Ramon a bit, but this was the first time he'd ever heard Larry utter a word of criticism about Tina and Lucy.

"I'm not," Ramon replied. "They are what they are."

"Yup," Larry agreed, "chips off their father's old block."

Growing up, that was something Ramon had worried about, too—that someday he'd behave the same way his father had. Today, for the first time, he realized he hadn't been wrong to be worried about that, but he'd always been focused on the wrong father. Now that he knew the truth, he understood that Sergio Gomez and Frank Muñoz were cut from the same cloth and both bad news, but if Ramon Muñoz turned out to be the kind of man Larry Rogers was, he'd be just fine.

When Sylvia turned up half an hour later with a bag loaded with teriyaki chicken, the three of them shared a surprisingly lighthearted evening together. By the time it was over, Ramon was pretty sure that Larry didn't know a thing about Sergio Gomez. And that night, when Ramon called Molly to wish her good night, he didn't tell her, either.

CHAPTER 26

BEAVERTON, OREGON

Friday, January 3, 2020, 5:30 a.m. (PST)

AJ Wilson had three strikes against him on the day he was born. His mother, Mia, always claimed she had been at war with her parents by the time she was in junior high. At age fifteen, after her mother's death, she had run away from home. She'd ended up in LA doing all the wrong things with all the wrong people. She'd married briefly and badly. When the marriage ended, Mia was left alone with a newborn baby to care for.

At that point she wound up working the streets and doing drugs. She and her son lived in a ramshackle house with several other women, some of whom also had children. The landlord happened to be their pimp, and rent for their rooms came out of their take, not his. The women took turns looking after each other's kids.

As the children grew older, and with their mothers working nights, the kids banded together. Their school attendance was intermittent at best. When money and food were scarce, they looked out for one another. On days when AJ did go to school, his mother was often still asleep when he got home, and he was careful not to disturb her.

One night, however, when it was well after dark and she was still asleep, he tried to wake her, but it didn't work. As soon as he touched her hand and felt how cold it was, AJ knew his mother was dead. He was only in the sixth grade, but he knew enough to suspect this was probably an overdose. He dialed 911. The EMTs showed up first, and the cops came next, followed by people from Child Protective Services. A social worker named Ms. Bonham helped AJ gather up a grocery bag of belongings to take with him, and off he went to a temporary foster home—"emergency fostering," she told him.

AJ had met kids at school who were in the system. From the stories he'd heard, he knew that some foster homes were okay while others were terrible. It was almost midnight on Thursday night when the social worker dropped him off. For the next three days, he stayed with a family that was fostering three other kids, two of them older and tougher than he was, so at night AJ lay in bed, barely sleeping and clutching his bag of goods for fear someone would steal it.

Then on Sunday afternoon, there came a knock on the front door. When the woman of the house opened it, AJ saw two people standing on the porch—the same social worker who had dropped him off earlier in the week and a tall, thin Black man with grizzled gray hair and gold-framed glasses. AJ was sent to his room while the newcomers were ushered into the living room. Sometime later they asked AJ to join them. And that was the moment when AJ's life changed for the better—when Ms. Bonham introduced him to the old man.

"I'm not sure if you've ever met Mr. Hiram Jones before," she said, "but he's your grandfather, your mother's father."

"Glad to meet you," the stranger said gravely, holding out an immense hand. "You can call me Gramps."

It took AJ a moment to figure out what was expected. Finally, at his foster mother's urging, he stepped forward and shook hands.

"When officers were going through your mother's things," Ms. Bonham explained, "they found a note saying that if anything happened to her, Mr. Jones should be contacted and asked to take charge of you."

"I came to get you as soon as I heard," Hiram said. "Those were your mother's last wishes, and I'm willing if you are."

AJ stared at this man who was a total stranger to him. According to his mother, her father had disowned her, and yet here he was, standing there offering AJ a future where he might not need to spend another sleepless night clutching his possessions.

"Where's that?" AJ asked. "Where's home?"

"Aloha, Oregon," Gramps said. "It's near Portland."

"Aloha," AJ repeated. "Is it like Hawaii?"

"Not exactly."

Even though Mia had been estranged from her father for years, on the day her son was born, even though she was married at the time and before she'd even left the hospital, she'd written the note and signed it in front of witnesses. She had kept the original and mailed a copy home to Hiram in Oregon. Never expecting anything would come of it, he had nonetheless kept the note.

Hiram was a man who believed in doing his duty— from the time he enlisted in the navy at age eighteen until now, in his sixties driving a mail truck for the US Postal Service. When cops finally got around to doing their next-of-kin notification, he'd understood that his duty now was to care for his orphaned grandson. He had boarded the next available flight from Portland to LAX.

He had arrived in LA with his copy of Mia's note in hand, and learned that the cops had located the faded but brittle original in Mia's underwear drawer. Together those two pieces of paper provided compelling evidence about Mia's final wishes.

AJ cut straight to the heart of the matter. "When would we go?" he asked.

"Tonight, if possible," Gramps said. "I want to get you enrolled in school as soon as I can."

"Okay," AJ agreed, "sounds good."

At the time, California's foster-care system was already stretched to the breaking point, and AJ wasn't the only one concerned about those tough older boys in the foster home—so was Ms. Bonham.

When Hiram Jones showed up with Mia's letter in hand, she instantly recognized that he would be able to offer the boy far more than Child Protective Services could. And as far as her caseload went, having AJ become someone else's problem with no muss or fuss seemed like a good idea. In the end, i's may not have been properly dotted and a few t's left uncrossed, but somehow Ms. Bonham managed to streamline the process. Hiram and AJ had flown from LA to Portland that very night.

Of course, it hadn't all been smooth sailing. For a kid who had grown up in Southern California, ending up in cold, damp Oregon was almost like landing on another planet. The skies were always gray and dreary.

It rained—all the time. It was only October, but if AJ had happened to own a winter coat, he would have put it on the minute they left the airport terminal.

Gramps had taken the next day off work and gone through the long, drawn-out ordeal of enrolling AJ in school, but once he got there, he hated it. Most of the kids in his previous school had been African American or Hispanic. That wasn't the case in the Aloha/Beaverton school district, where AJ's face turned out to be the only Black one in his sixth-grade classroom. Everyone else was white or Asian or Hispanic. Not only that, but it soon became apparent that what had passed for sixth-grade achievement levels back home in LA didn't work in Aloha—which definitely didn't resemble Hawaii at all! Before the end of that first week, while they were out at recess, one of the other kids had asked AJ if he was dumb or what. Naturally, AJ had lit into the kid in what, to the adults involved, had all the appearances of an unprovoked attack.

Summoned to the school to retrieve AJ from the principal's office, the boy had expected Hiram to raise hell with him on the way home. That wasn't the case.

"What happened?" Gramps had asked mildly.

"The other kid called me stupid."

"So what?" Gramps had replied. "You can either use that as an excuse, or we can choose to do something about it."

"Like what?"

"Like getting you a tutor to help bring you up to grade level," Gramps said. "We're also going to start playing catch every day after I come home from work because, come next spring, I'm signing you up for Little League."

"Why?" AJ had asked. "I don't even like baseball."

"You'll like baseball a hell of a lot more than you like fighting, and so will I."

"But I don't know anything about it."

"Trust me," Gramps said. "You'll learn."

As promised, Gramps hired a tutor whose focused attention worked wonders as far as AJ's schoolwork was concerned, but the real magic sauce that transformed the boy's life was Little League. Gramps turned the backyard of his small bungalow into a mini baseball camp. He put up a collection of nets to keep balls from straying into the neighbors' yards and windows. He found a used pitching machine online and bought it so AJ could practice hitting the ball. And rain or shine, they played catch for hours on end after school and on weekends.

Some kids might have balked at Hiram Jones's version of fair-minded tough love, but AJ thrived on it. By the time he walked onto a baseball diamond some six months later, AJ was reasonably confident about his skill level. Looking around, he quickly realized that the guy everyone looked up to—the one who called the shots on the team—was the pitcher. From that moment on, that's what he wanted to be, and now, six years later, he was.

He'd won a spot on Beaverton High's varsity baseball team as a sophomore. His junior year, with him as the star pitcher, the Beavers had walked away with the state championship. This year he hoped to do so again, not that he needed another championship under his belt. AJ had already been promised two full-ride athletic scholarships, one to the University of Oregon and the other to the University of Washington, but he was holding out, hoping for one from Arizona State University. If he was playing ball for the Sun Devils during spring training, maybe a Major League scout would spot him and make him an offer.

It wasn't easy for AJ to keep his pitching arm in shape during the off season, so his paper route had become a big part of his practice routine. Delivering papers had been Gramps's idea. He'd had a bicycle route when he was a kid, and he wanted AJ to have one, too. A morning paper route was a responsibility that made it impossible for a kid to be out running the streets late at night when getting into trouble was all too easy. It was also a way for AJ to earn some spending money. Except bicycle paper routes weren't exactly a thing anymore.

When AJ was fourteen, Gramps signed up for an auto-route, delivering both the *Oregonian* and the *Wall Street Journal* to houses in the Aloha/Beaverton area. They delivered eighty-five to ninety daily copies of the *Oregonian*, and fifty or so of the *Wall Street Journal*. The Sunday-only *Oregonian* subscribers numbered 135. For two years, they did the route together every day with Gramps doing the driving and AJ doing the throwing.

The two of them did a lot of talking on those long morning paper route drives, and it was during those that AJ finally learned the truth about his mother. Mia had been a difficult child from the beginning, but once her mother, Louisa, died in a car wreck, Mia was completely out of control.

Once AJ turned sixteen and got his driver's license, Gramps bought himself a new Prius and passed his elderly Civic on to AJ so he could drive the paper route by himself, unless Gramps, as he sometimes chose to do, went along for the ride. On those occasions, they reverted to their original roles with Gramps behind the wheel and AJ doing the throwing, because by then they had turned the whole paper route into a game of sorts.

AJ would exit the car in the middle of the street in front of a customer's house, wind up his arm, and then pitch the plastic bundled papers onto the porch. Papers that hit targeted doorknobs counted as strikes. A missed doorknob counted as a ball. So far AJ had never broken any windows, and only one customer had called to complain about the noise the papers made when hitting her door. (AJ no longer threw that customer's paper. Instead he walked it up onto her porch and dropped it in front of her door.)

On this cold January morning, AJ's pitches were golden, and he was well on his way to a no-hitter. Larry Rogers's home on NW Telshire Drive was more than halfway through AJ's route. Mr. Rogers was one of his favorite customers. For one thing, he was always good for a sizable tip. For another, he kept his house lit up with a porch light that came on automatically at dusk and switched off at sunrise. Porch lights made it easier for AJ to spot doorknobs.

AJ was out of the Civic, taking his stance and preparing to wind up when he saw a box sitting on the front porch. Obviously someone—Amazon, maybe—had made a delivery overnight. On a whim he decided to aim for the box instead of the doorknob, deciding on the fly that if he hit the box, it would count as a strike, too. So he did just that—he resumed his stance, took aim again, and threw.

CHAPTER 27

BEAVERTON, OREGON

Friday, January 3, 2020, 5:45 a.m. (PST)

Ramon had always been an early riser. Since he was the designated driver, and knowing Larry needed to arrive at Portland General at 6:30 a.m. for check-in, Ramon crawled out of bed even earlier that morning, showered, and was drinking coffee at his kitchen table while reading the online news when an explosion sent shock waves through the whole neighborhood. He raced out of the cottage to see what had happened as car alarms, including one he recognized as his own, went off up and down the street.

His cottage was in the rear left-hand corner of his parents' lot. As soon as he stepped outside, he smelled smoke and saw an ominous orange glow looming over the roofline of his parents' house. Ramon charged forward. As he reached the front yard, he spotted a pair of headlights stopped in the middle of the street with a male figure silhouetted before them. Ramon fully expected the guy to take off running. Instead he rushed toward Ramon clutching a phone to his ear.

"I'm calling nine-one-one," he shouted.

That's when Ramon realized who it was—AJ Wilson, his parents' paperboy. Ramon often crossed paths with AJ driving his aging Civic while Ramon was out doing early-morning runs.

Glancing toward the front of the house, Ramon was horrified to see that the entire front porch was already engulfed in flames. With his parents still inside, he skidded to a stop and reversed course.

"My folks are inside," he yelled over his shoulder. "I'm going to get them."

Ramon sprinted to the back door. Unsurprisingly, it was locked. Ramon had his own key to the deadbolt, but it was on his key ring inside the cottage, and there was no time to go after it. Instead he delivered three hard kicks to the door. It didn't open, but the lower panels finally gave way. He quickly scrambled through the opening and into the ear-splitting racket of a shrieking smoke alarm.

The house was already filling with smoke, but amazingly the lights still worked. He switched them on as he ran through the house toward his parents' bedroom. In the living room, flames had already penetrated the front wall. Glancing toward the hallway, Ramon saw his parents, still in nightclothes, hurrying toward him. On the far side of the living room they came to an inexplicable stop. While Larry tried to urge his wife forward, a panicked Sylvia suddenly seemed incapable of movement.

"Go!" Ramon shouted at Larry over the racket of the smoke alarm. "Head for the back door. I'll bring Mom!"

As smoke filled his lungs, Ramon willed himself to keep moving. When he reached his mother, he swept her into his arms, flung her over his shoulder, and made for the kitchen. He fully expected to have to shove her out through the hole in the back door, but Larry had had the presence of mind to unlock the deadbolt, leaving the door wide open.

Coughing and choking, Ramon staggered outside and headed for the street. As he neared the end of the driveway, it was all he could do to remain upright. He was close to falling when AJ stepped forward and relieved him of his burden. At that point, Ramon dropped to his knees and stayed there for the better part of a minute, coughing, choking, and gasping for breath. When the spasm finally ended, he looked around. Both his parents were safe, sitting on the ground side by side and watching in transfixed horror as their home went up in flames.

In the distance, Ramon heard wailing sirens signaling the approach of emergency vehicles. A cop car arrived first. A uniformed officer leaped out of the vehicle and ran toward them.

"Come on," he shouted, beckoning toward them. "You need to move back and make way for the fire trucks. Whose car is that?" he demanded, pointing at AJ's Civic. "Get that thing out of here!"

While AJ moved his car, the cop helped Ramon usher his parents to the far side of the street. By the time they reached their neighbor's lawn, Ramon realized his mother wasn't just coughing. She was clearly having trouble breathing. A fire truck arrived first, followed by an ambulance. Ramon raced in that direction and approached the first EMT he saw.

"Come quick," he shouted. "It's my mother. She can't breathe."

The EMTs took charge. Within a matter of moments, Ramon's mother was placed on a gurney and loaded into the ambulance with Larry climbing in after her. "Where are you taking them?" Ramon asked before the medic could slam the door shut.

"Portland General," was the curt reply.

Ramon nodded. That was the same hospital where Larry had been scheduled to have his knee replacement. *I guess that's not happening,* Ramon thought as the ambulance rolled away. "Is your mom going to be okay?" AJ asked when Ramon returned.

"I hope so," Ramon said, "but how the hell did this happen?"

"It had to be a bomb," AJ replied.

"A bomb?" Ramon repeated in disbelief. "Are you kidding?"

"I'm not," AJ said. "It must have been inside the box."

"What box?"

"When I pulled up, there was a cardboard box—a delivery box—sitting on the porch. I decided to use it for target practice and threw your dad's papers at it. As soon as they hit, the damned thing blew sky high."

After that, there was nothing more either of them could do but stand and watch in mute disbelief as Larry Rogers's mid-century modern burned to the ground. When firefighters sprayed water on it, the flames seemed to get worse.

Several minutes passed. "Where's your car?" AJ asked.

With his parents' cars in the garage, Ramon usually parked his 4Runner on the street. At this point, it was both out of sight and out of reach behind a barricade of fire trucks. "Over there," he said, pointing.

"Come on, then," AJ said. "We can't do anything here. I'll take you to the hospital."

Nodding, Ramon followed AJ to where he had parked the Civic. Once inside the vehicle, neither of them spoke for the next several minutes. AJ was the one who finally broke the silence.

"Who would do something like this to your parents?"

Ramon shook his head. "I have no idea," he answered. "None whatsoever."

All he could think about was watching the flames eat through his parents' house and wondering what, if anything, would be left.

"Well, it sucks," AJ said. "I'm so sorry."

At the hospital, Ramon directed AJ to drop him off at the entrance to the ER. "Thanks for the ride."

"Your car's not here," AJ pointed out. "How will you get back home?"

"If I even have a home," Ramon replied gloomily.

"Look," AJ said, "I gotta finish delivering my papers, but put my number in your phone. That way you can call me if you need a ride."

"Thanks," Ramon said, keying in the number.

"I'll give you my grandfather's number, too," AJ added. "His name is Hiram Jones. If you can't reach me, call him."

With the second number added, Ramon headed into the hospital. He spotted Larry on the far side of the ER's lobby. Some kind soul had taken pity on him and loaned him a pair of scrubs and some hospital socks, so at least he was no longer barefoot and wearing his pajamas. Sitting alone with his head buried in his hands, Larry Rogers was a picture of utter defeat. Ramon's mother was nowhere to be seen.

"Where's Mom?" he asked as he approached.

Larry raised a grief-stricken face. "Sylvia had a heart attack," he answered.

"How bad is it?"

"I don't know. They're running some tests—scans, they called them, but she's probably going to need surgery."

Ramon took a breath before sitting down next to Larry and putting a comforting arm around his stepfather's broad shoulders.

"It'll be all right," Ramon murmured softly. Those were the only words of solace he could summon.

"Will it?" Larry demanded. "If I lose her, what will I do? And what about the house? How bad is it? Will we even have a place to go home to? And what the hell happened? Was it a gas leak or what?"

That was when Ramon realized that Larry had been so focused on what was going on with his wife that he had no idea about what had happened at the house or the extent of the damage.

"It was a bomb," Ramon said quietly.

"A bomb?" Larry repeated in disbelief. "Somebody threw a bomb at our house?"

"Nobody threw it," Ramon explained. "A box was left on the front porch. The bomb was in that."

"What kind of box?"

"A delivery box. When AJ drove up . . ."

"The paperboy?" Larry asked.

Ramon nodded. "He threw your newspapers at the box. When they hit the box, it blew up."

"How's that possible?" Larry wondered.

That was one of the things Ramon had been wondering about during that long period of silence as AJ had been driving him to the hospital.

"I'm guessing someone placed it there during the night," Ramon said. "It was rigged so the slightest movement would set it off."

For a time Larry Rogers said nothing, but when he finally spoke it was in a voice filled with quiet fury. "That son of a bitch!" Larry muttered finally. "He's the one who did it, and she's the one he was after."

Ramon was taken aback. In all the years he had known Larry Rogers, he had never heard a single bad word escape the man's lips.

"Wait, you think Mom was the target?" Ramon asked in dismay.

"Of course she was!" Larry declared. "Who else? She's the one who goes out to get the papers every morning. If being hit by the morning papers was enough to set off that bomb, you can bet if she had picked it up to carry it into the house, she would have been blown to pieces."

"It sounds like you know who's responsible," Ramon ventured.

"Of course I do," Larry replied. "Your father. Who else? He swore on a stack of Bibles that he'd get her someday. Maybe the fire didn't kill her, but if she dies due to that heart attack, he will have succeeded all the same."

Ramon was still trying to sort things out. "You're saying my father threatened my mother?" Ramon asked. "Where? When?"

"The last time they were together," Larry replied. "They were at the jail. She had just told him that she wasn't going to post his bail, and that she hoped he'd rot in prison. He went berserk. He swore he'd get even with her if it was the last thing he ever did."

Ramon's mother had never mentioned a word to

Ramon about his father making that kind of threat, but then there were a lot of things his mother had never mentioned. The news wasn't especially surprising, however, because making threats was Frank Muñoz's second nature.

"But he's still in prison," Ramon objected. "How could he?"

"No, he's not," Larry said. "He's out on parole. He got out a couple of months ago. Your mother and I were told he was living in Las Vegas with his younger sister."

Something else Mom never mentioned, Ramon thought. It took several seconds for him to sort out what he should say next. Finally, the words came to him.

"All right, then," he said. "If that's the case, we need to go back to the house and tell the detectives what you just told me."

"No," Larry said.

"What do you mean, no?" Ramon objected. "If my father's a suspect in what happened, we need to tell them. I'm calling a cab."

Larry didn't seem to hear what he was saying. "Go ask one of the nurses if we can borrow one of those wheelchairs," he said.

"I'll get you one," Ramon agreed, "but let me call the cab first."

"Forget the damned cab!" Larry snarled, drawing alarmed glances from everyone in the room. "I don't want a cab! I need a wheelchair. It's ten after seven. We may be a few minutes late, but it's probably not too late for my pre-surgery check-in."

Ramon glanced at the clock on the wall. It was indeed ten past seven—ten minutes past the end of Larry's original knee replacement check-in time, but Ramon didn't understand. With everything else that had happened that morning, was he still thinking about going through with it?

"You can't mean that," he said.

"I most certainly do," Larry replied. "Your mom's been looking after me and my bad knees for years. Now she's the one who needs help. The only way for me to be there for her is to get my knees fixed, and that's what I intend to do. Now get me that damned chair!"

Ramon stared at Larry with new eyes, realizing that he had loved the man all along, but never more than in that moment.

"Yes, sir," he said, standing up and stuffing the phone in his pocket. "One borrowed wheelchair coming right up."

CHAPTER 28

BLYTHE, CALIFORNIA

Friday, January 3, 2020, 6:30 a.m. (PST)

The call came in at six thirty in the morning as Detective Juanita Ochoa was stepping out of the shower. She was just toweling off when her husband opened the door and stuck his head into the bathroom. "You've caught a case," he said, "make that a double."

Juanita had been a homicide cop for the Riverside County Sheriff's Office for the past six years. She didn't have to ask a double what. She knew what Armando meant.

"Where?" she asked.

"Northwest of town on Solar Farm Road," he answered. "I told them you're on your way, and don't worry about the kids. I already called Mom. She's on her way over to help with breakfast and get the kids off to school."

For Juanita, someone who had grown up mostly without family, that was one of the many blessings of living just down the street from your in-laws. Nana could always be counted on to drop everything and come on the run as needed. Armando was a captain with Blythe PD. Juanita worked for the sheriff's department. With two kids in elementary school—Gabe in third grade and Yoli in first—Nana's help was needed far too often.

"Breakfast before you go?" Armando asked.

"Better not," she answered. "Just coffee." Once in her vehicle and headed out, she radioed Dispatch. "What's the deal?"

"Two gunshot victims—young African American males, early to mid-twenties," was the reply. "One was shot from close range in the back of the head. The other one was shot in the back."

For Juanita, this was a familiar scenario, one that most likely meant a single shooter. When the first victim was shot, the second one had tried to make a run for it and hadn't succeeded.

"Who found them?"

"A guy named Mickey O'Rourke. He works maintenance at the solar farm. He was on his way home from work this morning and ended up needing to take a dump by the side of the road. Some kind of food poisoning, I guess. Anyway, he pulled over and climbed down to where a culvert goes under the road so he'd be out of sight. That's where he found the bodies. Deputies Lane and Rojas are already at the scene."

"Is Rudy coming with me?" Juanita asked.

Rudy Shepherd was her usual partner.

"Nope, he called in sick. Doc says he's got pneumonia. You're on your own on this one."

"Got it," Juanita said.

She arrived on scene fifteen minutes later. Solar Farm Road was a straight dirt track that ran north and south through seemingly barren wasteland. There were no commercial buildings or residences within miles of the place, so there wouldn't be any surveillance video coverage shedding light on what had happened.

Juanita pulled up and parked on the side of the road behind a collection of vehicles that included an older-model Ford pickup, two Riverside County marked patrol cars, and a van labeled RIVERSIDE COUNTY COR-ONER. Someone was sitting in the truck. The other vehicles were empty, meaning Juanita was late to the party.

Exiting her unmarked, she looked down the steep embankment and located the cluster of people standing in the bed of a dry wash. As Juanita made her way down the incline, Deputy Lane hurried up and met her as she reached level ground.

"Any idea how long they've been dead?"

"A while," he answered. "A couple of days, at least. I hope you brought your jar of Vicks."

Juanita paused to survey the scene. The two bodies, not yet covered, lay faceup in the wash's fine sand just inside the culvert's five-foot-tall opening. The bodies were several feet apart. One of them had obviously been shot several yards from where he lay. Seeing the trail of drag marks leading to the body, Juanita surmised that was the victim who had been shot in the back.

Finished with that initial visual survey, Juanita approached the culvert. As her nostrils were assailed by two separate odors—the pungent smell of human excrement mixed with the unmistakable scent of decomposition—she understood Deputy Lane's remark about needing her jar of Vicks. If Mickey O'Rourke hadn't been sick already, this would have done the trick.

Deputy Coroner Abigail Leavitt stood off to one

side, puffing away on a cigarette and dropping the ashes into a Styrofoam cup so as not to contaminate the crime scene.

"How'd you beat me here?" Juanita asked.

"I was in the neighborhood," Abby said. "Shall we?"

The two women approached the bodies together. This was Abby's show. Juanita stood to one side taking notes while the deputy coroner did her preliminary examination. She estimated the two male victims had been deceased for twenty-four to thirty-six hours. No wallets or ID were found at the scene or on either body. Both men showed indications of having worn jewelry—watches and rings—but those were no longer present. The missing items suggested robbery as a possible motive.

Both victims had been shot through and through, one in the forehead and the other in the back. On the second victim, the bullet had entered the body just under the left shoulder blade and exited through the chest, most likely impacting at least one or two vital organs along the way.

"Can you raise fingerprints?" Juanita asked.

"Yes, but not here," Abby replied. "That'll be easier to do in the morgue than it will be out here in the sand."

"Will you schedule the autopsies for today?"

"Sure can," Abby said cheerfully. "As far as I know, these two guys are first in line. Will you be joining us?"

"Yes, but I'll need to stick around here for a while. The CSIs should be arriving any minute, and I want to talk to the guy who found them."

While CSIs began photographing the crime scene, Juanita climbed back up to the road. O'Rourke was still sitting in his truck when she walked up to it and knocked on the driver's window.

"Can I go home now?" he demanded, rolling the window down, without actually looking her in the eye. Most of the time, that kind of evasion would have been suspect, but in this instance Juanita understood the man was beyond humiliated.

"Not quite yet. I'm Detective Ochoa," she explained. "Can you tell me what happened?"

"I left work a little before six—a couple of minutes early, I guess. I was having stomach cramps, but I figured I'd be able to make it home in time. I was wrong about that. I stopped here because I thought I'd be out of sight down inside the culvert, and that's where I found them."

"Do you know either one of the two individuals?"

"Never seen 'em before."

"Did you see anything unusual today—any unfamiliar vehicles or people who looked out of place?"

O'Rourke shook his head. "Nothin'," he said.

"You gave your contact information to the deputies?" she asked.

He nodded.

"You can go then, sir," she said. "I hope you feel better."

"Boy, you and me both!"

Back in the wash a pair of deputies was loading the corpses into body bags. No shell casings were found, but they located a slug in the blood-stained sand at the far end of the drag marks. Studying the projectile, Juanita thought it looked like a .22 LR, but that was just a hunch on her part. The ballistics folks would have to sort that out for sure.

The last part of processing the scene called for gathering up whatever litter there was to be found in the area, most of which would end up having nothing to do with the murders. When the trash had been properly bagged, Juanita excused herself and headed for Indio, an hour and a half away.

It was Friday morning without much westbound traffic on I-10. She spent most of the drive mentally reprocessing the crime scene until an overhead sign—one announcing the upcoming exit for El Centro—jolted her out of one reverie and into another. El Centro was where Juanita Moreno Ochoa had been born and where she had lived until she was twelve.

Her mom, Andrea, had gotten pregnant while still in high school and had raised her daughter as an unwed mother. Without so much as a high school diploma and with limited job skills, Andrea had supported her daughter by waitressing.

By the time Juanita was nine, she was accustomed to being left alone at night while her mother worked as a cocktail waitress in one of the rougher joints in town. Three years later, just after her twelfth birthday, she was awakened out of a sound sleep by someone pounding on the door. The two men she found standing there claimed they were police, but Juanita's mother had warned her daughter about not letting strangers into their apartment. Finally, one of them, Detective Philip Reyes, held his badge up to the peephole.

That's when Juanita finally opened the door, only to be given the awful news: Her mother was dead, shot in the course of an attempted armed robbery at the bar where she worked. Detective Reyes was the one who told her what had happened, and he was the one who held her while she sobbed her heart out. Later that night, once it was apparent that there was no one left to care for her, he was also the one who handed her off to a social worker.

Juanita often wondered what would have become of her that fateful night if someone other than Detective Reyes had come to the door. She doubted she'd be living the life she was today.

As the Indio exit appeared, Detective Ochoa switched on her turn signal.

No, she thought, *I would be someone else entirely, and I most likely wouldn't be spending my days chasing killers and witnessing autopsies.*

That was exactly how she spent the next several hours—standing in the Riverside County Morgue, observing the autopsies for the two victims whose fingerprints identified them as Dante Cox and Tyrone Jackson. The results were pretty well-foregone conclusions. For both young men the cause of death was listed as a gunshot wound. The manner of death was homicide. As for timing? Sometime within the last twenty-four to thirty-six hours.

Once the autopsies were over, it was time for Detective Ochoa to move on to the next part of her job—the worst part—delivering death notices.

CHAPTER 29

THE VILLAGE OF OAK CREEK, ARIZONA

Friday, January 3, 2020, 10:00 a.m. (MST)

Stu Ramey couldn't remember the last time he had crashed and burned like this. Thursday had been nothing short of brutal. Faced with multiple cyberattacks from around the world and missing several of their key players, High Noon's home team had managed to hold the line, but it hadn't been easy. All day long, he'd received updates from Frigg, letting him know that she was still on the job and accumulating information, but there hadn't been a spare minute for him to go through any of it, and now he was too tired.

As he was crawling into bed in the early hours of the morning, he summoned the AI. "I'm finally off duty," he told her. "I'll let you know when I'm available."

"I hope you have a restful sleep," she said.

He did, but the moment he stirred and sat up in bed at ten the next morning, a howler alarm sounded from the other room. Obviously Frigg had been monitoring his respiration and knew he was awake. Stu plugged in his earbuds.

"Okay, Frigg," he said. "You've got my attention. What's going on?"

"A bombing occurred at a private residence in Beaverton, Oregon, earlier this morning."

"What?" Stu said.

She repeated the same words but they made no sense to him. "Please explain. Who was bombed, and why would it be of any interest to us?"

"The situation would be more understandable if you had read the material I've been sending to you," Frigg said reprovingly.

What wasn't understandable to Stu Ramey was why he was being bawled out by a computer program first thing in the morning before he'd had a single sip of coffee. He glanced at his watch. He'd told Lance he'd be back at the office by noon, so there wasn't much time.

"All right," he consented, "go ahead and start sending. I'll read what I can before I go to work, but I'm going to need some coffee first."

The first document Frigg sent was a single sheet with a dozen names listed on it. Of those, Stu recognized two—Hal Holden and Jack Littleton.

"What's this?" Stu asked.

"It's the federal prosecutor's list of proposed witnesses for the 2003 trial of a former Pasadena PD officer, Frank Muñoz. Mr. Muñoz was arrested and sent to prison on a number of federal charges including police corruption, money laundering, and obstruction of justice."

Stu didn't want to inquire as to how Frigg had obtained the witness list in the first place. There was no point.

"You already told me Jack Littleton was dead," he

said, "but how did two local homicide cops get mixed up in a federal police corruption case?"

"They were called to investigate the 1997 homicide of Alysha Morgan, an exotic dancer at a Pasadena nightclub called BJ's, which, at the time, was the subject of an ongoing organized-crime investigation being conducted by the FBI. Another name on the witness list against Mr. Muñoz is that of Danielle Lomax, one of Alysha Morgan's fellow dancers and the only eyewitness to her murder. Ms. Lomax is also deceased. She was gunned down outside her workplace in St. Paul, Minnesota, on October 31, 2017. Her case, like Mr. Littleton's, remains unsolved."

Stu was beginning to get the picture. "Okay," he said, "of the twelve names on this list, two are dead and one nearly so, but why is this just a proposed witness list? Did any of these people actually testify?"

"They did not. Mr. Muñoz pled guilty and went to prison. He was released on parole on November 1, 2019, and currently resides in Las Vegas, Nevada."

Stu was starting to lose patience. Frigg seemed to be bouncing all over the map—Beaverton, Pasadena, St. Paul, Las Vegas.

"But about this bombing?" he asked. "I thought you said it was in Oregon."

"Yes," Frigg agreed, "in Beaverton. The bombing occurred at approximately 5:45 a.m. today at a private home located at 2514 NW Telshire Drive, which was completely destroyed in the ensuing fire. The residence belongs to Mr. and Mrs. Larry Rogers. Mrs. Rogers was formerly married to Frank Muñoz."

Wham! Just like that the light came on in Stu's head. Obviously Frank Muñoz was at the center of all this!

Frigg was unrelenting. Once his name had surfaced, the AI had tracked down the names and current addresses of everyone connected to the man and placed them on one of her watch lists.

"You knew about the bombing the moment it happened?" Stu asked.

"I did," Frigg replied, "and I believe I have identified the perpetrator."

"How?"

"It seemed likely that whoever was responsible for the bombing would exhibit an undue interest in the case. I hacked into several newsfeeds in the Portland area. Sites carrying advertising generally collect IP addresses on all visitors. One IP address located in Las Vegas, Nevada, has shown up ten—make that eleven—times so far this morning. I've identified the individual email address as FGMuñoz@LVNV.com."

"Frank Muñoz," Stu breathed. "He has to be our guy, but what do we do about it?"

"I would like to install a keylogger on Mr. Muñoz's computer," Frigg advised him. "I could set a trap so that the next time he searches for information on the bombing, the keylogger will download automatically."

Stu had to think about that. If Frank Muñoz was responsible for this whole series of violent events, shouldn't they do everything in their power to bring him down? The information Frigg had already gathered was damning, and a keylogger would no doubt reveal far more, but installing those was illegal. If Stu said yes, he would be encouraging Frigg to return to her old habits of coloring outside the lines. But what if he said no, and Frank got away?

"All right," Stu told Frigg finally. "Go ahead and do it, but don't get caught."

CHAPTER 30

PRESCOTT, ARIZONA

Friday, January 3, 2020, 9 a.m. (MST)

On Friday morning Chief Detective Biba went straight to the bull pen to check on his people. "What's going on with the vehicle abandoned in Quartzsite?" he asked Detective Morris.

"Our CSIs located several prints. They'll be running them through AFIS," she told him.

Biba nodded. If the two young thugs seen on the truck stop video had any previous criminal histories, the national Automated Fingerprint Identification System would be the logical place to find them.

"How long will that take?" Biba asked.

"Hopefully it'll get done today," Julie told him. "I asked them to put a rush on it."

"Any word on Ali Reynolds?" he asked.

"B. Simpson is having additional surgery today. Shirley Malone, the woman I spoke to in Cottonwood, said Ms. Reynolds is due to arrive sometime today and is expected to go straight to the hospital. I told them we'll be in touch tomorrow."

Biba sighed. He didn't like having to wait yet another day to interview the woman he considered his main person of interest in what had happened to B. Simpson, but wait he would. Eventually she would have to talk to him, and one way or another, he'd get to the bottom of this. In the meantime, he had other things to deal with, like the mound of paperwork covering his desk.

Sometime after two, with Biba still whaling away at his paperwork jungle, an excited Detective Flack dashed into his office. "Hey, boss," Steven crowed. "We've got something!"

"What?"

"AFIS just got hits on two of the prints from that stolen Subaru."

"That was quick," Biba said. "It has to be one of the fastest hits on record."

"Do you want the good news or the bad news?"

"Let's have the good news first. Who are they?"

"A pair of LA-based gangbangers—Tyrone Jackson and Dante Cox."

"And the bad?"

"They're both dead—shot to death in a dry wash somewhere near Blythe, California. A maintenance worker from a solar farm found the bodies in a culvert early this morning. Sounds like they've been dead for a day or so. No IDs were found at the scene, but the coroner was able to raise prints from both bodies. That's how we got the matches. Both victims were in the system."

"You've spoken to the detectives involved?" Biba asked.

"Not yet," Flack said. "But I've got a number."

"Hand it over," Biba said. "If we're dealing with another state, I should probably make the call."

He did. The phone rang several times before switching over to voice mail. "This is Detective Juanita Ochoa of the Riverside County Sheriff's Office. I'm currently out of the office. Please leave a message. I'll get back to you as soon as I can."

Biba left a message, then he sat at his desk for several long minutes wondering exactly how two dead gang-bangers from LA could have gotten hooked up with a spoiled rich bitch from Sedona, Arizona.

Finally he stood up and reluctantly headed for Captain Dunn's office. He didn't relish having to tell his supervisor that their high-profile vehicular assault case had now turned into a multistate homicide investigation.

Captain Dunn wasn't going to regard this as good news, and neither did Chief Detective Biba.

CHAPTER 31

BEAVERTON, OREGON

Friday, January 3, 2020, 10:00 a.m. (PST)

With his parents headed for separate operating rooms in the same hospital, Ramon did what he could. He needed to let his sisters know what was going on, but before he called either of them, he looked online to see if any additional information had been posted since AJ had driven him away from the house.

There wasn't much. Unfortunately, he found himself fact-checking almost everything he read:

> Authorities have confirmed that the early-morning incident on Beaverton's NW Tilshire Drive was indeed a bombing. Two individuals, residents of the home, have been taken to the hospital. No word on their condition is available at this time.
>
> No one has taken credit for the bombing, but it is not considered to be an act of domestic terrorism. The investigation is ongoing.

What the hell do the words "domestic terrorism" mean, then? Ramon wondered. *Having someone plant a bomb meant to burn down a house with people sleeping inside sure as hell seems terrifying enough, and since it's unlikely any foreign power was involved, didn't that make it domestic?*

A nearby neighbor who witnessed the bombing claims he observed an unidentified male toss a flaming device of some kind in the direction of the residence shortly before the fire broke out.

That unidentified male is AJ Wilson, Ramon thought, *and there was no "flaming device" involved. He was throwing newspapers, for Pete's sake.*

That's when he saw the photo. His cottage still stood, barely visible in the distance. The hazy foreground was punctuated by a single charred but upright stud, the only remaining remnant of the main house. Everything else was a pile of rubble, including the garage where his parents' two vehicles had been parked. The garage and the cars were gone, but the two plastic trash cans Larry kept on the far side of the garage appeared to be undamaged. He wondered why they hadn't melted. Had someone moved them?

At that point Ramon was too sick at heart to call his sisters. Feeling a sudden urge to see the damage for himself, he reached for his car keys before remembering that AJ had given him a ride. He was searching for a number to call a cab when the next sickening realization hit him—he didn't have his wallet with him, either.

For a moment, he panicked, then he remembered AJ's offer. He located AJ's number and dialed but after four rings, the call went to voice mail. With no other options in mind, Ramon dialed AJ's grandfather.

"Mr. Jones?" he asked tentatively.

"Yes," the man said warily. "Who's this?"

"My name's Ramon Muñoz. There was a fire at my parents' house this morning, and AJ gave me a ride to the hospital. He said I could call him if I needed a ride back home. I just tried, but he didn't answer."

"That's because the cops have taken him into custody," Hiram said grimly. "A witness said he saw AJ fire-bomb the house."

White neighborhood, Black kid, Ramon thought. *Naturally it's AJ's fault.*

Hiram sighed. "I'll be glad to come get you," he said. "Where are you?"

"Portland General," Ramon answered.

"How are your folks?" Hiram asked. "Are they going to be all right?"

"They're both in surgery, but I want to go check on the house."

"Hang in there, son," Hiram advised. "I know where Portland General is. I'm in Aloha, so it'll take some time for me to get there. I drive a white Prius."

"Good, I'll be outside the main entrance."

As Ramon headed for the door, his phone rang with Norm Williams's name showing on caller ID. Larry Rogers and Norm were old high school buddies, and Norm had long been Larry's insurance agent. He was also Ramon's.

"I just heard," Norm said grimly. "I'm here at the house, and one of the officers told me someone had been taken to the hospital. Are your folks all right?"

"My mom seems to have suffered a heart attack," Ramon told him. "She's in surgery, and so's Dad. He was scheduled to have knee replacement surgery today. Once we got to the hospital, he decided to go through with it anyway."

"Not surprised," Norm said. "Sounds like the Larry Rogers I know."

"What about the house?" Ramon asked, even though he already knew the answer.

"The adjustor isn't here yet, but clearly it's a total loss."

"Where are they supposed to go once they're released from the hospital?" Ramon asked.

"That's why I'm calling," Norm said. "One of my clients has a unit in one of the upscale assisted-living places here in town, but they also have a place down in Mesa where they stay during the winter. They're scheduled to be there until the middle of March. Ralph's a good friend of mine. I just talked to him and told him about what's happened. He's willing to let your folks stay in his place here on a temporary basis. They'll need to pay rent, of course. Meals are provided. They're not gourmet by any means, but served in a dining room. They'll have to pay for those, too."

"Sounds expensive," Ramon observed.

"Not compared to putting them up in a hotel," Norm said, "and the displacement clause in their home-owners policy will cover most of it."

"Fully furnished?" Ramon asked.

"Fully," Norm replied. "Not only that, it's all handicapped accessible, which sounds like something both your folks need right now. The thing is, Ralph would like to know yea or nay today if at all possible. What do you think?"

Ramon hadn't had time to consider where his parents would go after leaving the hospital, and he was grateful

Norm was working on the problem. And although he wasn't comfortable making that kind of decision on his parents' behalf, someone needed to do it. His handling it would mean one less worry for Larry. The fact that meals were included was a biggie. Ramon's mother was the cook in the family. Larry was utterly hopeless in the kitchen. That's what tipped the scales.

"Tell Ralph yes," Ramon said, "and if there's any fallout from that decision with my folks, I'll take the heat."

The call ended as Hiram Jones's Prius pulled up out front. "Where to?" he asked, once Ramon was inside. "The house?"

That's where Ramon had intended to go originally, but right now looking at the wreckage wasn't the point.

"Where did they take AJ?" he asked.

"Beaverton PD," Hiram answered. "I called but couldn't get any information. I'm guessing he'll call when he can."

"Take me there," Ramon said. "I've done some work with Beaverton cops. Did anyone mention the name of the detective handling the case?"

"Are you kidding?" Hiram asked. "I'm African American. Nobody told me nothin'."

"Well then," Ramon replied, "maybe they'll talk to me."

At the department, he and Hiram walked inside together. Luckily, the cop at the desk happened to be someone who recognized Ramon on sight.

"Hey," he said, "I heard about the fire—too bad. Are your folks gonna be okay?"

"Probably," Ramon answered. "But that's why I'm here. Who's the detective on the case?"

"Lew Wallace."

Detective Wallace was also someone Ramon knew

personally. They had met when the detective had been working sex crimes. As far as Ramon was concerned, Wallace was a good cop and a good guy.

"I need to talk to him," Ramon said.

"I'm pretty sure he's interviewing a suspect right now."

"That suspect is the reason I'm here. Please let him know I'm here."

The officer disappeared. It took several minutes, but finally he returned with the detective in tow.

"Tough day," Wallace said, shaking Ramon's hand. "I understand you were at the house this morning?"

Ramon nodded. "In the cottage out back. I just left my folks at the hospital."

"Are they all right?"

"They're both in surgery, but they should be okay."

"I'm going to need to interview you, but right now . . ."

"Right now, you're interviewing AJ Wilson," Ramon interrupted. "And there are a few things you need to know about him. No matter what your eyewitness says, AJ didn't throw that firebomb. He delivers newspapers, and my folks are on his route. That's what he threw at the house—my dad's packet of newspapers—the *Oregonian* and the *Wall Street Journal*. There was a box sitting on the front porch. When the papers hit the box, it exploded. That's what started the fire—whatever was in the box."

Wallace studied Ramon's face for a moment, then glanced in Hiram's direction. "Who's this?"

"I'm Hiram Jones, AJ's grandfather," Hiram said.

"He's also the man who picked me up from the hospital and gave me a ride here," Ramon added.

"Glad to meet you, Mr. Jones," Wallace said. After

a pause he added, "I guess you'd both better come on back."

Wallace led them to a cubicle and then pulled up an extra chair so they could all sit. "How do you know about the box?" he asked.

"AJ told me about it when I came running outside, right after the bomb went off. He called nine-one-one while I went back into the house to help my folks."

"If he's innocent, why didn't he hang around long enough to mention any of this to officers on the scene? Why did he take off?"

"Because he took me to the hospital," Ramon replied impatiently. "Dad rode in the ambulance with Mom, but my car was stuck behind the fire trucks with no way for me to get it out, so AJ offered to give me a lift. Once he dropped me off, he went out to finish delivering his papers."

Wallace shook his head dubiously. "I suppose you know that's the same story AJ told me," he said, "about throwing the newspapers and having the box explode. But how much did those papers weigh? Seems like it would take one heck of a throw to hit something hard enough for . . ."

Ramon cut Wallace off in midsentence. "Do you happen to follow Beaverton High baseball?" he asked.

"I'm more into football and basketball," the detective admitted, "so no, not much. Why?"

"Because last year the Beavers' varsity baseball team won the state championship. AJ Wilson was only a junior, but he was also their star pitcher, and this is how he keeps his pitching arm in shape during the off season—by throwing newspapers onto porches and trying to hit his customers' doorknobs. And you're right—he does have one heck of a throw."

That remark seemed to win the day. "All right." Wallace sighed. "Wait here."

Ramon and Hiram remained in place even though the detective was gone for the better part of an hour, but when he returned, AJ was with him.

"He can go, then?" Hiram asked.

Wallace nodded. "He's been a big help." Hiram stood up, and so did Ramon, but Wallace shook his head. "Not you," he said. "As long as you're here, we should get your interview out of the way."

"But I don't have my car," Ramon objected.

"Not to worry," Wallace said. "When we're done, I'll give you a ride wherever you need to go."

In the interview room, Ramon related the story again, beginning to end. This time the interview was being recorded, and for the most part, Wallace just listened. Only when Ramon ran out of steam did the detective finally begin asking questions, and there weren't many of those.

"AJ mentioned seeing an unfamiliar vehicle in the neighborhood the last several mornings," Wallace said. "What about you?"

"I haven't been out running for several days in a row," Ramon admitted. "We had out-of-town company."

"And do you know of anyone who would wish your parents harm?"

That was a question Ramon was more than ready to answer. "I do, actually," he said. "Frank Muñoz, my mother's ex-husband. He's a disgraced ex-cop who was recently paroled from the Lompoc Federal Correctional Complex after being in prison for the past fifteen years."

Wallace gaped at him. "Do you really think your father would be capable of something like this?"

The issue of whether or not Frank Muñoz was Ramon's father was too complex to deal with right then, so he didn't challenge Lew's entirely understandable assumption.

"I do," Ramon replied. "I didn't know anything about it until this morning when my stepdad told me. After my father was arrested, he expected Mom to bail him out. She refused. He didn't take it well, and he threatened her."

"Threatened to kill her?" Wallace asked.

Ramon nodded.

"That may be what your stepfather said," Detective Wallace countered, "but what do you think?"

"I personally believe Frank Muñoz is the scum of the earth."

Wallace paused a beat before saying anything more. "All right, then. Do you have any contact information for him?"

"We're not on good terms," Ramon answered. "Supposedly he lives in Las Vegas, but since you're a cop, if he's on parole, you should be able to find him."

The interview ended shortly after that. When they stood up, Wallace asked, "Do you still need a ride?"

Ramon nodded. "Please. My car's at the house—at least I hope it's still there. It was parked out on the street."

"Let's go, then," Wallace said. "With ATF still on the scene, you'll need some help getting past the crime scene tape."

Even though Ramon had already seen a photo of the charred remains of the house, it was still a shock to see it in person.

"How could it burn as fast as it did?" Ramon mused aloud as he stared at the wreckage.

Wallace pointed at a guy wearing an ATF jacket and talking on a phone. "Why don't we go ask him? Come on."

The detective opened the car door and exited the vehicle with Ramon hot on his heels. The ATF guy appeared to be about to tell them to get lost, but once Lew flashed his badge, he underwent a change in attitude.

"What can I do for you, Detective?"

"This is Ramon Muñoz," Lew explained, "and this is his parents' place. I brought him by so he could pick up his vehicle. Is that it?" he asked, tipping his head in the direction of the parked 4Runner, the only non–law enforcement vehicle visible on the street.

Ramon nodded. "Yes," he said.

Lew turned back to the ATF agent. "Seems like the fire burned pretty fast and furious, doing a lot of damage in a short period of time. Any idea what caused it?"

The agent glanced in Ramon's direction, but eventually he answered. "One of our accelerant-sniffing dogs alerted on the front porch," he said gruffly. "We've gathered samples to bring to the lab, but one of the firefighters told me that pouring water on the fire made it burn even hotter, so my best guess would be some kind of homemade napalm."

Someone called the agent by name just then, and he hurried away.

"If my father did this, he really meant for my mom and her husband to die," Ramon murmured. It was a tough pill to swallow.

"Yes, I believe he did," Wallace said quietly, "and if you hadn't gone back into that house to bring them out, he might well have succeeded."

CHAPTER 32

Frank had spent an almost-sleepless night awaiting the big event—his finale. Sal had said it would happen in the early-morning hours. Then, when he finally did fall asleep, he was so far under that he didn't awaken until after eight, far later than planned. Fully expecting to be able to take a victory lap and wanting to see the results of his handiwork, he logged on to his computer and got ready to see how things had turned out. He entered *bomb/beaverton* into his search engine and immediately hit pay dirt:

BEAVERTON NEIGHBORHOOD ROCKED BY EXPLOSION

A quiet Beaverton neighborhood was rocked by a massive explosion early this morning when a bomb was detonated on the front porch of a home on NW Telshire Drive.

Although the home was extensively damaged in the blast and resulting fire, no one was seriously injured although one resident was transported to the hospital for observation due to a possible medical emergency.

At this time Beaverton PD is investigating the incident, and agents from the ATF are also at the scene. A spokesman for Beaverton PD told reporters that it is unlikely that the incident is terrorist-related.

One person of interest was taken into custody at the scene, but police are asking that anyone seeing unusual overnight activity in the area contact Beaverton PD at their non-emergency number.

This is a developing story. Please check back for updates.

By the time he reached the bottom of the brief article, Frank was livid. One person was injured in the blast? That was the best Sal Moroni could do for ten thousand bucks? And who had been taken into custody? Was it someone who would spill the beans?

As far as Frank could tell, Hal Holden remained among the living and now so did Sylvia. Still, rather than fly off the handle and raise hell with Sal, Frank waited, hoping that subsequent news reports would tell him what he wanted to hear. That didn't happen. Midafternoon found him writing a furious message into Sal's draft file.

What the hell?

Sorry. Someone screwed up.

Do you think? Someone
screwed up AGAIN! Hal
Holden is still alive and so is
Sylvia. I think it's time for two
refunds instead of just one.

> I'll take care of it.

Which, give me my money back or finish
the job? You'd better do something
about this, or I'll blow the whistle on
your whole damned operation.

> Are you threatening me? If I go
> down, you go down.

Then you'd better figure out how to
deliver that refund. By my calculations
I'm out twenty thou with nothing to
show for it. And you'd better make it
fast. Sometime soon, I may be heading
out of the country.

With that, Frank slammed the lid shut on his laptop. Throwing on some clothes, he headed for the gym. He spent an hour walking on the treadmill, still seething. All this time he had thought Salvatore Moroni was the real deal, but maybe he was wrong. What if everything he'd heard about him pulling off that hit in Montenegro was just so much bull? What if this was nothing but a scam, one that raked in ten thousand bucks a pop?

After walking for a while, Frank began to get a grip and realized that what he'd said to Sal had been little more than an empty threat. Sal was right. If someone squealed on Sal, he'd return the favor. At this point Frank had far more to lose than Sal. After all, Sal was still in prison; Frank wasn't, and he wanted to stay that way.

What's gone is gone, he advised himself as he stepped off the treadmill. *Just let it go.*

CHAPTER 33

PHOENIX, ARIZONA

Friday, January 3, 2020, 12:00 p.m. (MST)

The last-minute itinerary Cami had put together for Ali's trip home worked flawlessly. Ali had boarded her flight in London and stayed awake long enough to have her plane-fare breakfast. Once that was cleared away, she had leaned her seat back, donned her eye mask, wrapped herself in her blanket, and slept for the remainder of the flight.

To speed up the deplaning process, Ali had traveled with a single carry-on, leaving the rest of her luggage for Cami to drag home later. While working her way through customs at LAX, she tried phoning Sister Anselm to see what was up with B.'s surgery. Feeling uneasy when her call went to voice mail, Ali dialed the office in Cottonwood.

"How are things on the home front?" she asked.

"Yesterday was a tough day back in the lab, but things seem to be under control now," Shirley said. "But I wouldn't recommend talking to Stu. He's Mr. Growly Bear today. On the bright side, I just heard from Cami.

She flies home to Phoenix tomorrow afternoon and has booked the shuttle, so no one will need to drive down to pick her up."

"I tried calling Sister Anselm to check on B.," Ali said, "but she didn't pick up. Is she all right? Is he?"

"Sister Anselm is probably busy," Shirley replied. "There was a terrible accident down in Cochise County last night. She and Sister Cecelia were both called away."

"What happened?"

"A Suburban loaded with thirty migrants was going the wrong way on I-10 and crashed head-on into a semi. People with serious injuries ended up in every ER within a fifty-mile radius."

"And all of them in need of patient advocates," Ali breathed.

"Exactly," Shirley agreed. "She was concerned about leaving B. on his own in advance of today's surgery, but he told her not to worry. With you on your way home, and with Hal's daughter there to look after him, B. said she and Sister Cecelia should go take care of people who needed their help more than he and Hal did."

"Have you had any word on the surgery?"

"Not yet," Shirley answered. "It was scheduled to start at nine, but I don't know if it did."

Just then Ali reached the head of the customs line. "Thanks, Shirley. I've gotta go. I'll call the hospital."

Minutes later, in a shuttle on the way to the FBO, Ali managed to get through to the hospital, where she learned that B. was out of surgery and in recovery. By the time she got there, he'd be back in his room.

Relieved, Ali boarded her charter flight. While Phoenix-bound, she used the aircraft's Wi-Fi to deal with some routine High Noon business transactions, then she spent the rest of the time answering the batch of texts and emails that had come in during her twelve-hour hiatus from electronic communication. Sometimes she missed the world where mail came and went on a once-a-day basis rather than at all hours of the day or night.

Once in Phoenix, she drove her rental car straight to the hospital, where she was relieved to find B. in his room, awake and in good spirits. The fractures in his upper arm had been set with no rods needed and the damaged shoulder had been replaced. Due to the meds, he was feeling no pain.

"What does the doctor say?" she asked.

"That I'll be almost as good as new after three months of intense physical therapy."

"How's Hal?"

"Stable, but still critical and still on the ventilator," B. said. "I guess you heard that Sister Anselm was called away?"

"I did," Ali answered. "Shirley told me about the wreck down in Cochise County. Did the doctor say when you might be released?"

"Tomorrow, most likely."

"And is anything going on with the investigation?"

"Nothing much," B. said. "Biba seems to be focused on you and likely to remain so, but I spoke to Stu a little while ago. He and Frigg have launched an investigation into Hal as the possible target, and he claims they may be onto something. My big concern is this: If they do come up with something incriminating, how do we pass that information along to law enforcement without blowing the whistle on Frigg?"

"Not to worry," Ali assured him. "We'll figure it out."

They chatted for the better part of two hours. When B. grew dozy, Ali took her leave. On her way out of the hospital, Ali detoured through the ICU. Inside Hal's room, she caught sight of a middle-aged woman napping in the visitor's chair positioned next to the bed. Ali left without disturbing either of them.

Ali drove north, her mind returning to what B. had said. If she and B. were the focus of Biba's investigation, that meant Hal Holden's part of the equation was officially being ignored, and it sounded as though Stu and Frigg were addressing that issue. Despite Shirley's warning about Stu's black mood, she called him anyway. As soon as she asked about the Holden inquiry, he became downright evasive.

"I'm not sure," he said guardedly. "Frigg has been working on it all day, but I've been too busy to read her updates."

Knowing Stu, that seemed highly unlikely, but Ali didn't call him out on it. "I'm on my way home from the hospital, just passing the prison north of Phoenix," she told him. "How about if I stop by the office so we can talk?"

"I'd rather meet you at my place," he said.

Meet at home instead of the office? Ali wondered. That also seemed out of character but rather than ask why, she settled for an easier question. "What time?"

"Five thirty?" Stu asked, but he didn't sound at all happy about it.

"All right," Ali said. "See you there."

CHAPTER 34

LOS ANGELES, CALIFORNIA

Friday, January 3, 2020, 1:00 p.m. (PST)

Detective Juanita Ochoa had been a homicide cop for the Riverside County Sheriff's Office for going on six years now, and for her, making death notifications remained the most challenging aspect of the job.

Once Deputy Coroner Leavitt identified the victims using AFIS, Juanita's next order of business was notifying their families. Tyrone had been living with his grandmother in LA. Locating her was easy, but finding Dante's wife, Malika, wasn't. Juanita finally learned that Malika was in LA County's Century Regional Detention Facility serving a six-month sentence on a drug-possession charge.

Before leaving, Juanita confirmed that Armando would collect the kids from Nana's house once he got off his shift. Just after two, she keyed the address of the correction center into her GPS and headed for LA.

By then she knew that between them, her two victims had a total of five kids. Dante's children—two boys and a girl—were nine, seven, and five. They had been living in foster care ever since their mother was sent to lockup. Tyrone's two kids, a five-year-old son and a three-year-old daughter, lived with Tyrone's grandmother, Ella Mae Jackson, in East LA.

Given that sad reality, it was only natural that, during her solitary drive, Juanita's thoughts turned once more to Detective Philip Reyes. The terrible night she met him marked the beginning of Juanita's own sojourn in foster care. Nonetheless, long after her mother's killer had been caught and sent to prison, Phil and his wife, Lila, stayed in touch with Juanita, faithfully sending her birthday cards and Christmas cards, usually with a gift card or two enclosed. She loved the ones for Target, which allowed Juanita to purchase new clothing and even new shoes on occasion, rather than always having to wear hand-me-downs, the main staple of foster-care attire.

Once Juanita had access to an email account, she and Phil had maintained a regular correspondence. He always encouraged her to stay in school and assured her that failing high school algebra the first time around wasn't the end of the world. When she graduated from high school, he suggested she enroll in the local junior college and helped track down the financial assistance that made that a reality.

But then, during her second year at Imperial Valley College, the unthinkable happened. Phil and his partner had been called to the scene of a vehicular homicide when Phil suffered a major coronary, and EMTs already on the scene were unable to resuscitate him. When Lila had called Juanita to tell her what had happened, she also asked if Juanita would be willing to say a few words at Phil's funeral.

236 J. A. JANCE

That was how, at nineteen years of age and with her knees trembling beneath her, Juanita Moreno stood in front of a standing-room-only crowd in El Centro's All Saints' Catholic Church, telling how, on the night of her mother's murder, Phil had appeared in her life, becoming both an avenging angel and a knight in shining armor for a child who had lost everything. She had ended her remarks by saying, "Someday I hope to be a cop just like he was."

Juanita had been considering that course of action for several years, but it was at Phil's funeral that she finally stated her intentions aloud and in public. Now, fourteen years later, she had been a police officer for eleven years, six of those in homicide. She and Armando had been married for seven years and had two kids. Phil Reyes was the one Juanita always credited for all those many blessings in her life.

Each day when she went to work as a cop, two badges went with her. The one she carried in her ID wallet and flashed as needed was her own, while the other was Phil's. Lila had given it to her on the day of her husband's funeral. That one Juanita kept in her purse as a constant reminder of the incredible impact his life had exerted on hers. And that was what she prayed for as she drove—that she'd be granted the ability to be the same kind of blessing in the lives of those two grieving families as Phil had been in hers.

Unfortunately, that wasn't easy or even possible, at least not with Malika Cox. When she appeared in the visitation room, every inch of her orange-jumpsuit-covered body bristled with anger and resentment. Once the guard directed her to sit, she did so, glaring at Juanita with her arms folded across her chest.

"What's this all about?" she demanded.

Juanita pushed one of her cards across the table. Malika studied it for a moment without touching it. "What do you want with me?" she demanded. "I ain't done nothin'."

Juanita took a breath. "I'm sorry to have to tell you this," she said, "but your husband was found shot to death early this morning outside Blythe. According to the coroner, he most likely died sometime in the early hours of January second."

Malika's eyes widened. "You serious? Dante dead?"

"Yes," Juanita answered. "I'm afraid he is."

"Why you tellin' me, then?" Malika wanted to know. "What you 'spect me to do about that when I'm locked up in here?"

It was not the kind of response Juanita had anticipated. "I have a sworn duty to notify next of kin," she began, "and if you'd like me to reach out to your children . . ."

"Good luck with that," Malika spat back. "They be in foster care and nobody tol' me where they took 'em, so you can take your so-called sworn duty and shove it. Dante's always gettin' hisself in trouble, and I was fixin' to get me a divorce. I woulda done it, too, once I got enough money together, but if he be dead, this ain't got nothin' to do with me." With that she turned back to the guard. "I'm ready to go back now," she announced. "We be done."

Malika stood up and huffed from the room. Watching her go, a stunned Detective Ochoa's heart ached for Dante's kids. She had done her duty and informed Malika. Eventually she'd tell the children, too, but not today. Finding them would involve negotiating countless bureaucratic hoops. Right then Juanita didn't have time. She still had to deal with Tyrone's family.

Ella Mae Jackson, Tyrone's grandmother, was listed on his driver's license application as Tyrone's next of kin. That detail struck Juanita. If Tyrone had once been married, his wife's name wasn't listed, nor were the names of either of his parents. As far as blood relations went, his grandmother was it.

Ella Mae's home turned out to be a small, well-kept bungalow on South Wyman Avenue in East LA. The house was surrounded by a chain-link fence, and the hard-packed dirt of the front yard was littered with numerous toys—a faded yellow Big Wheel, a rusty wagon, and a deflated wading pool along with a selection of balls in varying sizes. Given that, it was reasonable to assume that not only did Tyrone and his grandmother live there, but so did his kids.

At least they're not in foster care, Juanita thought as she let herself into the yard. The front door was opened by a sprightly, gray-haired Black woman dressed in a floral housecoat. She greeted Juanita with a ready smile.

"May I help you?"

A wide-eyed toddler, a little girl, stared up at Juanita from behind the woman's colorful robe. The sight of the child made Juanita's heart hurt.

"I'm Detective Ochoa with the Riverside County Sheriff's Office," she said, displaying her badge. "It's about Tyrone."

Ella Mae's hand went to her throat. "Oh, my! Tyrone? Is he all right?"

"I'm afraid he's not, Ms. Jackson," Juanita told her. "May I come in?"

Wordlessly Ella Mae ushered Juanita inside and

motioned her toward a threadbare sofa. The interior of the house was small but tidy. An assortment of indoor toys was confined to one corner of the room. An old-fashioned Formica kitchen table with a high chair positioned beside it occupied the dining room space.

"You come with me now, Skye girl," Ella Mae said, scooping the little girl into her arms. "Let's go get you a snack."

Ella Mae deposited the child in the high chair and then disappeared into the kitchen, returning moments later with a box of Goldfish in hand. After dumping some of those onto the tray, she returned to the living room and sat down facing Juanita.

"Tyrone is dead?" she asked.

Juanita nodded. "He and his friend were both shot to death."

"Dante?" Ella Mae asked, supplying the name without needing to be told.

Juanita nodded again.

Ella Mae shook her head. "I always knew that boy was trouble, him and that worthless wife of his. I told Ty to stay away from them, but he wouldn't listen."

Ella Mae fell silent after that, sitting with both hands in her lap, slowly shaking her head from side to side. Juanita had expected tears, but there were none. It was as though Ella Mae regarded this terrible loss as one of life's inevitable hardships—something to be endured, and the older woman's quiet dignity touched Juanita's heart. No doubt the poor woman had been largely responsible for raising Tyrone and had most likely done so without complaint. Now she would shoulder the burden of raising his children with the same unflinching acceptance.

"You said you found them today," Ella Mae resumed at last, "but when did this happen and where?"

"The coroner believes both victims died in the early hours of January second. The bodies weren't found until six this morning when they were spotted in a wash northwest of Blythe. Did either Dante or Tyrone have connections in Blythe—friends, relatives, or associates living in the area?"

Ella Mae shook her head. "Not that I know of," she said.

"And when's the last time you saw your grandson?"

"That would be on Monday," Ella Mae answered. "Monday morning. I was cleaning up after breakfast when a call came in on my phone. Tyrone's was broke, so he was using mine. When I answered, I recognized Dante's voice before I gave Ty the phone. He listened for a while, then he said, 'Great, tell Eddie I'm in.'"

"Who's Eddie?" Juanita asked.

Ella Mae shook her head. "No idea, but when Tyrone handed me back my phone he said, 'I'm gonna be gone a day or two, Granny,' he says, 'but don't you worry. I'm gonna get us some money to pay off all them Christmas bills.' A little while later, Dante showed up, and off they went."

"That's the last time you saw him?"

Ella Mae nodded. "When he didn't come home that night or the next, I started thinking something was wrong—that something bad had happened. Now I know I was right."

By then, however, Juanita wasn't really listening. She was focused on something Ella Mae had just said. If Dante had called Tyrone's grandmother's phone and then gone on to call Eddie on the same phone he'd used to call Tyrone, maybe she had a digital trail to follow.

"You said Tyrone took Dante's incoming call on your cell phone?"

"Yes, ma'am," Ella Mae answered. "He most certainly did."

"Could I see the call history?"

In reply, Ella Mae reached into the pocket of her robe and produced a phone. After switching it on and locating her call history, she handed the device to Juanita.

"The call from Dante came in around nine on Monday morning, just after Ty-Ty left for his friend's house," she said.

Juanita found the proper record and jotted down the number. "Had Tyrone been using your phone for a day or two?"

Ella Mae nodded. "Several," she said. "His phone broke just before Christmas—he dropped it somewhere and busted it to pieces. He wanted me to buy him a new one, but I had already used up my money for the month. I told him I'd help him out once my check came in, but by then he was gone."

"Is there a chance any of these other calls were made either from him or to him?" Juanita asked, handing the phone back to its owner.

Ella Mae studied the list with a frown before reading off several other numbers that didn't have names attached and were unfamiliar to her. Juanita quickly wrote them down, knowing as she did so that they might hold the key to what had happened. At that point, Skye finished her Goldfish and began fussing to get down. The disruption gave Juanita an excuse for making a graceful exit.

"Thank you for all your help, Ms. Jackson," she said. "I should be going, but here's my card. If anything comes up that you think I should know, please call. I'm so sorry for your loss, but believe me when I say that I will do everything in my power to bring Tyrone's killer or killers to justice."

"Thank you," Ella Mae said. "I hope you do."

It was full-on Friday night rush hour by then, and I-10 was wall-to-wall traffic. Rather than drive straight home, Juanita headed for the department's main office in Riverside. She was eager to hand her list of phone numbers over to the tech unit to see what, if anything, they could do about tracing them without actually having a warrant in hand.

On the way, she called home to check on Armando and the kids. They were home and having pizza. Next she dialed her direct number at the office, and listened to several voicemail messages. The last one, which had come in more than an hour earlier, caused the hair to stand up on the back of her neck.

"This is Chief Detective Warren Biba with the Arizona Highway Patrol in Prescott, Arizona. I need to speak to you concerning the two dead bodies located in your jurisdiction earlier today. We got a hit on their prints in AFIS and believe they're the same individuals who committed a case of vehicular assault on I-17 on New Year's Day. Here's my number."

Juanita called him back immediately. "Thanks for being in touch," he told her. "What can you tell me about your vics?"

Juanita told him what she knew.

"It sounds like a pair of fine, upstanding young citizens have now met their maker," he responded.

Having just left the home of Tyrone's grieving grand-mother, Biba's sarcastic remark rubbed Juanita the wrong way. For him Tyrone and Dante were suspects while for her they were victims.

"Any devices found at the scene?" Biba asked.

"None—no ID, no wallets, and no jewelry either," Juanita replied, making no mention of the phone numbers she had collected from Ella Mae's phone. As lead detective on the case, she made the determination about what information could be shared and what couldn't. For now, those phone numbers were hers.

"What can you tell me about your incident?" Juanita asked.

"On New Year's Day, an airport-bound limo was forced off I-17 by another vehicle," he said. "No one died in the incident, but the two occupants both suffered serious injuries. The assailants then drove another mile down the highway where they set fire to one stolen vehicle and escaped in another. That one was later found abandoned in Quartzsite, making me believe that your dead guys are my assailants."

"Two occupants," Juanita mused. "So which of them was the target or was it both?"

"Undetermined at this point," Biba responded. "No solid suspects, either, although the one victim is a big deal in cybersecurity with a ton of life insurance. I'm thinking his wife might be good for it, but we don't have anything concrete."

Now that Juanita was asking the questions, Biba wasn't exactly forthcoming, leading her to suspect that she wasn't the only one holding back information.

"Sorry," she said. "I've just arrived at my destination and have to go in."

Hanging up, she hurried into the building, where she handed her list of phone numbers over to the tech team and let them go to work. In the meantime, Juanita went online and did some sleuthing of her own. Using newsfeeds and police reports, she was able to follow the trail of Biba's incident, starting with the theft of the Subaru in Vegas on New Year's Eve and then crisscrossing much of Arizona before ending in the bloodbath at the entrance to a culvert outside Blythe, but her case had started days earlier than that—on Monday, with Dante and Tyrone still alive and well in LA.

This crime spree must have required planning and coordination. How exactly had Dante and Tyrone made their way from LA to Vegas? Juanita hoped once she figured that out, maybe everything else would fall into place.

An hour later the tech crew came through, confirming that the Monday morning call on Ella Mae's phone had been placed from a device registered to Dante Cox. With that news in her possession, she headed for Blythe. She didn't know any warrant-friendly judges in the city of Riverside on a personal basis, but she had one on-call in Blythe—Judge Emmett Carruthers. When cops there needed warrants, he was their go-to guy. And even though she was arriving home at a reasonable hour, she wouldn't call tonight. Carruthers was a good guy, but there was no sense in pissing him off on a Friday night.

CHAPTER 35

LONDON, ENGLAND

Friday, January 3, 2020, 10:00 p.m. (GMT)

Cami had barely managed to hold her head up during the afternoon sessions.

She had spent both breakfast and lunch in meetings with representatives from two different France-based companies. She would be returning home with letters of intent from each for switching their cybersecurity needs over to High Noon.

In other words, Camille Lee would return from her first-ever international conference with two possible sales to her credit. She doubted anyone would have seen that coming. She certainly hadn't. And for the first time in her life, she had to admit that in this case, her mother's insistence on Cami's being fluent in French had made all the difference.

Once the last session ended, Cami was toast. Telling Angela that she was done for the night, she went up to the suite, stripped off her clothing, and crawled into bed where she fell fast asleep—for hours. At ten p.m., not only was she wide awake, she was famished. Throwing on some clothes and leaving her name badge on the dresser, she headed downstairs to the bar.

Naturally the place was filled wall to wall with people. Spotting a solitary seat at the bar, Cami threaded her way through the crowd to that, placing her directly in front of the brightly lit liquor display. When the barman came by, she ordered a glass of Pinot Grigio and also asked for a menu. After ordering the green pea and salmon salad, she settled in to sip her wine.

For as long as Cami had known B. Simpson, he had been off globetrotting almost on a weekly basis, coming and going without ever exhibiting any obvious ill effects from jet lag. It annoyed her to think that she was still being laid low by it. After all, she was decades younger. If B. could do it, why couldn't she?

Eventually she took out her phone and scrolled through her texts, including a long one from Stu, which she found especially informative. Before her departure for London, he had installed a temporary duplicate of Frigg's text-vanishing software on her phone so that any text messages sent while Cami was overseas were all of the vanishing variety. They were readable only once, after which they disappeared, leaving no trace behind.

It's looking more and more like Hal Holden was the target instead of B. Frigg thinks she's on the trail of the people behind the attack. Local cops still have their eye on Ali.

Okay on B.'s shoulder, but Hal's closed head injury could have him on the vent for months.

> Getting glowing reports on your
> performance with B.'s presentation.
> Good for you, but I'd still like to know
> where that damned tech blogger,
> Adrian Willoughby, is getting his info.

As Stu's text vanished into the ether, Cami sent an immediate reply:

> I'd like to know that, too, but in
> the meantime, I'm coming home
> with letters of intent from two
> new customers.

Just then the barman approached bearing Cami's salad along with a napkin-wrapped bundle of silverware. She rested her phone on the bar and stared at the food in front of her. A filet of perfectly cooked salmon lay on a bed of brightly seasoned green peas. The mint flavoring on the peas was accentuated by two sprigs of mint arranged like crosshairs on top of the salmon.

"Buon appetito," the barman said with a cordial smile, keeping his words properly aligned with Il Bar's Italian-themed ambiance.

Focused on the food, Cami hadn't noticed that the person next to her at the bar had moved on until someone said, "Excuse me, is this seat taken?"

Cami glanced up to see none other than Adrian Willoughby himself, rocks glass in hand, lurch onto the stool next to hers. She had known all through the conference exactly who he was from the dossiers Frigg had created. During sessions and breaks, she had observed him from a distance, wondering if and when he would make an approach. Evidently now was the time.

"It's not taken," she said, giving the somewhat-tipsy newcomer what she hoped was a believably welcoming smile. "Let me get this out of your way," she added, picking up her phone and slipping it into a pocket. "I don't believe in taking calls or answering texts while I'm eating."

"Good idea," Willoughby muttered. "My mum's old-fashioned. Whenever a dinner guest pulls out a phone at the table, she hits the roof. She claims bringing phones to the table is bad manners, but then again, chewing out your guests isn't exactly behaving yourself, either."

"Your mother and mine would probably get along famously," Cami said, raising her glass of wine, "so let's drink to mothers, especially ones who are always peering over our shoulders."

Willoughby had arrived with an almost-empty glass in hand. After touching his glass to Cami's, he polished off the remainder of his drink, and then pushed the glass to the edge of the bar in search of a refill. When the barman appeared, Willoughby ordered a double and put the drink on his tab. Cami had thought from the outset that the man was inebriated. A double would make things worse.

"You're from the States, right?" he asked, noticeably slurring his words.

Willoughby had been in the back of the room when she'd done her presentation, so clearly he already knew the answer to that question, but Cami played along.

"Yes," she answered. "I'm from Arizona."

"That's where you live now," he said, "but where are you from originally—China?"

"California," she responded.

"How's the conference been treating you?"

If he was going to make some kind of play for her

and push came to shove, Cami still had her wasp spray handy, tucked away in the pocket of her blazer. In the meantime, however, it suited her purposes for Willoughby to think she was something of a dim bulb, and that was how she answered.

"Pretty well, I guess," she said with a noncommittal shrug. "It's my first, though, so I don't have much to compare it to."

"When do you head home?"

"Right after the closing luncheon tomorrow."

"Not hanging around to do a little sightseeing?"

"We're a bit shorthanded at work right now," she said. "I need to get back."

"Too bad," he said. "I'm single. You're single. I was going to offer to be your tour guide."

I'll bet you were! Cami thought.

Very few females had been in attendance at the conference. Of those, Cami was by far the youngest and most attractive. No wonder he was trying to put the moves on her.

"Sorry," she said, "no can do."

"Shorthanded because of B.'s injury?" Willoughby asked.

Cami wanted to ask how he knew about that. Instead, she merely nodded.

"How's he doing?" Willoughby inquired.

Cami could tell he was trying to act as though he and B. were great pals, but Cami wasn't falling for that line of bull, and she avoided answering the question by taking a long sip of her wine.

"Can I get you a refill of whatever you're drinking?" he offered.

He was smarmy. Cami understood smarmy. At that

point she was almost hoping Willoughby would pull some kind of groping stunt that would give her an excuse to deploy her wasp spray. On the other hand, she was curious. Clearly the man was already drunk. Once he had another one or two, maybe he'd spill the beans about what was really behind his very public grudge match with B. Simpson. She also knew that a second glass of wine wasn't going to hurt her.

"Sure," she said. "Why not? I'm having Pinot Grigio."

Willoughby ordered wine for her and another scotch for himself. When their drinks came, Cami's was delivered with a head shake from the barman and a disapproving glance in Willoughby's direction. She wanted to tell the bartender that she was more than capable of taking care of herself, but she didn't. When it was time for another round, the bartender cut them off. Willoughby was prepared to argue the case, but Cami talked him out of it.

"Let's just pay and go," she said. He made a bid to pay for her dinner and her first glass of wine, but the barman made sure that didn't happen. The fact that he signed his tab to his room told her he was staying at the hotel.

As they left the bar, Willoughby was clearly having difficulty walking, and Cami took his arm to steer him toward the elevator.

"What floor?" she asked.

"Third," he slurred, shambling to the back of the lift and leaning against the wall. Once the car began to move, Willoughby swayed dangerously and once more Cami was forced to steady him. "What's your room number?"

"Three thirty-four," he mumbled. "At least I think that's what it is."

When they reached the door to his room, he tried

the key several times but was unable to slip it into the slot. "Give me the key," she told him. "You'll never be able to make it work."

"Thanks," he said, handing it over. "I may have had a tiny bit too much to drink."

You think? Cami wondered.

Willoughby leaned against the wall for support while Cami slid the key into the slot. Once he let go of the wall, he would have fallen if Cami hadn't been there to grab him. She guided him inside and over to the bed. Once there, he toppled face-first onto the bed and instantly began to snore.

Cami stood there for an indecisive moment, looking down at him and considering her next move. She could have just left him there, but she still wanted to know more about his vendetta against High Noon in general and B. in particular. Rather than leaving, she walked over to the door and pushed it shut. Returning to the bed, she carefully eased Willoughby's cell phone out of one pocket and his wallet out of another.

Adrian Willoughby might have been a world-renowned cybersecurity expert, but his cell phone password was pathetic. Cami's third iteration of his birthday—3121984—opened the door to his entire life, and it turned out that wasn't pretty. Scrolling through texts and email, it didn't take long for her to suss out that George Smythe himself, the guy who passed himself off as a gentleman's gentleman, was paying the freight for Willoughby's publicity campaign against B., and knowing who was behind it would make it possible to put suitable countermeasures in place.

But that was only half of it. Using her cell phone to take screenshots, Cami spent the next two hours continuing to scroll through his texts, emails, and contacts, and copying the ones she considered to be most pertinent. It turned out that Willoughby was being paid to supply information on B. Simpson's operation to not one but two different firms, both of them known to be among High Noon's fiercest competitors. But that wasn't all, not nearly.

Adrian's personal life was in shambles. Frigg had already uncovered the fact that his wife, Marissa, had filed for a divorce, but texts and email correspondence revealed that she was playing hardball in terms of alimony, child support, and child custody issues. Marissa didn't care how long the divorce negotiations took. Adrian did because he just happened to have a very pregnant girlfriend who wanted to be married before her baby arrived in two months' time, to say nothing of a brand-new female acquaintance, one recently selected from a dating site where Adrian was still passing himself off as single.

Feeling sorry for the three different women who'd had the misfortune of becoming entangled with such a scumbag, Cami decided to do something about it. In the email correspondence dealing with the pending divorce proceedings, Cami located an email address for Marissa's attorney. Then she went back through all of Willoughby's texting and email history, taking a second set of screenshots dealing with him and his current crop of lovebirds.

Then she wrote a long email to the attorney.

To Whom It May Concern:

I recently had an encounter with Adrian Willoughby in a hotel bar here in London where, after attempting to pass himself off as

single, he ended up inviting me up to his room.
I accompanied him upstairs because by then he
was too inebriated to make it on his own.

Once in his room, he immediately passed out,
and I decided to take a look at his phone to
see who he really was. As a public service to
his wife as well as to the other women involved
with the man, I am attaching jpegs of what I
found there. You're welcome to use the material
as you see fit.

I would like to remain anonymous in this matter.
To that end, the address used to send this
message will no longer be valid once you have
read this message, and the email itself will also
disappear within a matter of minutes. I suggest
you immediately download and copy any of the
attached information which you feel might be
of use.

Sincerely,
A Concerned Friend

After attaching the jpegs, Cami pressed Send, hoping as she did so that the material she'd just provided
would make Adrian Willoughby's life far more complicated than it already was, maybe enough so that he'd
be obliged to pay more attention to his own business
and less to whatever was going on at High Noon Enterprises.

Finished with Willoughby's phone and wallet, Cami

returned both items to his pockets without disturbing him in the least. Then, after leaving the room key on his dresser, she exited the room.

On Saturday morning when Adrian woke up, Cami suspected he would be seriously hungover, but ultimately that would be the least of his problems.

CHAPTER 36

COTTONWOOD, ARIZONA

Friday, January 3, 2020, 4:00 p.m. (MST)

All day long Stuart Ramey had operated under a dark cloud, second-guessing and regretting his earlier decision to allow Frigg to install that keylogger on Frank Muñoz's computer. Telling Ali he'd been ignoring the AI's messages was a little white lie. In actual fact, he had put Frigg on a time-out when he left for work, telling her he'd let her know when he was ready to hear from her, and he still wasn't, primarily because he had yet to land on his next course of action.

On the one hand, Frigg's way of tracking down the killer had been nothing short of inspired, but using a keylogger to do so was strictly illegal. If law enforcement learned about that, there was a good chance Stu would end up in jail. At the very least he'd be fired. High Noon couldn't afford to have someone with a conviction for illegal hacking on the payroll. But Stu also knew that once Ali showed up at the house, he was going to have to tell her that he had stepped out of line, because what he had done affected not only his future but maybe High Noon's as well.

That spurt of late-afternoon texting with Cami had raised his spirits for a time, and he was especially gratified to know that she'd be returning from the conference with letters of intent from two new customers, but as the time for him to head home and face the music approached, Stu's sense of unease returned. Trying to settle his nerves, before leaving the office, he put in a pickup order for some comfort food from his favorite pizza joint. When it came to pizza, Stu's all-time favorite was the meat-eater's special. Ali's was pepperoni. As a peace offering, that's what he ordered.

After a short stop to pick up his pizza order, Stu hit the road. That was when he finally checked in with Frigg, and when he learned that earlier in the day the two suspects in the I-17 incident had been found shot to death outside Blythe, California. That was big news, of course, but not enough to relieve his anxiety. And arriving home to find Ali's rental car already parked in his driveway didn't help, either. As she exited her vehicle, the appraising look she aimed in Stu's direction made him think she already knew what he needed to discuss.

"Come on in," he invited. "I brought pizza," he added unnecessarily. Ali followed him into the house, threading her way through racks of humming CPUs in both the garage and family room that kept Frigg's formidable brainpower up and running.

"How are things at work?" Ali asked, once they arrived in the kitchen.

For once Stu was grateful for small talk. "It hasn't been easy," he responded, "but we're getting by."

He cleared a space on the island wide enough to hold the box. Looking around the kitchen, he was ashamed by how messy it was. Had he known he was going to have company right after work, he would at least have done the dishes.

Over pizza, without mentioning the keylogger, Stu filled Ali in on everything Frigg had so far been able to glean about the various investigations, including the early-morning bombing in Beaverton, Oregon. He finished by explaining how all of the incidents seemed to lead back to a single individual, a guy named Frank Muñoz.

"What do we know about Frank Muñoz?" Ali asked.

That question went to the heart of the matter. "A lot more than we should," Stu admitted ruefully. "I'm afraid I had Frigg install a keylogger on his computer."

Ali was aghast. "Are you kidding?" she demanded.

While they'd been talking, Stu's cell phone had been sitting quietly on the kitchen island next to the pizza box. Before Stu could reply, the device began buzzing in place. With a sigh, Stu reached over and picked it up. "Frigg," he barked, "I told you I didn't want to be interrupted."

"Sorry, Stu," Frigg replied. "I thought this was too important to wait. And good afternoon, Ms. Reynolds, I hope you had a pleasant journey."

There was no point in asking how Frigg knew Ali was in the room. She simply did, but Ali was still too dumbstruck by the unwelcome news about the illegal hack to bother responding.

"Should I put this material up on one of the screens in the family room?" Frigg continued. "That way you can both see it."

"I suppose," Stu conceded. "Give us a minute."

Taking their plates along with them, Stu and Ali moved to the family room sofa.

"All right," Stu said. "Go ahead."

What the hell?

Sorry. Someone screwed up.

Do you think? Someone screwed up
AGAIN! Hal Holden is still in the land of
the living and so is Sylvia. I think it's time
for two refunds instead of just one.

I'll take care of it.

Which, give me my money back or finish
the job? You'd better do something
about this, or I'll blow the whistle on
your whole damned operation.

Are you threatening me? If I go
down, you go down.

Then you'd better figure out how to
deliver that refund. By my calculations
I'm out twenty thou with nothing to
show for it. And you'd better make it
fast. Sometime soon, I may be heading
out of the country.

Ali was mystified. "What are we seeing here?" she
asked finally.

"This is Frank Muñoz communicating in an email
draft file with someone named Salvatore Moroni, a guy
who appears to be running a murder-for-hire operation
and who has likely been arranging and managing this
whole series of hits."

That was when Ali got it. "The only reason we're able to see this conversation is because of your key-logger?"

"Yes," Stu answered. "I had Frigg install it earlier this morning."

Ali reread the words on the screen, letting them sink in. "That sounds very much like a confession," she said at last.

Stu nodded. "Yes, it does."

"And totally inadmissible!"

"That too," he agreed.

Just then the words vanished, and the screen went blank. "Where'd that go?" Ali demanded. "Frigg, did you do that?"

"I did not," Frigg replied. "Mr. Muñoz simply closed the file, but I took a screenshot. By the way, that's how he and Mr. Moroni communicate— through draft files on an email account to which they both have access. The two of them are able to log in on it, as can Mr. Moroni's daughter, Rochelle, who, according to her IP address, also resides in Las Vegas."

"Who exactly is Salvatore Moroni?" Ali asked.

"He's supposedly ex–organized crime, currently doing life without parole inside the Lompoc Federal Correctional Complex for murdering four of his for-mer associates. It would appear that he's up to his old tricks—arranging hits for a price, and doing so from behind bars."

"But how does that work?"

"Apparently he has outside help," Frigg replied, "most likely his daughter."

"And he's doing all this over the Internet? How does

that work?" Ali asked. "I didn't think prisoners were allowed access to electronic devices."

"I doubt prison authorities are aware this device exists," Frigg answered.

"But none of that matters anyway," Ali continued. "Even if none of this is admissible, I'm assuming you've kept a copy."

"Of course," Frigg replied. "I've placed the original in Mr. Muñoz's permanent file. That is the correct terminology, is it not, Stu?"

"Yes," Stu agreed wearily. "That's what it's called and usually as a joke, but Ali's right. This confession doesn't do us a bit of good. It's both inadmissible and illegal. If we were to take this to the cops, we're the ones who would end up going to jail."

"But Frank Muñoz just said he's getting ready to leave the country," Ali objected, "so we'd better figure out a way to make anything that is admissible available to law enforcement without blowing our cover."

With that, Ali stood up. "I'm going home now," she announced. "Go ahead and continue collecting material, Frigg, but I want you to collate it into two separate files—what's legal for us to have and what isn't. Once I review what's legal, I'll see if we have enough information leading back to Frank Muñoz to build a believable case against him."

"Of course, Ms. Reynolds," Frigg said at once. "It will be my pleasure. Where would you like me to begin—with the murder of Alysha Morgan?"

"Wait," Ali said. "Who's she?"

"Alysha Morgan was murdered in a nightclub parking lot in Pasadena, California, in 1997. The investigation into that homicide appears to be what put three people in Frank Muñoz's crosshairs—Jack Littleton, Hal Holden, and Danielle Lomax-Reardon."

By now Ali's head was spinning. She didn't know who Danielle was, either, but she was sure she was about to find out.

"Yes," Ali said at last, "by all means start with Alysha."

CHAPTER 37

BEAVERTON, OREGON

Friday, January 3, 2020, 4:00 p.m. (PST)

By the middle of Friday afternoon, Ramon's already bad day got infinitely worse. He had called his sisters as soon as he got back to the hospital after his interview with Detective Wallace. Lucy immediately hopped in her car and arrived at the hospital while their mother was still in recovery. Tina chose to fly in, and Ramon had agreed to pick her up at PDX.

"You stink." Those were Tina's first words when she climbed into Ramon's 4Runner. "You should shower."

How about 'thanks for picking me up'? Ramon thought.

There were any number of things Ramon might have told her about having to carry people out of burning buildings or about not being allowed inside his cottage other than to get his car keys because the investigation was ongoing. He could have said those things, but he chose not to.

"Sorry about that," he responded mildly. "I've been a little busy."

"Was it really a bombing?" Tina wanted to know. "Who would do such a thing?"

"No idea," Ramon replied.

Not only did he suspect their father, he was also privy to some inside dope concerning the investigation, but he wasn't prepared to pass any of that along to "the girls." He could be trusted to keep his mouth shut. He doubted that was true for either one of them.

"And Larry went ahead with his surgery, even though Mom just had a heart attack?" Tina demanded. "You'd think he'd have the good sense to reschedule."

"I'm sure he had his reasons," Ramon said. *Good ones, too,* he thought.

Tina's interrogation continued. "What's the deal with the house?"

"It's a total loss," he answered.

"So where are the folks going to go when they leave the hospital?"

"I've been in touch with their insurance guy," Ramon told her. "He's found an assisted-living place where they'll be able to sublet a unit on a temporary basis."

"Assisted living," Tina huffed. "They're too young for assisted living."

"It's what they need right now," Ramon told her.

"But . . ."

"No buts," Ramon said, cutting her off. "It's a done deal."

"Shouldn't we all have been in on that discussion?"

"I'm the one who was here," Ramon told her. *Like it or lump it,* he thought.

"If we can't be at the house, where are Lucy and I supposed to stay?"

"Lucy found a hotel," an exasperated Ramon replied.

"I suggest you bunk with her." *Because you're sure as hell not coming home with me!*

By then Tina's nose was clearly out of joint. The remainder of the drive was done in silence.

Once they arrived at Portland General, Tina went straight to their mother's room while Ramon went to Larry's. The rooms were on different floors, and Ramon was grateful for that bit of physical separation.

Ramon had visited the room earlier, but Larry had been too groggy to talk. This time, when he arrived, Ramon was amazed to see that a pair of physical therapists had Larry up and walking. Ramon waited until the attendants finished getting Larry back into bed.

"Isn't it a little soon for you to be up and about?"

"I guess not," Larry told him. "My surgeon told me that these days most knee-replacement patients go home either the same day or the next. I told him about what happened both with Mom and the house, so he's made arrangements with the insurance company for me to have five days in a rehab facility. I believe Mom's doctor will be able to do the same for her. After that, I don't know where we'll go."

"Not to worry," Ramon told him. "I've got it handled. I've been working with Norm Williams, and it's all arranged. When the time comes for you to leave rehab, you'll be able to stay at an assisted-living place for the next three months."

A look of immense relief flashed across Larry's face. "Thank you," he said. "I've been worried sick about it. Norm's a good guy. So are you."

The silence that followed that small compliment was a comfortable one.

"I'm sorry the house is gone," Larry resumed finally.

"Before I had to take early retirement, your mom and I had talked about remodeling the place. Now we'll have to."

"I guess so," Ramon agreed.

"But the truth is," Larry went on, "I'm really grateful for that bomb."

Ramon looked at him in astonishment, thinking he must have misheard. "Really?"

"Really," Larry replied. "Mom's doctor said it probably saved her life. Her heart attack came on with no advance warning. If the EMTs hadn't been right there when it happened, she probably would have died."

Ramon nodded. That was vintage Larry Rogers. No matter what, he always managed to find the bright side.

Yet another silence ensued. It went on for so long that Ramon assumed Larry had drifted off to sleep. Although they were no longer chatting, Ramon's reluctance to deal with his sisters kept him where he was. When Larry spoke again, his voice caught Ramon off guard.

"Your father used to beat her, you know," Larry said quietly.

"I know he beat me," Ramon said with anger surging in his chest. "I didn't know he beat Mom, too."

"You weren't supposed to," Larry said. "He was always careful to hurt her in places where it didn't show—so people wouldn't know what was really going on. She stayed with him years longer than she should have, but once she could see he was on his way to prison, she managed to make a clean break of it."

"Why did she stay for so long?" Ramon asked.

"I believe she felt she owed him."

Ramon hesitated before asking the next question. "Because of me?"

Larry nodded. "Exactly," he said.

Ramon let his breath out. "So you know about that?"

"I knew about all of it," Larry replied, "about the rape, the unexpected pregnancy, and the shotgun wedding. She told me the story long before we married. When did you find out?"

"Just last week," Ramon answered. "I've wondered about it for years, but I finally got around to doing a DNA test."

"Did you talk to Mom about it?" Larry asked.

"I did," Ramon told him, "right after the girls left."

"Good," Larry said. "It's about time we got all that bad old stuff out in the open, but it doesn't change a thing between you and me, Ramon. As far as I'm concerned, you've been my son all along, and if Frank Muñoz did this, then the two of us are going to work like hell to see that he gets exactly what he deserves."

CHAPTER 38

SEDONA, ARIZONA

Friday, January 3, 2020, 7:00 p.m. (MST)

When Ali arrived home, Bella was overjoyed to see her, acting as though Ali had been gone for years rather than only a couple of days. It took a while to shower and change out of her travel clothes into a comfy pair of sweats. At that point, plagued by jet lag, Ali took herself to bed but not to sleep. Propped against a mound of pillows with Bella cuddled next to her, she opened her iPad and summoned both Frigg and Stu for an online call.

"Okay," she said once they were there. "Tell me about the murders of both Alysha Morgan and Danielle Lomax-Reardon, so I'm on the same page with both of you."

Frigg delivered a short overview of both, along with Frank Muñoz's subsequent incarceration on federal police corruption charges. After listening to those, Ali had a far better idea of where things stood.

"From here on out," she said, "all I want at my fingertips is open-source material I can freely share with law enforcement."

"Understood," Stu said.

"We know from the keylogger that Frank Muñoz is most likely responsible for what happened on I-17," Ali went on, "but for now let's leave Hal and B.'s situation out of the equation. Warren Biba isn't going to accept any assistance from us, so there's no point in wasting time. And we should probably take a pass on Jack Littleton's case as well. Yes, we believe what happened to him is connected to everything else, but as long as his manner of death remains undetermined, I doubt anything we find will be enough to jump-start reopening the investigation into that."

"Which leaves us with today's bombing in Beaverton and the murder of Danielle Lomax-Reardon," Stu concluded.

"I'm guessing the bombing is all hands on deck, so let's leave that one alone for now, too," Ali said. "Instead, let's concentrate on Danielle's case. From what you just told me, she's been dead for almost three years. I'm betting there are some homicide cops up in St. Paul who would welcome a new lead of any kind."

"But again, for your purposes, we'll be starting with Alysha's murder?" Frigg inquired.

"Correct," Ali confirmed, "starting there."

The first file that flashed on the screen was an archived copy of an old newspaper article dated July 20, 1997:

GUILTY VERDICT IN ALYSHA MORGAN HOMICIDE

After a weeklong trial and twelve hours of deliberation spread over two days, a jury in the

Pasadena Superior Court found accused killer Zeke Mathias Woodward guilty of second-degree murder in the 1997 parking lot shooting of exotic dancer Alysha Morgan.

The prosecution maintained that Ms. Morgan was the victim of a premeditated homicide, which would have called for a sentence of up to life in prison without parole. Instead, the jury found him guilty of second-degree murder, where sentence guidelines come in at twenty years to life.

During the trial, the victim's good friend and fellow dancer, Danielle Lomax, testified that as she and Alysha were leaving the strip club where they both worked, Woodward was lying in wait in the parking lot and ambushed the victim when the two women stepped outside.

BJ's, the troubled adult entertainment venue where both women worked, was shuttered three months after the homicide when the owner, Betty Jean Parmenter, was taken into custody by the FBI as the result of an ongoing racketeering investigation.

After the verdict was read, the lead investigator on the case, Pasadena homicide detective Jack Littleton, told reporters that he was disappointed with the second-degree verdict. "Alysha suffered through multiple instances of domestic violence, and when Woodward brought that weapon to the parking lot, he did so with the clear intention of murdering her."

Over the course of the trial, several of Ms.

> Morgan's fellow dancers, including Ms. Lo-
> max, testified that prior to the homicide, the
> victim often exhibited signs of bruising on her
> body, leading them to believe that she had been
> subjected to repeated instances of domestic
> abuse at the hands of her boyfriend.
>
> Sentencing in Mr. Woodward's case is
> scheduled for two weeks from today.

"Presumably Jack Littleton and Hal Holden were both involved in this case?" Ali asked.

"Correct," Frigg replied.

"But there's no mention of Frank Muñoz," Ali objected.

"Correct, but there should have been," Stu said. "Show her, Frigg."

The next item to appear on Ali's screen was an archived copy of a handwritten police report from one of the officers on the scene. Approximately thirty names were listed there, and Frigg had helpfully highlighted the name of Frank Muñoz.

"But that's the only place where his presence appears in the investigation," Stu said.

"Wait," Ali objected, "you're telling me an off-duty cop from Pasadena PD was present at BJ's the night of the homicide and that he was never interviewed? That makes it sound as though Hal and his partner were covering for him."

"Frigg thinks they were covering for the FBI," Stu replied.

"The FBI?" Ali echoed.

"That is correct," Frigg agreed. "When I examined the unredacted information from the investigation into the mob-related activities at BJ's, I learned that an FBI investigation was already underway at the time of Alysha's murder. If Muñoz had become involved in the investigation as a potential witness, his presence there might have derailed what the FBI was doing."

At that point Frigg's briefing veered into material she shouldn't have been able to access, the court reporter's version of Danielle Lomax's testimony in front of the grand jury. In it, she spoke about her affair with Frank Muñoz and his involvement in the illegal gambling activities going on inside BJ's, including his admission to Danielle in which he stated he had received a generous payoff from Betty Jean Parmenter for warning her in advance of an upcoming vice squad raid.

"So Danielle Lomax and Frank Muñoz were having an affair and she testified against him in the grand jury hearing?"

"Correct," Frigg supplied, "although I believe that part of the story may not qualify as open-source material."

"Probably not," Ali agreed, "but I think we can agree that someone who would go on an all-out revenge rampage so many years later is one angry dude—angry and dangerous. I wonder if physical abuse might be part of why she was willing to come forward and testify against him. What was Danielle doing at the time of her death?"

"She was serving as the executive director of Dahlke House, a domestic violence shelter in St. Paul, Minnesota," Frigg answered.

"Where are you going with this?" Stu asked.

"Women who make battling domestic violence their life's work usually have good reasons for doing so lurking in their own personal histories. Is there anything in Danielle's homicide investigation to suggest she was abused by her husband?"

"Would you like to see transcripts from Mr. Reardon's police interviews?"

"Yes, please," Ali said.

At the time of Danielle's murder, Danielle's husband, Luke Reardon, had submitted to several police interviews, including one done on the evening of the homicide. In all but the first he was grilled about his marriage to Danielle. Were there any issues, monetary or otherwise, in their relationship? His answer to that question was a resounding *no*. At one point, the lead detective, Amos Anderson, asked Luke about Danielle's previous romantic entanglements.

Reardon: When we met, we both had past relationships, and we agreed they were best left in the past.

> Anderson: So you're not acquainted with any of her previous boyfriends?

Reardon: No, I'm not. Like I already told you, Danielle's previous boyfriends were none of my business.

> Anderson: Have you ever harmed your wife in any fashion?

Reardon: Absolutely not.

Anderson: No physical altercations?

Reardon: None. And how could I possibly have done this? You already know I was out trick-or-treating with our boys at the time this happened.

Anderson: You could have hired a hit man.

Reardon: (a barely audible snicker) I don't know what the going rate is on hit men these days, but I doubt I could afford one.

"It sounds as though Luke Reardon wasn't even aware of Frank Muñoz's name, much less of his relationship with Danielle," Ali observed.

"He could have lied about that," Stu suggested.

"Why would he?" Ali retorted. "If someone was grilling me about my involvement in my spouse's death, and I happened to have some other suspect in mind, you can bet I'd say something."

"What about the Reardons' financials?" Stu asked.

"Everything appeared to be in order," Frigg supplied. "No credit card debt to speak of. The amounts of life insurance weren't excessive. They had recently purchased a home and carried enough insurance on each of them to cover the mortgage in the event either of them died. In addition, they each had $100,000 insurance policies that were purchased shortly after the birth of their first child."

"What did Danielle do between the time of Frank Muñoz's trial and her death?" Ali asked.

"She attended UCLA on a scholarship and graduated with a BA in sociology and a master's in psychology. She was hired as a victim advocate by Minnesota's Department of Public Services and moved to St. Paul in 2008. That's where she met and married Luke Reardon. In 2014 she was named executive director of the women's shelter where she was working at the time of her death."

"Let's get back to Frank Muñoz," Ali interjected.

"Very well," Frigg agreed.

The next article that flashed onto the screen, one from 2005, covered his guilty plea.

FORMER PASADENA OFFICER
GUILTY OF CORRUPTION

Former Pasadena police officer Francisco Muñoz surprised everyone today by pleading guilty to multiple federal charges minutes before his trial in federal court was scheduled to get underway.

Mr. Muñoz had been an eleven-year veteran of Pasadena PD when he was swept up as part of an FBI investigation into the notorious and now-defunct mob-owned strip club known as BJ's. He was accused of multiple counts of police corruption, money laundering, and obstruction of justice, and pled guilty to all of them in the course of today's court proceedings.

Under current sentencing guidelines, he

could spend the next twenty-five years in federal prison. Sentencing is set for two weeks from today.

Unable to post bail, Mr. Muñoz has remained in custody from the time of his arrest until today's court appearance. Any sentence given by the court will most likely be reduced by time served.

"Okay," Ali said, when she finished reading that one. "Frank Muñoz is off to prison while the three people who sent him there are free as birds. We still have no idea what he had against his former wife, but as far as the cops who put him away . . ."

"He has motive out the kazoo," Stu supplied.

Ali nodded. "And ditto for the ex-girlfriend who probably helped them. So now we need to track down a cop who'll see all this the same way we do."

"Good luck with that," Stu said. "It sounds like a tall order."

CHAPTER 39

BLYTHE, CALIFORNIA

Saturday, January 4, 2020, 7:00 a.m. (PST)

Detective Juanita Ochoa had arrived home from Riverside in time to tuck the kids in bed, but she was up and out of the house bright and early the next day, well before the Saturday morning cartoons came on. The Blythe Municipal Golf Course wasn't a private country club, but Judge Emmett Carruthers treated it as though it were. Every cop in town knew that he and his pals had a standing tee time there at seven every Saturday morning.

The guy in the pro shop knew the drill. When Juanita told him she was a cop looking for Judge Carruthers, he handed her the key to a golf cart. "They're probably on the tee box at the par three, waiting for the guys ahead of them to clear the green," he told her.

At that early hour, it was downright freezing in the open golf cart, and Juanita wasn't dressed for it. By the time she reached the par 3, she was chilled through. As soon as she pulled up, the judge, who was dressed for the weather, complete with a tartan wool hat, separated himself from his buddies and came over.

"Hola, Detective Ochoa," he said cheerily. "What have you got for me this fine morning?"

Juanita handed over the warrant request she'd prepared the night before. He scanned through it briefly. "Have you got a pen?" he asked.

Because she believed in being prepared, Juanita had the needed pen in her pocket. He signed off on the document, using the roof of the golf cart as a writing surface.

"There you go," Judge Carruthers told her with an encouraging smile as he returned both the signed warrant request and the pen to her waiting hands. "Happy hunting."

"Thank you," she said.

Minutes after arriving at the golf course, Juanita Ochoa was on the road, once again headed for Riverside. She'd heard about more than one case being solved by detectives obtaining a single telephone number. She only had one warrant now, but once she knew the next number Dante called on Monday morning, she'd put in a warrant request for that one, too.

Juanita understood that this kind of coordinated crime didn't happen in a vacuum, and with any kind of luck, following the lines of communication would eventually reveal all the players. Her only concern now was how long it would take for phone providers to respond to the tech team's requests for information. While she waited on that, Detective Ochoa planned to go to work on the complex process of locating the foster home or homes where Dante's children were currently being housed.

She had started doing the next-of-kin notifications, but she had yet to finish them, and finish them she would. Not only did she owe that to Dante Cox's kids, she also owed it to Detective Phil Reyes.

CHAPTER 40

SEDONA, ARIZONA

Saturday, January 4, 2020, 8:00 a.m. (MST)

Ali awakened a little past eight to the welcome scent of brewing coffee. With her body on no known time zone, she'd slept fitfully at best. Bella had already abandoned the bedroom and was eating breakfast by the time Ali staggered out of bed, pulled on her robe, and made her way to the kitchen.

"What would you like?" Alonzo asked.

"Just coffee for now," she told him, "and maybe French toast a little later. I've got something I need to attend to first."

Armed with her coffee, she headed for the library, where a fire was already lit in the gas-burning fireplace. While tossing and turning overnight, going over everything she'd learned in her mind, something else had dawned on her. Maybe they had this whole thing wrong. Yes, Hal Holden, Jack Littleton, and Danielle Lomax had sent Frank Muñoz to prison, but he wasn't the only one. Those same three people had also been instrumental in locking up Alysha's killer, Zeke Woodward. Maybe someone besides Frank Muñoz was out for revenge.

After settling in front of the fire, Ali summoned Frigg.

"Good morning, Ms. Reynolds," Frigg said when she answered. "I hope you slept well."

"I did," Ali lied. "Thank you for asking."

"What can I do for you?"

"What can you tell me about Zeke Woodward, Alysha Morgan's killer? I trust he's still in prison."

Frigg's voice returned a moment later. "Mr. Woodward was sent to prison for second-degree murder in 1997 and given a twenty-year-to-life sentence. He served his time in the California Correctional Institution in Tehachapi, California. On October 1, 2019, Mr. Woodward was granted compassionate release into the custody of his daughter, Monique Haynes, and her husband, Rodney, who live in Blaine, Washington. According to Mr. Woodward's medical chart, he suffers from stage-four lung cancer and is currently receiving hospice care at his daughter's residence."

The irony of his release date wasn't lost on Ali. Frank Muñoz and Zeke Woodward had been released within a month of each other.

"What can you tell me about Zeke's daughter?"

"Monique Haynes is employed as an RN at a hospital in Bellingham. Her husband works for the US Border Patrol."

"Can you provide me with Monique's phone number, please?"

"Of course," Frigg replied. "Home or work?"

"Both."

With the numbers in hand, Ali hesitated for a moment. It wasn't that early in the morning, but if Monique had worked a night shift, a phone call now might awaken her. However, Ali's reluctance about making the call was about more than just timing. She was still wrestling with what she should say when she finally squared her shoulders, keyed the Haynes's home phone number into her phone, and pressed Send.

A woman picked up after two rings. "Hello," she said, her voice flat and sounding more than a little impatient.

"Is this Monique Haynes?" Ali asked.

"Yes, it is, but who's this? If you're calling because you want to buy my house, I'm hanging up now."

Ali had received her own share of spam calls offering bogus real estate deals, and she understood Monique's truculent attitude.

"Please don't hang up," Ali put in quickly. "My name is Ali Reynolds from Sedona, Arizona, and this has nothing to do with real estate. I've been asked to look into the possibility of wrongdoing at the Pasadena Police Department around the time your father was arrested and convicted. I know he's been released and is staying with you, but I was wondering if it would be possible for me to have a word with him."

"Possible wrongdoing?" Monique repeated. "What kind of wrongdoing?"

"I've reason to believe that another Pasadena PD officer, a dirty cop, was at BJ's on the night the Alysha Morgan homicide occurred. Interestingly enough, that officer's name never came up in the investigation nor did he testify for the prosecution. I believe someone may have been hiding something, and I'd like to speak with your father to find out if he has any insights into that."

There was no immediate reply. Knowing it could go either way, Ali kept quiet.

"All right," Monique said at last. "Mornings are usually better for him. By late afternoon he's generally too tired to talk. Let me see if he's willing to speak to you."

In the background, Ali heard the sounds of movement as the phone was carried from one room to another. Finally Monique spoke again, leaving the phone uncovered so Ali could hear both sides of the conversation.

"Hey, Dad," she said. "There's a lady on the phone named Ali something or other. She's from Arizona, but she'd like to talk to you about possible wrongdoing on the part of Pasadena PD at the time you were arrested. It has something to do with a dirty cop. I told her I'd ask, but you don't have to speak to her if you don't want to. Do you want to talk to her?"

There was no audible answer, but he must have agreed.

"Okay," Monique said into the phone, "I'm putting you on speaker."

"What kind of wrongdoing and what dirty cop?" Zeke asked. His voice was weak and hoarse. The effort of speaking even that many words resulted in a fit of coughing.

"Someone who was at BJ's the night you got arrested."

"Who's that, Frank Muñoz?" Zeke asked at once.

His words caught Ali by surprise. The fact that Zeke had immediately hit on Muñoz as the dirty cop in question was striking.

"So you were already aware that Frank Muñoz was a dirty cop?" Ali asked. "How did you learn that?"

"I knew he was a cop because Alysha told me," Zeke replied. "Didn't find out about the dirty part until later on along with everyone else."

"And how did Alysha know Muñoz was a police officer?"

"Danielle told her," Zeke answered. "Why wouldn't she? Them two women was friends, and friends always talk about they's boyfriends."

"Did Alysha tell you anything else about him?"

"She said something about him beating the crap out of Danielle on occasion, but then again, who am I to talk?" Zeke gave a brief chuckle that morphed into another spasm of coughing,

Ali took a deep breath before asking her next question. "Do the names Jack Littleton and Hal Holden mean anything to you?"

"Sure," Zeke said at once. "They's the cops that arrested me and locked my ass up. I ain't got no problem with them—they was just doin' their jobs." That statement was followed by more coughing. At that point Monique intervened on her father's behalf.

"He can't talk any more right now," she said, taking charge. "It's wearing him out."

"Please tell your father that I said thank you," Ali told her. "He's been very helpful."

Because he had been—Zeke Woodward had just told Ali exactly what she needed to know. Danielle Lomax had indeed been the victim of domestic violence, but not at the hands of her husband. Her abuser had been none other than Frank Muñoz himself, and now Ali had someone who could attest to that fact, as long as Zeke Woodward didn't die first.

Uncertain of her next move, Ali opted for food before action and headed for the kitchen. By the time she had polished off Alonzo's French toast, she had decided. Back in the library, she summoned Frigg once more.

"Can you give me the name for the lead detective on the Danielle Lomax-Reardon homicide?"

"That would be Lt. Amos Anderson. He's now Captain Amos Anderson, the head of St. Paul PD's Homicide Unit," Frigg replied.

"Phone number, please," Ali requested, "and just the general number for the department. Today I need to go through proper channels and up the chain of command."

With that number in hand, she dialed. When an operator answered, she asked to be connected to the homicide unit.

"My name is Ali Reynolds," she told the next person who came on the line. "I'd like to speak to whoever was the lead detective on the Danielle Lomax-Reardon homicide investigation," she said.

"I believe that would be Captain Anderson, but he's not in at this time. Can I help you?"

"No, I need to speak to him directly. I have a possible lead in this case. Would you please ask him to give me a call?"

The guy on the phone took the message, but Ali was left wondering if Anderson would call her back. She hoped so. The promise of a possible lead in a long-cold case could be pretty enticing, but there was no telling if or when he'd respond. After hanging up, Ali hurried into the bathroom to shower. She wanted to be in Phoenix so she could be on hand whenever the doctors got around to releasing B. All the same, she took her phone into the bathroom with her and left it on the floor close enough to the shower so she'd be able to answer if it rang. If Amos Anderson did reply right away, she didn't want to miss the call.

CHAPTER 41

ST. PAUL, MINNESOTA

Saturday, January 4, 2020, 9:30 a.m. (CST)

Amos Anderson was outside, hard at work, and using his spanking-new snowblower. He had cleared both his driveway and the walkway to his front porch, adding several inches of the light fluffy stuff to the existing six-foot-deep canyon carved into old frozen snow. Now he was working on the sidewalk in front of the house. However, with a frigid air mass due to come down out of Canada, Saturday night temperatures were predicted to plunge well below zero. He wanted the new snow cleared away and a layer of deicer laid down before that happened.

He didn't mind being out in the cold. Because he spent most of his days locked in a downtown office, he loved any opportunity to be outdoors. With both of their sons out of the house now, Bonnie, his wife, kept hinting that maybe they should sell the house and downsize to a condo. That way, she said, Amos wouldn't have to worry about snow in the winter and yardwork in the summer, but the truth was, he loved working in the yard. It was something that helped manage the constant stress that came with working homicides. Some of his pals were big on ice fishing, but summer or winter, fishing had never been Amos's thing. In the winter, sitting in shacks and drinking schnapps or beer just didn't grab him. In the summer there were always mosquitos.

Given a choice, he'd take mowing the lawn, raking leaves, or blowing snow over fishing every single time, and most especially in this instance when the snowblower in question happened to be the latest and greatest. His old workhorse one had finally bitten the dust after the first big snowstorm in December, and he'd gone out and splurged on a new one. That was the other good thing about having both boys grown up and out of the house. Now that he and Bonnie were no longer forking over money for tuition, room rent, or food for two college-aged boys, they had a lot more discretionary income at their disposal, and Amos had really wanted that snowblower.

When his cell phone vibrated in his shirt pocket, he shut down the machine and removed his gloves in order to answer. Seeing the phone number, he sighed. If the office was calling him first thing on a Saturday morning, that probably meant they'd caught a case overnight.

"Hey, Cap," Sergeant Rod Toomey said, "how's it going?"

Toomey was the homicide squad's desk sergeant.

It was fine until now, Amos thought. "What's up?" he asked.

"An odd call just came in from a woman in Arizona, someone named Ali Reynolds," Rod answered. "She asked to speak to you. She claims she may have a lead in the Danielle Lomax-Reardon homicide."

Amos heard the quick catch in his own breath. So did Rod Toomey.

Every homicide cop has that one case that—solved or not—stays with him forever. For Amos, Danielle Lomax-Reardon's murder was it. He had been the lead on the case, partnered with a newbie member of the homicide squad named Russell Thomas. It had been Russ's first case, and it was a bad one.

Amos recalled being summoned to the scene. They had arrived at the address and found Danielle's bloody, bullet-shredded body lying among a scatter of pumpkins from a ruined Halloween display on the front porch of Dahlke House, a local women's shelter.

Upon seeing the bloodied body, Russ had lost his cookies, staggering off the porch and barfing into a nearby hedge. He'd been embarrassed as all hell about that, but Amos had told him not to worry—assuring him that first cases were often like that and that over time seeing dead bodies would become an everyday occurrence. It had been true for Amos once and eventually it was true for Russell Thomas as well.

The two detectives had remained at the crime scene for the next hour and a half. When the ME did his thing, there had been no need to transport the victim to a hospital for lifesaving care because Danielle had been pronounced dead at the scene. For Amos, the worst part of the night came later—after they left the crime scene and went to the victim's home to notify her family.

Like the front porch of the shelter, the Reardons' home, too, had been fully stocked with Halloween decorations both inside and out. A pair of glowing jack-o'-lanterns were stationed on either side of the door. A fake skeleton lounged on the porch rail, while more jack-o'-lanterns leered through every window.

That night Luke Reardon had answered the door as a happily married man, something that changed the moment he saw their faces and badges. He had invited them into a house where the living room was strewn with an assortment of Halloween debris. Two Darth Vader costumes had been abandoned just inside the front door. The coffee table in front of the sofa was covered with candy and cookies dumped out of two plastic jack-o'-lanterns.

Even this many years later, Amos remained grateful that they had arrived late enough that Danielle's sons were already in bed before they delivered the awful news. Nonetheless, he knew that their visit that night had forever changed the Reardon family's approach to celebrating Halloween.

Naturally Amos and Russ had put Luke Reardon under an investigatory microscope, but eventually they had cleared him. He and the boys had still been out trick-or-treating at the time of Danielle's shooting, and several neighbors had time-stamped phone camera footage that verified his alibi. Detectives had also looked at current and former romantic partners of women who were clients and residents of Dahlke House, but they had never identified any viable suspects. Eventually the case went cold.

"Hey, Cap," Sergeant Toomey was saying. "Are you there?"

Amos's quiet moment of introspection had lasted long enough for the desk sergeant to think the call had been disconnected.

"I'm still here," Amos said quickly. "Sorry. Please text me the number. I'm outside clearing the sidewalk. I'll make the call when I'm back inside."

Off the phone, Amos stuffed it back into his pocket and donned his gloves once more. Then he forced himself to finish the job—blowing the sidewalk from fence line to fence line before returning the blower to its pride-of-place storage spot in the garage. After that he methodically sprayed a layer of deicer on all three of the cleared surfaces. But the whole time he worked, he was wondering, *Is this a real lead, or is it some kind of joke?*

He didn't want to get his hopes up, but still.

In the house Amos retreated to his den, where he closed the door before placing the call. He and Bonnie were expecting company for dinner that night. If this was something that would entail Amos's going into the office on a Saturday, there'd be hell to pay. Still, he was relieved that when he finally did dial the number, a woman answered after only one ring.

"Is this Ali Reynolds?"

"Yes."

"Amos Anderson here with the St. Paul Police Department," he said. "I understand you wanted to speak to me."

"I did, and I do. Thanks for calling back."

"I believe this concerns the murder of Danielle Lomax-Reardon? May I ask about your connection to the case? Do you happen to be a friend or relative?"

As he asked the questions, Amos had pen and paper in hand and was ready to take notes.

"No," Ali replied, "I'm no friend or relation of any kind, but I may have a lead on her killer. Were you aware that Danielle was involved as a witness in a homicide that occurred in Pasadena, California, in 1997?"

"Yes, I was," Amos answered, surprising even himself at how many details of Danielle's case he could recall off the top of his head. "I believe the homicide was a domestic, and Danielle was good friends with the victim. I've always assumed that the death of her friend had something to do with her ending up working with victims of domestic violence. That's what she was doing here in St. Paul at the time of her death—running a shelter."

"I think her choosing to work with battered women had more to do with her own personal history than it did with what happened to Alysha Morgan," Ali Reynolds asserted.

That brought Amos up short. "Danielle a victim?" Amos objected. "We never found anything to corroborate those kinds of issues between Danielle and her husband."

"I wasn't referring to Luke Reardon," Ali said. "Does the name Frank Muñoz mean anything to you?"

"Not that I remember," Amos said. "I'm calling from home, so I don't have access to any of my files, but that's not a name I recognize. Who's he? And how do you have access to all this information?"

"Earlier this week my husband was on his way to Sky Harbor Airport in Phoenix, Arizona, riding in a limo driven by a retired Pasadena police officer named Hal Holden. Someone deliberately veered into their vehicle and forced them off Interstate 17 north of Phoenix."

"Is your husband all right?" Amos asked quickly. "And how's the driver?"

"They were both seriously injured," Ali answered. "My husband should be released later today. Hal remains on a ventilator. However, the two young men believed to be responsible for the wreck, Dante Cox and Tyrone Jackson, were later found shot to death in the desert outside Blythe, California. Those two homicides are being investigated by Detective Juanita Ochoa of the Riverside County Sheriff's Office."

Amos continued to jot down notes, but he still had no idea where this was going.

"The man in charge of the I-17 investigation, Captain Warren Biba of the Arizona Highway Patrol, has decided that my husband was the intended target, and he has focused his entire investigation on the idea that I'm the one responsible."

"Are you?" Amos asked. The question came out involuntarily, and he was surprised that Ali's answer was preceded by a hint of laughter.

"No, I'm not," she said, "but if you'll pardon my going all O. J. Simpson on you, I thought someone should go in search of the real killer by taking a look at Hal as the intended victim, and that's what we've done."

Amos wanted to ask who she meant by using the word "we," but the woman was still talking, and he didn't want to interrupt.

"By searching through online sources, we've discovered that Hal and his partner, Jack Littleton, were the lead investigators on the murder of a young woman named Alysha Morgan. Danielle, one of Alysha's friends, was also an eyewitness to the shooting. She testified for the prosecution at the trial that sent Alysha's killer, Zeke Woodward, to prison."

Amos felt his eyes beginning to glaze over. "This is all very interesting, Ms. Reynolds," he said, "but I don't see . . ."

"Hold on," she said. "I'm getting there. By searching through media sources involving those three names, we've learned that subsequent to that trial, an FBI investigation shut down the nightclub where both Danielle and Alysha had once been employed, and that's where we encountered Frank Muñoz.

"At the time of Alysha's murder, he was an eleven-year veteran of Pasadena PD and a regular customer at the nightclub. He was later swept up in the FBI operation and arrested on charges of police corruption, money laundering, and obstruction of justice, among others. Hal Holden, Jack Littleton, and Danielle Lomax all testified against him during grand jury proceedings. They were scheduled to testify against him at trial, but he pled guilty and went to prison. However, during her grand jury testimony, Danielle admitted to having carried on a long-term relationship with the defendant.

"Since the car wreck on Wednesday," Ali continued, "here's what we've learned. A couple of months ago Jack Littleton died of a single gunshot wound to the head in his home in Pasadena. Word on the street is that he committed suicide, but the ME ruled his manner of death as undetermined. As you know, Danielle Lomax-Reardon is also deceased. Hal Holden is on a ventilator, and, as of yesterday morning, the house belonging to Frank Muñoz's ex-wife, Sylvia Rogers, burned to the ground in the aftermath of a fire bombing in Beaverton, Oregon. The ex-wife wasn't injured by the bomb, but she was hospitalized with a heart attack."

Amos started to ask a question, but Ali plunged on.

"A little while ago, I spoke with a man named Zeke Woodward."

"That would be Alysha's convicted killer," Amos supplied.

"Correct," Ali responded. "He's out of prison now on compassionate release due to a case of terminal lung cancer. He told us that when Danielle was involved with Muñoz, she was also a victim of domestic violence."

At long last, finished with her recitation, Ali fell silent. It was several seconds before Amos said anything more. "Where exactly is this Frank Muñoz right now?" he asked.

"After serving sixteen of a twenty-five-year-to-life sentence in the Lompoc Federal Correctional Complex, he's now out on parole and living in Las Vegas, Nevada."

"When did he get out?"

"November of last year."

"Danielle died close to three years ago," Amos objected. "Since he was still in prison back then, how could he be responsible for that?"

"We believe he may have obtained the services of a murder-for-hire operation."

"Wouldn't that require substantial amounts of money," Amos asked. "How could a recently released ex-con afford it?"

"I don't know," Ali answered. "My researchers and I have only been able to examine public documents. We don't have a way to examine his financials."

"Do you happen to know the name of the person handling the bombing investigation?"

"No, but I can get it."

"And who was assigned to the Jack Littleton case?"

"I'll get that name for you, too."

"Text the information to this number, along with the name of the guy from the Arizona Highway Patrol who has you in his crosshairs."

"I will," Ali said. Then, after a slight hesitation, she added, "You probably shouldn't mention to Warren Biba that you've spoken to me."

"Do you think?" he asked. "Not my first rodeo, you

know. And while you're at it, feel free to send along anything else that turns up on your end."

"I will," Ali said, "but there is one more thing. We've heard a rumor that Muñoz may be planning to leave the country sometime in the near future."

"Not if I have anything to do with it," Amos declared. "I always say, if it walks like a duck and quacks like a duck, it probably is a duck. You've made a pretty good case here that this Muñoz character is a dangerous individual. He may or may not be a serial killer, but I can sure as hell make sure he doesn't leave the country until we're certain about that."

Amos hung up the phone, then he folded the paper containing his notes and stuffed it in his pants pocket. He was on fire. Every instinct in his body was screaming that Ali Reynolds was onto something. This wasn't just a lead. Frank Muñoz was potentially prime-suspect material, but in order to verify any of this, he needed to be at the office making official inquiries from an official phone.

With that, he lunged out of his chair and went looking for Bonnie. She was in the kitchen, already working on dessert for the night's dinner.

"We've caught a case," he said. He didn't tell her it was an old one.

"Dinner is at six," she warned him. "If you're not home on time tonight, St. Paul PD's Homicide Unit will have another case to work. Got it?"

"Got it," he said. "I hear you loud and clear."

CHAPTER 42

SEDONA, ARIZONA

Saturday, January 4, 2020, 10:00 a.m. (MST)

When Ali got off the phone with Amos Anderson, she didn't do a happy dance, but it was a near thing. With the exception of the so-called rumor about Muñoz possibly making a run for it, she believed she'd said nothing that could lead back to Frigg. And it sounded as though she'd gotten through to the man—as though he was determined to do something about all this. From the way he'd instantly recalled the details of Danielle's investigation, that unsolved homicide was something that had stayed with him.

Ali didn't have the phone numbers Amos had requested readily at hand, so she called Frigg, got the needed numbers, and texted them to him. Then she finally finished getting dressed. B. called while she was still in the bathroom.

"Release is supposed to be sometime around noon," he informed her.

"I'm almost on my way," she told him. "I'm just putting on makeup."

"Drive safe," he said.

She was slipping on her shoes when the doorbell rang and Bella began to bark. Since Alonzo was there, she didn't bother to answer it, but then he appeared in the bedroom doorway a moment later.

"Two cops are at the door," he said. "Two detectives, Julie Morris and Steven Flack. They want to speak to you."

"Time for Warren Biba's engraved invitation," she muttered under her breath as she followed Alonzo back to the front door. Bella was still barking, and Alonzo collected the dog on his way past.

"May I help you?" Ali asked the two people standing there. It was cold on the front porch, but this wasn't a social call, and she didn't invite them in.

"We'd like to ask you to come down to headquarters in Prescott for an interview."

"A voluntary interview?" she asked.

"Of course," Detective Morris said.

"Then I'm choosing not to come," Ali replied. "My husband is being released from the hospital today, and I need to go pick him up. Furthermore, I have no intention of speaking to anyone without my attorney present. We'll need to set up an appointment in advance in order to make that happen."

"But . . ." Detective Flack began.

"No buts," Ali said. "I've told you I want my attorney in attendance, so unless you're placing me under arrest, we're done here."

With that, she closed the door and left them standing there.

Since Warren Biba obviously believed Ali to be a murderous bitch, she might just as well act like one.

CHAPTER 43

ST. PAUL, MINNESOTA

Saturday, January 4, 2020, 12:00 p.m. (CST)

On his way to the department, Amos called Detective Thomas. "Don't tell me I've caught a case," Russ said. "It's Saturday. I'm supposed to be off this weekend."

"We have caught a case and you won't believe which one. We have a brand-new suspect in the Danielle Lomax-Reardon homicide."

"No shit!"

"No shit. Get your ass into the office. We've got work to do."

"My kid's playing hockey right now, but I'll call my wife to come get him. I'll be there in twenty."

The roads had been plowed, and there wasn't much traffic. People were staying home. During the drive, Amos prioritized how to handle all the cases. Naturally homicides—Danielle's and the maybe/maybe not homicide of Jack Littleton—went to the top. Third would be the bombing in Oregon. The vehicular homicide attempt would come in last, and Amos would talk to Warren Biba when he was damned good and ready.

Having decided on how they'd organize the cases, Amos sorted out how he and Russ would share the wealth when it came to making phone calls, but before making any calls, Amos needed to learn everything he could about Frank Muñoz, starting with his current location and the name and phone numbers of his parole officer. If Muñoz was planning on leaving town, his PO either knew about that or didn't. Amos needed to know which was which.

As a high school kid enchanted with all things *Star Wars*, Amos Anderson had dreamed of becoming the next George Lucas. With that in mind, he had persuaded his folks to cough up enough money to send him to a two-week-long fine arts summer camp in Green Bay, Wisconsin. The short film he and his team members had produced had been dreadful, and Amos had learned that making movies was far harder than it looked. As a result, by the time he enrolled in college, Hollywood and moviemaking no longer beckoned. Entering his junior year, Amos declared himself a criminal justice major and began the journey of becoming a cop.

But one part of that long-ago fine arts experience remained. Amos's screenwriting coach had been a true believer in storyboards. As a detective, Amos had gone through an endless supply of three-by-five cards to get the job done. Whenever he was deeply involved in an investigation, he'd lay cards out on the dining room table in order to visualize how people and events were somehow connected.

Now, as captain, cards on tabletops were blessedly a

thing of the past. Against one wall in his office, where his predecessor had kept a display of his awards and honors, Amos kept a movable bulletin board that he used for casual announcements and reminders, along with an ever-changing gallery of cartoons culled from local newspapers. On the other side, the private side, was a whiteboard. He used that in the dark of night when he drew diagrams to help guys in his unit sort their way through knotty cases.

Even before Russell Thomas arrived that morning, Amos had already deployed the whiteboard. Across the top in bold all-caps he had written the name FRANK MUÑOZ. On the next line down were the names of all the people presumed to be Muñoz's likely targets and potential victims: Danielle Lomax-Reardon, Jack Littleton, Hal Holden, and Sylvia Rogers. Under three of those were the names and phone numbers of the applicable investigators. Someone in Records had tracked down a copy of Jack Littleton's autopsy. Under his name were two separate listings—Ray Hollingsworth, the Pasadena PD detective assigned to the case, and Dr. Loren Sanderson, the current head of the Los Angeles County Department of Medical Examiner-Coroner. Off in the lower right-hand corner of the board were the names Dante Cox and Tyrone Jackson. Amos was sure they were part of all this. As of yet, however, there was no way to tell how or why.

When Russell showed up, Amos was on the line with someone inside the federal penal system who was able to give him the name and phone number for Frank Muñoz's parole officer—Miriam Baxter. Amos dialed her number as soon as he had it, but his call went straight to voice mail: "This is Miriam Baxter. If this is an emergency, please hang up and dial nine-one-one. In the meantime, I am out of the office on personal business until Monday, January sixth. You're welcome to leave a message, but I won't be able to return your call until I'm back in the office."

Amos left a message anyway. "My name is Amos Anderson, captain of the homicide unit at St. Paul PD in St. Paul, Minnesota. One of your parolees, Frank Muñoz, has surfaced as a possible person of interest in one of our cold cases. Please give me a call at your earliest convenience."

"Who's Frank Muñoz?" Russ asked.

"Turns out he was Danielle's abusive boyfriend back when she was living in California and long before she came to St. Paul and married Luke Reardon."

"How come his name never surfaced in our investigation?" Russ wanted to know.

"When I asked Luke about Danielle's previous relationships, he never mentioned this guy. Maybe he didn't even know about him. When he and Danielle met, she was walking the straight and narrow here in the Twin Cities. She probably didn't want to admit that she'd been involved with someone who ended up doing time."

"And we know about him now because?" Russ inquired.

"Because a woman from Arizona, a lady named Ali Reynolds, called in a tip."

Russ studied the board. "Who are all these people?"

Amos gave him a quick overview.

"How can I help?"

"By contacting Pasadena PD and talking to the detective assigned to Littleton's case, a guy named Ray

Hollingsworth. He needs to be in the know about what's going on. In the meantime, I'm going to call Luke Reardon. I want him to be aware that we're reopening the case. Our investigation may have cleared the guy in his wife's death, but that's not true in the court of public opinion. I know for a fact that he's been living under a cloud of suspicion ever since."

For going on three years Luke Reardon had called Amos on almost a monthly basis to check on the progress of the case. As a result, Amos had no difficulty locating his number. When Luke answered the phone, it was clear Amos's name was in Reardon's contacts list as well.

"Amos," Luke said uncertainly, "has something happened?"

"I believe so," Amos replied, relieved to know they were still on a first-name basis. "I wanted to let you know that as of this morning the investigation into Danielle's death is officially back on track."

"Really? Why?"

"Because we've identified a possible suspect."

"Who?" Luke asked.

Ignoring the question, Amos continued. "I'm calling to give you a heads-up. You already know Detective Thomas. He and another detective, I'm not sure which one, will probably be dropping by later to ask some uncomfortable questions."

Luke groaned aloud. "Don't tell me I'm back on the suspect list."

"You're most definitely not," Amos assured him. "As I said before, we've identified a new suspect, but my investigators will be looking into Danielle's love life back before you met."

"I don't know much about that," Luke admitted. "She put herself through school working as an exotic dancer, but that part of her history wasn't something she was proud of, and we never really talked about it. We worked on the premise that what either of us did before we met was none of the other's business. Why bring it up now?"

"Sorry, Luke, as part of what's now an ongoing investigation, I can't discuss this any further. I simply wanted you to be aware that it's all about to come raining down on your head once again."

"Okay," Luke said. "Thanks for letting me know."

After that call, Amos dialed the Riverside County Sheriff's Office. It took some time to locate Detective Ochoa. He caught up with her as she was driving back home to Blythe after doing a next-of-kin notification. And that's where Amos got his first piece of good news. Detective Ochoa had managed to pick up a search warrant for one of her victim's phones, and Riverside's tech team was busy examining the phone's call history in hopes of finding out how Ochoa's two dead guys fit into the Frank Muñoz picture.

Amos's last call that morning was to Beaverton PD. It was Saturday morning, but when he asked for Detective Wallace, the call was put through and answered immediately.

"Detective Wallace here. Can I help you?"

"My name is Captain Amos Anderson, head of the homicide unit at the St. Paul Police Department in St. Paul, Minnesota. I'm calling about your bombing."

"What about it?"

"I believe either the bomber himself or, at the very least, the person behind the bombing may be the same individual responsible for a nearly three-year-old unsolved homicide here in my jurisdiction."

"Does your suspect have a name?" Wallace asked.

"Frank Muñoz," Amos responded.

"I'll be damned!" Wallace exclaimed. "That's the same name someone gave me yesterday. Are you aware my intended bombing victim is Muñoz's ex-wife?"

"I am now," Amos said, "but can you tell me who pointed you in Muñoz's direction?"

"His son, Ramon. Evidently there's no love lost between them. He says his father is out on parole and living in Vegas."

"I know that, too. I've placed a call to his PO. She's out of the office until Monday, but you need to know there may have been several additional victims on Frank Muñoz's personal hit list."

"Hit list?" Wallace echoed. "Are you serious?"

"Absolutely," Amos replied. After that he went on to give yet another quick overview of the various cases and individuals involved.

"Lots of victims and lots of jurisdictions," Wallace observed when Amos was finished.

"Yes," he answered. "With one exception, I've got calls in to all the jurisdictions involved."

"Sounds like this calls for a task force," Wallace suggested.

"Maybe it does," Amos agreed.

"Since you're the one pulling it all together," Wallace went on, "I hereby nominate you to take the lead."

"Thanks," Amos said with a short laugh. "It would appear I already am."

CHAPTER 44

LAS VEGAS, NEVADA

Saturday, January 4, 2020, 2:00 p.m. (PST)

Now that Frank had adjusted to the idea that he was leaving town, he could hardly wait to do so. In fact, he was more than slightly anxious. Sylvia wasn't dead, and that was a big problem. What if she pointed the finger at him? Yes, it had been years since he'd threatened her, but if he remembered, maybe she did, too. He needed to get out of Dodge as soon as possible. On this Saturday afternoon, his scheduled Monday meeting with his PO couldn't come soon enough.

Trying to keep his growing anxiety at bay, Frank began dealing with logistics. The apartment came fully furnished. All he needed to take with him was his clothing, and there wasn't much of that. He'd come out of prison with the clothes on his back and little else. Since then he'd only added a few necessities, but if he was flying to another part of the world, he'd need to look like an ordinary traveler. To do that, he had to blend in. International travelers always carried luggage—large checkable suitcases and/or roll-boards—with clothing and toiletries packed inside them. With that in mind, Frank devoted Saturday to shopping.

His first stop was Walmart, where he bought two matching pieces of rolling luggage—a big one and a smaller carry-on. He also found a cheap shaving kit and stocked up on a few toiletries to go inside. In addition he grabbed a supply of underwear since he wasn't sure whether his favorite brand, Jockey boxers, would be available where he was going.

He was about to go looking for pants and shirts when something stopped him. He hadn't ever done any international traveling, so he wasn't sure of all the procedures, but if someone went through his luggage and found nothing but brand-new clothing, that could raise red flags. New underwear? Yes. New everything else? No.

While trying to get a grip on where he might end up, Frank had done some online searches about Indonesia. It was near the equator and mostly tropical. This was early January and what passed for winter weather in Vegas. The only people navigating the Strip in shorts and Hawaiian shirts were snowbirds from the Midwest. The people decked out in jackets and sweaters were all locals. There were plenty of long-sleeved flannel shirts currently on sale at Walmart, but very few of the short-sleeved variety.

Fortunately, Frank had learned Vegas was long on consignment shops—places where used upscale clothing could be purchased for pennies on the dollar. Since the best bargains were to be found on off-season items, he was able to locate everything he needed in three different shops.

When it came time to leave town, he'd take along

what fit in his luggage and abandon everything else. Rather than cabbing it from home to the airport, he'd leave his mother's Honda parked in its assigned spot and take a taxi from Hi-Roller to the airport. His rent was paid in advance till the first of February. With any kind of luck no one, other than his pesky sister, would miss him much before then, and by the time they did, Frank would have vanished.

Vegas was the kind of place where such things happened all the time. People who went there wanting to disappear did exactly that, and so would Frank Muñoz.

Finished shopping, Frank dropped his purchases off at home and then headed to the gym. He wasn't really expecting to hear from Nicholas, but when he checked in the back room, the attendant flagged him down.

"Hey, Frank," he said, "someone just dropped off a package for you."

Knowing it had to contain his travel documents, Frank settled into the back room's deserted lounge area to peruse them. Among them he found two separate but very legitimate-appearing passports, one in the name of Frank Manuel Ortega and the other for Frank Camacho Rios. There were two sets of flight documents. On Monday night, Mr. Ortega was booked on an American Airlines red-eye, departing McCarran International at 11:01 p.m. and arriving in New York City around 8 a.m. New York time. Almost three hours later, at 10:50 a.m., Mr. Rios was scheduled to depart onboard a Qatar Airways flight, arriving in Jakarta two days later.

Frank counted up the hours and was appalled. *Thirty-three hours in economy class?* he objected. *Couldn't Nicholas do better than that?*

His first instinct was to get on the phone to Nicholas and complain, but he didn't. Instead, he sorted through the rest of the contents. There was a prepaid Visa card for Mr. Rios along with a reservation for a two-day stay at the Jakarta Airport Hotel. There was also a handwritten note from Nicholas saying that Frank's next set of documents would be waiting at the hotel.

Once Frank had finished sorting through the details, he realized that, given the time constraints, Nicholas had probably done the best he could in terms of the flight arrangements. If thirty-three hours in economy was the price for his freedom, Frank was good for it.

"Tell Nicholas I said thank you," Frank told the backroom attendant on his way out.

Back at the apartment, he pulled up Sal's email draft file:

> Leaving town Monday night. I'll need that
> refund before then.

With that sent, Frank allowed himself to feel almost giddy. This called for a celebration, so he booked a table for one at Gordon Ramsay Steak and called a cab to pick him up. Once there, he treated himself to an exceptional meal. While in Lompoc, he'd watched endless cooking shows, learning all about beef Wellington without ever dreaming he'd have a chance to taste it. That night he did. When dinner was over, he took another cab back to his apartment.

Once upon a time, Frank wouldn't have passed through a casino without stopping off at the poker tables. In the private room at BJ's, he'd always been able to hold his own, and he was feeling lucky right then.

There was a possibility he might have won a bundle, but he decided not to risk it. These days, winnings in Vegas ended up being reported to the IRS, and Frank wanted to keep a low profile as far as all those three-letter agencies were concerned.

Back home, he checked the computer file. Sal's reply was brief:

Working on it.

Realizing he needed to accept that as good enough in the same way he'd accepted the prospect of that multiday airplane trip, Frank erased the draft file, went to bed, and went to sleep.

CHAPTER 45

BLYTHE, CALIFORNIA

Saturday, January 4, 2020, 6:30 p.m. (PST)

On Saturday evening, Juanita Ochoa was back home in time for dinner. She tried to put a good face on things, but Gabe was smart enough to figure it out.

"Are you sad, Mommy?" he asked.

Caught unawares, Juanita nodded. "I guess I am," she said.

"How come?" he persisted.

She sighed. "Not every family is as happy as we are, and that makes me sad," she told her son. She was grateful when Gabe took her answer at face value without asking any more questions.

Being both a mother and a cop wasn't an easy tightrope to negotiate, especially at times like this when the realities of doing the job left her feeling broken. Knowing she was barely holding it together, Armando waited until after the kids were in bed before he asked for more details about her day.

"I had to track down the location of the foster home

for Dante's three kids," Juanita said. "Rashid, Marwan, and Luwana, ages nine, seven, and five. They've been in foster care for months, ever since their mother went to jail."

"So I'm guessing you drove straight there and told them?" Armando asked.

Juanita nodded. "I'm glad I did, because no one from Dante's family had bothered to reach out to them, and their foster mom had no idea."

"You talked to all three of them?"

Juanita nodded again. "At the same time," she added. "It wouldn't have been fair for Rashid to be the one to share the news with the younger kids, so I had the foster mother bring them into the living room at the same time. When I told them I was a police officer and that I was there to talk to them about their father, Rashid came right out and asked, 'Is our daddy dead?' I told him yes. Then he wanted to know, 'Did he get shot?' I told him yes, again. And then he said, 'Are you going to make sure whoever did it goes to jail?' I said yes to that, too."

"I'm sure you will," Armando said. "And I'm equally sure that going to see them brought up a lot of bad old stuff for you."

Armando knew all about the years Juanita had spent in foster care. He also knew about Philip Reyes.

"It did," Juanita admitted. "Their foster home seems nice enough. I could tell the foster mom really cares, and it's a blessing that the three of them are there together, but still . . ."

"Life as they once knew it is over," Armando said, finishing the sentence for her.

Juanita nodded.

"And if and when you catch their dad's killer, you'll want to give them that news, too."

"Yes."

"And after that," Armando continued, "I suppose you'll want to keep an eye on them."

"That too," Juanita agreed.

"Big surprise there," Armando said. "I can't imagine you'd do any less."

It wasn't until later, when they were getting ready for bed, that she remembered the rest of it—the part she hadn't mentioned. "I forgot to tell you. I had a long conversation with a cop from St. Paul, Minnesota, a guy named Amos Anderson. He's working on a cold case homicide, a shooting dating from 2017. He thinks it may turn out to be a possible murder for hire. He thinks my two murders may somehow be linked to that and to three other incidents as well."

"Three?"

"One supposedly self-inflicted gunshot wound where the manner of death was ruled as undetermined and two attempted homicides—a vehicular assault and a fire bombing. He thinks Dante and Tyrone may have been part of the hired help on the attempted vehicular homicide."

"What do you think?"

"I'm not sure, but I'm hoping we'll know more once the tech crew in Riverside finishes analyzing Dante's phone records. I asked Anderson to keep me in the loop, and I told him I'd do the same."

CHAPTER 46

PHOENIX, ARIZONA

Saturday, January 4, 2020, 12:30 p.m. (MST)

"Sounds like you told Biba's people to go piss up a rope," B. said when, after arriving at the hospital, Ali informed him about her encounter with the two detectives.

"I guess I did," Ali replied. "Since it was supposedly a 'voluntary interview,' I told them I was otherwise engaged and that I'd do it sometime when I can have my attorney present."

"I'm surprised they didn't arrest you on the spot."

"So am I, but they didn't."

"Which defense attorney do you have in mind?" B. asked. "Gavin James, by any chance?"

Gavin was a Phoenix-based attorney who had come to their aid when their friend Archbishop Gillespie had been under threat.

"He's the only one I know on a personal basis," Ali said. "Just in case, I called him on my way down and gave him a heads-up, letting him know I might require his assistance."

In terms of leaving the hospital, they soon learned that B.'s expectation of being released around noon was too optimistic. While they waited, they made a pilgrimage to Hal Holden's room where his haggard daughter, Sheila, reported that his condition remained unchanged and the doctors had no idea when he might be able to be taken off the ventilator. She said that his ribs were healing but the lung itself was bruised and that could take weeks to heal. They were expecting to wake him from his induced coma sometime soon.

As they left Hal's room, B. shook his head. "Poor guy. He has it a lot worse than I do."

As part of the release process, Ali was given a detailed lesson in properly wrapping B.'s injured arm at bedtime so he wouldn't damage his new shoulder while sleeping. The wrapping lesson was followed by a mandatory trip to the hospital's pharmacy to pick up meds. All things taken together, it was midafternoon before they finally headed north.

At home, Alonzo helped them into the house. Bella was beyond ecstatic to have B. back home. Earlier in the day, Alonzo had called asking if B. had any requests for dinner, and he had asked for lasagna. By the time the meal was over, B. was ready to call it a day, but getting him ready for bed was more challenging than either of them had expected. Once B. was finally undressed, properly wrapped, medicated, and in bed, Ali was worn out, too, but since it was too early to go to bed, she collected Bella and retreated to the library where she dialed Stu's number.

"How are things?" he asked.

"It's been a long day," Ali admitted, "but we're home and fed and B.'s in bed. What's happening on your end?"

"Cami dropped by the office and told Mateo that she had 'fixed Adrian Willoughby's wagon.' I'm not sure what that means, and I guess I'll have to wait until I see her in person to hear all the details."

"What about Frank Muñoz?" Ali asked. "Have you made any progress on him?"

"As a matter of fact, we have," Stu said. "He's getting his departure lined up."

"I'm guessing you learned that through the keylogger," Ali offered.

"Yup," Stu replied. "From the draft file. He sent a note to Moroni saying he's leaving Vegas on Monday night."

"Any idea where's he going or how?"

"My best guess would be that he's flying rather than driving because he'll be looking for a destination that will put him beyond the reach of the US Marshals Service," Stu answered. "To that end, I've had Frigg check all scheduled flights departing Las Vegas after five p.m. on Monday. So far, Muñoz doesn't have a reservation on any of them. That would suggest that, if he's leaving by air, he's either flying private or traveling under an assumed name."

"Flying private costs money," Ali observed. "So does creating fake IDs so you can fly under an assumed name. Does Muñoz have a job?"

"Not that we can tell. Frigg took a look at his financials and tracked down a checking account in his name. In his draft file message to Moroni he complained about being out twenty thousand dollars, presumably for prepaid hits that didn't work out. Wherever that twenty thousand bucks came from, it didn't pass through his checking account."

"Any credit cards?"

"A debit card only. Twice a month he makes a three-thousand-dollar cash deposit into the checking account and then uses debit card transactions to pay his bills. Frigg has been able to examine that checking account's complete history, and she brought today's activities to my attention because they were so unusual."

"Unusual how?"

"Muñoz went shopping."

"That's unusual?"

"He's not big on cooking and takes most of his meals at a neighborhood diner. What shopping he does do is generally little more than a trip to a drug-store or grocery, but today he went on an extensive shopping spree that started at Walmart followed by visits to several consignment stores. Today's debit card purchases came to almost two thousand dollars. By the time he was finished, there was still some money in his account, but not that much considering that his next influx of cash isn't due until the middle of the month."

"Sounds like he's draining that account," Ali suggested. "Any idea what he bought?"

"According to the receipts, he came away with two pieces of luggage, toiletries, and a whole bunch of underwear as well as an extensive new wardrobe," Stu replied.

"What else do we know about him?" Ali asked.

"Quite a bit," Stu said. "It turns out Las Vegas is video surveillance central. Frigg has been able to hack into several security systems—not only the one inside his apartment complex but also several others in the near neighborhood. By using facial rec software and splicing video segments together, she's been able to access enough archived footage to monitor most of his comings and goings from the time he moved into the complex. She's also able to keep tabs on his current movements."

"That sounds cool," Ali said, "and more than a little creepy."

"In addition, although Muñoz has a vehicle, he seldom uses it. Most of his traveling is done on foot. His usual stops are the diner where he takes his meals, and a nearby gym—Hi-Roller Fitness—which he visits on a daily basis. Frigg noted that on days when he makes his bank deposits, he often walks directly from the gym to the bank."

"Are you suggesting that those cash deposits may be coming from the gym?"

"That's how it looks," Stu agreed. "Since gyms usually collect money rather than dispense it, Frigg believes we might have stumbled onto a possible money-laundering operation."

Ali had a hard time getting her head around that. "A money-laundering gym?" she asked. "Are you sure?"

"Seems like," Stu said. "Hi-Roller has several other locations in Vegas, all built with the same footprint and with identical interior designs and equipment, including top-of-the-line video surveillance equipment inside and out. Interestingly enough, the Alta location—the one Muñoz uses—is the only one where none of that high-end surveillance equipment is operational."

"If they're hiding things, maybe Frigg's right about the money laundering," Ali conceded, "but whatever the gym is up to at the moment isn't our concern right now. Frank Muñoz is. We know he's trying to skip town, and we need to keep that from happening."

Once the call with Stu ended, Ali considered what she'd just learned, searching for a way to pass this vital and very timely information along to law enforcement without being obliged to answer too many questions about how she'd obtained said information. She still wasn't sure how she'd deal with that when she dialed Amos's cell phone. She was beyond relieved when he didn't answer, allowing her to simply leave a message.

"We had one of our operatives keeping tabs on Frank Muñoz's movements today," she said. Calling Frigg an operative was a stretch, but still . . .

"Looks like he bought luggage and a whole wardrobe refresh," she continued. "As far as I'm concerned, that rumor of his leaving town soon is pretty much verified. Thought you'd want to know."

Ali didn't go into any more detail than that. If Amos was the kind of cop she thought he was, he'd be far more interested in using the information she'd just given him than he would be in tracking down the source.

She hoped she was right about that because, if she was wrong, she'd not only just put Stu, Frigg, and herself at risk, what she'd done might well spell doom for High Noon itself.

CHAPTER 47

BEAVERTON, OREGON

Saturday, January 4, 2020, 8:00 p.m. (PST)

Ramon showered before he went to the airport to collect Molly, but as soon as she climbed into his 4Runner, her reaction was similar to Tina's but without the barbed sarcasm. "You smell like smoke," she said.

"Sorry about that," he replied. "The folks' place may be the one that burned, but plenty of smoke got into mine as well. It's going to take time to get rid of it."

"Time along with plenty of soap and elbow grease," Molly observed. "So how are things?"

"Dad's supposed to be transferred to a rehab facility on Monday. He'll be there for five days before moving into temporary digs at an assisted-living place where he and Mom can stay for the next two and a half months. After that, who knows?"

"Are they going to rebuild?"

"Absolutely."

"How long will that take?"

"Anybody's guess," Ramon answered. "Six months at

least and maybe longer, depending on finding a contractor and getting all the permits."

"I was thinking about that on the plane," Molly said.

"Thinking about what?"

"About where they're going to live," she replied. "Originally your dad built the cottage for someone who couldn't get around. It comes complete with a walk-in shower, grab bars, and an ADA toilet, none of which you need, and all of which they do."

"You're suggesting they move into my place?"

"I am," Molly said with a laugh, "but only after you get the smoke out."

Molly's laughter was one of the things Ramon loved about her. "If they're in my place, where am I supposed to go?"

"Well," Molly said quietly, "you could always move in with me." Her statement was followed by a long silence. "Are you going to say something?" she prodded.

"Are you saying what I think you're saying?" Ramon asked at last.

"Look," she said, "while I was with my mom, I had plenty of time to think about lots of stuff—important stuff. She almost died, Ramon, and she still might. I knew as soon as I met you that you were the one for me. I want us to get married, and I'd like to do that while Mom's still around to come to the wedding."

"Let's be clear," Ramon said. "Are you asking me to move in with you or are you asking me to get married?"

"Both, I think," Molly said with a small giggle.

Ramon wasn't laughing. "I was planning on asking you over Christmas," he began, "but then . . ."

"But then Mom got sick, and I went to California," Molly finished. "Well, I'm here now. Maybe it's not cool for the girl to ask the boy to marry her, but I did, and I'm waiting for an answer. Is it yes or no?"

"It's a yes," Ramon said, "most definitely yes, but between now and the time we tie the knot, there are a few things you need to know about me."

"What kinds of things?" Molly asked.

"In the last couple of days I've gathered some disturbing information about my family background—some bad stuff I never knew before, and unless I'm sadly mistaken, it's going to get a lot worse before it gets better."

CHAPTER 48

BLYTHE, CALIFORNIA

Sunday, January 5, 2020, 9:00 a.m. (PST)

Juanita awakened late on Sunday morning to the distinct aroma of pancakes wafting through the air. Obviously Armando was in the kitchen, serving up Sunday breakfast. She'd had trouble falling asleep the night before, and she was grateful he'd let her sleep in. She was pulling on her robe when her phone rang with Roxanne Lugo's name on caller ID.

Roxie was the standout star of the Riverside County Sheriff's Office tech unit. In a world where it often took days or weeks to track down cell phone records, she was often able to achieve almost instantaneous results. When Juanita had handed the warrant for Dante Cox's phone over to Roxie the day before, she'd been hopeful answers might come quickly, but not this quickly.

"Roxie, good morning. What have you got for me?"

"Edward Gascone," Roxie replied, "aka Big Eddie."

"Who's he?"

"He's the guy Dante called as soon as he got off the phone with Tyrone on Monday morning. I already checked with Records, and Big Eddie is someone who, as they say, is known to law enforcement. Little stuff, mostly—several DUIs, resisting arrest, and various drug charges, along with some gang-related activities. I've got an address for him in Whittier. Would you like to have what I found?"

"Absolutely, please text it to me."

"I assume that means you'll go after another warrant on his number, too?"

"You'd better believe it," Juanita replied. "I don't have Judge Carruthers on speed dial, but close. Are you working today?"

"I wasn't supposed to, but for you I'll make an exception."

"All right," Juanita said. "I'll see you as soon as I can."

By the time Juanita entered the kitchen, the kids were gone and Armando was clearing up. "Where did everyone go?" Juanita asked.

"Grandma has summoned all the cousins for a play-date at her house," Armando told her. "I heard your phone. Do you have to go in?"

Juanita nodded. "Roxie, the tech unit's whiz kid, just came up with a name for a person of interest in my double homicide. I'm going to need another search warrant, then I'll need to drive over to Whittier and talk to the guy."

"Not alone, I trust," Armando said.

"Definitely not," she told him. "Doing death notifications solo is one thing. Meeting a possible suspect is not."

Juanita knew that not only did Judge Carruthers always golf on Saturdays, he also went to church every Sunday. After filling out the warrant request, she caught up with him at Blythe's United Methodist Church where he was finishing up leading a Bible study class.

"Not you again," he grumbled. "Another one?"

"Yes, please," she said, handing over the paperwork. "With any kind of luck, we're building a daisy chain of phone numbers that will lead to a suspect."

With the new warrant in hand, she called her partner at home. Rudy sounded terrible. "What's wrong with you?" she asked.

"Doc says I've got a case of walking pneumonia. I hear you're working that double homicide," he answered. "Having any luck?"

"Some," she said. "I just picked up a second search warrant from Judge Carruthers for the phone of a guy who lives in Whittier. I was hoping you'd be up to driving over and talking with him."

"Sorry, not today," Rudy replied. "You'll have to grab somebody else."

"Will do," Juanita told him. "In the meantime, get well."

As Juanita headed for Riverside, she thought about giving Amos Anderson a call to let him know what was going on, but she decided to put that on hold until after she talked with Big Eddie.

At headquarters, she dropped off the warrant and then checked with investigations to see who was on call. The guys working out of Riverside tended to look down on "substation" folks who worked out in what they called "the boonies." Juanita was happy when she ended up with Matt Dorsey as her ride-along. He was a younger guy, new enough on the job that he had yet to develop a full case of snark.

On the fifty-minute drive from Riverside to Whittier, Juanita briefed him on the double homicide near Blythe as well as the possible connections to the several other cases involved.

"Wow," he said. "This one is all over the map."

The address Roxie had provided was to an apartment building in the 5800 block of Comstock Avenue. As they approached the intersection of Comstock and Beverly, Juanita and Matt both fell quiet, understanding that things were likely to become dicey. When cops knock on suspects' doors, things can go south in a hurry.

The building appeared to be older but in seemingly decent repair. Big Eddie's apartment was at the end of a long corridor on the third floor.

"I'll knock," Juanita told Matt. "You're backup."

Arriving law enforcement officers don't announce their presence with tentative taps, and Detective Juanita Ochoa had fully mastered the "cop knock."

"Open up," she announced, pounding on the door. "Riverside County Sheriff's Office!"

After that, both she and Matt stood there, primed for action and waiting for the door to open. It didn't. In fact, nothing at all happened. There was no sound from inside the apartment. Eventually Juanita knocked again, harder. This time a door did open, but it was the one on the opposite side of the corridor.

An older woman dressed in a robe and fuzzy house slippers appeared in the doorway. "If you're looking for Ed, he's not home. Who are you?"

Juanita held out her ID. "I'm Detective Juanita Ochoa with the Riverside County Sheriff's Office," she explained.

The woman glanced at Juanita's ID briefly and handed it back.

"Ed's not in any kind of hot water, I trust."

"No," Juanita lied. "We'd just like to ask him a few questions."

"He took off for Vegas for a couple of days," the woman said. "He does that on occasion. Left Tony with me."

"Tony?" Juanita asked.

"His parrot," the woman answered. "Used to belong to his mother, but she left it to Ed when she died. Damned bird must be old as the hills, and it jabbers away constantly. I don't understand a word of it, but Ed tells me Tony speaks Italian."

"Any idea when Mr. Gascone will return?"

"Nope, he comes and goes as he pleases. He's got a lady friend who lives in Vegas—Rochelle something or other—and he spends quite a bit of time with her. Don't think he's ever mentioned her last name. Can I give him a message?"

Juanita started to give the woman one of her cards but decided against it. Her cards clearly said HOMICIDE DETECTIVE in black and white, and the less said about homicide right then, the better.

"Not to worry," Juanita said. "We'll stop by again later."

As Juanita and Matt left the apartment complex, she felt that peculiar sense of letdown cops always feel when an anticipated confrontation comes to nothing.

"Sorry to drag you all the way here for no good reason," she apologized.

"No problem," Matt said. "Being out driving beats sitting around in the squad room waiting for something to happen."

Back at the department and after Juanita and Matt

parted company, she detoured over to the tech unit where, as promised, Roxie was at her desk.

"Hey," Roxie said, "glad you stopped by. There's more to come, but I've got some preliminary results on that second warrant."

Juanita wasn't surprised. Phone companies were notorious for stalling when it came to complying with warrants. In fact, it seemed to be standard operating procedure industry-wide, but the responsibility for following those procedures usually landed on the people at the bottom of the food chains—the technicians doing the actual work—and when it came to charming technicians, Roxanne Lugo was an expert.

"What did you find?"

For an answer, Roxie handed over a computer printout. "A list of recent calls. Details on cell tower location as well as text and email data will come in separately."

Juanita studied the list. Most of the calls were to or from area codes she recognized as being in the LA area, but a whole flurry of them were from a number with an area code of 702.

"Where's this one?" Juanita asked, pointing.

"That would be Las Vegas, Nevada."

Juanita felt a jolt of excitement. "A neighbor told me Ed Gascone was in Vegas visiting his girlfriend. Can you track down that number?"

Several minutes of typing followed. Eventually Roxie spoke again. "This leads back to a cell phone belonging to someone named Rochelle Moroni. In addition to her cell, she has a landline that lists an address on 7th Street in Vegas. Does that help?"

"Are you kidding? Of course it helps! One of Big

Eddie's neighbors said he has a girlfriend named Rochelle. What can you tell me about her?"

"Hang on," Roxie said, "let's check with Records."

A records search in both California and Nevada took the better part of an hour and turned up nothing. Rochelle Moroni had no criminal history whatsoever. In fact, there wasn't even so much as a traffic violation.

"So what's this Little Miss Perfect doing hanging out with a bad boy like Big Eddie Gascone?" Roxie asked.

"No accounting for taste," Juanita replied.

"What are you going to do about this?" Roxie asked. "Head up to Vegas to question him?"

Juanita glanced at her watch. It was already mid-afternoon. In order to cross state lines to interview Eddie, she'd need to go through channels and across desks, a journey best navigated on weekdays during office hours rather than late on a Sunday.

"I think I'll tackle that tomorrow," she said. "What we have so far is still pretty thin—just that single connection between Dante's phone and Big Eddie's. How long before you have location info on his phone?"

"No telling," Roxie replied. "It's soup to nuts. Could be a matter of hours or a matter of weeks."

"All right, then, I'm going home. If I leave now, I'll be able to spend some time with my kids. This week I've been gone more than I've been home."

"Do that," Roxie said. "In the meantime and just for the hell of it, I'm going to go online and do a deep dive into both Big Eddie Gascone and his gal pal, Rochelle. What's showing in Records may not be the whole story. I'll take a look at what the Internet has to say."

Three hours later, Juanita's whole family was cuddled up on the massive leather sofa in the family room watching *America's Funniest Videos* when a call came in from Roxie. Juanita went into the other room to take the call.

"What have you got?"

"Rochelle Moroni may be a law-abiding citizen, but her father's a different story."

"Who's her father?"

"His name is Salvatore Moroni. He's a former organized-crime kingpin who moved from New Jersey to Vegas back in the eighties. Twenty years ago, while Rochelle was still in high school, Salvatore went to prison for knocking off some of his former associates. He was convicted on four counts of first-degree murder and four counts of conspiracy to commit. He's in prison doing life without."

"What prison?" Juanita asked.

"Lompoc Federal Correctional Complex."

A wave of goose bumps passed over Juanita's body. "Holy crap!" she exclaimed. "You may have just cracked the whole case."

"What do you mean?" Roxie asked.

"Frank Muñoz, the guy we're looking at as being the epicenter of this whole flurry of cases, was paroled from Lompoc just a couple of months ago. It's been suggested that he might be working with someone doing murders for hire."

"So maybe Muñoz and Moroni met up and started collaborating while they were both in the prison," Roxie suggested.

"Possibly," Juanita agreed. "Muñoz was still incarcerated when the first homicide occurred in St. Paul. He's out on parole now, but if he and Moroni are still working together, how do they communicate?"

"Easy," Roxie answered. "Via computer. I've gotten a look at Big Eddie's email accounts and found something curious."

"What's that?"

"Of the four accounts accessible by his phone, only one of those appears to be active. The other three are blank with no correspondence at all coming or going."

"Maybe he deletes his messages," Juanita suggested.

"I'm sure he does."

"Can you get them back?"

"No," Roxie replied.

"Why not?"

"Because they were never sent," Roxie said. "Have you ever heard of 9/11?"

"Of course, everybody has. Why?"

"The 9/11 coconspirators communicated with each other by having jointly registered email accounts on their various devices. By posting messages in email draft files, anyone with access to that account could read the content and then erase it completely simply by deleting the draft file. Deleted sent messages never completely disappear. Deleted draft files do."

"I'll need more warrants for those accounts, won't I?" Juanita said after a moment of consideration.

"Yes, you will," Roxie said, "and I'll text you those IP addresses right away."

"Thank you," Juanita told her. "I'll tackle Judge Carruthers first thing tomorrow. In the meantime, I believe it's time to give Amos Anderson a call."

"Who's he?"

"A captain at St. Paul PD in St. Paul, Minnesota. He was the lead detective on the first case in this whole series, the murder of a woman named Danielle

Lomax-Reardon, who was shot to death on her way home from work. It turns out she was also Frank Muñoz's ex-girlfriend. So the idea that Muñoz and Moroni might be collaborating on all of this doesn't seem at all far-fetched."

"So we're getting someplace then?" Roxie asked.

"I think so," Juanita agreed. "Let me know the moment that location info comes in. It doesn't matter if it's day or night—just call."

"I will," Roxie said. "I promise."

CHAPTER 49

ST. PAUL, MINNESOTA

Sunday, January 5, 2020, 9:00 p.m. (CST)

By late Sunday evening, Amos was still in his office. He had a headache and his eyes hurt. The interview Russ had done with Luke Reardon the night before had come up empty. Danielle had evidently edited her connection to Frank Muñoz out of her relationship with the man who became both her husband and the father of her children. Considering Muñoz's character and criminal history, that was entirely understandable.

Amos and Russ had spent hours combing through the Internet, tracking down everything they could find on Frank. Some of what they'd found, including his current address on Shadow Lane in Las Vegas, came from sources accessible to law enforcement only, but most of that came from sites open to the general public. Nothing they'd found served to move the investigation forward.

Based on the message Ali Reynolds had left on Amos's cell phone the night before, they had checked reservations for all commercial flights scheduled to leave Las Vegas's McCarran International over the course of the next two weeks. Frank Muñoz's name appeared in none of them. A similar check with local FBOs indicated that he wasn't due to depart on a private flight, either.

"I'm done," Amos told Russ finally. "Let's give it up for tonight. Tomorrow's another day."

That was when his phone rang. "Amos Anderson."

"Detective Juanita Ochoa here," she said. "I think I've got something."

To Amos's ear, she sounded excited. "Hold on while I put you on speaker." Together he and Russ listened to the whole story. By the time Detective Ochoa finished relating everything she and Roxie had pieced together, the two St. Paul detectives were excited and reenergized, too.

"All of this adds up as far as I'm concerned," Amos said. "Do you need any assistance in going after that next warrant?"

"I don't think so," Ochoa replied. "Since this all came out of my original warrant, it's probably best if I go back to the same judge for the one on Rochelle Moroni."

"While you do that, Detective Thomas and I will see what we can dig up on Papa Moroni, but we'll be doing it on the Q.T. We won't make any direct inquiries to Lompoc. I don't want to alert him or anyone who might be aiding and abetting him to the fact that we're on his trail. But here's something else you should know, Detective Ochoa. We've learned Muñoz may be planning to skip town in the near future. I've reached out to his parole officer to see if she's aware of that. If we can nail him on a parole violation, he'll automatically be shipped back to Lompoc to serve out the remainder of his sentence. That'll give us several more years to build a case."

"I don't want to wait years to build a case," Juanita Ochoa objected. "I want this solved now."

"Believe me, so do I," Amos told her.

"What next?" Russ asked once the call ended.

While Amos considered his answer, he shuffled back through the batch of notes he'd been making along the way. Finally he spotted the name of someone he'd originally discounted.

"Assuming we manage to nab Muñoz, one way to start building a circumstantial case against him is to show that he exhibited patterns of abusive behavior in the past. The only witness we know of for sure who can attest to that is Zeke Woodward, an ex-con living in Washington State and currently in hospice care."

"Hospice?" Russ asked. "So he's on his way out?"

Amos nodded in agreement. "And he most likely won't be around long enough to testify at trial."

"You're looking for something like a deathbed declaration?"

"Yes, I am," agreed Amos. "It might not be admissible but I'd like you to fly there to get it for us."

Amos and Russ hadn't worked together as partners for years, yet they had easily slipped back into being able to read each other's minds.

"Ali Reynolds, our source in Arizona, is the one who located Zeke in the first place. I'll text you her information. Since he talked to her, maybe he'll agree to talk to you, too. This time, though, I want that interview recorded."

"Got it," Russ said, getting to his feet. "If I get the go-ahead . . ."

"Book the flight and go," Amos told him. "If admin gives you any guff about it, have them check with me."

CHAPTER 50

LAS VEGAS, NEVADA

Sunday, January 5, 2020, 1:00 p.m. (PST)

As far as Frank Muñoz was concerned, Sunday seemed to go on for damned ever. Football was on, but not even the game between the Vikings and the Saints could hold his interest—he was too antsy and restless. He'd heard nothing more from Sal, and nothing from Rochelle, either. At this point there was no sign of his promised refund, and the clock was ticking. He was dealing with a sense of urgency no one else seemed to share.

Finally, unable to stand it any longer, he sent what he hoped sounded like a friendly reminder:

> Any news on that refund? I'll be checking out of here tomorrow night, and I really need to have it.

Then, to keep from just sitting there, staring at the unchanging words in the draft file, he left his apartment and moseyed over to Hi-Roller. An hour or so of walking on the treadmill would do him a world of good, especially since, starting tomorrow night, he'd be spending the better part of the next three days on board airplanes with his body crammed into an economy seat.

He stopped off at the diner for a tuna melt on the way home, and then spent the evening doing nostalgic channel surfing, wondering if there would be anything worth watching on TV in Indonesia once he got where he was going.

A little before midnight when Hi-Roller was due to close, Frank ferried his luggage over to the gym and left it with the backroom attendant. After returning to his apartment, he gave himself a mental pat on the back. It was late enough that he hadn't seen a soul coming or going. Now with his luggage safely stowed, he was good to go except for one last thing—that damned refund.

CHAPTER 51

COTTONWOOD, ARIZONA

Monday, January 6, 2020, 2:00 a.m. (MST)

Stu was in the office and manning a nighttime shift when the next howler came in.

"You need to see this," Frigg told him.

Pulling the file up on his iPad, he saw another segment of pieced-together video surveillance footage. In it someone resembling Frank Muñoz appeared to be transporting two pieces of wheeled luggage—a larger one and a smaller—out of his apartment, through the apartment complex, and into a business.

"When did this happen?" he demanded.

"A little over an hour ago," Frigg answered. "I spliced the footage together before sending it."

"And where is the luggage now?"

"Inside the Hi-Roller gym on Alta."

"What about Muñoz? Where's he?"

"Back in his apartment."

Stu sighed. Obviously the man's departure was now imminent. "Thank you, Frigg," Stu said aloud. "Keep him under surveillance and let me know right away if he goes anywhere else. In the meantime, I'll try to figure out what to do next."

Between looking after B.'s medical needs and juggling the many well-wishers who had stopped by the house to see B. on Sunday, Stu knew that Ali's day had been difficult. He suspected that once B. had gone to bed, Ali had, too. The last thing Stu wanted to do was disturb her, but with clear evidence that Muñoz's departure was imminent, he didn't think he should sit on that information until later in the morning. If he called Ali, there was a good chance she'd be upset with him for waking her in the middle of the night, but there was an equally good chance that she'd be even more upset if he didn't.

Taking a deep breath, Stu settled on option one and dialed. Ali answered the call in a whisper. "Hold on," she said.

Stu heard shuffling noises as she got out of bed. "Okay," she said a few seconds later. "I'm in the other room with the door closed. What's wrong?"

"It's Muñoz," Stu said. "He's moved his luggage from his apartment to a different location. It looks like he's making a run for it tonight or tomorrow. Do you want Frigg to send you the footage?"

"No need," Ali said. "I'll take your word for it. I'll pass this information along to Amos Anderson immediately if not sooner."

"There's a problem with that," Stu objected. "The footage we have came from a whole series of illegal hacks. What are you going to tell him?"

Ali thought a moment before she answered. "I'll use the same ruse I did before—that the information came from one of our operatives."

"That's what you're calling Frigg these days?" Stu asked. "An operative?"

"It worked last night when I left him a message," Ali said. "I'm guessing it'll pass muster this time, too. Is there anything else?"

"Well, yes, there is," Stu admitted. "I had a long talk with Cami yesterday evening. We've all been hearing rumblings about Covid possibly causing a worldwide pandemic. She said the last day of the conference was devoted almost entirely to talk about how restrictions to international travel might impact the cybersecurity industry as a whole. That got me to worrying about how it might affect High Noon in particular, so rather than just worry about it, I posed the question to Frigg."

"What did she say?" Ali asked.

"She says that there are currently no known therapeutics that can be used to combat Covid, which suggests that mandatory travel restrictions may well be imposed. Her calculations indicate a 97.6 percent certainty that a pandemic similar to the Spanish flu of 1918 is inevitable."

"How do we weather a storm like that?"

"I don't know," Stu said. "Let's figure that out after we finish dealing with Frank Muñoz."

CHAPTER 52

ST. PAUL, MINNESOTA

Sunday, January 5, 2020, 10:00 p.m. (CST)

Once Russ's travel plans were sorted, Amos went home. Bonnie was already in bed. Amos understood why. He'd been late to dinner the night before. Even though he'd turned off his phone and done his best to play host for the remainder of the evening, no doubt he was still in the doghouse about it. Not wanting to wake her, he closeted himself in his study and spent the next couple of hours digging into Salvatore Moroni's background.

He had grown up in Camden, New Jersey, with family connections that made him third-generation Mafia. By the late seventies he was in the top tier of the local mob and was expected to end up as the big boss. Then several of his compatriots had closed ranks, hoping to push him out and install someone more to their liking in his place.

That's when Sal and his family had decamped to Vegas where he gradually created a whole new set of mob-related connections. Meanwhile, back home in

Jersey, the hits started coming. One by one the guys who had taken Sal down came to grief in blatantly violent fashion, with package bombs being Sal's preferred method of exacting revenge. In view of what had just occurred in Beaverton, Oregon, on Friday morning, Amos found that part of Moroni's history especially compelling.

Eventually, after one of Sal's hired hand-bomb-delivery guys had ratted him out, the feds put it together and came calling. Moroni had been charged and convicted on four separate counts of murder in the first degree and conspiracy to commit. Amos found it interesting that the snitch had died of a self-inflicted shotgun blast within days of Sal being transported to Lompoc. After reading the chronology, Amos couldn't help but think Moroni had orchestrated the snitch's death as well.

What all those early cases had in common was a deeply personal link to Salvatore Moroni. What were the chances that, once he'd settled his own scores, Moroni had taken what he'd learned along the way and turned it into an ongoing business venture?

The more Amos thought about it, the more it made sense. Sal already had considerable experience in organizing long-distance hits, and he probably had a whole catalog of people willing to do his bidding if the price was right. Not only that, if he got caught, what was the worst that could happen to him? He was already serving life without. Death sentences were occasionally still imposed, but they were seldom carried out. In other words, the worst that could happen was the possibility of receiving yet another life sentence. Big deal.

At that point Amos's phone rang with the name of the Beaverton detective showing on caller ID.

"Hey, Lew," Amos said. "How's it going?"

"Hope it's not too late to call."

"Not to worry. It's not. What's going on?"

"Our CSIs found all kinds of newspaper and plastic confetti that tend to corroborate the newspaper boy's story of detonating the bomb by hitting that cardboard box. It was powerful enough that anyone holding the box when the bomb went off would have been blown to smithereens."

"So that kid saved somebody's life," Amos observed.

"He sure did," Lew agreed. "A sharp-eyed crime scene tech also located a metal fragment with what looked like a serial number that turned out to be from the bomb's triggering mechanism. I just heard back from the ATF on that. Their lab got a hit. It came from a lot of air-bag-triggering devices that went missing from an inventory supply room at an automobile air-bag manufacturing company in northern Utah back in 2008. Another triggering mechanism from that same lot was used in a 2010 unsolved out of Snohomish County, Washington. The victim in that firebombing was Marlene Harris. Her husband, Kevin, was county attorney at the time, and the couple was in the midst of what was supposed to be an amicable divorce."

"That obviously turned deadly," Amos put in.

"That's what investigators thought, but they weren't able to prove it. From what I've been able to learn, Kevin had moved out of the house and was living in his own apartment. He insisted the bomb was actually intended for him since the incident occurred at his residence rather than hers. According to both him and their daughter, Marlene stopped by his place that evening in order to return one of his pens—a misplaced Montblanc—that had turned up when she was cleaning out dresser drawers. To be fair, bits of a shredded Montblanc turned up in the wreckage."

"Which suggests he may have been telling the truth."

"Maybe," Lew agreed. "He resigned his position within months of her death and committed suicide a little over two years later."

"So he may have been responsible after all," Amos said.

"The investigators always figured he was good for it, but as I said, they couldn't prove it. It looks as though they never identified any other suspects, and her homicide remains unsolved. But now that this latest bombing has a connection to that one . . ."

"Have you reached out to anyone in Snohomish County?" Amos asked.

"Not yet," Lew replied. "I thought the person doing that should be the head of our task force as opposed to one of the grunts, but I can help you with that. The current county attorney there is Richard Pressley. I just texted you two phone numbers—his home number and his cell."

"Thanks, Lew," Amos said. "I'll get right on this."

And he did—without a moment's hesitation. It was now nearly eleven in St. Paul. It was also Sunday night, but it wouldn't be all that late in Washington State, and as far as Amos was concerned, this couldn't wait until morning.

The man who answered the phone didn't start out with a friendly greeting. "Who's calling?" he wanted to know.

"My name is Amos Anderson, head of the homicide

unit at St. Paul PD in St. Paul, Minnesota. I'm calling about one of Snohomish County's cold cases."

"The sheriff's office has a cold case squad—" Pressley began, but Amos cut him off.

"This is about the murder of Marlene Harris," Amos said. "I'm looking into a series of crimes that have occurred over a period of years and in several jurisdictions. The ATF has just linked a firebombing that occurred in Beaverton this past Friday morning with the one that killed Marlene Harris."

Pressley's turnaround was instantaneous. "I was just out of law school and working here as a beginning prosecutor when that happened," he said. "How can I help?"

"I'll bring you into the full picture in a second, but first maybe you could answer a couple of questions. I believe Kevin Harris served as county attorney. Did any of his cases ever get kicked over to the feds?"

"Not that I know of," Pressley replied. "Why?"

"Because we think the link between our cases and yours may lead back to a murder-for-hire enterprise operating out of the Lompoc Federal Correctional Complex. I was wondering if any of the defendants he successfully prosecuted ended up there."

There was a momentary pause before Pressley replied. "Kevin did send someone to Lompoc—not somebody he prosecuted, but something he uncovered. A local superior court judge, George Rappaport, was taking bribes. Kevin found out about it and brought in the feds. Rappaport pled guilty to the charges and did seven years."

"In Lompoc?" Amos asked.

"In Lompoc."

"Where is he now?"

"His wife stuck by him through the whole ordeal. Now I believe they're living somewhere out in the San Juans."

"Where's that, somewhere in Mexico?"

"The San Juan Islands are here in Washington State, but you still haven't told me what this is all about."

"I was just getting around to that," Amos said. "I believe there's a good chance someone other than Kevin Harris was responsible for his wife's death."

The phone call lasted for another hour. It ended with Pressley asking if he should send investigators out to interview Rappaport.

"Not just yet," Amos told him. "If he gets wind that you're launching a new investigation, he might alert Moroni down in California. The situation with our suspect seems to be coming to a head. I'd like to have him in custody before we tackle your case."

"Fair enough," Pressley said. "But I want to get this sorted. Kevin Harris is the guy who first hired me, and I looked up to him. The rest of the world may have thought he was responsible, but I didn't, and neither did his daughter. Still I'm pretty sure that's what killed him. He couldn't stand living in a world where everyone thought he was a killer."

That story sounded all too familiar to Amos Anderson. Exactly the same thing had happened to Luke Reardon. It just hadn't killed him—at least not yet.

Amos went to bed then and was sleeping soundly when his phone, still on its charger and sitting on the bedside table next to his head, chirped him awake. Bonnie, with an exasperated sigh, pulled a pillow over her head and turned onto her side. Seeing Ali's name on caller ID, Amos slipped out of bed, hurried out into the hallway, closing the door behind him.

"What's up?" he asked.

"We believe Muñoz is on the move," Ali reported. "We don't know when he's leaving or where he's going, but a couple of hours ago, he spirited two pieces of luggage out of his apartment and stored them at a local gym."

"Sounds like he's on his way out, all right," Amos agreed. "Can whoever you have following him keep up the tail?"

There was a slight hesitation in Ali's voice, enough to make Amos wonder about it.

"Unfortunately I can't," she resumed. "Our operative has been called away due to a family emergency."

"Okay, then," Amos said. "I'd better get in touch with his parole officer and see if there's anything she can do."

CHAPTER 53

LAS VEGAS, NEVADA

Monday, January 6, 2020, 3:00 a.m. (PST)

Miriam Baxter was shocked to be awakened at three a.m. by her landline phone. She had taken her cell along on her five-day R & R at the Grand Canyon, but she hadn't bothered trying to use it. It was common knowledge that cell phone coverage on the South Rim was virtually nonexistent. That meant there had been a slew of messages waiting for her once she got back home, but she was putting off answering any of them until morning. So who was calling her unlisted number at this ungodly hour? Without glasses, the caller ID window was a hopeless blur.

"Hello?" she said, as she fumbled to find her specs and put them on.

"Miriam Baxter?"

"Yes, who's this?"

"My name is Amos Anderson. I'm captain of the homicide unit at St. Paul PD in St. Paul, Minnesota. I'm calling about one of your parolees."

"Which one, and couldn't this wait until a more reasonable hour?"

"Unfortunately it can't," Amos replied. "The parolee's name is Frank Muñoz, and I have it on good authority that he's about to leave town and maybe the country. Has he mentioned any travel plans to you?"

By now Miriam was sitting up in bed and paying attention. "Muñoz is one of my recent additions," she said, "but I don't recall his mentioning anything of the kind. Hold on a sec." She moved the phone away from her ear long enough to call up her calendar app. "His regularly scheduled monthly appointment is this afternoon at three. Maybe this travel arrangement came up recently, and he intends to tell me then. What's all this about?"

Soon after Amos began relating the story, Miriam grabbed the steno pad she kept on her bedside table and began taking detailed notes. The call lasted for the better part of an hour.

"All right," she said when Amos finished. "I see where you're going with this. All you have now is circumstantial. You're hoping that if I bust him on a parole violation, he'll be in custody long enough for you to build your case or cases, whichever that might be."

"Correct."

"All right," Miriam continued. "I happen to have a number of undercover cops that I can deploy in situations like this. Is Mr. Muñoz still at his apartment?"

"As far as I know."

"I'll put a tail on him first thing, but if he really is leaving town, and most especially if he's flying, our most effective outcome would be to have him taken into custody by an air marshal after he boards the aircraft and prior to its taking off. At that point there'll be no question about his intention to leave my jurisdiction. Of course, if he comes in this afternoon and requests permission to travel somewhere . . ."

"Then all bets are off," Amos put in. "But what happens once he's taken into custody?"

"He'll be transported to the Clark County Detention Center and held there until authorities at Lompoc get around to sending someone here to pick him up."

"How long will that take?"

"A week to ten days," she replied, "maybe longer, depending on their having available personnel. If you want to interview him about your case, I'd recommend your coming to Vegas to do so in person. I have jail connections here that I won't have once he's back inside a federal facility. In the meantime, I'll keep you apprised if anything happens on this end."

"Thanks so much."

It was after four before the phone call ended. Miriam didn't bother trying to go back to sleep. Instead, she got dressed, made herself a cup of French-press coffee, and headed for the office. Once there, she retrieved Frank Muñoz's file and sat down to study it.

Muñoz was relatively new to her roster. She had met him face-to-face only twice before—in November and December. Today's meeting would be their third. Her own notes verified much of what Amos Anderson had told her—that Muñoz was a former cop who had gone to prison on a collection of federal charges. Nothing in Miriam's previous interactions with the man had led her to believe he was inherently dangerous or likely to reoffend. But if Anderson was right and Frank had been using a murder-for-hire operation to wreak revenge on people he believed had wronged him, Miriam wondered, where was he getting the money?

He had told her that he was currently living on funds from a small inheritance left to him by his mother who had passed away while he was incarcerated. He also said that he was participating in an unpaid apprenticeship program at Hi-Roller Fitness, which, upon completion, would qualify him to work as a personal trainer in one of their facilities. The gym mentioned in the apprenticeship program was the exact location where Anderson had indicated Muñoz had dropped off his luggage.

"Let's see about this," Miriam told herself, picking up her phone. It was just past six in the morning at that point, and a Siri search on her phone reported that that particular Hi-Roller location had just opened its doors for business. Miriam pressed the Call button.

"Hi-Roller Fitness," a voice answered. "How may I help you?"

"I'd like to speak to whoever is in charge of your apprenticeship program."

"Our what?" The person on the line seemed puzzled.

"Your apprenticeship program," she repeated, "the one you use to develop certified personal trainers."

"Just a minute, let me check."

The call was placed on hold. For the next minute or so, Miriam was subjected to the usual drivel about her call being very important to them. Eventually the original attendant came back on the line.

"I just asked my manager. He says he doesn't know anything about an apprenticeship program and doesn't think we have one."

Liar, liar, pants on fire, Mr. Muñoz, Miriam thought

to herself. *Sounds like Amos Anderson is on the right track.*

What she said aloud to the attendant was, "Thank you very much. I really appreciate the help."

Her next call was to Bradley Whitman. Of all the undercover operators she'd used, he was by far the best.

"Good morning, Brad," she said when he answered. "Sorry to call so early, but I've got a job for you."

CHAPTER 54

BLYTHE, CALIFORNIA

Monday, January 6, 2020, 9:00 a.m. (PST)

By nine o'clock Monday morning, Juanita Ochoa was parked in the waiting room outside Judge Carruthers's chambers, warrant requests in hand. The requests targeted the four empty email accounts the tech unit had located on Big Eddie's devices and would allow investigators access to the IP addresses and locations of those accounts as well as to whatever messages they might contain.

"You're becoming quite the pest," Carruthers growled at her. "What's the deal here, and why are you requesting warrants on email addresses no one is using?"

When she explained what Roxie had told her about the 9/11 conspirators using draft files to communicate, he was amazed.

"Really?" he asked, as he scribbled his almost-illegible signature in the proper place. "I had no idea, but there you go. If there really is a criminal conspiracy going on here, I hope these help put a stop to it."

With signed paperwork in hand, Juanita headed for

Riverside. She wanted these new requests to land at the very top of the tech unit's heap. Fortunately Roxie beat her to the office.

"Am I ever glad to see you," she said. "I was about to give you a call."

"Why? What's up?"

"Take a look at this," Roxie said, calling up a screen on her monitor.

Juanita studied the screen but couldn't make sense of what she was seeing. "What is it?"

"That's a cell tower in Quartzsite, Arizona, where Big Eddie Gascone's cell phone was pinging at 11 p.m. on January first. He was in that area for a total of one hour and thirty-six minutes. Now look at this one." Roxie called up another screen. "This tower is northwest of Blythe."

"That's the crime scene," Juanita breathed.

"Indeed it is," Roxie agreed, "and he was there from 1:14 a.m. to 1:58 a.m. on January second, long enough to shoot your two victims and then drag one of them back into the culvert."

Juanita could barely contain her excitement. "We've got him, then!" she exclaimed. "Where did he go next?"

"Straight back to Whittier," Roxie answered, "but would you like to know where he is now?"

"Where?"

Roxie called up another screen. "Guess where that is?"

All Juanita could make out was a maze of streets. "No idea."

"That's the closest cell tower to Rochelle Moroni's place in Las Vegas, Nevada."

"He's there right now?"

"Yup," Roxie said. "He arrived at that location early yesterday afternoon and spent the night."

"Holy cow!" Juanita said, rising to her feet. "If I want to interview him, it sounds like I'd better get a move on."

Detective Ochoa left the tech unit's office and went straight to the homicide unit, where she laid out her case to the commander in charge. He thought what she had was too thin for an arrest warrant, but he agreed that an interview with Big Eddie Gascone was definitely in order.

An hour later, Juanita was on her way to Las Vegas, Nevada, with Detective Matt Dorsey once again riding shotgun. Yesterday had been a dry run for both of them. They both hoped today would be more fruitful.

CHAPTER 55

LAS VEGAS, NEVADA

Monday, January 6, 2020, 7:00 a.m. (PST)

Frank Muñoz rolled out of bed on Monday morning and went straight to his keyboard. To his immense relief, Sal had left him a message:

> R. will have the refund available for you by
> eleven a.m. today. She doesn't want to walk
> around carrying that kind of cash. She'd like
> you to stop by her place and pick it up. Address
> to follow.

Frank didn't need the address. He knew exactly where Rochelle Moroni lived. Because he didn't really trust Sal's daughter, he had followed her home after one of their previous interactions, but Sal didn't need to know that.

> Please send.

Once Sal's reply came in, an elated Frank Muñoz deleted the draft. A late-morning pickup left time enough for him to do a quick workout, grab some breakfast, and still be on time for the appointment with Rochelle. Once he had his money in hand, he'd keep his mandatory visit with his PO and then go straight to the airport, where, after clearing security, he'd spend the next few hours awaiting his scheduled departure.

Frank was quite sure the authorities would frown on his leaving the country with twenty thousand bucks in cash, nor did he want to have a packet of cash sitting in plain sight in his checked luggage. With that in mind, on his way back to the apartment, he stopped off at a drugstore and bought several paperback books—not that he intended to read them. Reading had never been Frank's thing, but lacing the pages with hundred-dollar bills would be a good way to keep his traveling money out of sight and out of mind.

CHAPTER 56

ST. PAUL, MINNESOTA

Monday, January 6, 2020, 9:30 a.m. (CST)

After talking to Miriam Baxter, Amos had gone back to bed and, to his astonishment, had fallen fast asleep. The next thing he knew, it was 9:30 a.m. Bonnie was shaking him awake and handing him his phone.

"I found this in the bathroom," she told him. "It rang as I was getting out of the shower, so I went ahead and answered. A Detective Raymond Hollingsworth from Pasadena PD is on the line. He says it's urgent."

Amos was grateful Bonnie had let him sleep in, but he hated to sound so groggy when he answered the phone, especially considering this was the detective assigned to investigate Jack Littleton's case.

"Amos Anderson here," he said, hoping he sounded more chipper than he felt. "How can I help you?"

"Sorry it's taken a while to get back to you," Hollingsworth said. "After you called the other day, I went back through our case log. At the time of Jack Littleton's death, officers responding to the scene regarded it as a clear case of suicide. For one thing, there was an open file on his computer with only two words in it: 'I'm done.' Looked like a suicide to them. When the initial autopsy revealed an elevated blood-alcohol level, no further tox screening was deemed necessary."

"So how come his manner of death came up as undetermined rather than suicide?"

"There was blood spray on his hands and clothing, of course," Hollingsworth continued, "but some blood evidence was found on the inside of the palm of his right hand. Since he was right-handed and would have held the weapon in his right hand, that inconsistency should have raised red flags, but it didn't—at least not enough.

"Some lines of inquiry were conducted after the autopsy, but no actual persons of interest or suspects were ever developed. I had received a message from a so-called concerned citizen a day or so before you called in, but I didn't take that one too seriously. After your call, however, I went back through the case file and discovered that although his clothing had been checked for blood evidence, it was never checked for gunshot residue. So I ordered a GSR."

"Wait," Amos asked. "His clothing wasn't checked for gunshot residue at the time? Isn't that Crime Scene Investigation 101?"

"It is," Hollingsworth said, "and I have no idea how or why it was overlooked in this case, but it's fixed now, and the results just came in. Guess what? Gunshot residue was found on his shirt—around the neckline, on the collar, and on the shoulders of his shirtsleeves, which is consistent with being shot in the head. However, no GSR was found on the cuffs of his shirt or on the lower portions of his shirtsleeves."

"So the shot wasn't self-inflicted."

"No, it wasn't," Hollingsworth agreed. "The ME's office is changing Littleton's manner of death to homicide even as we speak, so what can you tell me?"

At that point, Bonnie appeared in the bedroom and handed Amos a cup of coffee. He thanked her with a grateful thumbs-up.

"We're zeroing in on a guy named Frank Muñoz," Amos answered, "a dirty cop Littleton helped send to prison years ago, but I have to tell you, everything we've got is circumstantial."

"Tell me about it," Hollingsworth said wearily, "because circumstantial beats the hell out of what I've got at the moment, which happens to be a big fat nothing."

CHAPTER 57

COTTONWOOD, ARIZONA

Monday, January 6, 2020, 9:00 a.m. (MST)

With Alonzo at the house to look after B., Ali headed in to work on Monday morning. She had almost a week's worth of backlogged paperwork to get through. She was still in transit when Stu called with Frigg's latest report.

"Sal just told Frank his refund will be ready for pickup by eleven a.m. this morning," Stu told her. "He even included his daughter's address, but what should we do now? We can keep track of him as long as he's in or around his apartment complex, but once he leaves that, we'll be blind."

"All this information came from Munoz's draft file?" Ali asked.

"Yup."

"That keylogger is still off limits," Ali declared, "so there's nothing we can do with it. I already told Amos about the luggage situation. He's aware that we're unable to maintain any further surveillance."

"So the ball's in his court, then," Stu muttered.

"Yes, it is," Ali agreed, "but he's a dedicated homicide cop out to solve a very cold case. I say we stand aside and let him do his job."

"I hope you're right about that," Stu said before he signed off.

So do I, Ali thought. *So do I!*

By midmorning she was knee-deep in paperwork when Shirley poked her head into Ali's office. "Sheila Rafferty is on the line."

Ali's instant fear was that Hal Holden's daughter was calling with bad news. "Put her through," Ali said.

"Good morning, Sheila," Ali said. "How are things?"

"He's still on the ventilator, but he's stable, awake, and upgraded from critical condition to serious. We're able to communicate by writing on a whiteboard. I had to tell him what happened. He didn't remember anything about the wreck."

"What's the prognosis?"

"The doctor says that cases like this usually require up to two more weeks on a ventilator. After that he would normally be sent to a rehab center, but Dad raised hell about that. He wants to go home. When the doctor told him that would require the services of a full-time nurse, Dad wrote, 'HIRE ONE!' I have to get back home for work. I tried to explain that hiring a private nurse would be prohibitively expensive, but he wrote, 'I CAN PAY WHATEVER IT COSTS!'

"I thought he was nuts, but then he had me log into his bank accounts. It turns out he's right. My father has more money than I ever would have thought possible. He can easily afford to hire whoever he wants. In fact, I just got off the phone with Sister Anselm to see if she has any suggestions about possible candidates."

Ali was incredibly relieved. "This is all excellent news," she said, "and you can be sure that anyone Sister Anselm recommends will be top drawer."

"It is good news," Sheila agreed. "But here's what I want to know. If my father is sitting on bank accounts that come to more than seven figures, why the hell was he driving an airport limo in the first place?"

For a moment, Ali didn't answer. She was thinking about her own father. Bob Larson had always been gregarious, and in retirement, he had loved being busy and useful. When his diminishing mental capacity began robbing him of all those things, he'd lost his reason for living. With that realization, Ali had the answer to Sheila's question.

"Your dad was probably lonely," she said, "lonely and bored. He was working because he wanted to, not because he had to."

"If he hadn't been out on the road that morning," Sheila objected, "none of this would have happened."

With what Ali knew about Frank Muñoz, she suspected that he would have come after Hal one way or the other, no matter what. It might not have been on I-17 on New Year's morning, but it would have happened sometime, somewhere.

"I haven't heard anything more about the investigation," Sheila said, changing the subject. "Have you?"

There was a lot going on that had nothing to do with Warren Biba's investigation, and Ali couldn't talk about any of it.

"Not really," Ali hedged. "I'm sure someone will get back to us in good time."

"I hope so," Sheila said.

"So how long can you stay?" Ali asked.

"I need to be back in DC in time to go to work a week from today."

"If you need anything in the meantime, we're here," Ali told her.

"Thank you."

As the call ended, Ali glanced up to find Stu standing in the doorway.

"I think we're okay," he said.

"How come?"

"Frigg spotted someone—an unidentified male—messing with the back of Muñoz's car. She's pretty sure whoever it was attached something inside the back bumper."

"A tracking device, maybe?" Ali asked hopefully.

"That's Frigg's best guess," Stu replied.

"Good," Ali said with a smile. "Sounds like Amos Anderson has someone working the case."

CHAPTER 58

LAS VEGAS, NEVADA

Monday, January 6, 2020, 8:00 a.m. (PST)

Bradley Whitman had been employed by the DEA in LA for twenty-seven years, most of it undercover. In many cases, undercover work and marriages don't go hand in hand, but Brad had been lucky on that score. Emmy had stuck with him through thick and thin.

Emmy was an only child raised by parents who had both been in their forties when she was born. In retirement, Brad's in-laws had moved to Vegas and settled in Sun City Summerlin. By the time they both passed on, they had left their mortgage-free home to their only daughter and heir. At the time, Emmy had been fifty-five and Brad fifty-seven, which meant they both qualified for Sun City's fifty-five-plus age requirement.

What to do next had been a no-brainer. Brad retired from the DEA. They had sold their LA house for a bundle and moved to Vegas full time. Which was fine as far as it went, but for Brad, once a LEO, always a LEO.

When he heard about a possible part-time gig doing undercover work for parole officers, Brad signed on and loved it. Working for POs let him keep his hand in without being nearly as dangerous as working for the feds.

After Miriam Baxter called him that morning, he gathered the information he needed to do the job—address, photo, and vehicle license and registration—and went to work.

In the old days, keeping a suspect under surveillance in traffic would have required a whole team of officers. Now, with a bit of high-tech assistance, Brad could do that job single-handedly. After locating Muñoz's Honda in the apartment complex's parking lot, it took only a moment for him to affix a magnetic tracking device to the inside of the vehicle's back bumper.

With that done, he grabbed a newspaper and a cup of coffee from his car and went in search of the complex's pool. It was fenced with a key required for entry. He was making a show of searching his pockets for a missing key when a bundled-up maintenance man gave him a questioning look as if to say, "Why would anyone go to the pool in the dead of winter?" But Brad had a ready answer for that. He pulled a pack of cigarettes out of his pocket, pointed to an upstairs apartment, and shook his head.

Nodding his understanding, the maintenance guy let Brad inside. Once there, he located a lounge chair that afforded an unobstructed view of his target's front door. With the newspaper in one hand and a lit cigarette in the other, Brad settled in to wait, and it didn't take long. Twenty minutes later, Muñoz's door opened, and the man himself appeared.

He traversed the second-story breezeway and then disappeared into a stairwell. Emerging at the bottom of that, he set off between buildings. Brad expected Muñoz to head straight for the car. Instead, he left the complex on foot, sauntering down Shadow Lane toward Alta as if he didn't have a care in the world.

There weren't many people out walking on this chill winter morning, and Brad had no trouble keeping his target in sight while maintaining a discreet distance. He watched while Muñoz entered a gym, the same one where he'd left his luggage hours earlier. Brad stationed himself at a bus stop across the street and waited. As time ticked by, Brad worried he'd screwed up. What if Muñoz had grabbed his luggage, left via a back door, and taken off in some other vehicle? Eventually, though, Brad's patience won out. More than an hour later, an empty-handed Muñoz exited the gym and entered a diner two doors down the street. As Muñoz settled in for breakfast, a chilled Brad Whitman did the same after crossing the street and entering the restaurant from the opposite direction.

Once breakfast was over, Muñoz paid his bill and left the restaurant in a purposeful fashion. Leaving enough cash on the counter to cover his tab, Brad followed suit. This time there was no mistaking where he was going— Muñoz made straight for the Honda. When he exited the parking lot, Brad let the tracking device do its work. Even so, he was still close enough that when the Honda turned off East Oakey Boulevard onto South 7th Street, Brad was able to casually drive past and pull up in front of a residence two houses farther down the street.

From there he used his vehicle's mirrors to keep the Honda in view. Muñoz exited the vehicle, walked up to the front door, rang the bell, and was ushered inside. With Muñoz out of sight, Brad made a quick U-turn and moved one house closer. Then, camera in hand, he waited again. After the better part of an hour passed, he sincerely regretted the second cup of coffee he'd had before leaving the diner.

At last the door to the house opened, but Muñoz didn't reappear. While Brad snapped photos, a woman dressed in a brightly colored tracksuit exited the home, hurried over to Muñoz's Honda, and climbed into the driver's side. She appeared to be several inches shorter than the suspect and had to spend several seconds adjusting both the car seat and rearview mirror. She was still doing that when the garage door slid open. A white Lexus emerged and immediately turned left onto 7th. When it turned left again onto Oakey, the Honda wasn't far behind.

Brad was close enough to see that the man behind the wheel wasn't his target, and for a moment, he was stumped. If Rochelle Moroni and Big Eddie Gascone had just left the residence, where was Muñoz? Had he spotted the tail and managed to give Brad the slip, or was he waiting inside for the couple to return?

Needing to know for sure, Brad left his own vehicle. Opening the trunk, he pulled out a bright green vest, a hard hat, and a clipboard. Then, armed with a lanyard proclaiming him to be an employee of Southwest Gas, he went straight to the front door where he rang the bell twice, to no avail. When no one answered the second time, he let himself into the backyard through a side gate.

As soon as Brad peered in through the patio sliders, he knew something was wrong. Furniture was tipped over—a recliner lay on its back while a shattered glass coffee table sat on one edge. A broken floor lamp leaned drunkenly against one wall. Obviously a violent struggle had taken place inside the room, and Frank Muñoz was nowhere in sight.

Brad tried the patio door, and it slid open. Luckily, no alarm sounded. He raced through the house with his weapon drawn, clearing each room as he went. Eventually there was only one possible conclusion—Frank Muñoz had left the house, most likely in the back of the Lexus and probably not of his own free will.

Rather than call for backup and spend the next half hour trying to explain what was going on, Brad chose another option. Using the tracking app on his phone, he saw that Frank's Honda was a mile or two away and merging onto northbound I-15.

Racing back to his vehicle, Brad followed. Once he, too, was on northbound I-15, he hit the gas, hoping to close the gap between him and the moving blue dot that represented the Honda, which by then had already passed the Las Vegas Motor Speedway and was heading into the open desert.

Brad's personal vehicle, the one Emmy called his "midlife-crisis car," was a bright red Ford Mustang that didn't mesh well with undercover operations. For those he generally borrowed Emmy's Hyundai Elantra. It didn't have quite the same acceleration as the Mustang, but eventually it got the job done.

As the speedometer passed the speed-limit mark and

kept rising, Brad began hoping a traffic cop would pull him over. After all, he was out here on his own, and bringing along another officer—even an inadvertent one—might level the playing field. At the moment it was two against one, but there wasn't a cop car in sight.

Just for safety's sake, Brad dialed Miriam's number. She didn't answer, but he left a message, telling her where he was and letting her know the address of the place where Muñoz had lost him. That way, in case something bad happened, if someone had to come looking for him, they'd at least have a starting point.

Ahead of him, the blue dot slowed and exited the interstate, heading northbound on Highway 93, aka the Great Basin Highway. That roadway traveled through one of the most desolate and unpopulated areas of the whole country. Some seventy miles north of the Highway 93/I-15 intersection lay the tiny burg of Alamo, with nothing but miles of empty desert in between.

By the time Brad himself turned onto Highway 93, there were no other vehicles in sight. Brad hit the gas pedal again. Fifteen minutes later he noticed that the blue dot had turned off the highway to the right and was now moving east into what appeared to be trackless wilderness. Before Brad reached the turnoff himself, he noticed a speeding vehicle approaching from the opposite direction. As it drew closer, Brad could see it was white, but it wasn't until the vehicle roared past in the southbound lane that he knew for sure it was a Lexus—the same Lexus—with two occupants inside, a man behind the wheel and a woman in the passenger seat. If Muñoz was in the vehicle, too, he was nowhere in sight.

Brad did a gut check. Should he turn and follow the Lexus or head toward the stationary blue dot that indicated the current location of the Honda? Eventually, he went with the second option. Minutes later a roadside sign warned of an approaching side road. At the turnoff, Brad spotted a street sign, the letters of which had been totally obliterated by barrages of bullets. The primitive roadway leading away from the sign looked barely passable. Since it seemed to head directly toward the Honda, however, Brad had no choice but to follow it. As he eased Emmy's precious Elantra onto the rutted dirt track, he knew that his wife would be pissed as hell if he damaged her beloved sedan.

A hundred yards from the turnoff, the road curved slightly to the left to cross a dry wash bed, then it continued east, but beyond the wash the road was worse than before. Brad estimated that by then he had to be within half a mile of the Honda, but when the Elantra threatened to high-center on the rock-strewn roadway, he decided to park and walk. Once he did so, he spotted numerous places where undercarriages of passing vehicles had scraped over rocks and overturned boulders, making him wonder if whoever had been behind the wheel of the Honda had been worried about damaging it.

After rounding another sharp curve and crossing another wash, Brad spotted the Honda parked up ahead and stopped directly in front of a padlocked gate with a sign that said No Trespassing. Even from that far away Brad noticed that the Honda's two back tires were flat, and he also spotted what appeared to be a motionless person slumped in the driver's seat.

Once Brad reached the vehicle, he peered inside and spotted Muñoz, sitting with both hands at his side and his forehead resting on the steering wheel. The door was locked. Brad pounded on the window, but there was no response. Muñoz was either unconscious or already dead.

Desperate to gain entry, Brad located a baseball-size rock and used that to create a large enough hole in the passenger-side window so he could reach inside and unlock the door. Once the door was open, Brad spotted an empty syringe lying in the footwell of the passenger seat. This wasn't a gunshot wound or a stabbing—what most likely ailed Frank Muñoz was a drug overdose.

On the subject of drug overdoses, Brad was a walking encyclopedia. Twenty years earlier his older brother Jimmy—a homeless drug-addicted vet living on the streets in San Francisco—had been found dead next to a dumpster. Jimmy had died long before the emergence of the miracle drug Narcan.

Working undercover on the mean streets of LA, Brad had encountered any number of overdosed people—several of them already dead. Once Narcan came on the scene and was made available for use by law enforcement, Brad had availed himself of the necessary training. From then on, he never went anywhere without a vial of that tucked in his hip pocket.

Part of the Narcan training entailed learning the telltale signs, and in that parked Honda Brad saw them all. Despite the noise caused by the breaking window, Muñoz remained unresponsive. His fingernails and lips were blue; his breathing thready and irregular. At this point the man was still alive, but if the drug used turned out to be fentanyl, Brad feared Muñoz might already be past the point of no return.

Grabbing him by the shoulder, Brad wrestled him out of the vehicle and onto the ground. Tilting his head back to check his eyes, Brad spotted the pinprick pupils that were another dead giveaway of an overdose in progress. With that final confirmation, Brad pulled out his tiny bottle of nasal spray, opened it, and sent a gentle squeeze into the unconscious man's nostrils. Knowing it would take two or three minutes before there was any kind of reaction, Brad sat back to wait.

That's when he noticed that, in the process of dragging Muñoz out of the vehicle, his wallet had somehow fallen onto the ground. Not one to miss an opportunity, Brad picked it up and sorted through the contents. As he did so he noticed something odd. The driver's license featured Frank Muñoz's photo, all right, but the name on it was listed as Frank Manuel Ortega. There were several credit cards and other IDs under that name as well as a preprinted boarding pass for an American Airlines flight departing Las Vegas at 11:01 p.m. and arriving at JFK in New York City at 8:00 a.m.

Miriam Baxter was right, Brad thought as he replaced the contents before returning the wallet to Muñoz's pants pocket. *This guy was definitely about to break his parole.*

Other times when Brad had administered Narcan, he had found himself hoping that the people he saved would somehow find a way to live happier, more fulfilling lives. This time he wanted to save Frank Muñoz for no other reason than to have him face justice for what he had done. When the man jolted awake seconds later, Brad Whitman was inordinately pleased with himself for getting the job done.

CHAPTER 59

LAS VEGAS, NEVADA

Monday, January 6, 2020, 12:00 p.m. (PST)

When Frank came to, he was momentarily confused. Where was he? Why was he lying on the ground? And who was this stranger kneeling next to him? What had happened?

But then, gradually, it all came back. He had gone to Rochelle's to get his money. She had said it was on its way and told him to have a seat. She had offered him coffee, which he had accepted, but as soon as he started drinking it, he hadn't felt right. When he tried to leave, some other guy had shown up, and things had gotten physical. After that, he remembered nothing.

"Where am I?" he asked.

"In the desert off Highway 93," the stranger said, "probably some forty miles north of Vegas."

"How'd I get here?"

"No idea," the guy replied. "I was out doing some hiking and found you sitting passed out in your car with an empty syringe in the footwell. I figured you had come out here to end it all, but maybe things aren't as bad as you think. Now you've got a second chance. If it weren't for me and my little spray bottle of Narcan, you'd be dead by now."

"I'm not suicidal," Frank declared. "I didn't do this. Somebody else did."

"You mean someone tried to kill you? If that's the case, we should call the cops."

"No cops, please," Frank said. "I know who they are. I can handle this."

"Are you sure?"

"I'm sure."

"At the very least, you should go to an ER and get checked out."

"No cops and no ER," Frank insisted. "I'll be okay."

At that point he fought his way up to a sitting position. "What time is it?"

The guy checked his watch. "Just past noon. Why?"

"I need to get back to town. I've got an important appointment at three." Frank attempted to rise to his feet. He wouldn't have made it if the man hadn't helped him. Once upright, he was forced to lean against the side of the car in order to stay that way.

"You won't make it to town in this," the guy told him, aiming a solid kick at a seriously flattened tire on the Honda, "unless you happen to have an extra spare in the trunk."

That's when Frank noticed that the Honda's two rear tires had both been sliced open. "Crap!" he said, reaching for his phone. "I'll need a tow truck."

"Good luck with that, too," the man said. "No signal

out here, but I'll be glad to give you a lift back to town. The problem is, my car is back down the road a ways. Can you walk that far?"

"I'll make it," Frank said determinedly. "Let's go."

The uneven road made walking more of a struggle than he had anticipated. His legs felt like rubber beneath him, and bouts of vertigo sent the world spinning. Had it not been for his companion's steadying arm, Frank would have fallen on his face.

"By the way, Mr. Ortega, my name's Brad," the guy said. "Glad to meet you."

Frank was startled. It took a blink for him to realize that according to the ID in his wallet, he was now Frank Ortega as opposed to Frank Muñoz, but that wasn't something this stranger should know.

"Wait," he said, "how do you know my name?"

"Before administering that dose of Narcan I checked your wallet to make sure you weren't carrying a medical ID alert card."

Frank was relieved. It sounded plausible enough, but still . . . "How come you're walking around out here in the wilderness with a bottle of Narcan in your pocket?"

"I'm EMS," Brad explained. "Years ago my older brother died of an overdose. I carry Narcan with me wherever I go, on the job and off."

"Oh," Frank said.

They finally reached Brad's car. Doubting he could have taken another ten steps, Frank fell gratefully into the passenger seat.

"Where to now?" Brad asked once they were both belted in.

Frank gave him the address for the Shadow Lane apartment complex. While Brad put the car in reverse and looked for a place to turn around, Frank leaned his seat back, closed his eyes, and pretended to be asleep. Brad was all about asking questions; Frank needed to think.

Rochelle and her pal had tried to kill him, but he understood they hadn't taken that kind of drastic action on their own. In demanding his money back, Frank had threatened to take Salvatore Moroni down, and Sal had responded in kind. So what the hell was Frank going to do about this? Let it go? Absolutely not! Frank's whole existence was all about revenge. He'd get even this time, too, but not until after he was safely out of the country.

Somewhere during the drive Frank dozed off after all. Twenty or so minutes later the sound of Brad's voice awakened him.

"You're sure you don't want me to take you to an ER?"

They had just pulled up in front of Frank's apartment complex. "I'm sure," he insisted. "I'll be fine. Thanks for the lift and for everything else, too. I owe you."

"No problem," Brad replied cheerfully. "Glad to help."

Upstairs in his apartment, Frank went straight to the shower. When he came out and while still wrapped in a damp towel, he went online and looked up an anonymous Crime Stopper's tip line on the Internet. Once on the site and having been issued a secret one-time-only passcode, he carefully keyed in the names of the email accounts whose draft files he had used to communicate with both Sal Moroni and

Rochelle. Beneath the accounts, he added the following message:

> Salvatore Moroni, an inmate at the Lompoc
> Correctional Complex in Lompoc, California,
> is running a murder-for-hire scheme with the
> help of his daughter Rochelle, who lives in Las
> Vegas, Nevada.
>
> His hits are carried out through communications
> left in the draft files of the email accounts
> listed below. There may be other accounts
> involved, but these are the only ones I have
> access to.

Once his email went out, Frank felt relieved. Sal had betrayed him, and Frank had returned the favor. He didn't know how often anyone checked traffic on the tip line, nor did he know how long it would take for someone to take some kind of action, but he doubted it would occur instantly.

After that, and because Frank had no intention of taking the computer with him, he set about reformatting the hard drive. Eventually someone was bound to go searching through his computer, but by then all incriminating evidence would be long gone.

At two thirty on the dot, while the computer was still reformatting, a cab picked Frank up at the complex's Shadow Lane entrance and dropped him off at the US Probation Office on S. Las Vegas Boulevard in plenty of time for his three o'clock appointment.

Rather than use the elevator, he took the stairs, using the time in the stairwell to calm himself. He couldn't afford to look nervous or ill at ease. Miriam Baxter was a nice enough lady, he supposed, but a bit on the dim side. He was grateful she called him into her office immediately without leaving him cooling his heels in her waiting room.

This visit was no different from the earlier two. The PO was cordial enough, repeating many of the same questions she had asked him previously: How was he doing? How was his apprenticeship going? How soon would that end so he could have a regular paycheck coming in? Was he having any difficulties with other individuals at the gym or with other residents of his apartment complex?

He answered her questions promptly and cheerfully, assuring her that everything in his life was just hunky-dory. The appointment ended at half past three, and by four Frank was back at Shadow Lane where the computer had completed its reformatting process.

He spent another hour in the apartment before walking out and closing the door behind him for the last time. Then he walked over to Hi-Roller for a final workout. The attendant in the back room got off at six. For a hundred bucks, he was willing to drop Frank off at the airport on his way home.

Frank arrived at the airport at 6:30, several hours early for an 11 p.m. departure. After checking both bags, he headed for the security line. When it was his turn, he forced himself to not hold his breath as a TSA agent examined his ID. Moments later, without even so much as a pat-down, a triumphant Frank

Ortega was walking down the concourse toward the gates. Nicholas Fratelli had come through for him. Frank was free. All he had to do now was find a decent place to have some dinner and wait for his flight to be called.

CHAPTER 60

ST. PAUL, MINNESOTA

Monday, January 6, 2020, 3:00 p.m. (CST)

Miriam Baxter's phone call to Amos came in a little before three his time. "How soon can you get to Vegas?" she asked.

"Why? What's up?"

"I just heard from Bradley Whitman, my undercover guy. Frank Muñoz is booked on an eleven p.m. flight, leaving Vegas for New York City, flying under the assumed name of Frank Ortega. There's no way to tell where he's headed after that because that reservation is probably under a different name, but here's the point. I've still got him under surveillance, and he's due in my office for his regular monthly appointment at three my time.

"I'll have undercover operatives sticking to him like glue until he gets to the airport. From there, air marshals will take over. Once he boards the aircraft and flight attendants close the Jetway door, he'll be in violation of his parole. At that point the air marshal on board the plane will take him into custody. If you'd like to have some personal one-on-one time with your prime suspect before he heads back to Lompoc, you'd better get here in a hurry."

"I'm on it," Amos said.

"You might also be interested in knowing someone tried to kill him today."

"Are you kidding?" Amos demanded.

"Not at all. After our discussion this morning, my tail on Mr. Muñoz followed him to a residence belonging to one Rochelle Moroni. Does the name sound familiar?"

"It certainly does."

"She, along with an associate believed to be one Big Eddie Gascone, got into a physical altercation with Muñoz inside her residence. Apparently they overpowered and restrained him before driving him out into the desert, administering what should have been a fatal drug overdose, and leaving him to die. If Brad Whitman hadn't shown up on the scene when he did with a vial of Narcan in hand, Muñoz would be dead by now.

"While Brad was waiting for the Narcan to kick in, he took a look inside Muñoz's wallet. That's where he discovered Frank's phony ID as well as his flight information. Based on all the above, I've asked Las Vegas PD to bring both Ms. Moroni and Mr. Gascone in for questioning on suspicion of kidnapping and attempted homicide. If they're not already in custody, they soon will be."

Minutes later, off the phone with Miriam Baxter, Amos began checking the Internet for flights to Las Vegas. The only direct one available was due to leave MSP at 6:55 p.m. Amos charged upstairs to administration. If Travel had given him any guff, he would have purchased the ticket on his own nickel. Fortunately, that wasn't necessary. With his boarding pass in hand, Amos hurried home to break the bad news to Bonnie that he was heading for Las Vegas without her.

"You do know what this means," she said sometime later, as she drove him to the airport.

"What's that?" he asked.

"I understand this trip is all about Danielle Lomax-Reardon," she told him, "but you'd better believe that the next one will be all about me. Once you break this case, Captain Anderson, I'm serving notice that's what I'm owed—a trip for two to Vegas with a minimum five-day stay in a deluxe suite at the Bellagio."

"Done," Amos said. "I'll pay that debt with a happy heart."

He was out of the car, checked in, and waiting in the jam-packed security line when a text came in from Miriam Baxter:

Interview is over. Muñoz never mentioned his travel plans. Color me surprised. He also didn't say a word about someone trying to kill him today. Interesting.

That detective you mentioned to me earlier, Juanita Ochoa, from the Riverside County Sheriff's Office, showed up at Rochelle Moroni's residence while officers were there executing a search warrant. I've asked her to stop by my office so I can bring her up to date. In the meantime, please send me your ETA.

After replying, Amos hurried to the gate. During the flight, he occupied himself with making notes for his upcoming interview with Muñoz. With no physical evidence linking the man to Danielle's death, Amos would need a full-blown confession. Obtaining one of those seemed unlikely.

Amos's flight lasted a little over three hours, but for him it felt like an eternity. When the plane finally landed and Amos turned on his phone, there was a new text from Miriam:

> I'm at your gate. Muñoz has arrived at the airport. He has cleared security, had dinner, and is at his gate. He's on a different concourse, so we shouldn't cross paths with him. I've reserved a TSA conference room for our use in the interim, and we'll have access to a regular interview room once Muñoz is in custody.

Amos found himself smiling. He liked Miriam Baxter's style. She didn't need flocks of squad cars with blaring sirens to get the job done. No, Frank Muñoz's apprehension would be a lot more low-key.

When Amos exited the Jetway, a woman leaning on a cane smiled in his direction, giving him a small wave. Dressed in proper business attire, Miriam Baxter was a fortysomething, somewhat stout woman with gray-flecked brunette hair and a ready smile.

"How did you know who I was?" Amos asked after they shook hands.

"You'd never be able to make it undercover," Miriam told him. "Everything about you screams *cop*."

"Where do we stand?"

"Muñoz is still at his gate, but I've obtained a search warrant for his luggage and his apartment. That one is being executed as we speak. His two bags were collected from the conveyor belt on their way to the plane. They're waiting for us in the conference room. I thought we'd sort through them together."

Amos had been impressed by Miriam Baxter from the start. Now he was even more so.

"Do you have any checked luggage?" she asked.

"Nope," he told her, "just this carry-on."

"All right, then," she said. "Come along."

She led him through the airport to a part of the terminal that was closed to the general public. Once there she used a key card on a door that opened into a surprisingly plush conference room. Two covered plastic bins designed and sized to hold individual pieces of luggage sat on a table in the middle of the room. Both were secured with nylon straps that came complete with a password-protected locking mechanism.

It took several minutes for Miriam to get the room's video equipment work-wise and to unlock the security straps.

"Shall we?" she asked, lifting the first lid.

"Please," Amos murmured.

Donning gloves, Miriam began sorting through the larger of the two bags. It was packed full with neatly folded lightweight clothing, much of it seemingly new, along with several equally new-looking paperback books.

When they hit the bottom of that bag, Amos shook his head. "Looks like we're coming up empty."

"I wouldn't be so sure about that," Miriam replied. "Look here."

Holding the newly emptied bag up to the light, she

pointed out a place along the bottom of the interior of the case where someone had used a sharp instrument to cut a long but almost invisible slit in the lining. It was a craftsmanlike job. The two layers were held together by strips of Velcro. Once the Velcro strips were parted, Miriam reached inside and pulled out a file folder—one that contained a passport as well as a slew of credit cards and other forms of ID.

"Bingo," she said. "Get a load of this."

All the items in the folder bore the name of Frank Camacho Rios, but the accompanying photos featured Frank Muñoz's face. Along with the IDs and credit cards, Miriam found a printed boarding pass for a Qatar Airways flight due to leave JFK at 10:50 a.m. on Tuesday, January 7, bound for Jakarta. That, too, was in the name of Frank Rios.

While Miriam went through the process of videotaping each separate item, Amos focused on the passport.

"This is one excellent fake," he said, "and work of this quality doesn't come cheap. Did Muñoz have a job?"

"Nope," Miriam declared, "not as far as I know. Supposedly he was participating in an unpaid apprenticeship at Hi-Roller Fitness, but I found out this morning that no such program exists. Based on what we're seeing here, I'm going to assume he has access to some unknown source of cash—lots of it."

Amos thought about that. "When Muñoz went to prison originally, he could have gotten a reduced sentence had he spilled the beans on certain organized-crime-based enterprises. He pled guilty to the charges without becoming a snitch and, according to one of my sources, while in custody, he was under what appears to have been mob-related protection."

"Maybe he still is," Miriam suggested, "and maybe that protection includes some spending money."

Once the luggage contents had been properly inventoried, Miriam collected the credit cards and IDs and returned them to the folder. They were loading the repacked luggage back into the evidence bins when someone knocked on the conference room door.

"Who is it?" she asked.

"Sammy," a woman's voice replied. "I brought you a present."

Sammy turned out to be a very attractive young woman. "This is Samantha," Miriam explained. "She's one of my undercover operatives. What do you have for me?"

Sammy handed over a clear plastic evidence bag containing what appeared to be a package of Fritos. Opening the bag, Miriam peered inside for a moment before extracting a cell phone.

"Muñoz's?" she asked.

Sammy nodded. "He dropped it into the dumpster out behind Hi-Roller just before he left for the airport. The SIM card is missing."

"We'll need a separate search warrant for this," Miriam said.

"Yes, ma'am," Sammy agreed. "I'm on it."

With everything sorted and put away, Miriam looked approvingly around the room. "I believe we're done here," she said. "I'm starved. We still have plenty of time before Frank's plane is due to take off. How about if we have a bite to eat? It's going to be a long night, and we'll need to keep up our strength."

There were several upscale restaurants in the terminal, but Miriam led the way to a Shake Shack. Halfway through dinner, her phone rang. After answering, she spent a long time listening in silence.

"Of course they both lawyered up," she said finally. "No surprises there, but I'm here at the airport with a colleague of yours, Amos Anderson. Care to join us?" Another brief silence followed before Miriam added, "We're at the Shake Shack in Terminal 1. We'll wait for you here."

"Juanita Ochoa?" Amos asked as she stowed her phone.

"Yes, indeed," Miriam responded. "She's on her way."

CHAPTER 61

LAS VEGAS, NEVADA

Monday, January 6, 2020, 10:45 p.m. (PST)

As Frank settled into his aisle seat, 26C, he let out a sigh of relief. He wasn't dead. Rochelle and her pal, Eddie, hadn't turned over his refund, but they hadn't succeeded in killing him, either. The documents Nicholas had supplied had gotten Frank past TSA scrutiny here, but he'd have to go through the same agonizing process in order to board the Qatar flight. In the meantime, once the plane took off, he planned to sleep.

Naturally the people seated in the A and B seats of his row didn't arrive until the last minute, and then there was a big fuss because there wasn't room for the woman's carry-on. The lack of space wasn't Frank's fault. He had checked everything.

Eventually the last passenger filed into his seat, and the flight attendants made their door-closing announcement. That's when everything went to hell. Someone tapped Frank on the shoulder and said, "Mr. Muñoz, you're going to need to come with me."

Frank should have said the guy was mistaken, but he didn't. "What's this all about?" he asked.

"I believe you know what it's about."

Frank wanted to argue further, but the man's uncompromising stare and the air marshal badge clenched in his fist said this was no mistake. Frank was done. Someone had squealed on him, but who—Rochelle, maybe? She had known he was leaving town, but she didn't know where he was going or what flight he'd be on. Besides, she thought he was dead. That left only one possibility—Nicholas Fratelli.

Slowly Frank unfastened his seat belt and got to his feet. He was conscious of all the curious eyes and several cell phone cameras focused on him as he made his way down the long, narrow aisle. Within minutes his name and face would be all over the Internet.

A flight attendant stood poised at the door, waiting for the Jetway platform to return. Once the door finally opened, Frank knew this marked the end of the road for him. The easy thing would be to make a run for it. No doubt the air marshal was armed, and a bullet in the back might be a preferable alternative to going back to prison. In the end he simply walked toward whatever was coming.

At this hour of the night, the concourse was far less crowded than it had been hours earlier. Frank expected to retrace his steps. Instead, the marshal directed him to a locked door that opened with the swipe of a key card. Beyond the door a metal staircase led to yet another locked door. This one opened onto the tarmac. Outside, an idling cop car with blazing lights and an open back door awaited them.

"Hands," the marshal said.

Frank knew what that meant. A moment later, a pair of handcuffs snapped shut around his wrists. After that, an invisible hand on the top of his head propelled Frank into the waiting vehicle, which then sped away. When it stopped soon after, a door leading back into the same building was opened by none other than Brad—the guy who had saved his life with that dose of Narcan.

"You!" he said accusingly.

"Yup," Brad replied with a grin. "When it comes to parole officers, Miriam Baxter believes in going the distance."

The parole officer, Frank thought. *So maybe she wasn't as stupid as I thought.*

"You were following me?" he asked.

Brad nodded. "All day long, from the moment you left your apartment this morning. Fortunately for you, I put a tracker inside the back bumper of your car. Otherwise we wouldn't be having this conversation. Come on."

As Frank allowed himself to be led through a part of the airport that clearly wasn't open to the public, he tried to remain calm. He could live with a parole violation, but if that anonymous Crime Stopper's tip was ever traced back to him, he'd be going to prison under an inmate-imposed death sentence. Salvatore Moroni would see to it.

Brad ushered Frank into an interview room, removed the cuffs, and left him there. Frank had been in rooms like this before and knew the drill, so he leaned back in the chair, took several deep breaths, and prepared to play the game whichever way it went.

When the door opened again, as expected, Miriam Baxter entered. She was followed by two people Frank didn't know, a man and a woman. The woman lugged an extra chair into the already crowded room. While she sat on that in one corner, Miriam and the man seated themselves side by side, facing Frank across an intervening table.

If this is all about a parole violation, who the hell are these other people? Frank wondered.

"Good evening, Mr. Muñoz," Miriam said affably. "I'll make the introductions as soon as the recording equipment is operational."

Having said that, and much to Frank's dismay, she placed two items on the table in front of them—the file folder he had carefully concealed in the bottom of his larger checked bag and the cell phone he had tossed into a dumpster before leaving Hi-Roller.

It took the better part of a minute for Miriam to adjust the video equipment to her satisfaction.

"All right, then," she said finally, "we'll get started. This interview is commencing at 11:52 p.m. on Monday, January sixth, in a TSA interview room located at McCarran International Airport in Las Vegas, Nevada. I'm Parole Officer Miriam Baxter. I'm here to interview Frank Muñoz about a possible parole violation. The other officers in the room are . . ." She pointed first at the man.

"My name is Amos Anderson," he said. "I'm captain of the homicide unit at St. Paul PD, in St. Paul, Minnesota. I'm here investigating the October thirty-first, 2017, shooting death of Danielle Lomax-Reardon."

Danielle! Frank suddenly felt as though he was free-falling through space.

Miriam pointed at the second woman, who spoke next. "I'm Detective Juanita Ochoa of the Riverside County Sheriff's Office, in Riverside, California. I'm here investigating the shooting deaths of Dante Cox and Tyrone Jackson. These two individuals are suspected to have been involved in a pair of attempted vehicular homicides that occurred in Arizona on January one. They were later found shot to death in the desert outside Blythe, California."

"Very well," Miriam said. "We should probably begin by reading Mr. Muñoz his rights."

Miriam Baxter's lips were moving, but Frank didn't hear a word. He knew it was over for him. If they'd already put this much together, he'd be a lifer now—for however long he lasted.

Once Miriam stopped speaking, the room went dead silent for a moment, and Frank was the one who broke the silence. "I want an attorney," he croaked.

"Very well, then," Miriam said with an unconcerned shrug. "This interview ended at 11:54 p.m. Mr. Muñoz, you will be transported to the Clark County Detention Center and held there until you can be returned to Lompoc. In the meantime, someone will put you in touch with a public defender."

Miriam stood up then, walked over to the door, and knocked. When the door opened, Brad stood waiting outside. In that moment, there was no one in the world Frank hated more than the son of a bitch who had saved his life. This was all his fault. Dying of a drug overdose would have been infinitely better than bleeding out on a prison shower room floor with one of Sal's henchman's shivs stuck in his gut.

Holding a pair of handcuffs in one hand, Brad beckoned to him with the other. "Come on, Mr. Muñoz," he said. "Let's go."

That's when Frank realized what he had to do. Brad was armed. He could see the bulge of the holster under his arm. Frank understood he'd have to be quick, but suicide by cop was preferable to what awaited him in Lompoc.

Frank stood up and sauntered toward the door, doing his best to look unhurried and casual. Two feet from the door, he lowered his head and charged forward, catching Brad full in the gut. Frank heard the air whoosh out of the man's lungs as he fell backward. Brad should have smashed the back of his head on the tile-covered concrete floor, but that didn't happen. While attempting to grab Brad's weapon, Frank inadvertently broke his opponent's fall, and they both went down together.

The two men were about the same age and build, but Brad recovered faster than Frank expected. They grappled for several long seconds, but finally, without ever laying hands on the gun, Frank found himself pinned to the floor. As handcuffs once again snapped shut around his wrists, Frank Muñoz grabbed for the only option he had left.

"Take me back inside," he managed. "I want to talk. I'll tell you everything."

"Wait," Miriam objected. "I thought you wanted an attorney."

"I've changed my mind. I don't want an attorney. I want a deal."

"What kind of deal?"

"Don't send me back to Lompoc."

"Very well," Miriam said with a smile. "It may take time and it depends on what you have to tell us, but I do believe that can be arranged."

CHAPTER 62

THE VILLAGE OF OAK CREEK, ARIZONA

Tuesday, January 7, 2020, 6:51 a.m. (MST)

Frigg's next howler arrived at 6:51 a.m.

"What the hell?" Stu muttered sleepily. Days of working short-staffed had gotten to him, and he had been dead to the world. "What now?"

"Frank Muñoz was taken into custody in Las Vegas, Nevada, last night at 10:59 p.m. Pacific time," Frigg announced.

"Taken into custody," Stu repeated, sitting up. "How do you know that? Are you sure?"

"My facial recognition software located a YouTube video showing him being escorted off an aircraft at McCarran International Airport in Las Vegas. He's just now been booked into the Clark County Detention Center. Initially he's being charged with nothing but a parole violation. Several other unspecified charges are said to be pending."

"You did it, Frigg," Stu breathed. "You got him fair and square. I'll let Ali know."

Stu had given Frigg strict orders that during B.'s

recuperation time at home, she was not to contact Ali directly, but that didn't keep Stu from sending her a text.

> Munoz is in custody. Just booked
> into Clark County Detention Center
> in Las Vegas.

Ali called a moment later. "Is this for real?"

From the hollow echo of her voice, it sounded to Stu as though she was once again speaking to him from inside her bathroom.

"It's real as far as I can tell, but that's all I know," Stu answered.

"How did you find out?"

"Frigg's facial recognition program found a You-Tube video showing him being escorted off an airplane by an air marshal. That happened around eleven p.m. His actual booking didn't take place until just minutes ago."

"I'm going to call Amos and find out what's going on," Ali said. "I'll get back to you."

She called Stu back a few minutes later. "My call went straight to voice mail," she reported. "I guess I'll see you at work."

"You won't see me there today," he said. "Cami's back, so I'm off, but keep me posted."

Once the call ended, Stu went back to sleep.

CHAPTER 63

LAS VEGAS, NEVADA

Tuesday, January 7, 2020, 12:00 a.m. (PST)

The interview resumed at 12:01 a.m., this time with Frank Muñoz handcuffed to the table. Much to Amos's amazement, the man admitted to all of it— to hiring a fellow prisoner named Salvatore Moroni to arrange contract hits on the people who had wronged him—Danielle Lomax-Reardon, Jack Littleton, Hal Holden, and Sylvia Rogers.

"So you're admitting to hiring someone to murder each of those individuals?" Miriam asked.

"Yes," Frank replied.

"How much did each contract killing cost?" Miriam wanted to know.

Muñoz tried to hedge on that, but Miriam called him on it.

"You're fresh out of prison, Frank. You don't have a job, and you've invested $40,000 in a not-entirely-successful hit man, and probably another ten in two first-rate sets of fake IDs. So either tell us the whole truth, or the deal's off. You go straight back to Lompoc to await trial on the charges to which you've just admitted. Which is it?"

After a moment of reflection, Frank finally came clean about the rest of it—about that original payout for keeping quiet. Unlike the first time around, this time he did name names, including his dealings with William Banks and the paymaster arrangement with Nicholas Fratelli at Hi-Roller. Amos knew that information alone would attract the attention of the FBI and launch yet another complex investigation.

The interview ended shortly after five in the morning Pacific time—two hours later on Central. Having done two all-nighters in a row, Amos was brain-dead. His hotel was a Hilton Garden Inn well off the Strip. With the help of the GPS in his rental car, he made it to the hotel, but once in his room, he kicked off his shoes and flopped down on the bed, where he slept fully clothed.

His eyes popped open again hours later when a maid knocked on his door. The clock on the nightstand said it was ten to eleven. From the undisturbed appearance of the bedding, he hadn't moved from his original position for five hours. When he reached for his phone, it was dead as a doornail. Once connected to a charger, Amos found he had missed several calls and messages, but he ignored them in favor of his first priority—getting home as soon as possible.

A call to Delta told him there was only a single seat left on the 1 p.m. flight to Minneapolis–St. Paul. That one happened to be in first class, but he booked it without hesitation. He'd duke out the first-class issue with Travel later on. To his way of thinking, there were two equally important reasons for him to be on that first flight out.

One of those had to do with securing an arrest warrant for Frank Muñoz and initiating extradition proceedings. During his last exchange with Miriam Baxter, she had advised him that it would probably be easier and faster to have Muñoz extradited from a jail cell in Vegas than it would be once he was returned to federal custody. The fed's first fallback position would be to return him to Lompoc, which might cause Muñoz to retract his confession. The other concern was that once back in prison, especially Lompoc, he'd be a dead man walking. Signed confessions from people who failed to survive long enough to testify in court didn't count for much.

But that was only part of Amos's justification for his first-class ticket. Full details of Muñoz's arrest had not yet been made public, and Amos wanted to deliver that news to Luke Reardon in person. There was still no hint as to the identity of Danielle's shooter, but for now at least, and after a long, frustrating wait, justice was about to be served to the man who was ultimately responsible for her death.

Amos didn't bother showering or changing clothes. Five minutes after getting off the phone with the ticketing agent, he was out of the hotel and on his way to the airport. Once through security and at his gate, he saw that his phone's charge was still in the red zone. The only available seat with an electrical outlet happened to be next to a bank of slot machines. They were very noisy, but that was fine with Amos. He needed to make several calls, and the racket from the slots gave him privacy.

The first call was to Russ. Next up was Lew Wallace in Beaverton, followed by a call to Raymond Hollingsworth in Pasadena. Both of those calls were complex, requiring a good deal of explanation. Once first-class passengers were cleared to board the aircraft, he realized he had yet to call Bonnie to say he was on his way home.

"How did it go?" she asked when he called.

"Let's just say you can start booking a hotel for that Las Vegas junket I owe you."

"You mean you solved it?"

"I didn't solve it," Amos replied. "We all did. You know how you're always saying it takes a village to raise a kid? This was a case that wouldn't ever have been solved without the cooperation of a whole bunch of people in several different jurisdictions."

As passengers continued to file onto the plane, there were still two people on Amos's call list—Ali Reynolds and Warren Biba. He chose Ali.

"Sorry to take so long to get back to you," he apologized. "What I can tell you is this. As of now our mutual friend is currently in custody in Las Vegas, and I'm on my way home to St. Paul to arrange for extradition proceedings."

"Does Warren Biba know?" Ali asked finally.

"Not yet," Amos answered. "I was going to call him next, but I'm on an airplane, and they're just now closing the cabin door. I'll be in touch with him later on tonight after I get home."

"That's all right," Ali said with a laugh. "The longer he has to wait, the better."

CHAPTER 64

BEAVERTON, OREGON

Tuesday, January 7, 2020, 11:00 a.m. (PST)

Sylvia Rogers was still hospitalized, but Molly Braeburn and Ramon Muñoz celebrated the second day of their engagement by facilitating Larry Rogers's move from the hospital to the rehab facility, something that required an emergency shopping trip for suitable clothing.

Getting Larry out of the wheelchair and into the front seat of the 4Runner wasn't easy, but they made it work. Ramon had intended to leave the hospital and go straight to the rehab facility, but Larry begged to be driven past the burned-out wreckage of his home. Ramon complied, even though it was against his better judgment, and he wasn't wrong about that, either. His stepfather had always been a stoic kind of guy, so Ramon was taken aback when Larry burst into tears when he first caught sight of the charred remains.

"Sorry, Dad," Ramon murmured, patting Larry on the shoulder. "We'll get through this."

Larry shook his head. "This is awful. It's going to

take months to rebuild, maybe even a year. Sylvia and I have somewhere to stay until the end of March, but what's going to happen after that?"

"How about if you stay at my place?" Ramon asked. "It's still smoky and grimy, but Norm has a cleaning crew scheduled to come air it out."

"If we're there," Larry objected, "where will you stay?"

"That's the thing," Ramon said. "I'm moving into Molly's place. We wanted to let you and Mom in on the good news at the same time, but you're hearing it first. I popped the question to Molly on Saturday night on our way home from the airport. Or rather, she asked me, and we both said yes."

"You're getting married?" Larry asked.

"Yes, we are," Ramon answered. "We haven't had time to find a ring, but we've set a date. We're getting married on Valentine's Day."

"That soon?"

"Yes, that soon," Molly interjected. "The last few months have made it clear to both of us that we don't know how much time we'll have, and we don't want to waste any of it."

Larry thought about that before nodding. "Then congratulations to both of you," he said. "Does that mean I might end up being a grandpa someday soon?"

"Not immediately, I hope," Ramon countered, "but that's the general idea."

"I'm delighted," Larry said, "and your mother will be thrilled. Once you drop me off at rehab, you'd better go back to the hospital and give her the news. If Sylvia finds out I've been sitting on this without telling her, she'll have my ears."

CHAPTER 65

ST. PAUL, MINNESOTA

Tuesday, January 7, 2020, 8:00 p.m. (CST)

Bonnie had been waiting in the cell phone lot when Amos's plane landed, and it was ten past eight when they pulled up outside Luke Reardon's home. The first time Amos had come there, the whole front of the house had been alive with Halloween decorations. Now several strings of colorful Christmas lights still lingered on the front porch.

At the airport, Amos had offered to drop Bonnie off at home before continuing to the Reardons' place on his own, but she had insisted on driving him. "Don't worry," she had assured him. "I'll wait in the car."

As Amos trudged up the sidewalk toward the front door, he felt successful but not triumphant. He was there to deliver important news concerning the continuing tragedy that had been central to this young family's life for years. Frank Muñoz might finally be held accountable for what he had done, but two boys would still be growing up without their mother, and Luke was living without his wife.

Given all that, when Amos rang the bell, he was surprised when the door was opened by an attractive brunette, who appeared to be somewhere in her mid-thirties. "May I help you?" she inquired.

Amos whipped out his badge. "I'm Amos Anderson, with the St. Paul Police Department," he said. "I'm the captain of the homicide unit. Is Luke home? I'd like to speak to him, if I may."

"He's upstairs overseeing the boys' bedtime," the woman said. "I'm Francine Mosier, his fiancée. Is this about Danielle?"

Amos nodded.

"Come in and have a seat," she invited. "Luke will be down in a few minutes."

She ushered Amos into the living room where an assortment of partially filled boxes testified to the fact that someone was engaged in the unwelcome but necessary task of denuding a still partially decorated Christmas tree. Amos sat, and so did Francine.

An awkward silence ensued. Francine eventually filled the conversational void by answering the question Amos hadn't asked.

"Luke and I met two years ago at a grief support group," she explained. "We were the youngest people there. Everyone else was in their sixties and seventies. We were in our thirties and we'd both just lost the loves of our lives with no advance warning. My fiancé died in a car crash three weeks before our scheduled wedding, and Danielle . . ." She fell silent. "I'm sure you know all about Danielle," she added.

"Yes," Amos agreed somberly, "I'm afraid I do."

Just then he caught sight of Luke Reardon descending the stairs. "Did I hear the doorbell?"

"Yes," Francine replied. "Captain Anderson is here to see you."

Luke stopped short at the bottom of the stairway with one hand maintaining a white-knuckled grip on the banister. "Is there news?" he managed.

"Yes, there is," Amos answered. "Frank Muñoz was taken into custody in Las Vegas late last night. This morning he supplied us with a full confession, admitting to contracting with a murder-for-hire outfit not only for Danielle's death but in three additional instances as well. He's currently in jail on a parole violation with other charges pending. I came home to obtain an arrest warrant and to initiate extradition proceedings."

Wordlessly, Luke dropped onto one of the stairs, and Francine hurried over to join him, taking one hand in hers.

"You mean it's finally over?" an anguished Luke whispered in disbelief.

"Not *over* over, I'm afraid," Amos replied. "I'm sure you and the boys will be back in the public eye while the case makes its way through the courts."

"But maybe people will finally stop blaming me," Luke said. "I'll be able to look strangers in the eye on the street without wondering if they think I'm a cold-blooded killer."

"They never should have to begin with," Amos said.

"But they did," Francine said.

"I know," Amos said, "and I'm sorry." He got to his feet then. "I'm also sorry about dropping by without calling, but I was on my way home from the airport and wanted to give you the news before any of this hits the airwaves. And although it may have been a long time coming, I've never forgotten about you or Danielle."

As Amos started toward the door, Luke managed to get to his feet and offered his hand. "I know, and thank you for that," he said tearfully. "Thank you so much."

Amos almost said, "It's my job," but something stopped him. That would have been a lie. Helping people like Luke Reardon was far more than a job for him. It was a sacred trust.

He left the house and hurried back to the car, which, because of the biting cold, Bonnie had kept idling.

"Are you all right?" she asked as he slipped into the passenger seat and closed the door.

"Not really," he admitted.

"Let's get you home, then," she replied. "What you need right now is a stiff drink, a bite of supper, and a good night's sleep."

Amos noticed that she hadn't asked for any details. They both knew he'd tell her about the case eventually, but not right now—not tonight. It was still too raw.

"Luke's engaged," Amos added as Bonnie put the car in gear. "His fiancée was there at the house."

"The woman who answered the door?"

Amos nodded.

"Was she nice?" Bonnie asked.

"Very."

"I'm glad to hear it," Bonnie declared. "After everything this family has been through, it's about time something good happened to them."

CHAPTER 66

BLYTHE, CALIFORNIA

Wednesday, January 8, 2020, 9:00 a.m. (PST)

Juanita Ochoa had stayed in Vegas long enough to be present for the Muñoz takedown on Tuesday morning, but once he was carted off to jail, she and Matt Dorsey headed home, this time with Matt at the wheel and Juanita asleep in the passenger seat. As far as their own cases were concerned, staying on in Sin City made no sense. Big Eddie Gascone was in custody, all right, but not in theirs, and once he lawyered up the possibility of their coming away with a confession had gone away, too.

Matt drove her as far as the substation in Blythe where an on-duty deputy was drafted to drive him on to Riverside while Juanita went home to spend the remainder of the afternoon and evening in the welcome warmth of her family.

The next morning she was up and dressing for work when Armando brought her a cup of coffee. "I thought you'd take the day off," he said, with a frown.

"No such luck," she replied. "I have to drive over to

Riverside so Matt and I can meet with the district attorney. With Eddie Gascone in custody in Vegas, we're going to need both an arrest warrant and an extradition warrant to get him back here. I'm hoping Bill Fordham will be willing to sign off on both."

Fordham was the Riverside County district attorney.

"Do you have enough to make a homicide charge stick?" Armando asked.

"I'm not sure," Juanita told him. "The most damaging thing we have so far is the cell tower information from Big Eddie's phone. That clearly places him at the crime scene at the time Dante and Tyrone were murdered. There's a possibility we might even have the murder weapon, but that's not a sure thing."

"Might have?" Armando wanted to know.

"While the Las Vegas cops were executing a search warrant on Rochelle Moroni's home, they located a loaded 9mm Glock in a guest bedroom. We're hoping it will turn out to be the murder weapon, but there's no telling how long it will take for their ballistics folks to get back to us."

"I wouldn't worry about that," Armando said with a laugh. "As a prosecutor, Bill Fordham has a reputation for getting things done. He'll light a fire under somebody's butt."

"After we meet with him, I'll go on to East LA."

"To notify Tyrone's family?"

Juanita nodded. "After that, I plan to come home and put my feet up."

"You've earned it," Armando told her.

In Riverside, DA Bill Fordham lived up to his advance billing. He was determined to get the ball rolling, and as Matt and Juanita left his office, he was on the phone rattling someone's chain about the progress on the ballistics situation. While Matt went back to headquarters, Juanita headed for East LA on her own.

When she arrived at Ella Mae Jackson's home, Juanita was dismayed to find a funeral home's black SUV parked outside the residence. Obviously she had arrived within minutes of the family's leaving for Tyrone's funeral. Not wanting to intrude, Juanita was on her way back to her car when Ella Mae, dressed all in black and wearing a hat, stepped out onto the porch and called out to her. "Detective Ochoa?" she said. "Are you here for the funeral?"

Turning around, Juanita caught sight of Tyrone's two orphaned children. Skye was decked out in a deep blue long-sleeved dress. Next to her stood a boy of five wearing a very grown-up-looking black suit, complete with a clip-on bow tie.

"Sorry, no," Juanita stammered, staying where she was. "I've been out of town. I didn't realize the funeral was today, but I do have news. I wanted you to know that a man named Big Eddie Gascone is currently in custody."

"Tyrone's killer?" Ella Mae asked, placing her hand over her heart.

"We believe so, yes; we're in the process of extraditing him back to California."

"Praise God," Ella Mae uttered, dashing forward and folding Juanita into a heartfelt hug. "Thank you so much."

As Ella Mae had hurried forward, the two children had followed. "Who's she?" the little boy asked.

"This is Detective Ochoa, Ty-Ty," Ella Mae answered.

"She's with the police. She thinks she's caught the man who took your daddy away."

Ty-Ty held out his hand. "Glad to meet you," he said seriously.

"I'm glad to meet you, too," Juanita managed, "but I won't keep you."

With that she fled the scene, barely managing to reach the privacy of her vehicle before her roiled emotions overcame her. A block or so away, she pulled over to allow a blinding storm of tears to play themselves out. Only then did she head home.

Halfway there, Juanita's phone rang with an unknown caller.

"Detective Ochoa?" a woman's voice asked.

"Yes?" Juanita answered uncertainly.

"I'm Marcia Holmes, the acting US Attorney here in Nevada. I'm calling to express my sincere thanks for securing that search warrant on Rochelle Moroni's phone number. Between information gleaned from that phone and from devices collected from a second search warrant on Rochelle's residence, the FBI now has at its disposal a cache of material concerning her current mob-related activities and connections."

"You're welcome," Juanita said, "but I never would have been able to do so if Tyrone Jackson's grandmother hadn't shared that one critical phone number with me."

"It turned out to be a veritable gold mine," Marcia said. "So far we've been able to ascertain that Ms. Moroni and Mr. Gascone have worked together for some time, functioning as the outside facilitators for her father's prison-based operation. When their operatives, Mr. Jackson and Mr. Cox, messed up, Mr. Gascone tried to get rid of them in a cover-up attempt gone horribly wrong. By the way," she added with a laugh, "it's always the cover-up that gets you.

"So here's what's happening on our end. I've been in touch with your DA. He and I are facilitating the extradition request on Mr. Gascone. The necessary ballistics tests on Mr. Gascone's Glock have been expedited and the results on that have been forwarded to the Riverside County Crime Lab."

"That all sounds like good news," Juanita suggested after the short pause that followed.

"Well, yes," Marcia said, "but I'm calling to give you a heads-up—an apology in advance, as it were."

For the first time in the course of the conversation, Juanita was alarmed. "An apology?"

"We have struck a deal with Ms. Moroni. She's agreed to tell us everything she knows. Before any details of this investigation are made public, she will have disappeared into witness protection."

Juanita was offended, but this was an all-too-common occurrence. Cops did the hard work of catching crooks. Prosecutors cut deals, getting the goods on some criminals while letting others get away with murder.

"That's not fair," she said.

"No, it's not," Marcia Holmes agreed. "The elites exist in a separate universe. Rochelle Moroni was born a Mafia princess, which makes her a valuable commodity. Big Eddie Gascone is a grunt and therefore expendable. But I want you to know that you and that other young woman—the one in your tech unit . . ."

"Roxie?" Juanita supplied.

"Yes, Roxie," Marcia said. "You've both done outstanding work here, and if you ever tire of the Riverside County Sheriff's Office, I'm pretty sure I could help you locate suitable positions in the land of the feds."

"Thank you," Detective Ochoa said. "I'll keep that in mind."

But even as Juanita said the words, she knew she wouldn't take advantage of Marcia's offer. Family was important to her. Juanita was happy to stay right where she was, in Blythe, California, a place where her kids could grow up with cousins scattered all over town and with a loving grandmother living just down the street.

CHAPTER 67

ST. PAUL, MINNESOTA

Thursday, January 9, 2020, 9:00 a.m. (CST)

Danielle Lomax-Reardon's murder may have vanished from public view for an extended period of time, but by Thursday morning, her name made for headline news all over the city. An abusive former boyfriend named Frank Muñoz had hired a contract killer to slaughter her on the front steps of her place of employment, Dahlke House, a local shelter for battered women. The irony of that wasn't lost on anyone. Danielle had perished as a result of the same deadly violence from which she was trying to protect others.

Captain Amos Anderson was at his desk. The Frank Muñoz case had blown up into a jurisdictional free-for-all. Even though he had made what appeared to be a comprehensive confession, everybody wanted a piece of him. For the first time, investigators at St. Paul PD had finally identified the man who had shot Danielle dead. Unfortunately, the actual triggerman was already beyond the reach of the legal system. He'd been murdered by a girlfriend's angry ex-husband a year earlier.

Karma, Amos thought. *What goes around, comes around.*

Regardless, the case was closed at last. Both Amos and Russell Thomas would finally be able to move on. At that point the desk sergeant appeared, accompanied by a young Muslim woman wearing a headscarf. The new arrivals came to a stop in Amos's doorway.

"Ms. Baan Ibiri to see you, sir," the desk sergeant said.

Who is this woman? Amos wondered. *A witness, perhaps?*

Puzzled, Amos got to his feet. "Do have a seat," he invited. "How can I be of service?"

Baan settled into her chair. "Three years ago, I was trapped in a violent marriage. On Halloween night of 2017 I attended my first-ever domestic violence support-group meeting at Dahlke House. While there, I met Danielle Lomax-Reardon and heard her story. No one in the investigation ever said her death was related to domestic violence, but I for one was sure her husband killed her."

"He didn't," Amos said.

Baan nodded. "I know that now, and so does everyone else, but what happened to her that night changed my life forever. I took my children and left my husband. For several months we lived in one of the apartments at Dahlke House, and now, much to my amazement, I am the executive director."

Amos was surprised. "You have Danielle's job?" he asked.

"Yes," Baan said, "and it's in that capacity that I've come to see you today. We've decided to hold a candle-light vigil in Danielle's honor on the steps of Dahlke

House tomorrow night. We've asked Luke Reardon and his sons to attend, and we'd like to invite you and Detective Thomas to be there, too."

For a moment Amos Anderson was too moved to speak. "Thank you," he murmured at last. "I'd be honored to attend, and I'm sure Detective Thomas will be as well."

CHAPTER 68

SEDONA, ARIZONA

Saturday, January 11, 2020, 7:00 p.m. (MST)

It was Saturday evening on Manzanita Hills Drive. B. was still in recovery mode, and so was Ali. Earlier in the afternoon, they had heard from Hal Holden's daughter, who had told them that her father's recovery was proceeding well and that he was finally off the ventilator. On Sister Anselm's recommendation, she had hired a retired LPN who would be available to oversee Hal's care at home once he was released from the hospital.

Now, with visitors and well-wishers gone for the day, B. and Ali were enjoying a quiet evening next to the fire in the library when a howler from Frigg came in over Ali's iPad.

> Salvatore Moroni was found unresponsive in his cell in the Lompoc Correctional Complex and has since been declared deceased. His death is being investigated as a possible suicide.

After reading the message aloud to B., Ali grabbed her phone, dialed Stu, and put the call on speaker. "Is that really true?" she demanded. "Is Moroni really dead?"

"As far as we can tell," Stu replied. "So far the deceased has not been publicly identified while attempts are made to contact his next of kin. Corrections officials have been referring to him by only his prison ID number."

"Which Frigg just happens to know," Ali observed.

"Yes," Stu said. "She does, and since his daughter is supposedly now in witness protection, I don't think that next-of-kin notification is going to work out very well."

"Any word on the cause of death?"

"With the autopsy pending, the preliminary cause of death is strangulation due to hanging."

"How's his hyoid bone?" Ali asked. "Did he happen to hang himself the same way Jeffrey Epstein supposedly did?"

"Too soon to tell," Stu answered. "Anyway, if someone calls to notify you, remember, we're not supposed to know."

"Got it," Ali said. "Mum's the word."

As the phone call ended, B. gave his wife an appraising look. "The three of you really stirred up a hornet's nest this time," he observed, "but it sounds like a lot of bad guys are now off the streets and/or out of commission as a result of your efforts."

"The three of us stirred up a hornet's nest?" she replied indignantly. "We never would have gotten involved in any of this if you and Hal hadn't wound up in the hospital. Fortunately, for all concerned, we didn't get caught."

"Fortunately," B. agreed with a fond smile. "And believe me, no one is happier about that than I am."